DARK SANITY

PAUL L. CENTENO

Cover illustration by Greg Opalinski.

ISBN-13: 9781497470880
ISBN-10: 1497470889
Library of Congress Control Number: 2014906247

DEDICATION

I dedicate this novel to my father, Raymond Centeno. I would have never been able to complete it without your motivation. Thank you for always believing in me, inspiring me, and supporting my dreams.

CONTENTS

PART I
DREAMTIME

PROLOGUE
THE WILD, WILD EAST

The unmerciful sun blazed. Though it looked relatively normal, with the exception of a few black spots, the same could not be said for Earth; the planet lay on the brink of death, sizzling due to an unnatural heat wave that existed for thousands of years. Australia was the only continent where the intense temperature was slightly less severe, primarily around the Northern Territory.

Deep in the arid wilds, near Kings Canyon, a red-eyed cicada clung to the lower bark of a mulga tree's trunk, singing its rasp song. Crickets and birds sang too. A black-breasted buzzard landed in its nest atop the boughs of a tree in the dry wilderness, a dead ibis in its beak. Upon settling down, it laid the carcass next to its two chicks.

The chicks squealed anxiously as they tried to poke their bills into the dead ibis. Their mother, however, blocked them while puncturing the corpse. She began to feed her chicks by regurgitating the bird's flesh into their tiny beaks. Their squealing finally calmed down when they finished eating.

A long silence fell, broken only by the howl of a starving dingo. It knew the buzzards weren't too far, and it could smell the remaining flesh of the dead ibis. The mangy animal circled the buzzards' tree with a growl.

It stopped when a cryptid beast made itself visible by the mulga tree. The bulky carnivorous animal with thick fur advanced in a quadrupedal galumph. Whatever it was, it wasn't native. It lingered, sniffing the air, as though it had sensed something other than the dingo lurking around.

The creature rose on its hind legs, standing twelve feet tall. It continued sniffing, gazing at the eastern region of the wilderness. Since it didn't see anything, it lowered itself back to the ground with a clamorous stomp. It was about to leave and hunt the dingo when an ear-piercing shell zoomed through the cluster of trees. The creature roared viciously as its shoulder tore open with blood.

Unaffected by the wound, the beast turned around and charged through the wilderness. It rose and pounded a tree in its way, continuing to thump forward. Then another shell pierced the beast's skull. The animal croaked in a high-pitched bawl, which died out when it fell flat on the barren land.

"Yer may be gettin' old, Flint," said Joey Stalls, "but yer aimin' ain't."

Flint Cross kept his Winchester rifle leveled, still aiming at the beast's head. The brim of his hat shaded his wrinkled forehead as he squinted at the fallen beast. He had a scruffy, grayish goatee that looked just right on his aged face.

"Nice shot, dad," said Tom Cross, a fair skinned and clean-shaven pretty boy with his father's sky-blue eyes.

"I know," said Flint, winking at his son.

He loved nothing more than being in the wide open outback of Australia, hunting. Flint knew that the world had fallen centuries—maybe millennia—ago, but there were still animals in the wild to track and shoot. Although fruits known here as bush tucker did justice, he yearned for a bit of meat. And, of course, the game made it worthwhile. As an old man, it had become his goal to be a great hunter. In fact, it was his goal *because* he was old. Getting older disheartened him since it meant that he'd have to eventually retire and would be forgotten in this world, like the rest of the continents that withered and died long ago. So hearing his son and best friend give him a compliment made him smile. In the end of it all, he wasn't just a father, friend, or lucky shooter—he was a cowboy.

"Heya, Flint," said Joey. "Are ya gonna check ta see if it's still alive?"

Flint placed the Winchester rifle on his shoulder and approached the animal, spurs chinking. Reaching the beast, he placed a boot atop its head.

"Come on, you chickens," he said.

Joey, a younger man with a bushy yet handsome mustache, stepped up first. Tom, who was a mere teenager, hesitated but joined them.

"Bloody hell," said Joey. "I never thought I'd live ta see a yowie."

"Don't be so superstitious," said Flint.

"Then what is it?" asked Tom, starring at the massive dead creature with a face of revulsion.

"It's just an oversized bear," said Flint.

"Bears ain't native 'round here," said Joey.

"Hardly anyone or anything is native here anymore. In fact, you're the only one with an Aussie accent," said Flint, extending his hand with a smug smile.

Joey sighed. "Shucks, looks like I'm broke again. I shoulda never made that bet wit ya," he said, pulling out a few dented coins and slapping them onto Flint's hand. "But I've gotta say, tha bet was worth it."

"Worth's the name of the game, Joey," said Flint.

Currency was no longer in effect in this aged world of death. But it still had meaning to people who had it. Money became a great symbol of worth to those who were still alive in Australia. Though there wasn't a real economy, coins were exchanged for gambling or making purchases because people like Flint saw them as tokens—artifacts to remember the days when civilization meant something.

Flint slung his rifle on his back and unsheathed a skinning knife from his belt. "Now comes the fun part," he said. "I'll let you do the honors, son."

"Me?" said Tom, wincing.

"Don't be such a wuss, Tommy," said Joey, chuckling.

"I'm not a wuss!" snapped Tom.

Stepping forward with a nauseated expression, he unsheathed his weapon and dug it into the bear's fur, beginning to skin it.

"Grah!" roared Joey.

Tom fell on his rear while the others laughed.

"*Dad,*" said Tom moodily.

"Sorry," said Flint, coughing over a laugh. He glared at Joey, gesturing him to stop. He then gave his fifteen-year-old a helping hand. "Are you all right?"

Even though Tom felt embarrassed, he gave a faint nod.

"All right," went on Flint, playfully twirling his dagger between his fingers. "Let's get to work and bring us home some food."

"I reckon ya keep tha head as a trophy," said Joey.

Flint wore a devious grin, amused by the suggestion. Joey and Tom assisted him with the skinning by severing its limbs. The carcass soon turned into piles of blubber. Upon finishing, the trio rinsed their hands using the water in their wineskins. Flint stood up first, producing a loud whistle. Three horses emerged from a basin, trotting over. He rubbed his mare's mane, taking a break. In the meantime, Joey tied up stacks of blubber on his stallion. Tom did the same with his mustang, though he carried less. Flint noticed his son struggling, so he came over and assisted him.

"Thanks, dad."

Flint winked at his son, patting him on the back. They continued to load the meat on the horses. Once done, they mounted their steeds. Joey noticed the bear's head that lay behind Flint and chuckled softly.

"Crikey," said Joey, "I was just kiddin' about tha trophy!"

"Your point?" replied Flint, raising an eyebrow.

Joey was impressed by his decision to take the head. Tom, on the other hand, gasped when he saw it.

"Mom's gonna freak out when she sees that."

"Maybe," said Flint, shrugging. "But when she sees the food we've got, she'll make due." He pulled the reins of his mare. "Let's go!"

The trio started to ride through the wilds. Departing the dreary region didn't take them long. Upon leaving, they rode alongside Kings Canyon. The horseback riders felt a calm breeze as they traveled across the frontier, the sun beaming against them. Despite its vicious glare, they rode headlong through the barren expanse of the wild, wild east.

CHAPTER ONE
THE COWBOY'S VOW

Central Australia's scorched terrain appeared endless as Flint Cross, Tom Cross, and Joey Stalls rode through it. The draught savanna fluttered while the three horses galloped forward. Feeling the wind push him along, Tom let out a skyward cheer. Flint tilted his head and glanced at his jubilant son with a smile.

"I think Tommy's gonna make a fine ranger huntin' wit us," said Joey. Flint nodded at him.

"You really think so?" asked Tom.

"Yep," said Joey. "There ain't nothin' better than a good ol' hunt; all ya have ta do is howl like a dingo, bite like a crocodile, 'n think like a maniac. Ya got tha howlin' part down. Now ya just gotta bite hard 'n be—"

"As crazy as me," said Flint.

The horseback riders laughed as they traveled past the savanna. The eastern expanse was a crusty yet radiant frontier. A dangerous wave of heat gripped the land, creating a blurry effect. Flint, however, had adapted to the temperature. He was one of the few who were immune to the severe heat. In fact, Tom and Joey were the same. Those who didn't adapt simply died.

The trio embraced the humid wind while riding farther into the northeastern wilds. In the distance were several mountains, or at least that was how they appeared to Flint from afar. When the riders traveled a bit closer, the rock formations became clearer, turning out to be gargantuan bornhardts.

Kata Tjuta—The Olgas—stood on the eastern region from where the trio rode. It was never a dull sight to Flint. The thirty-six dome-shaped bornhardts gleamed with an orange-red tinge. Not too far away from Kata Tjuta, they came upon a kangaroo hopping with a youngling in its pouch.

"Hey, Joey," called out Tom. "It's you!"

He laughed hysterically while Joey shrugged, grumbling under his breath. Flint joined in with his son, chuckling when he noticed the kangaroo carrying her joey.

"Funny," said Joey. "Gettin' back at me from earlier, eh?"

Tom grinned as he nodded, continuing to ride north with his father. It wasn't long until Kata Tjuta was far behind them. They eventually passed by a boulder sign that looked ages old. It was barely readable—*Wel o e to Al ce Spr ngs*. There was, however, a new sign carved on an arch of wood high above the dusty trail leading them to a town with several plantations:

Welcome to the town of Desonas!

Flint had never been happy about the withered world, but the town of Desonas was the one remaining remnant of civilization that made him whole—survivors from around the world had come here to avoid the deadly heat. He could already see the many ranches and plantations throughout the land, as well as tiny springs trickling with water. The horseback riders passed a few onlookers by the town's entrance. The women wore shabby Victorian dresses. Most of the men were even shabbier with dingy jeans and tattered, wide-brimmed hats.

Bystanders greeted the trio as they rode by. The townspeople in Desonas knew each and every resident by name, face, and reputation. It was a big town, but the folks helped one another since they were out in the middle of nowhere. Based on what Flint knew, no other civilization existed. The populace was unable to make a new settlement in Australia because most of the land had been ruined by the lethal heat. The Northern Territory was all that remained, so those living here in Desonas had to work together to survive. In fact, Flint referred to the townspeople as his second family, especially Joey.

"Howdy, Cross!" said Ronald Salomon.

"Good afternoon, Marshal," said Flint, waving.

Ronald Salomon, a six-foot-tall man clad in black clothes, was the town's marshal. He looked as old as Flint with gray shoulder-length hair and a thick, well-groomed beard. Marshal Salomon squinted on the veranda of his office as the black-spotted sun shone on his wrinkled face. He tipped the brim of his hat at Flint and his company, bidding farewell to them.

The buildings they passed by were rundown; no standing structure was taller than two stories. Among them was a church led by Preacher Harrison. Truth be told, Flint felt disturbed when he rode past the town's house of worship. But it wasn't due to the preacher. In fact, they were great friends. It was a rather odd sensation he experienced because he wasn't sure what to believe in considering that Earth was now a godforsaken planet. Yet there was something else lingering within him, a daunting notion that someone was calling out to him from above—a feminine whisper.

"Hamarah doesn't exist," he muttered to himself.

Gazing up, he only saw the black-spotted sun. Flint was gradually becoming delusional, he realized, stuck here on this dying rock. Thinking about why he'd thought he heard a woman's voice call out to him, he felt as though he'd forgotten something extremely important. This made him feel sick to his stomach. He dared not speak of this incident to anyone; he simply pretended to be the same as the others—a nonchalant, law-abiding citizen. He wiped sweat away from his brow and shook his head, trying to let go of these troublesome thoughts.

The trio kept riding through the town's dusty trail. They rode between two orchard plantations where many farmers attempted to gather fruit. Upon passing them, Flint led his company to a vineyard a short distance from his home. When the riders reached the homestead they pulled on the reins of their horses and came to a halt. Flint was the first to get off his steed, hitching its reins to a post. He then helped Tom and Joey unload their share of the bear's skin and meat, stacking them up on the porch.

"Son," called out Flint, getting ready to open the front door, "can you bring the horses to the corral?"

"Sure," said Tom.

He led the horses to a corral beside the barn. In the meantime, Flint opened the front door of his house and stepped inside with his new trophy. It was quiet inside. This made him sigh with relief. He then started wondering where he should put the animal's head when his wife appeared behind him and gasped in horror.

"Flint Cross," began Amanda, placing her hands on her hips. "Just what do you think you're doing bringing *that* into my house?"

"Our house, you mean?" he replied gruffly.

Marrying her was the one decision he regretted. He accepted many things in life, such as the dead world and its heat that could kill people if they didn't adapt. He accepted being a father. He even accepted his old age despite him being unhappy about it. But he could barely accept the reality of coming home to Amanda. Her close-minded attitude about his hobbies was enough to make him lose his temper and have a reason to hate her more.

"Are you actually planning on keeping that *thing* in my house?" said Amanda, stroking her black hair to the side. "It's disgusting!"

Joey couldn't help but laugh, giving Flint a sidelong grin. Amanda dared to watch her husband play taxidermist, her eyes widening in shock. She then noticed Joey bringing in some meat.

"So, you finally found some real food out there?" she asked.

"Obviously," said Flint, unprofessionally hammering the bear's head onto a plaque so he could hang it up on the entrance's wall. He knew it would make the house stink, but a part of him decided to do this just to spite his wife. "I handled the bear. Joey helped skin it."

"It took us a bit of time," said Joey. "But by God, we scored big!"

Sulking under her breath, Amanda stomped to the kitchen. Flint snorted when she left. Joey simply shrugged. Together they climbed a bench and hung up the trophy. Afterwards, they brought the skin and meat into the kitchen. Although uptight, Amanda took out a cooking knife and started cutting the meat to cure it. Tom entered the kitchen as soon as Flint and Joey finished placing their last stacks of meat on the counter.

"Hey, mom," said Tom.

"Welcome back, dear," said Amanda, kissing her son on the cheek. "How was your first day with the outlaws?"

Tom began, "It was—"

"Outlaws?" interjected Flint.

Upon hearing his father's tone of voice, Tom withdrew and kept his mouth shut. He hated when his parents argued, but he wasn't about to get in their way. Joey tilted his head, pouting at Tom.

"We just brought back a week's worth of food and you're calling us *outlaws*?"

"It was great, mom," intervened Tom before she could snap back at his father. "Dad took on a bear bigger than any animal I've ever seen in my entire life. I just wish skinning it wasn't so messy."

Joey chuckled while taking a seat at the kitchen table and said, "Well, I reckon ya hunt it next time."

"No thanks," said Tom, shaking his head.

"Ah, yer no fun," said Joey teasingly.

"My son's smart, Mr. Stalls," said Amanda, working on the meat. "And, in this town, smart is what's truly important." She smiled for a change, proud of herself, and asked, "Tom, dear, can you help me?"

"I'll do it," said Flint.

"No," said Amanda sternly. "Marshal Salomon would like to have a word with you. I think it's important."

"Really?" said Flint, looking skeptical. Amanda reassured him with a nod. He still wore a doubtful expression despite her nod. He grumbled under his breath and continued in an irritated tone, "Well, that's odd. I just rode past him on Donna; he didn't seem so anxious to speak with me when I saw him."

"Probably because he noticed that you'd just returned," responded Amanda in a mutually irritated tone. "Any man with manners would know his boundaries, unlike you and your hideous trophy."

"I knew you'd hate it," said Tom, curing the meat next to his mother.

Flint ignored his wife's remark. "Where is Sarah?" he inquired.

"She's in the vineyard making sure the grapes are all right," replied Amanda. "Check on her before you see Salomon."

Flint complied with a sullen expression on his face. He waved at Joey, patted his son, and then stepped outside. Heading over to the vineyard, he spotted his daughter gathering grapes on the far left side of the vineyard.

Sarah Cross, a petite young woman with red waist-length hair and light freckles on her face, strangely didn't resemble her parents. Although wearing a dress, she had the look of a tomboy. Flint, above all people, knew this. She continued harvesting grapes despite her father standing there.

"Still upset with me?" he asked.

"Dad, do you even have to ask?" she said without bothering to look back at him. Upon harvesting the last vine, she placed the grapes in her basket and faced her father with a frown. "You let Tommy go, yet he's five years younger than me. It's not fair."

"Sarah, turning twenty changes nothing," he said, trying to remain calm. "Life's just not the same for a woman out there. You know I considered it, but your mother would've killed me if you came along with us. She's already upset because I brought home a bear's head."

"*What?*" she said, less upset. "Can I see it?"

"Of course you can," he said. They started walking along the right side of the vineyard, not far from where the barn stood. "In fact, I'm pretty sure anyone who visits our home will see it," he added, winking.

"Mom was actually okay with this?" she asked in disbelief.

"*No,*" he said, "but I put it on display anyway."

"Oh my gosh," she said. "That must've *really* gotten mom riled up." Flint nodded at her as she excitedly went on, "Our neighbors will probably be jealous to see it when they come by for the festival."

"My thoughts exactly," he said smoothly, stopping at the corral and leaning against the splintery wood. "Listen, I need to ride Donna to see Marshal Salomon about something. Why don't you go take a look at my prize while I'm gone? You can tell me what you think when I come back."

"Okay," she said, hugging her father. "If you happen to see Jake, please tell him I said hi."

"I sure will," he said. "See you soon, darling."

After parting, Flint entered the dusty corral and mounted Donna, his mare. He tugged the reins and waved at his daughter while his horse galloped away. Flint glanced at the neighboring farms, which belonged to the Froehlich and Steward families. Even though the farms were a part of Desonas, the town square stood three miles away.

It was brighter and hotter outside, yet Flint didn't break a sweat. He was lucky enough to catch a nice breeze because of the ride. A piece of tumbleweed rolled across the dusty trail while his mare trotted forward. Flint guided Donna away from it and continued onward. He eventually reached the square and dismounted his mare, hitching her at a post beside the marshal's office. The door was already open. He knocked anyway before entering.

"Come in," said Marshal Salomon, his feet on the desk. "Ah, Cross. I was hoping you'd show up."

Flint entered, tipping his hat. "How are you, Marshal?"

"Not too shabby, my friend," said Salomon. "And yourself?"

"Just dandy, sir," he replied. "My wife told me you needed me. Is that true?" When the marshal answered with a nod, Flint continued, "You should've stopped me when I came back. Joey would've taken my son home."

"It's quite all right," said Salomon. "I don't expect you to be doing anything more today. Besides, I'm seeing your ugly face again at the festival. Right?"

Flint laughed. "I guess so," he said.

"But it's still good you came," said Salomon in a serious tone. "Speaking privately about this is what I had hoped for. And please, close the door."

"Sure," said Flint, closing the door behind him. When he did so, Salomon stood up from his seat and walked over to a window, peeping through the blinds. Flint raised an eyebrow. "Is everything all right, Marshal?"

"Yes," he said. "For now at least. There are two jobs I have for you. That is, if you're interested."

"I'm listening."

Salomon leaned against the wall beside a window and continued, "Well, I sent both my deputies over to the mine. The miners have apparently struck gold."

Flint's dull face lit up.

"Not *real* gold," said Salomon, chuckling softly. "They discovered a strange tunnel after an unforeseen earthquake. One of the walls collapsed; it led the miners down to a trail with metal we've never seen before." He noticed that Flint's lit up face changed to a frown but went on, "I was hoping—"

"Absolutely not," said Flint, scowling. "With all due respect, Marshal, I told you several times already that I'm not a miner, nor am I meant to be a deputy or overseer."

"Very well," said Salomon with disappointment.

"I made a vow long ago to protect this town...not help run it," said Flint. "Now, what's the second proposition you've got for me?"

"It's for your ears only," said Salomon. "Absolutely no one is to know about this. Not even my son knows. If you want to take Joey with you, that's fine. But under no circumstances are you to tell him the details. Do you understand?"

"All right, let me hear it."

For a second, Salomon looked like he might not proceed. "During one of my evening patrols I came across a dead Wakaya near Uluru. His chest had gun wounds."

Flint's eyes widened.

"I know," added Salomon, noticing his reaction. "But it gets worse. When I returned his body to the tribe, their chief told me everything."

"I'm surprised Yeramba even spoke to you," said Flint. "The Wakaya prefer isolation more than any of the other aboriginals. Who the hell would do such a thing?"

"I was getting to that," said Salomon. "Do you remember Browder?"

Flint stiffened. He looked as though he recalled a nightmare that he'd buried deep within his mind, hoping to never remember. The memory of Browder seemed like a lifetime ago. His heart pounded, and a strange sensation of nostalgia swept over him as if something else from his subconscious was trying to emerge. Flint managed to give a faint nod.

"Believe me, I had the same reaction," said Salomon. "That's right, after all these years he's finally resurfaced. But he's lost it. I mean, before Browder disappeared he already seemed to be losing it with those absurd stories of his past. And now, from what the tribe told me, his hallucinations have driven him completely mad. He was the best gunslinger we had until you took over. I don't even think I can take out Browder."

"Are you positive it's him?"

"No, but who else would do this?" replied Salomon. "Chief Yeramba said this wasn't the first time one of his people were shot. He's been finding corpses of his tribesmen for weeks."

"*Weeks?*" said Flint, distraught. "And Yeramba tells you this *now?*"

"It was kept secret between all the tribes," replied Salomon. "The tribesmen are calling him *wild demon*; they've been trying to hunt him down to honor their gods. Though, now that I've found a body, they had no choice but to come clean. We can't have outlaws like Browder terrorizing people, especially during the festival. That's why I need you to find him."

"If it's really Browder who's causing this, then they can't possibly expect to kill him unless they also have guns," said Flint.

"They don't know who Browder is," said Salomon, walking over to an empty cell. "I'm the one who's assuming that it's him based on what Chief Yeramba and his tribe have told me. To them, a wild cowboy has come to steal their souls for Wanambi. It's as simple as that. Now, are you going to help?"

"Of course," said Flint. "What kind of question is that?"

"Just making sure," said Salomon, smirking.

"As I said before, Marshal, I made a vow since Browder disappeared: to protect this town and its people with my life," said Flint, removing a

Peacemaker from his holster and spinning it with ease. "That includes the aboriginals. We're all in this together, and I'm not letting anybody down. Whether it's Browder or somebody else, something strange is definitely happening in the wilds. And if the aboriginals fail to stop Browder, then this problem will eventually affect us." Flint checked his revolver's cylinder—six bullets. He spun his revolver back into its holster and went on, "This is much more serious than you led on, Marshal. I should get Joey and leave right now."

"Wait a minute," said Salomon, taken aback. "Now?"

"Marshal, that maniac can attack anytime."

Salomon looked troubled at first but nonetheless agreed.

"Do any of the aboriginals know where Browder may be?" asked Flint.

"I doubt it. Otherwise they would've dealt with him already," replied Salomon. "Flint, if you're seriously planning to leave now, I strongly suggest you see them first. We both know they don't like outsiders, but I'm sure they'll comply once you tell Chief Yeramba that you're helping him and his tribe kill Browder—the wild demon." He shook Flint's hand with a slight expression of hope and said, "I wish there was more I could do, but I need to keep an eye on this town since my deputies are at the mine."

"Don't worry about it, Marshal," said Flint, waving his hand. "That's why I'm here." He headed for the door while adding, "I'll try to return before the festival. And trust me, if anything happens, you'll be the first to know."

"All right, good luck out there," said Salomon. "And, Cross," he called out before Flint left. "Thanks for helping."

"Protecting the people of this town is my life, Marshal," he said, exiting the office.

Standing on the veranda, Flint observed the dusty town. When thinking of Browder, he had a strange feeling that this town wasn't real. He was never one to be overly conscious of his surroundings or the inner depths of his muddled mind, at least from what he could remember. And that was the problem—he had little memory of his past. This sudden flash of self-aware tension hit him as though someone had shot him awake.

"Cross!" shouted a nearby voice. "Flint Cross!"

Flint's dilated eyes returned to normal. Upon breaking away from his daydreaming, he noticed Preacher Harrison approaching.

"Steve," he said warmly.

Preacher Harrison, an elderly man, gave out a hearty laugh and said, "Why, for a moment there you looked like you saw a ghost."

Flint hugged him and replied, "Not yet."

The preacher laughed and said, "One day, when the good Lord wills it, I'll be a ghost myself. But don't count on me visiting you. The good Lord said that after the end of days the faithful shall join Him—that time is coming very soon. Just look at the state of the world and you'll know in your heart that it's true."

Flint nodded at Preacher Harrison but wasn't entirely swayed by his words. Although he didn't understand why, something deep within his mind told him that he had unfinished business before leaving this dead world.

"It's not over yet," said Flint, gazing at the sky.

"I beg your pardon?" responded Preacher Harrison, surprised by the unexpected tone Flint used.

"I'm sorry," he said. "I mean, the end of days hasn't come just yet."

"Oh, I see," said Preacher Harrison, looking at him suspiciously. "Well, I just wanted to say hello. I'd best be going now. The good Lord is waiting for me to return to my prayers. Come by with your folks for once, eh?"

"I promise," said Flint, a bit embarrassed yet still shameless. "After the festival you'll see me with my wife. And don't worry, it won't be for a divorce."

Preacher Harrison chuckled and then waved goodbye.

Flint turned his attention back to the town square. Looking ahead, he spotted passersby walking along the grimy road. Some kept to themselves while others conversed quietly among one another. A few were sitting on the opposite side of the veranda, in front of a saloon called *The Wild Owl*. Meanwhile, the Steward family rode by on their stagecoach with goods they'd just received after trading with aboriginal herders. Even though there was a lot going on in front of Flint, he wasn't paying much attention.

"Browder," he muttered, drifting away yet again. He refused to believe Browder would go on a rampage, killing innocent people. "It can't be him," he said to himself. Just then, he noticed Joey's stallion hitched by the town's gun shop. Perfect timing, he thought. He stepped down the veranda, walked across the dusty road, and entered the store. "I'm impressed, you got back home pretty quick."

"Heya, partner," said Joey, crafting bullets. "Yeah, I left just a few minutes after you. So, what'll it be?" Glancing at a rack of various guns, he grabbed a Chassepot and went on, "This breach-loadin' baby is my finest rifle. I can also show ya my latest revolver. But, er, that face of yers is tellin' me otherwise. Somethin' on ya mind?"

"Yes," replied Flint despondently. "Marshal Salomon just told me that someone's been murdering aboriginals—the Wakaya. Now I'm not supposed to tell you this, but Salomon seems to think that the man responsible for killing them is Browder."

"*What?*"

"Yeah, I could hardly believe it myself," said Flint. "I guess your reaction is how most folks would respond, which is why you need to keep this a secret. The only reason why I told you this is because I need you to come with me. I'm not sure if I can stop an outlaw at my age, especially if he's Browder."

"I see," said Joey, startled. "Well then, what're we waitin' fer?"

He tossed his Chassepot to Flint, grabbed a Winchester for himself, and placed it in a gun scabbard. Flint, meanwhile, stocked up on bullets and slung a bandolier over his vest.

"Hey," pouted Joey, "yer payin' fer all that, right?"

"Consider us coming back alive as payment."

Joey rubbed his chin. "Hmm, yer always a thinker. I guess that's why I'm still followin' ya even though yer crazy."

They both chuckled.

"Anythin' else we need?"

"Some food for the journey would suffice," said Flint. "You still have some left over bush tucker, right?"

"Yep," said Joey, going downstairs.

"Get one of your knapsacks too," said Flint. "We can put the food inside." He raised his voice since Joey was in the cellar, "I'm going to take some extra ammo just in case!"

"Good idea!" said Joey, also raising his voice.

Flint noticed a double-action swing-out-cylinder magnum on the counter. He had never seen such a gun before. Flint peeked at the basement door—no sign of Joey—and put the gun in his left holster. The magnum barely fit, but he managed. After taking several more bandoliers of ammunition from beneath the counter, he walked over to the door leading outside.

Still waiting for Joey, he started feeling anxious. Pacing back and forth, he wondered whether the outlaw who'd killed the Wakaya was in fact Browder. If it *was* him, thought Flint, why did he vanish for so many years, and why did he decide to come back? Could he have a posse with him or is he acting alone? He snapped out of his daydreaming, hearing steps creak from behind.

"So," began Joey, finally coming back upstairs, "does Amanda know what we're plannin' ta do now?"

"Amanda?" replied Flint, staring blankly at him as if he didn't recognize the name.

Joey exploded with laughter.

"What's so funny?" asked Flint, irritated. "She knows how busy I can be with this line of work. Besides, if she starts worrying she can visit Salomon. He'd probably tell her something to calm her down."

"Have it yer way, partner," said Joey, tapping Flint on the shoulder. "Let's git outta here 'n find us an outlaw before tha festival." He exited his shop and reached his stallion, placing his knapsack on the saddle. "Time fer another long ride, Buddy."

Flint walked across the road and freed his mare from the hitch post. Buddy, Joey's black stallion, trotted toward Donna. The steeds stood beside each other until their masters tugged their reins. Together they galloped out of Desonas—south. Flint felt confident riding his horse into the desolate frontier. Joey, on the other hand, was so ecstatic with their adventure that he raised his rifle and cheered. He'd always been a bit strange,

Flint conceded, but that's what made Joey amusing, as well as a good co-hort to have in the wilds. To Flint, good company meant good security.

Most of the Northern Territory's terrain was flat. And though barren, tumbleweed rolled by during an occasional breeze. Fertile land was rarely seen outside of Desonas, but it did exist. In fact, Flint saw potential farm-land while he rode out. Much of Australia's terrain, however, remained without alteration since the aboriginals didn't want their sacred landscape changed. Another problem was that those few who dreamed of expanding their land were too nervous to take a risk. So, the continent remained bar-ren. Even the trees scattered throughout the wilds were withered.

If anyone still lived outside of Australia and traveled here, they would probably consider it to be a war-torn land. But to Flint, having an arid wasteland for a home was just fine—mostly because he didn't know any-thing else. As he traveled south with Joey, he noticed one of Earth's largest sandstone rock formations: Uluru, a site considered sacred by the aborigi-nals. It looked small from Desonas; however, it soared three-thousand feet high like a majestic citadel whose aim was to kiss the clouds. The sun had begun to set, but the reddish clutches of Uluru stood out like a mountain of fire.

"So, why didn't ya tell Amanda 'bout this expedition of ours?" asked Joey. "I mean, she is yer wife 'n all."

"You're joking, right?" responded Flint. To his surprise, Joey looked serious. "Didn't you see how she reacted earlier?"

"Well, I guess."

"Mind you, that was just a lousy trophy," said Flint. "Imagine what she'd say or do after telling her that I'm hunting an outlaw. She expects me to be up all night fixing the house for the festival when it can be done between her and Sarah."

"Good answer," said Joey. "But I'm still puttin' my money on a secret. Yer tryin' ta hide somethin' from me, aren't ya?" He winked at him. "Still dreamin' of that woman?"

"Wh-what?" stuttered Flint, slightly blushing. "N-no. I haven't dreamt of Hamarah in months."

"*Sure*," said Joey, guffawing.

"Why would I lie?" said Flint defensively. "She's just a damn fantasy. It's not like I'm being unfaithful to Amanda."

Joey's eyebrows twitched, a grin growing on his face.

"And I'll tell you this," went on Flint, "between you and me, I wish those dreams *would* come back."

"Heck, I'd freakin' wish fer tha same thing myself from tha way ya described her," said Joey, squeezing his chest and pretending he had huge breasts. "Ooh la la."

Flint sighed.

"Ah, I'm just kiddin' wit ya," said Joey with sympathy. "Listen, I know things aren't so grand between ya two, but she does love ya. And I know, somewhere in that crazy heart of yers, that ya love her too."

"Thanks for reminding me," said Flint. "Now I'll be able to sleep tonight."

They continued south until evening came, spotting several stars while the sky changed from blue to indigo. It became windier. A chorus of insects grew. And though still far off, Uluru now loomed twice as big to the riders.

The duo started riding southwest. Night swept over them like a breeze. Although the sun was out of sight, the severe heat persisted. The land remained silent and dreary. For the first time in a long while, being in the Northern Territory disheartened Flint. He strangely began to feel as if he didn't belong here; yet he had no idea why this feeling came over him. Flint wondered to himself, was this because he was tired? His discomposure, however, dissolved when he saw a lake up ahead.

"As much as I love being out here in the wilds, especially at night, I think we should stop by that billabong and let our horses rest for a few hours," said Flint.

"Our horses? Hell, what 'bout us?"

"Yeah, I suppose we can get some rest too," said Flint.

He nudged Donna toward a gulch in which the billabong lay. He then swung down from the saddle and hitched her to a bloodwood tree. Since it was the only one in walking distance, Joey hitched Buddy there too. The horses drank from the water while Joey helped Flint set up camp.

"Thanks."

"Anytime, partner," replied Joey. He took out some bush tucker and then sat down, eating the fruits while waiting for Flint to start a fire. "We gots plenty of food. Should I give a bit ta tha horses?"

"I'm touched you even thought of them," said Flint.

Joey shrugged. "Hey, I'm a nice guy."

"Yes, you are," said Flint, chafing a stone with twigs until the tinder lit up in a small flame. "They'll be fine. They can eat grass and drink from the billabong." He grabbed a few pieces of bush tucker and ate them. "These are really good."

"I only bring tha best of tha best."

"That you do, my friend," said Flint. He finished eating and then lay on a blanket by the fire. He stayed quiet, staring at the clear sky. He was beginning to feel ill-at-ease—a discomfort rising from his subconscious. "Joey," he called out in a low tone.

"Mmhmm?" he uttered, munching on a piece of fruit.

"Ever get the feeling that you were meant for more?"

"Eh?" said Joey, swallowing prematurely. "Whaddya mean?"

"I don't know," said Flint, sighing. "It's just...I get this weird feeling once in a while that I don't belong here. It makes me think I was meant for so much more."

"Kinda like wishin' ya was married ta that dream girl instead of Amanda?"

"I'm being serious," said Flint. "Sometimes I feel like something's missing—as if I left a part of my soul behind somewhere."

Joey tilted his head. "I could tell ya what I think," he said. "But I reckon ya don't wanna hear it."

"Try me."

"Easy," replied Joey. "Yer gettin' old." When he said that, Flint's eyebrows twitched. "It happens ta us all. I'm not as old as ya, but I'm gettin' there. We all want ta feel accomplished before we go, right?"

Flint kept quiet. He was upset, almost insulted. He knew what Joey said was true. Yet a part of him wanted to shrivel up in shame; instead he took a deep breath and attempted to keep listening.

"It's obvious yer not happy wit Amanda," said Joey bluntly. "It's makin' ya think 'bout everythin' ya done, wonderin' if things would've been different marryin' another gal."

"Maybe," muttered Flint, purposely trying to act unconvinced by Joey's thoughts even though he knew this was a fact. "I may not be happy with Amanda, but I'll never regret being a father. Sarah and Tommy are my life now. Still—"

"Come on, Flint," interrupted Joey. "Yer a great man. There ain't a lot of people out here who do what yer doin' fer tha folks in town. Heck, yer even helpin' those aborigines. Some folks don't realize it as much as others, but yer tha best ranger we've got."

"It's a thankless job whenever it comes to Amanda," said Flint grumpily.

Joey yawned and said, "She'll come around. Ya just keep being who yer are 'cus they'll always be people who depend on ya. Even tha Wakaya need ya. Hell, every tribe out here needs ya. And who's gonna stop Browder if it ain't us?"

Rubbing his scruffy goatee, Flint nodded.

"But we ain't gonna stop 'em in this condition," said Joey. "I reckon we git sum shuteye before ya lose it."

Flint chuckled softly. "Yeah, I can use a nap." He noticed that the horses were resting by the murky billabong. He yawned, stretched his arms, and lay on his blanket. "Have a good night, Joey."

"You too, partner," he said, turning sidelong and going to sleep.

A few hours passed. The land slowly changed and deformed. The billabong turned into a marsh. The land around Flint became green, filled with life. Even the landscape changed—Uluru no longer stood in the distance. Flint awoke, finding himself in a marsh located in Arnhem Land, northern Australia. His garbs were soaking wet since he'd been sleeping in the mire. Rain poured over him while he rose to his feet, confused.

"What the hell?" he said to himself, gazing at the lush terrain.

Joey and the horses were gone. He observed his surroundings carefully, spotting the very familiar Nourlangie Rock—a steep and jagged escarpment that looked like a fortress of nature. Though observing this sacred aboriginal site was incredible, Flint had no clue how he'd gotten here. The rain abruptly ended, and the clouds vanished, as did the black-spotted sun.

"Where did the sun go?" he said, dismayed. "How's this possible?"

He waded through the marsh while a wedge-tailed eagle flew over him. It squawked, gliding high above. Gazing at the bird, Flint felt as though it were staring at him. The eagle soon faded away, flying to the east. Not a second later, daytime became nighttime. Flint couldn't see anything except the primordial stars that shimmered in the firmament.

Fixing his eyes on them, he saw one move. Flint watched the star travel. He couldn't help feel that it symbolized his lost soul. Despite him not knowing how he ended up being here in this region, he felt calm by observing his soul as it began its journey into the unknown. Then the sun abruptly reemerged. When it rose along the hazy horizon, it cast a tremendous flare, vaporizing all life. Flint screamed as his skin melted off his bones.

He woke up screaming, on the verge of having a heart attack. Only six hours had passed, yet he felt that the dream had lasted forever. He was still tired but made do. Joey, on the other hand, awoke and got to his feet in a hurry while aiming his loaded rifle, uneasily scouting the area.

"What in tarnation happened?" asked Joey, distraught.

"Sorry," said Flint. "It was another one of those dreams." He sat up on the dirt and took a deep breath. "Sometimes I feel my dreams have a mind of their own."

Joey looked puzzled by his words, yawning.

"Tell me," continued Flint, "what do you think the world would've been like without those sun flares?"

Sighing with contempt, Joey splashed water on his face. "Civilization's gone, Flint," he said dismally. "Try ta think 'bout why we're out here. Desonas ain't safe wit Browder on tha loose. It's why we got our duty. Er, on second thought, yer tha real ranger 'round these parts. I jus' help ya when I can."

Flint accepted Joey's answer and knew it was true, yet he felt that there was something else. His dreams, he conceded, have been a link to some deep, vague part of his subconscious mind. However, he had no idea why he thought this.

"Thanks for listening," he said, getting up.

Joey nodded with a suspicious gaze. In the meantime, Flint packed his supplies. About a minute later, however, he stopped and stood stock-still.

"Somethin' wrong, partne...holy shit."

Dozens of aboriginals surrounded the camp. They were wielding knives and spears. Their skin was dark, and they had extensive paint on their bodies from head to toe. To Flint, the white paint made them look like skeletons from a distance; and though he felt this made him lack respect—cultural sensitivity to be precise, he nevertheless felt that those few who didn't have paint resembled brooding demons with the menacing gazes they wore. Utterly speechless, Joey dropped his gun. Flint, meanwhile, lifted his hands in the air.

"King Yeramba," he called out. "I need to see King Yeramba."

Most of the aboriginals glanced at one another with ferocious expressions. They walked closer to the duo, pointing their spears at them as if intending to attack. Flint heard aboriginals whispering among themselves but couldn't understand them. One finally approached, towering over Flint by at least two feet.

"No king. No chief. No tribe. We not like you. We tell Anangu many time. We one people," said the tall aboriginal.

"My apologies," replied Flint.

"I am Jatma," said the tall aboriginal, placing a hand on his chest. "I take you to Yeramba."

Flint bowed and signaled his comrade to follow, mounting their horses. The duo traveled at a slow pace with the aboriginals. Joey stared at them curiously. Many of them had no facial hair, though some did have thick untamed beards. What became most disturbing to Joey was that each aboriginal had a laced vine necklace on which hung teeth.

"Hey," whispered Joey, glancing at Flint. "Do ya suppose those teeth on their necks are from animals they hunted?"

"It's my understanding that before burying their family they remove at least one tooth and keep it for protection."

"Protection?" said Joey, flinching. "These people need protection?"

Flint noticed his partner wore an aghast expression and could barely keep himself from laughing. "It's believed that by doing so the spirits of their ancestors will watch over them," he said, smirking. "Now don't get all excited on me. This is just wilderness lore."

"Tch," muttered Joey. "Ain't nothin' gonna scare me."

Dawn came, and the sun began to rise. In due time, they arrived at Yeramba's territory. This region was less desolate with hummock-forming spinifex. More aboriginals were in the area, staring at their visitors.

"They don't look too happy," said Joey.

"Not with Browder running rampant around here," replied Flint. "In fact, the aboriginals are probably wondering if we've helped him."

The majority of the aboriginals kept to themselves such as those who played music. Four of them had didgeridoos, playing rhythmic wind sounds in unison while Jatma guided his two visitors through the settlement. Ahead of the aboriginal musicians stood a few naked warriors dancing, incense wafting alongside them.

"What's goin' on?" asked Joey, flabbergasted.

"Smoking ceremony," said Flint. "They're attempting to ward off evil spirits. It's usually forbidden for outsides to witness. Things must be really bad if—"

"Anangu," interjected Jatma, glaring at Flint. "No talk."

Flint complied. He waited patiently with Joey while the aboriginals danced to their wind music, smoke spreading. Even though Flint had been educated in the ways of the aboriginals, he hadn't seen an actual ceremony performed before. He was a bit startled at first but appreciated the tribal ritual, unlike Joey who looked dismayed by the dance.

In the meantime, the incense began to waft around them. More aboriginals joined the ceremonious dance and entered a wild trance. They encircled Flint and Joey, chanting in their native tongue.

"Uh," uttered Joey, slack-jawed, "are they plannin' ta cook us or something?"

"Patience," whispered Flint.

Though he wanted to speak with Yeramba, he couldn't help but feel the need to dance. Flint entered the same wild trance as the aboriginals. They suddenly looked like dark angels to him, glowing with their white paint. They were here to save him from this nightmarish world he lived in. He desperately wanted the trance to last forever; he wanted the dark angels to seize his old soul and resurrect him—to restore him to his former glory. Then he wondered to himself, what resurrection and former glory? Before he could figure this out, his thoughts dwindled, and he broke out of the reverie.

For some reason, Flint couldn't reenter the spiritual trance. It made him feel uneasy. He desperately wanted to be a part of it—to see the angels again, and to forget Amanda, his old age, and the ruined world. His children were the only reason why he desired to continue existing as Flint Cross. There was a great turmoil within him. He turned, noticing how serene Joey looked. He thought to himself, shouldn't Joey be the one in turmoil? Flint didn't have an answer; in fact, he no longer had answers to anything in life. Submerged in depression, he surrendered his inner revolt and simply waited for the dance to finish.

Just then, Flint noticed that the smoke covering the spinifex had begun to fade. When it disappeared, Yeramba became visible. He was naked, covered with exotic stripes of white paint. Sitting on the ground in silence while taking deep breaths, he abruptly opened one eye and glared at Flint like a madman. Then he shut the eye, inhaling smoke. The amount he consumed seemed a bit supernatural to the rangers.

"I fancy smokin' but goddamn," said Joey.

Flint kept quiet. Many of the aboriginals were dancing now, including Jatma. The four musicians kept blowing their didgeridoos in unison. Joey was beginning to enjoy hearing each sound they created from their instruments.

"Sit with me, Anangu," Yeramba finally said, his voice deep and loud. Flint obeyed, walking uphill with Joey. "Alone," he added sternly.

Hearing the aboriginal's tone of voice, Joey gulped heavily and stepped back. In the meantime, Flint warily approached Yeramba and sat opposite him.

"You go into the dreaming," said Yeramba.

"I have no idea what you mean," said Flint.

"Ah," said Yeramba, blowing smoke from his nostrils. "You think it coincidence to be here?"

Flint questioningly stared at him.

"Altjira has spoken," went on Yeramba, pointing skyward. "You come help, but no help if not align with spirits. Much help needed. Earth become ill by Wanambi's wild demon. Even mighty sun, created by Altjira, become corrupt. Dreamtime is same."

Listening to the aboriginal leader, Flint experienced another eerie flash of self-revelation; he had a bizarre feeling he'd forgotten something long ago that was imperative to remember. Yet nothing seemed logical about it.

"I'm here to stop the wild demon," said Flint. "But I am troubled. I can't seem to shake off this feeling that I don't belong here. Can you help me?"

"Dreamtime is answer," said Yeramba. "I help you go into Altjira's realm, Anangu. But first prove yourself. You same as Salomon. Though this not enough. Salomon is white soul; you is murky soul. Murky confuse me, and that cause trouble."

"What must I do to enter this *dreamtime* and remember?" asked Flint.

"Dreamtime source of creation, Anangu," said Yeramba. "It is birth and death—endless cycle in reincarnation. We enter and return to dreaming." Yeramba placed his bullroarer on top of a stone slab beside him and stayed quiet for a moment while Flint pondered whether Yeramba was insane. "Maybe you a dingo or goanna in the dreaming."

Yeramba momentarily opened his eyes and blew powder into Flint's face, making him cough violently.

"Ah, you is white dingo."

"What the hell did you just do to me?" scowled Flint, continuing to cough.

"Spirits," said Yeramba. "They protect Anangu. Return if stop Wanambi's wild demon and defeat him. Remember dreamtime. Spirits split over sun's illness—held in dreamtime past Alchera. Only if Altjira happy are souls awaken and heal."

"King Yeramba," began Flint, "do you at least know where this wild demon is?"

"No king," said Yeramba. "I told Anangu I no king. We all messenger of Altjira. We all have dreamtime. To answer question: let spirits guide you. Wanambi hides. Wild demon face us. Find him at rock of creation."

"Thank you," said Flint. He rose to his feet and tipped his hat even though Yeramba had his eyes closed. "May the spirits protect you and your people." He walked downhill and rejoined Joey. "Let's get out of here."

"Wait," he said. "What did that old coot say?"

"A bunch of gibberish," replied Flint, walking toward his horse. "The only thing he said that made sense, or at least I think so, was the rock of creation." He then pointed at Uluru, which stood miles away from them. "Browder is probably hiding somewhere there."

"Huh, I reckon tha shaman ain't as mad as tha marshal claimed."

"Trust me, what Salomon claimed isn't far from the truth," said Flint. He mounted Donna and went on, "It's just that he hasn't lost all his screws yet."

Joey laughed, scaling his horse. "I'm glad yer not gonna convert 'n run 'round naked."

"Hilarious," said Flint, giving a smile that lasted quicker than a flicker of lightning.

Clearing his throat, Joey asked, "Just us then, eh? No back up now that we know where Browder is?"

"Just us."

He tugged Donna's reins, making her gallop fast. Within seconds they were away from Yeramba's tribe, traveling closer toward the gargantuan rock formation known as Uluru. It was yet another hot morning. The sky was fairly clear with only a few clouds above. Upon looking east, Flint spotted an emu in the spinifex. The flightless brown-feathered bird stared at him when he passed by it.

Looking farther ahead, he saw Kata Tjuta's domed formation in the western region of the Northern Territory; though, it was quite far from his position. The ground was evermore dry and almost as red as Uluru. A big lizard lay still while the duo rode through the semi-desert land.

"That's a big mama," said Joey.

"Yeah," agreed Flint. He recalled Yeramba suggesting that he could've been a goanna in the dreamtime as he glanced at the laced lizard. It swiftly slithered and scuttled away. "It's been a long time since I've seen one."

They finally reached Australia's greatest landmark. Uluru—Ayer's Rock—had become a god among rocks, enduring Earth's primeval age without any marks of separation. Despite how mesmerizing Uluru looked, Flint wore a grim expression. He saw a cluster of bodies near one of the climbing areas.

"My God!" he cried out.

Flint dismounted Donna and rushed to aid the aboriginals. But it was too late; they were dead—gunshot wounds all over their twisted, stiffened bodies. Joey swung down his horse and joined Flint, gently patting his shoulder. He remained quiet, staring at the corpses.

"I was told long ago that the indigenous Australians used to refer to us as *drifters of the world*," said Flint, his face pale. "When the sun destroyed our land, we drifted like lost souls on Earth, desperately looking for a home. Then we invaded their territory. It took decades for the tribes to change and call us Anangu. This meant that we'd finally earned their trust." His fingers curled into fists as he added, "And now Browder is destroying that trust." Confused and furious, he asked, "Why is he doing this?"

"Only way we gonna know fer sure is ta find 'em," said Joey, grabbing his Winchester rifle and cocking it. "Though, I reckon we shoot as soon as we git sight of 'em or his band of maniacs; that is, if he has a bunch of cronies wit him."

"Right," said Flint warily. He hesitated, wondering which weapon to use. After thinking about it, he removed the magnum that he'd sneakily taken from the gun shop. He noticed Joey's slack-jawed face and couldn't help but grin. "Sorry, pal, you know how much I love these kinds of guns."

"That ain't no gun," said Joey. "As the aborigines would say, it's a damn demon. Try not ta lose yer head wit it."

"Relax," said Flint, observing the area. "Let's split up. I'll take this path. You go around and flank him."

"What if there's nobody ta flank?"

"Then we wait," replied Flint.

Joey agreed and sprinted as quietly as he could to the eastern side of Uluru. Upon seeing him leave, Flint started to ascend Uluru. The sun shone on Ayer's Rock, making it dangerously hot; however, Flint barely paid mind to the heat. His brown leather gloves helped him avoid getting burned while climbing Uluru's reddish granite. The only thing on his mind was the fate of the aboriginals.

"Damn it, Browder," he said to himself. "How could you kill them? *Why?*"

He soon approached a bluff that brought him to a wide area with two passages. The path on the left led to Uluru's peak while the right led to a cavern. Flint cautiously entered the dark cave. Fortunately for him, the sun gave him more than enough light to see. He saw a few petroglyphs inside the cavern. Some were illustrations of aboriginals dancing while others depicted them hunting animals such as bustards and kangaroos—at least this was how Flint interpreted the petroglyphs.

Captivated by the rock carvings, he'd forgotten to check the cave for signs of Browder or any possible goons. Luckily for him, no one was hiding inside. He exited the cave and took the other path. It was a narrow ridge, so Flint walked carefully. In due time, he reached halfway up the mountainous rock. A perentie lizard stood on a boulder; it was standing on its hind legs. As soon as it saw Flint, however, it scuttled away.

No one seemed to be on Uluru other than Flint and some wild animals. He nevertheless watched his back to make sure he wasn't being flanked by Browder. Although the heat didn't bother Flint, the sun's glare prevented him from looking skyward. The brim of his hat helped, but it wasn't enough. He eventually investigated a passage more shaded than others. Reaching a dead end, he sighed and took a deep breath.

Flint was about to give up searching Uluru when he heard a cluster of pebbles fall from above. At first he thought another animal scuttled like the perentie; then he noticed a humanoid shadow appear. He leaned against the jagged wall and stood still on the rickety trail, waiting for the shadow to move away. Upon gazing outward, he noticed the barren expanse below. Once again, Flint experienced an irrational feeling that made him question everything he knew from the environment to his very existence. His life suddenly became fictitious. Everything around him felt surreal and fake.

"This must be the effects of Yeramba's powder," he muttered. Pausing for a moment, he rethought what he'd just said. "No, that's not true. I've had this feeling before."

Snapping out of his eerie daydreaming, he found himself by the ledge. He turned around, realizing the humanoid shadow had vanished. Upon looking at the cliff above, however, he saw one of Browder's men walking away. He aimed his magnum at the goon and shot him without hesitation. The bullet blew off the outlaw's right arm and shoulder, causing him to scream and fall down from the edge, smashing against rocks. Normally, the backfire of a magnum would have jolted its wielder, yet Flint didn't even budge. He acknowledged this, wondering why it hadn't affected him. Nevertheless, he was impressed.

Flint had no idea how to gain higher ground other than rock climbing, so he holstered his weapon and climbed Uluru. The gloves he wore continued to protect his hands from the heat. He thought having them on might make it harder to free climb, but he didn't slip or have any trouble scaling the fiery-tinged rock. In fact, Flint climbed so fast that he reached the summit in a matter of minutes.

It was already early afternoon by the time Flint reached Uluru's peak. He lifted himself and rose to his feet, unexpectedly standing before Browder and his goons. They were glaring at him, hands hovering over their holsters. Oddly, Flint didn't feel threatened despite the fact that seven outlaws were about to shoot him. Instead he glared at Browder with utter hatred. With the exception of Browder, the small posse looked young. Browder appeared to be the only one who was around Flint's age. Yet he was clean shaven and clad in tattered garbs.

"Andrew Browder," said Flint. "It's been a long time. And honestly, I never thought I'd see your face again."

"Commandant?" said Browder, astonished. "Is it really you?"

Flint's grimace was wiped away, replaced by a baffled expression. "Commandant?" he replied in a perplexed tone. "What the hell are you talking about?"

"You don't remember?" asked Browder. "No, of course you don't."

"Do you have any idea what you've done, Browder?" said Flint, his hand moving closer to his single-action revolver. "You have murdered countless aboriginals for no reason! Are you planning to attack Desonas next?"

"Of course I am," answered Browder.

"Then it's as Marshal Salomon had suspected," said Flint.

"Salomon's just a pawn!" exclaimed Browder.

"A pawn?" responded Flint, even more confused. "I don't know how you've gained such a large supply of ammunition to kill the aboriginals and wage war against Desonas, but whatever you've planned ends today, Browder. I'm afraid you'll either have to surrender now or face the consequences."

"Who the fuck is this old man?" asked one of the goons.

"Steer your hand, Landers," replied Browder. "This is Etha—I mean, this is Flint Cross we're talking to. He's different from the others out here. We're no match for him."

"I'd listen to him if I were you," said Flint.

"You're joking," said Landers, laughing loudly. The other gunmen laughed with him. In the meantime, Flint's fingers drew closer to his revolver's handle. "It's seven to one," went on Landers. "This old fogy can't do anything."

Flint pulled out his single-action gun and, cocking the revolver, shot all six of Browder's comrades. There used to be a theory stating that nothing was faster than the speed of light; Flint, however, put that theory to the test. Landers didn't even have a chance to remove the smug look on his face. He lay dead with a contorted smile, along with his companions. Browder, who had his arms in the air, was the only one left standing.

"Don't shoot!" he pleaded.

"Browder," began Flint, "there's only one reason why you're still alive, and it's because my gun only has six chambers." He put his revolver away while simultaneously taking out his double-action magnum, aiming it at Browder. "But this one's loaded. And forgive me for being a bit anxious, but I'm rather itching to hear the sound it makes again. Start talking, and maybe I'll reconsider using it. Why have you killed the Wakaya?"

"You'd be doing the same if you remembered."

"That's not an answer," said Flint, shooting Browder's hat off. Once again, he felt the gun's recoil but didn't budge. Browder, on the other hand, cringed and showed his palms.

"Don't kill me!" he shrieked.

"I'm losing my patience," said Flint. "Give me an answer."

"You think you're in control?" replied Browder, rising and gazing at Flint harshly. "Not even Salomon's in control! It's all a sick game! Everything! And the worse thing is that there's not much I can do about it. But with you? Yes, with you there's a chance to leave this forsaken rock. We can work together like the old days."

"The old days?"

"Yes, you even saved my life once," said Browder. "I told you that I'd find a way to repay you. It's the only reason why I'm still here. How could you forget? Commandant, you must remember."

"Why do you keep calling me that?" scowled Flint.

"Do you actually think you're a cowboy?" said Browder. He laughed hysterically while observing Flint's clothes. "You're in the wrong era, pal. I can help you remember everything. We can still win the war and get back our freedom. But first you have to stop eating the greens; then you'll—"

Browder's head suddenly burst with blood and brains. Flint wore a ghastly expression as he saw the outlaw get blown away. He winced and aimed his gun past Browder's body, spotting Joey who had been creeping up on Browder for quite some time. Joey lifted his Winchester rifle, relieved.

"What the hell did you just do?" yelled Flint.

"What I came here ta do," answered Joey, startled.

Flint irrationally ran over to Browder, hoping he was still alive; however, seeing a lifeless body with a pool of blood brought him back to reality.

"Tha man was a complete lunatic, Flint," explained Joey. "He could've caught ya off guard 'n shot ya!"

"I had everything under control!" shouted Flint, enraged. His head throbbing, he pressed the magnum's cylinder against the temple of his head while he said, "I failed you...just as I've failed Hamarah."

"What did you just say?" asked Joey in a tone of disbelief, his accent a bit off.

Flint tensed up, gawking at what remained of Browder's face. Not even he remembered what he'd just said—or at least the latter of what he'd said. Flint took a deep breath, rising back to his feet.

"I had everything under control," he repeated.

"No, after that," said Joey, suspiciously gaping into Flint's eyes.

The throbbing pain in Flint's head worsened. It was so horrible that he could hardly see anything. He felt as if Yeramba had blown another dose of powder into his coarse face. Covered with sweat, his heart pounded. His panting became heavy—too heavy. A drop of blood trickled from his nose. Joey's voice sounded like gibberish as he gazed at the hazy vista. Then the pain abruptly subsided, Flint feeling normal again.

"Forget it," he muttered, wiping his nose. "I'm sorry I got upset."

Joey eased up, putting his rifle away.

"Browder's insanity got the best of me, that's all," said Flint. "You did the right thing. I told you to flank him, and we agreed to shoot on sight."

"Right," said Joey warily. "Well, let's git tha hell outta here, partner."

The duo carefully descended Uluru. They were quiet most of the way back home. Flint's mind, however, had never been more cluttered with outlandish thoughts. Even though Browder and his posse had killed innocent aboriginals, Flint couldn't help but ponder what the outlaw had meant by calling him Commandant. He wondered about what he may have forgotten. And if he did in fact forget something, was it significant? Or did Browder simply feed him lies in a vain attempt to survive?

More absurd was that Browder had told him to stop eating the *greens*. In folded palms, he held his remaining bush tucker as he rode back home, trying to figure out why Browder had told him to stop eating them. He didn't know what to do, so he slipped the bush tucker back into his pocket and kept quiet while following Joey. He had no logical answers to the questions plaguing him; though, somewhere deep down inside his gut, he had a feeling they would be answered one day, and that such explanations wouldn't be what he'd be hoping to discover.

CHAPTER TWO
THE STREAMING DREAM

Flint entered his home in the afternoon, haggard. He yawned when he stepped inside. Closing the door behind him, he noticed Sarah and Tom sitting in the hall looking fretful. Seeing their father, they hugged him. Flint closed his eyes for a moment, embracing them too.

"I was so worried," said Sarah.

"What happened, dad?" asked Tom.

"Long story," replied Flint. He rubbed his son's hair and kissed his daughter on the forehead. "Let's just say that the festival will be a peaceful night to remember."

Being with Sarah and Tom was the only true joy he had left. Not even being a cowboy made him feel content, even though it presented him with the freedom he needed. Freedom was the second most important thing to him after his children. Without such freedom in the world, he would rather die than be a slave or prisoner. Sadly, he felt he wasn't far from being a prisoner since Amanda was his wife. Flint cherished this very moment, holding his son and daughter. But the family reunion was short lived because Amanda entered the hall. He didn't even have to look at her to know that she was glaring at him.

"Flint Cross, where have you been?" she asked furiously.

"Save it, Amanda," said Flint. He let go of his children, removed his bandolier, and then walked away from his family. "I know everyone's coming over for the festival in an hour or so, but right now I'm really tired and need a nap."

"Don't you dare walk away from me!" yelled Amanda.

She grabbed his arm as though ready to tear it off. Flint, however, shoved her away with force. Amanda shrieked while pushed against the wall and then shriveled down to the floor. Tom and Sarah gasped when they witnessed what their father had done.

"I'm not in the mood to hear your bitching, so shut up," said Flint.

"I've had enough of your dirty little secrets," whimpered Amanda. "You can't just leave us whenever you feel like it and not say anything!"

"Looks like I just did," retorted Flint.

"Stop fighting," said Sarah. "I'm sick of this. Is it really so hard for the two of you to get along? I feel we're not a real family anymore."

Although nodding, Tom kept quiet, staring at the dusty mat on the floor while Amanda cried in the corner of the hall. Tom mutually hated the endless arguments between his father and mother, except he never knew how to express himself. He was a bit too reserved. Instead he let his older sister handle these problems.

"Everybody else is happy," continued Sarah. "Why can't we be happy too?"

Flint didn't respond or even look at his daughter. He felt ashamed, knowing in his heart that Sarah had a point; she was always honest, logical, and emotionally strong. Flint, however, merely responded with a grunt and went upstairs to his bedroom. He locked the door behind him, sighing. He thought to himself, today was supposed to be a memorable day; it was supposed to be about family. Flint heard Sarah's voice in his head, telling him to fix this horrible family feud. But, instead of fixing the problem, he ignored it. He simply took off his boots and hat, rested on the bed, and fell asleep.

The bedroom darkened. A shadow of a woman swept by from the door to the window on the other side. Then the floral wallpaper ripped off the walls, replaced with a nomadic design of Australian wildlife. At that moment the window reshaped into glass doors leading to a balcony, the beige drapes changing into sheer curtains.

Flint yawned, opening his eyes and rising from his bed. He noticed that the bedroom was different. Yet he wasn't surprised by this strange occurrence. Standing up, he put his hat back on and walked over to the balcony's glass doors through which he could see an ocean. The house he resided in was now on a beach. Opening the doors, he heard waves rising and falling. The sky was clear—not a single cloud in sight. It was a beautiful panorama, but more beautiful was the woman in front of him.

Leaning on the balustrade was a petite woman who wore a white gown with sexy curves, long black hair, and a tan complexion. Standing behind her, Flint caressed her shoulders. She looked no older than thirty. Despite the major age difference, Flint knew he'd always loved her, and she loved him. This was the woman he had longed for all his life. He was so enthralled by her beauty that he no longer cared about his family, especially Amanda.

"Hamarah," he whispered.

She touched his hand, facing him as the wind swept through her hair. "Yes, Ethan," she said, "it's me. I've been waiting for you to escape that awful town so you can find me."

"Escape?" he said. "You mean Desonas?"

"It's not safe there," she said. "In fact, nowhere in Australia is safe. Browder knew it, and that's why he lost his mind."

"How do you know about Browder?"

"Because you and I are one," she said affectionately. "I always know what's on your mind: what you're feeling and what you've seen."

Holding him close, Hamarah kissed his dry lips. Flint could hardly believe what he was experiencing—being able to see and hold the love of his life again; to feel her lips and hear her sweet voice was too good to be true.

"Is this real?" he asked.

She nodded at him.

"How long do we have together?"

Her eyes cast down, she answered, "Not long, I'm afraid. But I'll always be waiting for you to come back. All you have to do is remember and you'll be able to find me."

Gently holding her arms with a desperate look, he asked, "What must I remember?"

She stared into his eyes with an endearing gaze. Flint stared back at her, stroking her hair. He needed to hear her voice again, but all he heard were the waves of the ocean. Hamarah didn't respond. Instead she held him and kissed him passionately. Flint wanted the kiss to last forever. The longer he kissed her tender lips, however, the more difficult it was to feel the warmth of her body. Soon he couldn't smell her either. Then she was gone, like his memories.

Flint awoke on his bed. The room had returned to its original form. The withered floral-design wallpaper welcomed him back to his sad reality. He looked for the balcony, but it was merely a window again. Hamarah was gone. Sitting up on his bed, he felt lonely and depressed. He rubbed his eyes and then scratched his scruffy goatee, continuing to ponder about what had happened.

"She felt so real," he muttered to himself.

As he wondered about Hamarah, three voices emerged within his mind. One was telling him to leave this wretched, desolate town and find his soul mate. Another voice whispered that he was delusional, and that if he continued down this path of thought, he'd lose his sanity. The third voice was telling him that whether Hamarah was real, he had an obligation as a husband, father, and cowboy to protect his family and the people of Desonas. Flint desperately wanted to leave. The moral voice within him, however, overpowered his temptation to go. In the end, he felt that the dream was just a wild fantasy from his twisted subconscious. His life, despite how miserable it made him, was here with Amanda.

Since he'd gotten some rest, he felt it was time to go downstairs and eat something. When he put his boots on, he got to his feet and heard music from outside. That's when he realized it was evening—the townspeople had come to his family's festival. Feeling more energized after his nap, he grabbed his hat and left the bedroom. Upon opening the door, he heard several people talking. Going downstairs, he saw Joey playing poker in the kitchen with a group of men: Deputy Ted Thornton, Kevin Smith, and Martin Aleman.

Ted looked about Flint's age. He was clad in black and wore his deputy badge with pride. Like Joey, he had a thick mustache, except it was gray. The other two were a lot younger. Kevin had wavy blonde hair and was wearing overalls. Martin had red hair with freckles and also wore overalls. Flint came into the kitchen, joining them.

"Here's our hero!" said Joey. He stood up and patted Flint with delight while the others greeted him. "I told 'em all 'bout how ya bested tha beast!"

"Nice one, Flint," said Kevin Smith.

"Yes, I saw that thing as soon as I came inside," said Ted, shaking Flint's hand. "You're a terrible taxidermist,"—Flint chuckled at his comment—"but it's good to know you're still the best cowboy. Other than a koala, I never knew those critters lived here in Australia."

"Neither did I," said Flint. "In fact, Joey over here got all indigenous on me and thought it was a yowie."

The guests at the table laughed.

"Why don't you join us?" asked Martin.

"I'd like to, but I'm expected to be the host outside," said Flint. "Perhaps after I see how my other guests are doing I'll come back and take some of Joey's money."

Joey laughed. "Okay, see ya later."

Leaving the kitchen, Flint glanced at his trophy and thought about his dream. He couldn't get Hamarah out of his mind. This wasn't healthy, he conceded. Hoping that the festival would help him get his feet on the ground, he exited his house and stood on the porch, observing his company. People were square dancing to the music ranging from guitars, fiddles, accordions to harmonicas. Many families were dancing together. Even Preacher Harrison was dancing. Flint felt so happy to see his guests having such a great time that he finally stopped contemplating about his dream.

The women were clad in their nicest dresses with bodices while the men looked more rugged than usual. Flint, however, didn't mind their attire. What mattered to him the most was that they were having a wonderful time together. He spotted Amanda standing at the corner of the porch, speaking to Penny Tutherfield, the only doctor in Desonas. They giggled when Flint glanced at them. He tipped his hat at the doctor but didn't give his wife eye contact—he was still agitated by her attitude. She surprisingly kept quiet, not starting another fight.

Flint stepped down the porch and noticed two groups of men, who were mostly miners, creating commotion. One group arm wrestled while the other competed in a game of five-finger fillet.

"Hey, dad!" called out Tom. "You've gotta see this!"

Flint came over and greeted the gang of miners. He came just in time to see Daren Linko compete against Walter Hamel—owner of *The Wild Owl* saloon. Daren, recognizable because of his facial mutton chops, grabbed a knife on the wooden table, jabbing it between his fingers. The onlookers' eyes were wide open. Daren was pretty vicious and quick with the blade; he finished his pattern in ten seconds. Walter scrubbed his chin patch, grumbling.

"Beat that," said Daren smugly.

Walter, slack-jawed, took the knife and attempted to mimic Daren's pattern. He was, however, moving his hand too slow. The miners booed loudly at his cowardice. Despite them complaining, he continued moving the knife sluggishly. Eleven seconds passed, and he wasn't even half way finished. Walter sighed, giving his opponent eight coins.

"That's right, I own this game!" said Daren.

Gazing at him with an equally smug expression, Flint took a seat. Daren looked at him curiously but nevertheless stuck the knife into the center of the table, acting like he was done. Flint, on the other hand, cracked his knuckles while yawning.

"You don't own this game yet, Linko," said Flint.

The miners grew rowdy and cheered him on, especially his son. Daren, in response, arrogantly took back the knife.

"You're on, old man," said Daren. "Let's go with one round and see if you survive. But how much are you willing to wager, huh? One coin?" Some of the miners guffawed at Daren's sarcasm, yet Flint maintained his smug expression as Daren edged him on further, "Maybe two? Or is that too risky?"

"Twelve," said Flint.

Daren flinched. Though surprised, he remained steadfast and jabbed the knife in his usual reckless pace. Flint didn't blink once while his rival struck the knife between his fingers. Daren acted as though the knife were a plastic toy that could never harm him. This time he finished in nine seconds. Jamming the knife into the table, he praised himself.

"Who's the man?" said Daren. "That's right, I'm the man!"

Flint smirked, taking the knife. The spectators were silent as he put his left hand on the table. Then, in a rapid movement, he thrust it back and forth between his fingers. He repeated this and finished the pattern within seven seconds. It happened so fast that Daren dropped his coins in disbelief. Even the others at the table could hardly believe what they'd just witnessed. Flint's speed was almost inhuman.

"Dad, that was incredible!" said Tom.

"Thanks, son," winked Flint. He stood up, collected the coins, and patted Daren on the shoulder. "Better luck next time."

The miners laughed at Daren. The guests at the table now had the urge to challenge him again. In the meantime, Flint walked over to a table with food. By then, those who were dancing had stopped and took a break beside the bonfire, gleefully listening to the musicians play their instruments. Marshal Salomon, on the other hand, approached Flint.

"Cross," called out Salomon. "It's good to see that you and Joey made it back safely. Any good news or—"

Flint nodded at him despite the fact that he was uptight about the ordeal. "You don't have to worry about Browder anymore, Marshal," he said.

"Excellent," said Salomon, secretly handing Flint a pouch full of coins.

"I'm not sure if I deserve this, but thanks," he said. "Joey was the one who silenced him. I managed to take out his posse—seven of them; though, it's possible there can be more. I think it would be wise for us to keep our eyes open in case there are others still lurking around."

"Good idea," said Salomon. "At least Browder is out of the way. And who knows, maybe you *did* take care of all his goons."

"I don't know," said Flint, looking troubled.

Salomon stared at him curiously and asked, "Is something bothering you?" He wasn't getting a response, so he patted Flint on the shoulder.

"Listen, you did your best. Try to relax now. By the way, this is a splendid festival; though, I must admit, I was a bit worried that you wouldn't show yourself. Amanda said you were feeling sick."

"Sick of her, yes," scoffed Flint. "But don't worry about me. I'm fine. I wouldn't miss this festival if it were the end of the world."

A flash of suspicion arose in the marshal's eyes, caused by Flint's choice of words.

"Great," said Salomon. "You know, Flint, sometimes you say the strangest things. But I guess that's what makes you who you are."

"Right," said Flint.

Salomon let out a sigh and said, "Well, I guess I'll leave you to your guests and rejoin my wife. See you around, Cross."

"Stay close," said Flint.

"Huh?" uttered Salomon, intrigued.

"I've got a fancy speech coming up and would like everyone to be around when I give it," he said.

Salomon nodded with an amused grin, rejoining his wife who was talking to Amanda by the porch. Flint, meanwhile, took off his gloves, tucking them in his vest's pocket. He noticed the bear steak that Amanda and Sarah had prepared. The smell was intoxicating to him. Though, before he could grab a piece of the seasoned meat, Sarah came by with her fiancé.

"Good evening, Flint," said Jake Salomon.

"Jake," he said, shaking his hand. "It's always great to see you."

"Same here."

Jake Salomon, second deputy of Desonas and Marshal Salomon's son, was a twenty-two-year-old man who had green eyes, short brown hair, and a light beard. Although seeing him with his arm around Sarah didn't please Flint, he let it slide since they were engaged.

Flint hugged his daughter, gently kissing her forehead. "Are you two love birds having a decent time?" he asked.

"Of course," she said.

"Yes, it's been quite a while since we were all together," said Jake. "It's a nice feeling. I don't think this would've been possible without you,

Flint. In fact, I heard most of the food here is thanks to you hunting in the wilds."

"Ah, it's the least I could do," said Flint. His stern face unexpectedly blushed despite the fact that he was attempting to act manly in front of Jake.

"*Awww*, dad's blushing."

"Wha-what?" he stuttered. "No I'm not. It was nothing, really. Besides, I had Tom and Joey by my side. They helped a great deal. Which reminds me: can you tell Joey and the others who're inside to come out? I'd like to have a word with our guests."

"Sure," she said, returning to her house with Jake.

While continuing to listen to the entertaining music, Flint heard loud groans. Turning to his left, he noticed two men arm wrestling. Yet they weren't just any men; they were the Panzo brothers, also known as the titan-steel brothers. Brock and Bas Panzo were the bulkiest men Flint had ever known. A single look at them made him feel like he was in desperate need to get back in shape; though, he wasn't in bad shape for being fifty-nine years old.

More miners gathered to watch the titan-steel brothers continue to arm wrestle. Patrons stood behind them, flaunting their money and anxiously shouting out the names of their chosen bets to win. Even though money had little importance, the miners nevertheless loved to gamble. Flint came by to watch as the brothers grumbled, gnashing their teeth in an attempt to overpower each other. Eventually, even those who were playing five-finger fillet came over to watch.

To Flint, it had always been difficult for him to tell the difference between Brock and Bas; however, up close there was one thing that made each of them distinguishable, which was that Brock had a massive auburn beard while Bas had an auburn goatee. Other than that, they looked about the same: sweaty, huge, muscular, and hairy titans. It looked like their bulky arms were about to explode while moving from left to right.

The viewers were getting louder, except Flint who didn't know whom he wanted to win. He mutually liked Brock and Bas and knew they were equally strong. So, to him, it was literally impossible to determine who would win. After a long minute of grimacing and grumbling at each other, they let go and guffawed. Both of them grabbed their tankards, clashed them together, and drank their ale in great swigs. The guests, meanwhile, booed at the draw.

"How come you guys never go at it to the end," jeered Daren Linko. The other miners agreed with his complaint while he added, "We gotta know who's stronger!"

"My dad's stronger," said Tom boldly. The commotion ended right away as the miners looked at Tom. No one wanted to laugh out of respect for Flint, though they couldn't hide their grins; even Brock and Bas were finding it difficult to hold their laughter. "I mean it!" snapped Tom, noticing their reactions.

"My son's jesting," said Flint, chuckling.

"Show us what yer made of, cowboy," said Joey.

Flint swallowed, glancing at his best friend. He wanted to give him a dirty look; however, many of the guests joined in the excitement. With the exception of Sarah who felt rather fretful, they were eager to see this arm-wrestling match.

"Come on, Flint," went on Joey, "how 'bout takin' on Bas?"

"Yeah, dad," said Tom excitedly. "You're amazing at everything. And when you beat Bas it means you can take on Brock too!"

Flint sighed and began, "Well—"

"Excellent," interrupted Daren. "I'm wagering on Bas!"

"No betting this time, folks," said Marshal Salomon. "Flint's already tired what with the hunt. And we all know we're only here because of him, so let's cut the man some slack."

With the exception of Daren Linko, who wanted to win back the money he'd lost in five-finger fillet, the guests agreed. Flint didn't want to arm wrestle Bas; however, since his son and guests were so excited, he felt he had no choice but to comply. He placed his elbow on the table, followed by Bas whose biceps were triple the size of his. They gripped each other's hands and then looked at Brock.

The nod he gave was the signal for them to begin. The onlookers kept quiet while they watched with unintentional excitement, eagerly waiting to see Flint get tossed across the table. Bas attempted to pin him down. His arm, however, didn't budge. Flint expected to lose within seconds, yet he managed to push forward.

For a split second Flint felt as though time stopped. The viewers were silent. He could hear his heart pounding, sweating heavily. There was something wrong about this, he thought. How could he possibly have the strength to resist his hulk of an opponent? Without thinking on this further, he no longer resisted. He then felt time being restored, and Bas pinned his arm down so hard that it wouldn't have surprised anyone if a bone in his body had been fractured; though, he was strangely fine. Bas smiled, most of the spectators praising him.

"Dad, are you okay?" asked Sarah.

"Yeah, I'm fine."

Tom was disappointed and surprised. Apparently, he'd just realized that his father wasn't perfect after all. Joey patted Flint on the shoulder, proud of him, contrary to Amanda who rolled her eyes and sulked under her breath in response to their macho behavior. Some of the guests clapped, pleased to have witnessed such an event. Bas, meanwhile, was very impressed with Flint but said nothing. With the exception of Bas, no one acknowledged what had happened in that split second, and Flint hoped he'd keep it this way.

"Nice try," said Salomon.

"Thanks," replied Flint. He looked at Bas and said, "My goodness, you're an incredible arm wrestler."

"You're not bad yourself, Flint," said Bas.

"Right," said Flint, trying to sound diffident. He stood up and noticed that all his guests were present. If he had a speech as he'd told Marshal Salomon, then there was no better time to share it than now. "Well, before I retire with Doctor Tutherfield,"—Many of the guests laughed softly while Flint jiggled his right wrist—"I mean, before I retire to bed, I'd like to say a few things."

"Ya got two minutes," said Joey.

"Thanks," said Flint, smirking. "First, I want to thank all of you for coming. It means a lot to me that we're all here. I'd like to think that we're fairly close to each other by nature, but most of the time we're busy with our personal lives. A lot of you spend hours working hard in the mine or on your farms. It's never easy here, but I think we're doing just fine. So though we have our responsibilities every day, I'm grateful we were able to get together and have fun. In fact, gratitude is what this is about, which leads me to tell all of you how this festival came to mind."

Most of the people looked overly curious.

Flint continued, "Dreams are a gift. And we know how rare it is when we remember one, especially when it makes us realize what's most important in life. Odd thing is…I had this dream twice."

"That's very interesting, Flint," said Marshal Salomon. "When exactly did you first have this dream? What was it about?"

"It happened a couple of weeks ago, in the beginning of the month. In the dream, I found myself lying in the middle of some badlands after an explosion. It's kind of scary because I was dying." Several of the guests gasped. "I'm still here," he added, chuckling. "I don't know where I was. Though, there were a lot of people gathering around me. I think they were soldiers…it's hard to remember. Oh, and for some reason they called me Ethan."

Marshal Salomon glanced at Doctor Tutherfield who suspiciously glimpsed at him too while Flint spoke.

"I thought you said it's impossible for him to remember anything," whispered Salomon.

Tutherfield, slightly irritated, muttered, "These are just residual memories—grains. He can't possibly put the pieces together. The bush tucker will keep him in line."

"And if he stops eating it?"

"Why on earth would he do that?" she snapped quietly.

Snorting and looking back at Flint, he asked calmly, "And you had this dream twice?"

"Yeah," replied Flint. "I had it again last week. There was more to the dream, but sadly I can't remember. All I know was that these people tried to save me. Like I said, it's a bit creepy. But the bottom line is that I'm alive right now and mighty grateful. You're all family to me. It's a hard life out here. Yet we're doing great. And I wanted to show my gratitude by bringing us together. So, I hope you all have a wonderful night. And may we always remember today as a time to be grateful for everything we have."

"Amen to that," said Preacher Harrison.

Many of the townsfolk clapped at Flint who hugged his children. And, for the first time in months, Amanda approached Flint without screaming at him. She had teary eyes as she walked over to him. She surprisingly kissed his lips, and though Flint hesitated he kissed her back. The townspeople smiled and clapped. Then the musicians played their music again, and the guests continued dancing.

"I'm sorry for being hard on you," whispered Amanda.

"It's really my fault," said Flint. "Sometimes I act younger than Tommy and think I know everything, or that I can do anything I want."

"You're a stubborn man, Flint Cross," she said, kissing him again.

"But a man you can't get enough of," he said.

"For now," she said teasingly.

At that moment his stomach grumbled. He finally grabbed some meat and sat by a table with his wife, eating.

"How's the food?" asked Amanda.

"It's perfect," he said. "Thank you."

"I'm glad," she said, rubbing Flint's hand. "It's a good thing you found that bear. All we had was bush tucker. Everyone eats that, so getting this meat really made a difference."

Flint began to drift away when Amanda mentioned the bush tucker. He remembered what Browder had said to him: 'I can help you remember everything, Commandant. But first you have to stop eating the greens—' Then, instead of grabbing bush tucker from the bowl, he simply took another piece of bear steak.

"My trophy isn't so bad now, is it?" he said, raising an eyebrow.

"Don't push your luck with me, mister," she said sharply. "But I do admit that I'm happy you went hunting with Joey. By the way, how did Tommy do?"

"Honestly, I don't think Tommy was ready," he replied, swallowing a piece of meat. He noticed Amanda nod with a pretentious look on her face. There was nothing more he hated than her self-righteous attitude. "It's not like he did anything wrong. It's just—"

"He's too young and nervous," she said.

"I don't think age has anything to do with it," he said firmly. "But yes, he was nervous." A part of him wanted to mention Sarah—her tomboyish interest to hunt; however, he wanted to keep seeing Amanda in a decent mood, so he kept quiet about her wanting to join him. "Well, I think it's bedtime for me."

"So soon?" she replied in a disappointed tone. "I guess I'll stay here until our guests leave." She gave him a quick kiss on the lips. "Hope you sleep well."

"I will, thanks," he said, walking away.

Flint bade his guests goodnight and returned to his home, going upstairs to sleep. When he entered his room he sat on his bed and leisurely took off his boots, hat, and holster. He blew out most of the candles and lay on his bed, tucking himself under the soft sheets. Worn out by the festival, he fell asleep in a matter of seconds.

The candles on Flint's dresser started to melt rapidly. Meanwhile, the wallpaper withered and ripped apart, revealing prickled walls. The ceiling changed too, stalactite growing. Just then, water leaked down onto the floor. A shadowy figure swept across the room; yet Flint continued sleeping, unaware of the changes before him. Little by little, the furniture melted as if made of wax. Even the bed melted, lowering Flint to the now jagged floor. Within seconds, his bedroom turned into a cave. Waking up to this, he panicked and fell off what was left of his bed, onto the granite ground that had many puddles due to the dripping water.

"What the heck is this place?"

Flint looked for the door, noticing it had become a part of the cavern's wall. When he turned to find the window to escape this madness, he saw that it had become a large hole. He drooped through it, entering a faintly lit tunnel that led him to the exit. Leaving the cave, he stepped onto a lush grove. It was enclosed by an escarpment resembling the Kakadu wetlands of Australia. A waterfall wilted over Flint, flowing from the gargantuan canyon above.

"How the hell did I get here?"

Flint was flabbergasted by his surroundings. It felt so real to him. Yet the uncomfortable feelings within him brushed away when he spotted Hamarah. She was naked, swimming in the waterfall's plunge pool. Flint no longer cared where he was; he dived into the water and swam over to her as if his life depended on it.

"I knew you'd come back to me," she said.

He held her waist in the water, his hairy chest pressing against her breasts. "Hamarah," he began, "where are we?" She kissed him without replying. Even though he kissed her back with delight, he still couldn't accept what he was experiencing. "How is this possible? In dreams we never have control of what happens. Yet it feels so real here."

"That's because it *is* real," she said.

Hamarah pushed back her long, wet black hair. She stared at Flint with her soft eyes and held him. He gently caressed her body in the water, feeling her every curve. It was too good to be true, he thought.

"And you're real, too?" he asked.

"Of course I am," she said. "There is only one thing that isn't real, Ethan. Do you know what that is?"

Thinking about it for a while, he answered, "Desonas?"

Her face lit up as she said, "You must break free of that delusional town and rejoin me. There are only a few years left before the tribunal completes the gateway. Then the revolution will have been for nothing."

"Revolution? Tribunal?" he said, confused. "Browder said something about a war before Joey killed him."

Hamarah nodded.

"How can I find you?"

She didn't reply, making Flint feel anxious. He was frightened of waking up. In this eerie yet magical dream, he felt right at home. Old age didn't weigh him down. And best of all, he was free of Amanda—no longer the slave he felt he'd become in Desonas.

"I love you," she whispered. "I've always loved you."

Finally accepting this wondrous experience, he closed his eyes and kissed her. The longer they kissed, the more they sank. She pulled Flint deep into the plunge pool, embracing him. To Flint, there wasn't a better feeling than this. When he opened his eyes to gaze upon her beauty, she was gone; there was only darkness.

He awoke in his bed. The candles hadn't melted. Amanda was sleeping soundlessly next to him. For a moment, Flint wanted to scream. It was just a dream; yet it felt as real as this very moment, he thought. These experiences didn't make any sense to him.

Sadly for him, there was nothing he could do except continue sleeping. But this time it took him longer than ever to fall asleep again because he had so many questions plaguing his dreary mind—mostly about what Browder had told him, the strange stream of dreams that he'd been having lately, and his lost memories. He may have finally begun to remember a part of his past; however, there was still so much more to remember.

CHAPTER THREE

A BROKEN FAMILY

On the following morning, Flint decided to see the doctor about his dreams. He dressed formally, putting a duster over his clothes despite the heat, and made his way to the clinic on his mare. As soon as Flint reached the town square, he hitched Donna to a post and entered the building. The door chimed when he opened it. Behind a desk sat Doctor Tutherfield with her glasses on. She was writing something in a notebook.

"Good morning, Flint," she said warmly, putting the book in a draw. "What a surprise to see you."

"I'm sorry for disturbing you, Penny," he said, doffing his hat.

"Nonsense," she said. "You're always welcome. Besides, I don't have any appointments until the afternoon. I've just been updating medical charts. Pretty boring, I know. But I have to keep records. Anyway, what can I do for you?"

"Well," he began, "I was hoping you'd have enough time for another discussion. You know, like the ones we used to have last year."

Penny gulped heavily but tried not to look too distressed. "Of course," she said. "Have a seat. Make yourself comfortable."

He took a seat opposite Penny, handing her an ancient twelve-sided coin. Though dented and faded, the doctor was still able to make out an embossed depiction of a primordial queen on the fifty-cent coin's obverse.

"Oh, this is *very* nice. Thank you," she said earnestly. "You're always thinking of others before yourself."

"Except when it comes to my wife."

"I see," she said in a somewhat sad tone. "So, it started again?"

He gave Penny a faint nod, prompting her to take out a notebook with Flint's name on it. She took a moment to browse through her old notes and then flipped over to a page where she'd written comments about his dreams.

"How many times have you had that dream since our last session?" she asked, holding a glass of water and taking a sip.

"I dreamt of her twice last night—"

Penny almost gagged on her water.

"And before that," he continued, "about two months ago. So, all together, I've dreamed of Hamarah three times since the last session we had a year ago."

Her silence disturbed him.

"What do you think this means?" he asked, hoping she'd give him a reasonable response.

"I think the question should be redirected at you," she said.

"Me?"

She gently bobbed her head, waiting for him to answer the question he'd posed without trying to seem snooty.

"I don't know," he said. "It's scary because no one except me experiences this, and yet it's also enthralling since there's a part of me that longs to see Hamarah. Yet when I see her, I feel like a part of me is lost. I become desperate. The world changes almost every time when she's in my dreams. And I'm always aware, too. You know, the way you and I are aware right here. It always feels so damn real."

"But we went through this before, Flint," she said firmly. "You know it can't possibly be real." She exhaled and went on, "It's real in your subconscious, narcissistic mind because you yearn for it to be real. You're miserable with Amanda, so you've created an alternate persona of her."

"That's not true," he said, irked by her response. "I've never seen this woman before in my life and yet..."

"And yet she's there," said Penny curtly. "It's because you created her." Flint shook his head angrily while she spoke. "Flint, no one has the same dream over and over again. The only reason why you keep dreaming of this 'Hamarah' of yours is because you've invented her as a means to escape your unhappy marriage."

"But what if the dreamtime is real?" he said.

Penny stared at him blankly for a moment. "We all have the right to wonder, Flint," she finally said. "I don't know much about the dreamtime or if spirits exist in it. But if it makes you feel any better, I agree with you in the sense that we don't know what's out there. Despite how many people follow Preacher Harrison, the truth is no one really has an answer as to why we're here—irrefutable evidence, that is. Mind you, civilization as our ancestors once knew it is just wishful thinking for us. I don't even know what'll happen to us in the future."

"I'm not sure either," he said glumly. "But listen, whether the dreamtime has anything to do with this, what do you think I should do about these dreams of mine?"

"Honestly, I think it's time for you to let go of Hamarah," she said coldly. "If you're as self-aware as you claim to be in those dreams, you should tell her that you've moved on. You're a married man and have two children." Drinking the last of her water, she continued, "Nothing's going to change unless you put Hamarah behind you."

"Hmm...I guess you're right," he said pensively.

"Remember, this is just my opinion," she said. "Whatever you decide to do is your choice."

"Thanks, Penny," he said, getting up. "I appreciate your time and advice."

She nodded modestly. "I'm just doing my job the way you hunt and help others around town, cowboy."

"Do you think I'm one?" he asked.

"One what?" she responded, raising an eyebrow. "A cowboy? Of course, silly. You're the best ranger in Desonas. I think you're even better than Andrew Browder. It's unfortunate that he abandoned us. Gosh, how long has it been since he left? Eight years?"

"I think so. Who knows where he is," said Flint, lying. "Anyway, thanks again. Your advice helped me a great deal."

"I'm glad I could help," she said. "And please, come by anytime you want."

"Careful, I might take you up on your offer," he said playfully, waving and closing the door behind him.

Before returning to his horse, Flint stood still on the veranda for a minute. He took a deep breath, considering everything the doctor told him. Was he truly narcissistic? Was he losing his mind? Or were his dreams possibly a link to his past? Could it be that Hamarah existed, waiting for him somewhere on this godforsaken rock of death? He didn't know what to think. In the end, all he could do was return home and be a husband and father to his real family.

Over the next few weeks, Flint and his fellow townspeople continued working hard to keep their desolate town alive. It wasn't easy being a farmer, especially with such horrible heat scorching crops. They worked harder and harder as the weeks passed. And before they knew it, the month of December was already reaching its end.

Waking up on the twenty-fourth day of the month, Flint put on his clothes—neckerchief included—and went downstairs to the kitchen. After getting a glass of water, he took a seat and opened a journal filled with scribbled notes about his experiences and feelings. He drank some water while staring at a blank page, wondering what he should write. Shortly after thinking about it, he placed his cup on the table, grabbed his pen, and wrote in his notebook:

> The heat has gotten worse in December. It makes me feel Earth wants me to burn in despair. I long for the gift of freedom, yet I'm always shackled. All I've done this month is think about Hamarah.

I haven't been able to experience or remember any other dream with her. I feel utterly hopeless. I don't even have the peace of mind that I once had within my dreams. Amanda, over time, has become the house warden. She imposes her homebody rule with pleasure, but I'll never give in.

"G'day," said a voice by the kitchen door.

Flint jolted and immediately closed his book while looking up, seeing Marshal Salomon who tipped his hat.

"Well, you already brought yourself in," said Flint. "Have a seat."

Salomon pryingly gazed at him and sat down.

"What can I do for you, Marshal?"

"It's been about a month since that incident near Uluru," said Salomon. "So, I decided to visit Chief Yeramba to see how his tribe was fairing."

"And?"

"And they're very pleased with you," said Salomon. "Though, they told me something rather odd." He paused as Flint raised an eyebrow and then continued, "Do you remember the day when you went hunting with Joey?"

"Of course," said Flint. "That was my son's first trip."

"Well, get a load of this: according to the Wakaya, during a walkabout rite, one of them spotted a yowie."

"A yowie?" said Flint, startled.

"Yes," said Salomon. "Now, you and I both know yowies aren't real." Flint agreed with Salomon who then added, "At first I wondered if perhaps the one going on the walkabout had seen the yowie in…what do they call it?—dreamtime? Anyway, when I mentioned this, Chief Yeramba made it very clear to me that the adolescent saw it while awake. The aborigines don't lie, but it's a very strange tale."

"Sure sounds like it," said Flint, intrigued. "I wonder why Yeramba didn't tell me when I went there hunting for Browder."

Salomon shrugged at him.

"Anyway," continued Flint, "I can't imagine you came all the way out here just to tell me this story."

"No," said Salomon, grumbling. "Chief Yeramba, however, asked whether you would go on a walkabout, if I could talk you into prowling around the wilds to see if you find one or more of them."

"Yowies?"

"No, hyenas," said Salomon. "Yes, yowies."

Amused by the sarcasm, Flint let out a faint chuckle.

Salomon went on, "I know it's been about four weeks with only one sighting—mind you, it's just wilderness lore. But hey, this means more prehistoric coins for you to collect. That is, of course, if you're up for the task."

"Sure, why not," said Flint.

"Excellent," said Salomon, shaking his hand.

He handed Flint a shabby pouch of coins as he stepped out of the house and then took off on his horse. Upon his leave, Flint went back inside his house and grabbed his journal. He took it upstairs and hid it in a guest room. Walking through the hall, he noticed Amanda in her bedroom knitting a red shirt. While he passed by, Amanda looked up at him.

"Going somewhere?" she asked.

"Huh?" he replied, stammering. "Eh, just outside."

Flint didn't want to tell her his real intention, trying hard to avoid another argument. He smiled innocently at her until he was out of her sight. After passing the room, he rolled his eyes, rushed downstairs, and left the house. He trudged across his muggy ranch and entered the barn. Tom, organizing stacks of hay, turned around and waved.

"Hey, dad."

"Morning, son," said Flint, hugging Tom. He helped him organize the haystacks. Once finished, he asked, "Say, how about you and me spend the day exploring the old wilds? Maybe some game while we're at it?"

"That'd be great!"

"Perfect, just don't tell your mother," he said, winking at his son. "Let's get the horses prepped and have some fun."

They mounted their steeds and rode out of the barn, leaving the fertile homestead. Tom let out a skyward cheer despite it gradually getting cloudy. Flint thought to himself, it seemed Tom valued freedom as much as he. The duo left Desonas in no time, entering the humid wilds of the

Northern Territory. Flint took out his Chassepot rifle and stretched over to his son, letting him borrow it.

"Amazing," said Tom, holding the gun.

"I'll let you use it, but first we'll stop by the eastern springs," said Flint. Tom nodded and kept a similar pace with his father who added, "I'm sure there'll be plenty of dingoes or bustards; they always like resting there."

"Great," said Tom. "I can't wait!"

After galloping through the grassland for about an hour, they reached a region of springs. It was a vast field with small streams scattered around the arid terrain, resembling an oasis. Flint halted Donna, swooped down to the ground, and hitched her to a bloodwood tree. Tom mimicked his father and then shuffled through the trail with his father. They heard gentle streams ahead, as well as distant thunder. Though a storm seemed to be brewing, it didn't stop Flint from hunting and spending quality time with his son.

"So much for nice weather," he said, pulling out his Peacemaker and ducking.

Tom agreed. He then followed in his father's footsteps, getting to the ground while firmly holding his rifle.

"Here is good," said Flint, stopping and observing the dreary area. He pointed north and asked, "Do you see anything over there?"

Glancing around, Tom shook his head.

"Nothing? All right, let's move up a little more," whispered Flint while crawling, his blue eyes narrowing ahead.

They advanced through the wilderness as quietly as they could. Flint wasn't bothered seeing an occasional insect wriggle around in the soil, but Tom had a ghastly look on his face when he saw an orange-footed centipede squirm into the dirt. Tom stomped on the insect hard several times until it was utterly mangled. In the meantime, a cream pelt dingo scooted away with a speed that matched a cheetah.

"Son," murmured Flint while slack-jawed, looking like he'd witnessed an angel descend from the heavens.

"Sorry, dad."

"Unbelievable," moped Flint. "That was a dingo. Did you see its fur?"

Tom didn't respond, his eyes cast down at the grass; he felt responsible for scaring the animal away.

"I'm almost sixty years old and I've never seen one like that before."

Flint watched the white dingo until it vanished from his sight. He felt as though it came out of the dreamtime. Shortly after, Flint signaled Tom and continued to quietly move forward until nearing a spring. They heard water trickling as it started raining. Thunder boomed with a burst of cloud-to-ground lightning. Flint ignored it, observing the region.

"There," he said, pointing skyward. "See it?"

"Yeah," said Tom, gazing at a bustard. He attempted to aim his rifle at it. The bird was flying around in a circle, making it difficult for Tom since he had to keep moving with the bird. "Should I fire?"

"Only if you think you'll get it," replied Flint.

Tom hesitated and then gave his father a doubtful gesture. Flint smirked, letting out a faint chuckle.

"Maybe there're more below," said Flint.

Tom suddenly fired; the bird instantly flew away, as did several others by the foggy springs.

"*Ah*, you should've waited longer."

"Sorry, dad," he said depressingly.

"It's all right, son," said Flint. "This is just a fun game of hunting. Let's keep looking around. Any animal will do."

They continued searching the region. But for some reason they couldn't find any animals near them. The rain came down harder, mist forming around them. Still, this didn't stop Flint or his son from having quality time together. Tom eventually saw a wombat scurrying through the grass. He ran after it but slipped on the mushy land, falling down.

"Tom!"

Flint ran over to his son, expecting him to have a sprained ankle. Instead he found him chuckling. Seeing that his son was all right, covered in mud no less, he joined in the laughter. Despite the heavy rain pouring over them, they were having a great time. And before they knew it, evening came. Flint kept searching around with Tom. Finally, after a few more hours, they saw several more birds flying toward a flooded spring.

"Dad," muttered Tom, "I think those are them."

"You're right," said Flint, scouting ahead.

Tom knelt down beside his father, lifted up the Chassepot rifle, and placed its wooden stock on his shoulder.

"Easy, son, you don't want to miss them."

"Right," murmured Tom, aiming carefully.

He followed a bustard and remained steady, his eyes squinting, trying to see through the thickening mist.

"Patience," said Flint. "That's what hunting's all about."

Tom listened and continued tracing his target's movement. Then he took a shot, and the bird fell.

Flint stood up and shouted, "You did it!"

"I did?" said Tom in disbelief. "Whoa, I really did it!"

He cheered himself on. Flint, meanwhile, walked ahead to locate the dead bustard. As he approached the spring, another bird flew skyward. Flint swiftly drew his Peacemaker and shot it without even aiming. Tom watched the bird fall with a look of astonishment.

"How did you do that?" he asked.

"It's all about practice, my boy," replied Flint, winking at his son. "Now let's find these critters before it gets too dark." He holstered his revolver and walked through the wet marsh to pick up the birds. It was almost pitch-black outside, so it wasn't easy for him to locate them, but he eventually found the bustards by the spring. He mounted Donna shortly after putting the birds in his knapsack. "Time to go home and brag about dinner."

"Sounds good to me," said Tom.

The duo mounted their horses and rode back home. Not once did Flint see any signs of a yowie. It was midnight by the time they reached Desonas. The downpour became even worse. Fortunately for them, they were nearing their ranch. The horses galloped fast through the trail between the Steward and Froehlich farms, the rain not hampering them. Upon arriving home, the duo brought their steeds straight into the barn. When they finished putting away the saddles they locked the barn and ran to their house.

"Crazy storm," said Tom, panting.

"Not as crazy as your mother," replied Flint.

They entered the house, chuckling loudly. Their hearty laughter, however, died out when they saw Amanda standing by the hall with a grim face. Tom appeared as if he'd shrunk, taking a step back. Flint, on the other hand, stood proud while glaring back at his wife.

"It's past midnight," she said coldly. "There's a horrible thunderstorm outside, and you think it's okay to come back home laughing without even wondering how I felt about the two of you going out for hours?"

"Don't you even dare bring our son into this," said Flint, frowning. "I'm his father, and I wanted to spend quality time hunting with him." He tossed two bustards down by Amanda's feet, causing her to shriek. "Tom got one of them all on his own. You should be proud and happy that we're bringing some extra food home instead of always eating bush tucker."

"Is that so?" responded Amanda sardonically. "So, my bush tucker ain't good enough for the *high* and *mighty* Flint Cross?"

"Go screw yourself," said Flint, leaving the house.

"Dad, don't leave!" cried out Tom.

Flint heard his son call out to him but didn't care. He trudged across the sodden ranch, rain pouring over him. Not only did Flint feel he was drowning in despair, but the water drops felt like needles stabbing his body. He wanted to scream and leave, never to come back.

Though his conscience was telling him to go back home and ignore Amanda's selfish and infuriating behavior, he refused to turn around. A part of him felt like a child by walking out on his family so quickly. He thought, if it was so easy to leave, did he even deserve to be a father? Another voice within his mind told him that he wasn't acting like a child—he was acting quite his age. There was no need to return since Amanda wasn't the woman he loved. He owed her no loyalty or respect because she'd never given him any. This sudden realization made him feel that leaving was acceptable.

Since his key to freedom was in the barn, he decided to go in. His clothes were dripping wet when he entered. He quickly mounted Donna and left, riding to the town square. At first, his destination was irrelevant. In fact, he almost went out into the barren wilds again. Upon reaching The Wild Owl, however, he tugged the reins of his mare, halting her.

He heard lively music and merry banter coming from the saloon. It attracted him. Yet it was alcohol that became a priority for him. Being married to Amanda had made him so angry and miserable that he desperately wanted a way to forget about her. Alcohol seemed to be his one and only solution. He hitched Donna to a nearby post and entered the saloon. The townsfolk turned around—startled—when Flint barged in. He was dripping wet and looked like he wanted to shoot someone.

The Wild Owl appeared old and dull from outside. The interior, however, was brightly lit and roomy with many tables. The saloon was filled to capacity with patrons. Most of them were playing billiards and solitary while others conversed by the bar with Walter Hamel, owner of the saloon. With the exception of Marshal Salomon, Jake, and his best friend Joey, all the men Flint knew were there. Martin Aleman stood up, staring at him in dismay.

"Hey," he said. "Are you okay, Cross?"

"I'll live," said Flint, water dripping all over the floor while he approached the bar. "Hit me hard, Walt. I'm in the mood to let loose."

"Sure thing, pal," replied Walter, preparing a glass of whiskey behind the counter. When he gave the drink to Flint, he gazed at him and said, "Somehow I have a feeling you'll be staying here for a while."

"Right," said Flint sternly, gulping down the whiskey and slamming the glass on the counter. "Give me a bottle."

"Huh?" said Walter, hesitating. After seeing Flint's vicious-looking face, however, he refilled the glass and gave him a bottle of whiskey. "Here you go," he added. "Stay as long as you want."

"I don't mean to pry, Cross," said Martin, taking a seat beside Flint. "You tend to always be the one looking out for us. Yet this time it looks like something's troubling you."

"You're right," responded Flint. "And I appreciate your concern. But you know, someone once told me that whiskey is man's best friend." He patted Martin's shoulder. "Don't worry, kid. I'll be just fine."

Nodding warily, Martin returned to his table. When he sat down, most of the townsfolk carried on with their banter and gambling. Flint, in the meantime, continued to gulp down his whiskey.

"A few more of these will do it for me," said Flint groggily. "Then I'll be as good as new, right, Walt?"

"If you say so, cowboy," said Walter.

"What?" said Flint, annoyed. "I'm not entitled to a few drinks? I may go around helping others, but I'm as human as you. I have a right to some peace of mind too." He popped open the bottle and guzzled down the alcohol. After a few more minutes, he went on, "I had jus' abou' 'nough wid Aman'da. She al'ways wantin' me home...helpin' tha ran'ch—" Flint gave out a loud belch. "Hell, I ain't knowin' no m'ore than anyone—hic!—but I rec'kon I'm way in o'ver ma head, Walt—hic!—if ya kn'ow wha 'er mean."

"Flint," began Walter, "you know you're not much of a drinker. Why don't you give me that bottle and get some rest. I'll even let you stay upstairs for the night."

"Yer cra'zy," mumbled Flint, belching again.

"Okay," said Walter, sighing. "Have it your way."

Some of the patrons kept a sharp eye on Flint as he became more violent and drunk. Flint gulped down the rest of his bottle and slammed it hard on Walter's bar counter. He then took the empty glass, attempting to drink from it even though there was nothing left.

"Eh?" he uttered. "Wha kinda drin' ez zha?"

Like the bottle and glass, he felt empty. His mind was barely stable at this point. Though, what sanity remained didn't seem to help much. He became less sober and distant by the second. Flint felt the urge to scream again. He wanted to lift up all the tables and smash them apart. He wanted to pull out his gun and unload every bullet. It didn't matter to him if the bullets would end up in Amanda's skull or the wall. Then, quicker than a flash of lightning, his anger flushed away. Yes, he was as empty as the glass. He wanted to cry. Yet as depressed and ashamed as he was of himself, he didn't weep.

Flint nearly fell off his stool when he rose to his feet. He staggered, wobbling back and forth. For a moment it looked like he was waltzing.

Though most of the patrons tried to ignore his behavior, a few of them gazed at him with pity. They knew his marriage was a mess and understood why. No one looked down on him. In fact, the folks of Desonas admired him. They simply sympathized with his inner turmoil. Once again, Martin stood up to take action.

"Don't worry, Walt," he said, glancing at the bartender. "I'll get him home."

It was still pouring outside. Flint doddered through the batwing doors of Walter's saloon and tried going down the veranda's steps. He tripped over his crisscrossed boots and fell flat on his face over the muddy ground. The last thing he saw before passing out was Martin who came out of the saloon, reaching down to help him.

A few hours passed. Flint opened his eyes and found himself in a puddle of mud in a meadow. It was raining hard. The ground trembled violently when he rose to his feet, making him wobble around like a drunken oaf. Oddly, he was sober. Flint gazed at the sweltering sky and noticed the sun appeared twice its size and had black spots on it; there was also a wrathful aura of flame enveloping it. The heat was so intense it made his vision hazy.

Flint turned away from the sun. As he did so, however, he noticed that the meadow had vanished; wherever he was had become a wasteland. He gasped at the landscape. Just then, the ground beneath him turned into quicksand, seizing him. Flint sulked and squirmed in an attempt to free himself. Though, moving around only made it worse.

He realized his freedom had always been an illusion. To him, there was nothing worse than losing his autonomy. He was a prisoner to the wasteland, sinking into the quicksand. After being swallowed by it, he found himself in a swamp. Splurging out in a panic, Flint panted and thrashed about until he freed himself.

Wading in the mire, he said in a wheezing tone, "I don't know where the hell I am, but I'd rather be drunk again than be here."

Out of nowhere, it seemed to Flint, the same cream-furred dingo he'd seen earlier with his son appeared in the sludgy mire, staring at him. Its eyes had a gleam of intelligence, as if it were sentient and possessed by an enlightened spirit—at least that was how Flint felt when he saw it. The dingo trotted over to him, holding something in its mouth. Upon reaching him, it released the object. Flint gazed at the wrapped object on the mud and cautiously picked it up, confused.

"Is this supposed to be for me?"

The dingo bowed. Then it walked away and disappeared. Flint abruptly felt like a child as an innocent anxiety stirred within him. He quickly tore the wrapping apart. The gift was a small bullroarer. Being given this sacred present strangely made him think about how selfish he'd been lately.

"Everything has been about me," he said, holding the carved gift. "Is that what this is about?" He paused in thought for a moment. He gazed up at the sky, his pupils dilating as he went on, "Hamarah needs me; the rebels need me. The war isn't over yet." His eyes were no longer dilated. "Wha...what happened?" Whatever memories of his past that were on the verge of resurfacing faded away. Then, thinking hard about the gift he'd just received, he said, "Yes, I understand. I've been far too selfish as of late." He closed his eyes, allowing himself to fall into the swamp while he added, "Thank you, Yeramba."

Flint awoke on a guest bed in his home. Sarah and Tom sat next to him. He rose, feeling ashamed. Silence fell, punctured only by the pattering of rain drops falling against the window; it was the only sound in the room. Amanda wasn't there. Perhaps she was sleeping or simply didn't care about his condition, conceded Flint.

"Are you okay, dad?" asked Tom.

"Yes," he said quietly. "Listen, I'm sorry about leaving like that. This isn't an excuse, but sometimes your mother is ungrateful, and it really pisses me off."

"We were really worried," said Sarah.

"I know," said Flint. "I'm sorry. It was wrong and stupid of me to do that. I hope neither of you ever get into the habit of following in my footsteps, especially visiting The Wild Owl in the middle of a storm to get drunk." Feeling awkward, he rubbed his neck and asked, "So, who managed to bring me back here?"

"Martin and Kevin," answered Tom.

"Ah," said Flint, scratching his head. He wondered if his children were disappointed in him. They probably were, he thought. Flint anxiously wanted to try to make them forget about his imprudent mistake. Then he wondered about his dream—the message he felt Yeramba had given him. "I want you both to stay here for a moment."

Sarah and Tom had puzzled expressions while Flint left the room. He went downstairs, searching for his guns. When he reached the entrance hall, he grabbed his Chassepot rifle. He then pulled out his older Winchester rifle, which he'd used to kill the massive bear last month. Flint went back upstairs, rejoining his children. First he gave Tom the Chassepot; then he gave Sarah the Winchester.

"Whoa," said Tom in a tone of awe. Being able to keep the rifle that he'd used to hunt today was an amazing feeling to him. "Thanks, dad!"

"For me?" asked Sarah, hardly believing it.

Even though she'd always wanted to own a gun, she had never been given the chance to have one because of her mulish, strict mother. So, possessing the Winchester rifle was a dream come true for her.

"And don't worry, Sarah," began Flint, "one of these days we'll convince Amanda to let you come hunt with us."

"Thank you so much," she said, smiling. "You make us worry a lot, but you're still the best dad in the world."

Flint hugged his children and thought to himself, although he was experiencing a horrible marriage, at least something good had come out of it—his children. Despite the turmoil building up in his mind, he'd managed to find it in his heart to be a little humble. The Cross family still had their problems. Things never changed in Desonas. In fact, life in Australia would probably never change. During the month of December, however, Flint started to feel that everything would be all right.

CHAPTER FOUR

THE DEFILED MINE

It was another humid day. The sun blazed fiercely as if it were about to explode with a furious rage of flares. Flint sat on a bench in his porch, holding his journal. He occasionally glanced at the farm. For a brief moment he watched Sarah graze new cattle she'd bought from aboriginal herders; Tom was helping her. In the meantime, Amanda stayed inside washing dishes since the others had finished eating breakfast. Flint, who could hear the clatter of dishes, smiled when he looked at his children. Yet his face grew stern, focusing his attention back on his notebook:

> It's been three months and nothing has really changed, not even the weather. March has never been so hot, and yet it's warmer than ever. I'm longing for winter. But these days June isn't even cold anymore. At least we haven't had any violent dust storms. As I wrote, nothing much has changed.
>
> Most families here in Desonas are happy and content, but Amanda and I continue to have

meaningless arguments. Most of the time she's frustrated by me leaving to hunt with Joey. I will never give up hunting, especially since I've stopped eating bush tucker. Yes, that is what I meant to record here. I'm starting to believe that Browder was not insane.

My dreams have become more vivid. They are definitely not some narcissistic form of escaping as Doctor Tutherfield had suggested. Something different is happening. I don't know if Yeramba has the truth, but I'm convinced these "dreams" of mine are not simply random. I had one last night and Hamarah was there again.

Hamarah keeps telling me that I have to "remember" but I don't know what that means. Remember what? She hasn't been able to tell me yet. I'm finally convinced she's not a fantasy in my subconscious mind. It's even possible that she's waiting for me somewhere.

When I dream of Hamarah I feel that I belong with her. Sometimes I am at a beach, the barren wilds of Australia, or near some kind of aboriginal site in the dreamtime. I may not always know where those places are, but I'm certain they're real, like Hamarah.

The only reason why I haven't left to find Hamarah and spend my life with her is because of Sarah and Tom. They keep hoping things will get better between Amanda and me. But the truth is that it'll never happen, not as long as I keep having these dreams.

Flint started to hear distant thudding. He looked up, noticing his best friend approaching on his mustang. Joey tugged the reins of Buddy when he reached Flint's house, swooping down by the porch.

"Howdy, Flint," said Joey, saluting him.

"Morning."

"How's yer diary goin'?"

"It's a journal," said Flint sternly.

"Diary," coughed Joey.

"Journal," repeated Flint.

Joey gave out a hearty laugh. "Boy, how I love teasin' ya. So, are ya ready ta go huntin' sum bustards wit me, partner?"

"Of course," said Flint, rising from his bench. "After all, we still have to find out who's a sharper shooter."

"Twenty coins fer me," said Joey, mounting back on his horse.

"Deal," replied Flint, the lips of his mouth curling into a smirk. Entering the corral, he released Donna and prepared her saddle. He then whistled at his son. "I'll come back later. If your mother asks for me, tell her I'm with Joey."

"Okay," replied Tom. "Have fun."

Sarah was too far from her father to say anything since she was grazing the cattle, but she waved at him in the distance. Flint waved back after mounting his steed, excited to hunt bustards with his best friend. Before leaving, however, Walter Hamel approached the house on a dappled horse, screaming like a madman. He shouted so loud that Sarah rushed over to find out what was wrong.

"Cross!" he yelled out. "Cross!"

"Walter, calm down," said Flint.

"The mine," he said frantically. "It's horrible." He then started to stammer, "There was a cave-in. They're all trapped."

"Oh my God," said Sarah. "Jake's inside the mine!" On the verge of crying, she ran to get her horse. Flint, however, grabbed her arm. "Don't you dare stop me!" she shouted, pushing him away. "I'm going with you, and there's nothing you can do to stop me!"

Flint, startled by her reaction, replied, "Sarah, there's *no* way in hell I'm letting you or Tommy come. I don't even know if I'll be able to help them."

She ignored him, mounting her horse.

"Sarah?"

Nudging her horse, she rode out of the corral without another word, making her way to the mine.

"Sarah!"

"Whoa," said Joey, his eyebrows raising.

"Unbelievable," said Flint. "Tommy, I need you to stay here and watch the farm. If your mother asks…shit, I don't even know what to tell her anymore. Forget about it. Just keep an eye on the cattle and vineyard."

Tom complied, staying in the corral.

"Let's go!" said Flint urgently.

"Wait," said Walter. "Can't we leave from here?"

Flint shook his head. "Six miles south from here leads to a cliff," he said. "We'll have to leave from the town square and travel southeast."

"Gotcha," said Walter, following him.

The trio left, riding fast. Flint was hoping to spot Sarah; however, she was nowhere in his sight. The Steward and Froehlich families stood near their fences, startled when Flint and his companions passed them. There wasn't much they could do, especially since their children were not older than five.

Reaching the town square, they noticed Marshal Salomon standing near his office. He wore a frantic expression. Upon seeing Flint, he stepped down from the veranda and gazed at him in disbelief.

"Flint?" he said in a hopeful tone. "You're going to the mine?"

"I've already told you that I made a vow to protect these people, Marshal," said Flint. "I can't do this alone, though. Jake needs you now more than ever, and there's nothing you can do here except worry. Come with us."

Salomon hesitated but went into his office and brought out supplies: lassos, dynamite, and ammunition. He then got on his horse and joined the group.

Flint knew this was going to be a long journey, but he was prepared to do anything since Sarah wouldn't listen to reason. That's when he realized he wasn't actually traveling to the mine for the townspeople—it was for his daughter. This realization made him feel awful because it meant he was selfish and indifferent. He nevertheless rode toward the mine, earnestly ready to help anyone who might be in trouble.

The quartet eventually passed the massive rock formations of Uluru and Kata Tjuta. They occasionally spotted different animals such as hopping kangaroos, scuttling wombats, and even a bellowing koala bear that was clinging to a tree. Meanwhile, in the distance, they were able to see a girl horseback riding. Although they were gradually catching up to her, she was still far away.

"Cross, is that your daughter?" asked Salomon.

"No, it's Amanda," said Flint, making Joey laugh. "Who else would it be, Marshal? She left like a madwoman the moment Walter said that there was a cave-in at the mine. Apparently my daughter thinks she can save Jake and the others on her own."

"I see," replied Salomon, surprised. "Goodness, sometimes people do crazy things for love."

"And then some," said Joey, guffawing.

"Let's hurry and join her," said Flint. "I don't want anything happening to my daughter." The others complied, increasing the pace of their horses as he shouted, "Sarah!" She didn't look back. "Sarah!" She finally slowed down, allowing her father to catch up to her. "Are you crazy?" he yelled, staring harshly at her. "You'll get yourself killed traveling out here alone with nothing but a horse!"

"I'm not going home," she said firmly.

"I didn't say you had to," he responded, irked. Noticing she had her rifle, he gave her a bandolier. "Keep this in case we're attacked. The aboriginals reported dangerous animals in the wilds."

She took the ammo, not showing any signs of gratitude.

"You're crazy, you know that?" he added.

"I'm just following in your footsteps," she said.

Flint shook his head. "Yeah, I guess you are. Just…never leave like that again. I don't know what I'd do if something happened to you."

"Welcome ta tha team, cowgirl," said Joey.

"Thanks," said Sarah, smiling weakly. She then glanced at Walter and Marshal Salomon, giving them a quick nod of acknowledgement while riding south. "I only went to the mine once to see Jake, so I don't remember exactly where it is. But I think we're getting close."

"I reckon yer right," said Joey.

"Yes, good memory," said Flint. "I think we have to turn a bit more east though. It should be visible in about ten more miles."

"You mean you've been there before?" asked Walter.

"I passed by a few times with Joey while hunting," answered Flint. "But I've never gone inside, nor have I ever wanted to."

"Not a mining person, eh?" said Walter. Flint shook his head at Walter who added, "Me neither. I've always preferred running a business, which is why the saloon worked out just fine for me."

"Best saloon Australia has ta offer," said Joey.

"Cross," called out Salomon. "I know you've made it clear several times already that you don't want to work at the mine—obviously things are a bit different in this situation. Still, thanks for coming."

"Just doing my job, Marshal."

Midday arrived before the quintet knew it. When the sun started to set, they were finally able to see the mine. In the distance, they saw a massive pit. It looked as if a quake had torn the land apart, forcing a part of the ground to sink.

"Here we are," said Salomon. "Panzo Mine."

This mine, owned by the titan-steel brothers, was two thousand feet deep, bigger than the ancient Super Pit gold mine in Kalgoorlie, Western Australia. Upon arriving at the mine, Flint became more cognizant. How men could dig such a gargantuan pit was beyond him. It seemed unfeasible to him, even with the presence of the Panzo brothers; however, Flint wasn't about to become a detective when his friends' lives were at stake.

"Gettin' here is one thing," said Joey. "Gettin' down there is another."

"It's not as bad as it looks," replied Salomon. "Just follow me. I'll guide you down there safely."

"Be my guest, Marshal," said Walter, feeling distraught.

Flint and the others followed Salomon on their horses. They gently tugged the reins of their steeds, cautiously riding along the mushy side roads while descending corner ramps that resembled the ridges of a mountain. It took them twenty minutes to reach the bottom of Panzo Mine. They then searched around to see if anyone was there. Not a minute later,

Deputy Ted Thornton came over on his horse from the opposite side of the mine.

"Thank goodness you came," said Thornton. He noticed Sarah and her father right beside the marshal. "Flint? You're a sight for sore eyes."

"Where is Jake?" asked Sarah.

"He's…they're all buried inside," said Thornton grimly. "I tried using all the dynamite I could find, but it hasn't helped much. I'm sorry."

"All right," began Salomon, "let's split up. The mine has several entrances, which are all scattered around. I'll check around here. Walter, stick with me. Joey, you'll go east with Deputy Thornton. Sarah, check the westward entrances. Cross, you search the northern region. If any of you hear the slightest whisper from my son or the miners, come back to me immediately. I don't want any dynamite used until we know exactly where they are. Understand?"

Sarah was the only one who didn't respond.

"*Understand?*" repeated the marshal.

"Yes," she said, sulking.

"Off you go then," he said warily. With the exception of Walter, the others turned their horses around and left. "This area seems to be sealed tight," he went on. "It must've happened here. Come on, Walt, let's check southeast and go in from there."

Walter followed Salomon on his horse.

In the meantime, Flint rode north. Before going far, however, he nudged Donna to swerve west, glancing at Sarah.

"Are you going to be all right?" he asked.

She nodded. Flint knew the answer she'd give him, but as a father he felt the need to ask anyway. He tugged Donna's reins, making her gallop northward to an entrance in Panzo Mine. Flint dismounted his steed when he arrived.

"I'll be back soon," he said to his horse.

Donna nickered as he patted her snout. He then entered a tunnel resembling a cave. Its walls were a mixture of solid dirt and rocks with shafts keeping everything stable. Oil lamps, their lit wicks burning, allowed Flint to see the path on which stood carts filled with ore; they were scattered around the passage.

Flint ignored the shiny minerals and kept walking through the mine. The sun's light eventually dissipated, and the only light remaining was from the oil lamps. Silence fell, broken only by his footsteps while he treaded upon the mashed ground. When he descended down the path, an earthquake occurred. Though it was brief, it shook Flint up. He hesitated to go farther. For all he knew, the mine would fold and collapse, burying him alive.

"Hello?" he called out. "Is anyone in here?"

He heard his own voice echo in the dim tunnel. There were no responses. No one seemed to be inside the northern section of the mine. Dust fell from the dirt-covered ceiling, causing him to cough. When hearing distant sounds of shafts creaking, he grabbed an oil lamp and broke into a run.

Another quake occurred, dust falling on his clothes. He brushed the dirt off, sprinting toward the exit. The path illuminated as he drew closer to the entrance of the mine. His heart pounded while he wondered whether he'd make it in time. Upon getting out, he expected the tunnel to collapse at any moment. The northern sector, however, did not crumple.

"I hate mines," he muttered, still panting.

Mounting his horse, he rode south and returned to where Salomon was supposed to be waiting. He saw two entrances, one of which had been sealed. Yet when he arrived he heard a scratching noise emanating from a circle-shaped slab that blocked off the entrance.

Flint dismounted Donna, placed his lamp down, and approached the sealed mining shaft while trying to listen to the faint noise. Then, before he could even realize it, dynamite exploded inside. The circular slab blew off, soaring toward Flint. Normally, such a vast object would have crushed any person. Before it fell on Flint, however, he seized it with his hands, feeling it was as light as a gun when in fact it weighed hundreds of pounds. He threw the slab aside and stared at his palms in disbelief. In the meantime, Bas emerged from the mine, gawking at Flint.

"I knew there was something different about you," he said in a coarse tone. "But that's just between us."

Flint gave a faint nod, still dazed at what he'd done.

"Listen, Flint," continued Bas, "I don't know how Marshal Salomon convinced you to come here, but I'm mighty grateful because I think you're the only one who can help me get my brother back."

"What about the others?"

"I don't know," said Bas, looking troubled. "There's something down there, Flint. It took my friends."

Flint gazed at him, confused.

Bas went on, "Salomon's son and my brother were the only ones who weren't taken...at least for now."

"Bas, what the hell are you talking about?"

"You'll see," replied Bas, loading his shotgun. "You better arm yourself, Flint. There might be more of them. I tried blocking the path so it wouldn't come to the surface. But, since you're here, maybe you can kill it—or them." He cautiously walked into the mine, the barrel of his shotgun directed at the ceiling.

Flint grabbed the lamp and pulled out his magnum, following him.

"Good, you got yourself some light," said Bas, glancing at the oil lamp. "It seems to be afraid of light."

"You keep saying *it*," said Flint, perplexed. "What is this *it*?"

The titan-steel brother stayed quiet while he led him deeper inside. In the meantime, Flint pointed his magnum up.

"Bas," continued Flint, "I'm not going farther until you tell me what's down there."

"I don't know what it is," said Bas. "All I know is that it's not human. I don't even think it's an animal. But if anyone can kill this thing and save the others, it's you."

Flint felt nervous as he reentered Panzo Mine. It looked similar to the northern zone he'd gone into earlier except it was much deeper. There were shafts and carts and rocks with veins of titanium, which had never been seen before in Australia. It was getting darker inside. The narrow path they walked through led them down to a passage that no longer appeared natural. Metal of an unknown alloy replaced the wooden walls in the mine. Even the ground and ceiling were made of metal; it was a hidden structure.

"Did you and your brother build this?" asked Flint, slack-jawed, wide-eyed. He glanced at Bas who shook his head, causing his heart to skip a beat. "This can't be real. Where are Brock and Jake?"

"If they're still alive they should be waiting for me past the next door," said Bas.

Flint's heart pounded heavily again, his forehead covered with sweat. Something was unnatural about the mine—something awful. He nevertheless followed Bas until they reached a massive metal door. Flint thought it resembled the slab that had flown onto him when Bas freed himself, except this one appeared to be in mint condition.

"This is it," said Bas. "Are you ready?"

"I don't even know what we're up against!" snapped Flint.

"Listen, if Brock and Jake aren't on the other side, then I think we should seal this door and forget about the mine."

"*What?*" said Flint, glaring at Bas. "Have you lost your mind? Nothing has ever scared you before. You and Brock are the titan-steel brothers. Let's go in there, get the others, and kill whatever it is that may have taken them. All right?"

Bas gave a faint nod, aiming his shotgun at the door.

Flint noticed how focused Bas became and added, "It might actually be better if we get Marshal Salomon and—"

"Pointless," interjected Bas flatly. "He wouldn't last a second. I couldn't find or speak to Deputy Thornton, but I was hoping he'd tell Marshal Salomon what happened only in hopes that he'd convince you to come here. And don't worry, I haven't told anyone other than Brock about what *really* happened during our wrestling match."

Recalling that experience made Flint feel disconcerted. It seemed impossible, like how he'd caught the slab, not to mention him being in this warped mine of unknown origin—yes, all of this seemed impossible, he thought.

"Trust me, you're the only one who can help," said Bas.

"Okay," said Flint. "What do you want me to do?"

"With that secret strength of yours, I bet you'll have no trouble opening this door with one hand," said Bas. "Lower the lamp if you have to, but not your gun. When the door opens, back away as fast as you can or else you may end up like the others."

Flint nodded at Bas and approached the door. Lowering his lamp, he stared blankly at the metal door. He had absolutely no idea how to open it. Then he saw a hole on its right side, which was the size of a human fist. Flint placed his hand inside, feeling a knob. He turned it clockwise. While he twisted it, the door made a clicking sound and opened.

"Get ready," said Bas, grimacing.

He was a nervous wreck as the metal door swerved open. There was no one in the pitch-black tunnel. That, however, was the least of Flint's worries when he raised his lamp. Peeking inside, he noticed the walls were covered with patches of slime that resembled human mucus. Some of the ground was covered in gunk too. Flint was speechless.

"It spread this far already?" said Bas, looking horrified. "That's it, seal the door! Brock and Jake are done for. Hurry!"

"No," replied Flint. "This is your brother we're talking about, and Jake's my daughter's fiancé. He's the only man I can see her marrying. You can leave if you want, but I'm not going anywhere without them. So either get out or prove to me that you're a titan-steel brother."

"You've got balls," said Bas. "I'll give you that. But let's see if you still have them when you find what's in there."

Flint went inside first. His boots became sticky as he stepped on the slime. Stepping over it sounded like he'd been going through a tunnel of mud. Although he could hardly see anything, the lamp aided him. Bas trudged behind Flint, aiming his shotgun up. Both of them shuffled their feet while goo sporadically fell from the mucky ceiling.

They turned at a corner and entered a narrower chamber. The walls seemed to be inhaling as if they were alive. Flint glanced at the side, noticing bubble-like pods hanging along the walls. When he drew his lamp over to the inhaling pods, however, he realized that they were cocoons holding the miners. He gasped at the sight and felt the urge to vomit; yet he managed to take a deep breath and hold it in.

If what existed before his eyes had been a dream, then he was most certainly having a nightmare. But he knew this wasn't a dream, especially since Hamarah did not exist here. She was nowhere to be seen, and almost every time Flint had a dream, he ended up being in either a beautiful grove or beach with her. No, this wasn't the dreamtime; this was real. And reality was draining Flint of whatever sanity he had left.

"Still have your balls?"

"Bas, this isn't the time to be mocking me," said Flint. He glanced at a cocoon again. "I think your brother's inside that thing." Bas checked, realizing it was true. In the meantime, Flint walked across and noticed his daughter's fiancé imprisoned in another pod. "Jake's here."

"What should we do?" asked Bas, distraught.

They suddenly heard something hiss deep within the tunnel. At that precise moment, Bas turned and fired his shotgun. Flint aimed his magnum ahead but didn't shoot. Whatever dwelled inside continued to hiss. Bas fired again and started to reload his shotgun. As he did so, a shadow moved toward him. Glancing up, Flint saw a humanoid creature hanging on the ceiling, clawing its way to Bas.

Flint lifted his magnum and blasted the beast's chest just as it lunged at Bas. It fell down, screeching. It then growled, scuttling back into the shadows. The creature resembled a hunched man except it had greenish skin, needle-shaped claws, and lacked irises in the eyes.

"What the hell is that thing?" asked Flint, dismayed.

"I tried to warn you!"

"Here," said Flint, pulling out a sleek hunting knife and handing it to Bas. "Cut them free and get them out of here."

"What about you?"

"Someone has to find the others," said Flint.

Bas agreed, trying to cut his brother loose with the knife.

"It doesn't make any sense for it to be inside here," went on Flint, "but there's only one thing that creature could be—a yowie."

Bas raised an eyebrow. "Huh?"

"It's what the aboriginal people call a yeti," said Flint. "Problem is, I don't remember them talking about it putting its victims in cocoons."

"Then maybe it's not a yowie, or whatever they call that damn thing," said Bas, finally freeing Brock.

Flint shrugged, keeping his guard up.

After a minute, Bas removed Jake from the gooey cocoon and put him over his shoulders. He then attempted to heave his brother. "I'll be back in case you find the others," he said.

"Now you're living up to your name," said Flint.

Bas faintly smirked while he left the chamber. Once he was gone, Flint grabbed his lamp and continued walking through the slimy tunnel. Despite him going deeper inside, he didn't hear any hissing or growling.

"Not so vicious now with a bullet in your chest, are you?" he shouted.

Flint no longer felt nervous, nor did he feel as though he were in a horrible nightmare. He was feeling confident, especially since Bas had seen what he saw. Most importantly, he felt sane. Flint entered an antechamber and looked at the walls. This time he saw dozens of cocoons, which were holding the other miners captive.

"Holy shit," he muttered, staggering at the sight.

Flint glanced down, noticing blood. He quickly searched the chamber but didn't see the creature. The blood was his only lead. Cautiously following the trail, he noticed several familiar faces imprisoned: Kevin Smith, Martin Aleman, and Daren Linko. Bas returned just before Flint continued through another passage.

"Where're you going?" inquired Bas.

"I'm following its trail of blood," said Flint. "The others seem to be inside this room. Get them out of here while I hunt this thing down."

"All right," said Bas. "But be careful."

Flint nodded, entering the passage ahead. It was another narrow, dark tunnel. This was new territory that not even the miners had explored. Yet the walls looked manmade; they had panels with long vertical slits where steam exhumed. After observing the wondrous chamber, Flint crouched down and noticed more blood. He clenched his teeth, rose back to his feet, and trudged onward.

"Come out, you fucking monster!"

Once he reached the center of the chamber, the wall panels hummed, emitting light. Flint cringed, startled by the lights that flickered on. He aimed his magnum at them when the creature scuttled toward him from the oozy ceiling. Flint managed to see it from the corner of his eye. He swiftly targeted it and fired his gun, blowing off its left foot. It screeched in agony, plunging onto Flint and pressing him against the slime-covered floor. Flint tried to use the abnormal strength he had in his arms, pushing the monster away; yet it barely budged. That's when he realized that the creature had melded its limbs onto the ground, holding him in place.

There was nothing Flint could do except hold the monster back from sinking its teeth into his face. It jittered and screeched in a desperate attempt to eat him alive. Flint groaned loudly as he continuously tried to push the creature away. It gradually drew its mouth closer to him. Slime dripped down from the monster's mouth, splotching Flint's shirt and vest. Then, without another intake of breath, a bullet jammed right into the beast's forehead.

Sarah had just entered the chamber, aiming her Winchester rifle at the beast even though it had already loosened its grip on Flint. The creature was dead. Just before Flint could free himself, however, its body burst into a blob of ooze, enveloping him with its remains. Sarah shrieked, rushing over to her father who started drifting away into a coma.

"Oh my God, dad!" she cried out.

Flint heard his daughter scream for help and felt her holding him even though he could not move a muscle. None of this could be real, he thought. He was expecting to wake up in his room any moment now. But that wasn't happening. Instead he closed his eyes and gave up on figuring out what was real.

"We're coming!" exclaimed a voice behind him.

Just then, Bas entered the chamber with Salomon; however, Flint fell unconscious before anyone could ask him whether he was all right.

Several minutes passed. The sounds of people screaming filled Flint's ears. He could hear explosions, as well as feel the vibrations of what seemed to be a bomb going off. Then he heard the reverberation of bullets. He desperately wanted to open his eyes. Oddly, something prevented him from doing so. Flint couldn't see anything, yet he knew that the resonating environment was nothing more than a war-torn wasteland. Searing smoke brushed over him while he lay helpless to the screams and explosions.

Silence descended over the ruined terrain. It was near midnight. Flint could finally open his eyes. He lay beside a tree on a hillside. Strangely, he saw no signs of a war. Then he gazed at the sky. Countless stars were in the firmament, but Flint couldn't see the moon despite the fact that there were no clouds. He rose and looked ahead, seeing Hamarah by the hillside's ridge. She sat alone, stargazing. Flint walked up the hill and joined her.

"I dreamt of a war," he said. "So many people were helpless and frightened. Even I was afraid."

"That's because there *was* a war," she said.

"Why can't I recall anything?"

She didn't answer him.

"I want to remember everything," Flint went on. "You don't understand, Hamarah. It's as if someone has purposely removed a part of my soul. I feel as though my life has been one long dream. Being here in the dreamtime has become my reality—my freedom. Australia has become a prison to me."

Hamarah had a sad face, refusing to look at Flint. "I'm sorry, my love, but I can't help you," she said.

He sighed, deeply frustrated. "Hamarah, how can I put an end to the war if I'm always imprisoned?"

This time, she stared at Flint while placing her hands on his face. "If you truly want to end the war and help the people who have suffered, then you must first help yourself," she said enigmatically. "Always bear in mind that you must fully understand yourself before you can ever understand and help another."

She tenderly kissed him. He closed his eyes, kissing her back. To him, she smelled like lilac blossoms and felt as soft as silk. He desperately wanted to stay by her side and forget his life in Australia. Upon kissing her, however, he trembled and coughed out water.

Flint convulsed in a pond by a canyon, opening his eyes. Brock and Bas held him tight in the water. He choked and fidgeted. Realizing he had recovered, the titan-steel brothers brought him to the surface. Flint gagged and wheezed for air when he fell on the wet ground. Sarah ran to her father, hugging him. In the meantime, the others around Panzo Mine praised Flint, including Brock and Bas. All of the miners had, like him, recovered.

"Dad, are you all right?" asked Sarah.

"I think so," said Flint, still coughing. He spat out some water and then glanced at Brock and Bas. "Why drag me in the water?"

"Sorry," answered Bas, scratching his head. "We were just trying to clean that mess off you." He paused for a moment and said, "You remember, right?"

"Do I remember?" responded Flint, attempting to stand on his feet. He glanced at his drenched arms and then gazed at Bas with a distraught expression. "That wasn't a nightmare then, was it?"

Bas shook his head.

Flint couldn't help feel distressed. The only relief he felt at this point was seeing the miners among him.

"I don't know what the hell that thing was or why it was even in the mine," said Flint, faintly panting. "I'm just glad you're all safe."

"Ya sure had us worried, partner," said Joey, approaching him. He patted Flint on the back, which made him unexpectedly cough. "Eh, sorry 'bout that. Anyway, it's good ta see yer safe."

"Thanks," said Flint. He took a deep breath, holding Sarah tight. "But that wouldn't be the case if my daughter hadn't been around."

Sarah blushed and kissed her father on the cheek.

"Did you reseal that door, Bas?" asked Flint.

"Yeah, as soon as I got you out of there."

Marshal Salomon came over and firmly shook Flint's hand. "You saved my son and all the miners," he said proudly. "Once again, the town of Desonas owes you more than it can ever repay."

The miners, including Daren Linko, concurred. Brock and Bas praised Flint again. They even lifted him above their shoulders, making him smile and chuckle.

Salomon continued, "I think we can all agree on giving this man an award. How about it, Cross?"

"All I care about is a home for my daughter and son-in-law," said Flint.

"Then a house it is," said Brock. "Bas and I will build it with our company."

Sarah, shocked by this news, hugged and kissed Jake who appeared just as surprised.

"Though," added Brock, glancing at the darkening sky, "I reckon we return home before it gets too late."

"You read my mind, brother," said Bas. "Let's tidy up and get out of here!"

The miners, still horror-struck by what had happened to them, gathered their belongings and helped one another load their stagecoaches with whatever materials they had left. Most of the raw materials they'd unearthed were perfect for building homes, weapons, or coins should they create a new economy one day. Brock and Bas each managed their own stagecoach while Kevin Smith, Martin Aleman, Daren Linko, and Deputy Ted Thornton took the reins of the other stagecoaches.

Jake, meanwhile, approached Flint. "Bas told us how you barged in there. He said if he had a third titan-steel brother, it'd be you."

"He really said that?" asked Flint.

"Yes," answered Jake. "Thanks for saving my life."

"You shouldn't even be thanking me," said Flint.

Jake smiled and stayed beside Sarah. Noticing that Bas was ready to leave, Flint walked over to him.

"Tell me, what will happen to the mine now?"

"It's over," replied Bas. "But no worries, Brock and I will find another site. It'll be better than this one. I guarantee it." He then tugged his horse's reins. "See you in town."

"Take care," said Flint, waving.

"Cross," called out Marshal Salomon.

Flint turned around and noticed that the others were already on their horses, waiting for him to join them.

"Are you coming?" asked the marshal.

Flint hesitated for a moment and answered, "I'm sorry, Marshal, but there's something I need to do first." He could tell that his response wasn't going to fly with Sarah from the look on her face, so he decided to lie: "I promised Yeramba I'd help him tonight. Sarah, tell your mother I'll be home tomorrow."

"Are you sure about this?" she asked, giving her father a dubious look. "Mom's going to be worried. Can't your friend wait one more day?"

"I'm sure he can," replied Flint. "But I'm sure your mother can wait too." His choice of words made Sarah frown. Although she didn't argue, it was obvious to Flint that she went from being happy to sad in the blink of an eye. "I'll be fine. I promise."

"Okay," she said, trying not to sound too upset.

"Take care, partner," said Joey, saluting him.

Flint waved back, watching his friends ride off until they vanished from his sight. Only he and his mare stood by the canyon. He heard crickets and cicadas with an occasional hoot of a barn owl. A slight breeze brushed over him as he looked up at the partially clouded, starry sky. This had become his freedom; it was all he had left in life, he conceded. To be out in the barren wilds was a sanctuary compared to the penitentiary that he dared call Desonas.

"Why am I still living in this shithole?"

Overlooking the now derelict mine, he took a deep breath and gazed at the wide, empty expanse. He unexpectedly felt that the arid land of the Northern Territory had an eerie beauty to it. Yet without Hamarah, his one and only soul mate, Australia was as dead to him as the rest of the world. The time was coming when he would set out to find her. But where to? He had no idea.

CHAPTER FIVE
WAKING THE DREAMER

After an hour of solitude, Flint mounted Donna and left the canyon. He rode northwest toward Uluru. It was darker than usual. He could hear several animals prowling in the wilds as he rode across the vast plains of the Northern Territory.

Flint observed his surroundings. He appreciated the old, mystical-looking landscape. This desolate region was flat, covered with scorched grass. Trees were scattered throughout the land. Rarely did Flint see a pond. And of course there was Uluru. According to what the aboriginals had told him, its creation was believed to be one of Earth's birthmarks—a primordial behemoth of a rock that formed after the dawn of the dreamtime.

Most interesting to Flint was that he'd passed by these parts countless times and yet only now did he truly pay attention to the landscape's features. Several times since November he felt as though he was becoming more self-aware, but he also felt that he was losing his mind. This time, however, he didn't experience insanity. This particular kind of sentience had been growing more and more since he'd stopped eating bush tucker. He desperately needed to find out why this was happening to him, and he felt Yeramba was the only person who could help him.

He patted Donna and said, "Well, girl, it looks like I didn't lie to Sarah after all. In a way, Yeramba still has need of me. Although it's been a few months, he *did* tell me to return once the 'wild demon' had been taken care of. So I guess we'll pay him a visit."

Flint passed Uluru, riding farther west in the Northern Territory. It was only a matter of time before he'd reach Yeramba's tribe. Flint felt a few cool breezes as he journeyed through the wilds. It made him long for winter; the heat was finally getting to him. He wiped off the sweat on his forehead and nudged Donna to gallop faster.

He rode through a dry region covered with spinifex, wild flowers, and bloodwood trees. Dozens of desert oaks stood amid the northern frontier. Flint could see Kata Tjuta on his left; it looked undersized in the distance. Animalistic totems eventually became visible to Flint who thought they resembled fierce emus. He knew the Wakaya tribe lived somewhere in this region and kept searching around.

His first visit had been by escort back in November, so it proved difficult for him to find the tribe. Then he heard a distinct sound: Yeramba's bullroarer. It reverberated with the air as it twirled, changing and manipulating the sound of wind, which resembled vibrato melodies. Flint followed the natural synthesizer. It was dusk, but he finally saw the aboriginals on the grassland. Their dark complexions made it a lot easier for Flint's old eyes to spot them. He halted his mare, swung down, and greeted the aboriginal tribe by bowing before them. Jatma stood there too and mutually bowed.

Up on the hill sat King Yeramba who placed his bullroarer on the grass, gesturing at Flint to join him. Yeramba remained silent, inhaling smoke. Flint advanced and wanted to speak with him but decided to keep quiet; he simply waited until being spoken to.

"Anangu come back," Yeramba finally said. "This very good."

"Thank you," said Flint, feeling somewhat awkward by the warm welcome. He took his tattered hat off for a change and scrubbed his untidy, grayish hair. "So, you're not upset with me returning after three months?"

"Altjira spoke as Emu in dreamtime," said Yeramba who, as usual, had his eyes closed. "Much fear and confusion in your broken soul before.

Now, I see strong spirit. You defeat wild demon. Altjira honor this; we honor too, Anangu."

Flint smiled at him.

"It time you healed," continued Yeramba, inhaling smoke again. "You prepared for great journey?"

"I'm not sure yet."

"This be journey of soul, not journey of body," said Yeramba. "Maybe one day Anangu leave land, but not today. Now is dreamtime. Altjira guide me for teach wondering soul; creator beings help at spirit world that Anangu only see in the dreaming."

Flint took a deep breath, trying to be patient as he tried to understand Yeramba; however, barely anything was making sense to him.

"You understand if you remember past," said Yeramba. "Past gone but still here, hidden like treasure. We search mind and discover Anangu's past. Dreamtime show you it all," he said, opening his eyes. He stared sharply at Flint and asked, "You leave the tribe and rediscover soul now?"

"Yes," said Flint, accepting this as a mental journey. The moment he said that magical word, Yeramba blew powder into his face. Flint coughed violently and said in a wheezing tone, "Not again."

"Come to dreamtime," said Yeramba.

Flint tilted and fell sideways. His vision become hazy. Yeramba's voice sounded like a distorted hum. Bonfires diminished. Stars vanished. The aboriginals looked like wild, burning shadows. Whispers filled his ears. The faint voices were calling out to him. One of them called him *Ethan*. He soon felt groggy, closing his eyes.

One hour later, Flint awoke in the hummocks and rose to his feet. King Yeramba stood next to him. They were in front of Kata Tjuta, the rock mass of thirty-six bornhardts. The sky was cloudy; it looked as though it were about to rain.

"Good, you have awakened," said Yeramba.

"This is a dream, right?" asked Flint.

"Yes, we have entered the dreaming. We are in the realm of the dream-time. This is where your memories hide—deep in the mind like the distant stars; though, only you can retrieve them if you're able to slay Wanambi."

Flint dug his eyebrows inward, realizing that Yeramba spoke vastly better than before. "I have a feeling you're not Yeramba."

The aboriginal did not respond.

"Where is Wanambi?" he asked, irked.

Yeramba pointed skyward and said, "Mount Olga—what we call Kata Tjuta. But beware, Anangu, he is the king of all snakes and has become stronger than ever."

Flint sulked and started climbing the largest bornhardt. As he scaled it, the sun blazed down on his back, which seemed strange to him since it was a cloudy day. He looked up at the sky, yet he saw no clouds. Instead the clouds were beneath him. Flint gasped when he realized how high he suddenly was. For a split second he lost his grip but managed not to fall down. He groaned, attempting to reposition himself. After regaining control, he continued climbing and eventually reached the peak of what was supposed to be Kata Tjuta.

This area of Mount Olga made Flint feel as though he were standing on Mount Olympus. Kata Tjuta, outside the realm of his dream, was a colony of natural skyscrapers—the peak being higher than Uluru. In the dreamtime it was above the clouds. Flint, ready to confront Wanambi, observed the summit, his hand hovering over his holster.

"Come out, snake," he said, grimacing.

Looking ahead, he spotted a scaly creature on the ground. He walked over to the center of the peak, stepping on the already dead snake. The sight of the serpent made Flint feel nauseous; he was expecting to find Wanambi. As soon as he saw the dead snake, however, he had a feeling that Wanambi no longer existed—perhaps he never existed. Flint felt the snake was once him—a devious devil who had died long ago, and yet he'd managed to come back from the dead. But this time he wasn't the devil incarnate; this time he was a savior. He wondered, what did all this mean? Were they clues about his long forgotten past? Were these thoughts utter nonsense or did they actually mean something? And where did Hamarah fit into all this?

"I don't understand," he said to himself.

"Trust your mind, Ethan," said Yeramba. "The answers you seek are deep within you."

"Eh?" Flint noticed the aboriginal appear from the corner of his eye and felt suspicious, wondering how much Yeramba knew. "Is my name truly Flint Cross, or is this name some kind of joke someone created just to mock me?"

Staring at him, Yeramba replied, "You are Flint Cross as long as you will it. Names are mere labels; it is the body's inner spirit that defines us."

"But why can't I remember anything else? Why can't I remember the war or Hamarah?"

Yeramba pointed at the cloudy sky and said, "Your answer is beyond this world, Ethan. There is nothing left for you here on this wretched planet. You must break free of this illusion and leave."

Flint unexpectedly felt queasy, convinced that the person before him wasn't Yeramba. He bent down, vomiting, and fell sidelong to the ground, blanking out. After what seemed like a few hours, he awoke on Yeramba's hillside. It was past midnight. He removed the remaining powder around his nose while coughing. Then he sat up, gazing at Yeramba.

"Why did you tell me I had to kill Wanambi?"

Yeramba smiled and said, "Wanambi be fear. You fight fear and defeat it. You battle him with spirit. Dreamtime not always different from real, but sometime it distort with fear. In dream, enemy be fear—enemy be you."

"How can I be my own enemy?" asked Flint, unconvinced. "No, more importantly, how can I have fear of something that I can't even remember?"

"Ah, what body want be different from spirit," said Yeramba. "You very troubled soul, Anangu. You not aware of this trouble. Emu in dreamtime know. All spirits aware—only they. But today is victory; it be first day Anangu awaken."

"But what have I awakened from?"

"The dream," said Yeramba. He put his hands on Flint's shoulders and added, "Returning not coincidence. Rest. We talk in dawn."

Flint nodded, grabbed his hat, and walked away.

"Wait," he said abruptly, turning around. "I almost forgot."

Yeramba raised an eyebrow, listening.

"In Panzo Mine," went on Flint, "the miners were attacked by a mons…by a beast I've never seen before. I thought it might've been what your people call a yowie." He noticed that Yeramba had a pale face, though it may have been caused by the bonfire. "It resembled a man, but it was hunched with green skin and claws. I don't think it had eyes. Actually, it *did* have eyes; though, for some reason it looked blind. Do you think that was a yowie?"

"Anangu," began Yeramba in a befuddled tone, "you in dreamtime more than spirits led me believe."

Flint sighed out of frustration.

"Rest now, Anangu," said Yeramba. "Tomorrow is new day."

Flint left the hillside and rejoined his mare by a campsite. The tribesmen had surprisingly made a bonfire for him and his horse. He approached Donna, who nickered, and gently rubbed her fur.

"Sleep well, girl," he said to her.

Flint lay by the fire, trying to sleep. He thought of Amanda for a brief moment, feeling an ounce of shame for not returning home. A voice within him, however, told him that he deserved this freedom because he'd helped the miners. He then let go of his wife and tried to embrace the nature before him. With the exception of the insects' sporadic chorus, it was a quiet night. Flint felt safe among Yeramba's tribe. This was the first time he decided to stay with the Wakaya, or any tribe for that matter. The complex feelings within him were doused while he rested outside in the wilds. After a few minutes of listening to the sounds of wildlife, he fell asleep.

In the distance, Uluru sank into the ground. The landscape near it gradually changed into the East Alligator expanse of Kakadu, which looked beautiful unlike months ago when Flint had awakened to the burnt wetland that was near Nourlangie Rock.

He slowly awoke, finding himself on the painted rocks of Ubirr. Rising to his feet, he gazed at the lush vegetation surrounding him and noticed Hamarah who sat by the outcrops of rocks, watching the sunset. Flint smiled, relieved to see her. Upon joining her, he observed the floodplains and escarpments. Hamarah hummed a song when he sat down.

Flint calmly listened to her hum, also watching the sunset. After a while, however, he turned, gazing at his beloved soul mate.

"I'm starting to remember," he said.

Hamarah smiled, gracefully staring at him. "Once you remember, you'll never be able to go back," she said.

"I don't want to go back," he said, embracing her. "I want to find you."

She closed her eyes and leaned her head on his shoulder. "I'm so happy you've made up your mind. But this is only the beginning, Ethan. Your life will be in danger from here on."

"I had a feeling you'd tell me that," he said. "I'm prepared for the worst; though, I keep thinking about what Browder told me—his words have made me concerned. Please tell me, is there anyone whom I'm able to trust?"

"Andrew Browder was too paranoid; he had no idea who to trust when he woke up from the dreamtime," she said pensively. "If you ever have any doubts, confide in Yeramba."

"Thank you."

"I believe in you," said Hamarah softly. She gleamed at him with affection and gently kissed his lips.

Flint closed his eyes, holding her while the sun finished setting. Upon opening his eyes, he found himself back in Yeramba's territory. It was already dawn, and yet, to Flint, it felt as if only mere seconds had passed since he'd gone to sleep. He sat up, smelling the burnt residue of wood that belonged to his now lifeless bonfire. Smoke still lingered, creating a hazy effect. Most of the aboriginals were gone. Flint assumed they were hunting.

He then noticed Donna eating grass and felt hungry; he hadn't had an opportunity to eat last night. Putting on his hat, he walked toward the hillside. A few women and children smiled at him while he passed by. He, in return, tipped his hat. Eventually, he approached Yeramba who was currently the only male aboriginal there.

"Good morning," said Flint, doffing his hat. Yeramba remained seated and silent, smoke blowing out of his nostrils. "Do you do that every day?" he asked, amused.

"Spirits say Anangu remember past," said Yeramba. Before Flint could reply, Yeramba added, "This good. Much healing on mind, but too much break soul again. It be good to cleanse spirit. And, at time, let go of thoughts. Dreamtime same: we go to Altjira like birth. It source of healing on spirits and creator beings; we fly and journey but not remember."

"How come we may not remember?"

"If spirit remember all lives, spirit probably think always on many lives," said Yeramba meditatively. "This life very important."

"But if I can't remember my past lives, then how will it help me in this life?"

"Your spirit strong," said Yeramba. "It be like instinct of animal. We know soul from dreamtime—doorway to past lives. This true light guide us on what all must do."

"Does this mean that the war I experienced was from a past life?" he asked. Yeramba did not answer, causing Flint to feel anxious. "How about Hamarah? She feels so real. Is it possible she's still alive in this life?"

"I not have all answers, Anangu," said Yeramba. "I point you in direction; it guide you to find the lost. Only you, Anangu. You go now: desert of many gods."

Flint knew that the "desert of many gods" was the dead world itself. Yeramba apparently wanted him to leave this continent to find what he seeks. And while it was something he longed for, he knew deep down inside that he couldn't do that—not yet at least. Although he was willing to leave his wife, he could never abandon his children.

"You are ready?"

"No," said Flint. "I'm sorry, but I have a family. I can't just leave whenever I want. In fact, my wife is probably furious enough as it is because I spent the night here."

"Family important, Anangu," said Yeramba considerately. "Homage to Tjurunga—the ancestors place where Emu totemic body on Olgas— that be only thing more sacred than family. My eight wives knowing this as one law above love."

"Eight wives is a *lot* of love," said Flint, trying not to laugh. Ironically, Yeramba was the one who laughed. "Well, it's been a pleasure." He rose to his feet, doffing his hat. "My wife and children are waiting for me. Maybe we'll meet again someday, my friend."

"If creator beings will it," said Yeramba, pressing his palms together. "May white angel wake after dreamtime. Ride safe, Anangu."

"Thanks," he said. "Good hunting."

Flint waved goodbye to the aboriginals while approaching his mare by the smoldered campsite. Taking hold of Donna's reins, he tugged her to gallop northward. The morning was proving to be another beautiful day. Unlike the dreamtime, it was a clear sky with no clouds in sight. Traveling home, Flint saw a bustard flying. He smirked, spun out his revolver, and aimed at the bird.

"This one's for you, Joey."

He shot down the bustard with a single bullet and nudged Donna to canter over to where the bird fell. It was difficult for him to find it amid the grassland, but he eventually spotted it and placed its body in his knapsack. Gently tugging the reins, he continued to ride north. After three hours of traveling, he returned to Desonas. Strangely, he saw a group of horses standing by the hitch rail of Steve Harrison's church. Some of them belonged to the miners.

"What the heck?"

He couldn't remember the last time so many people were at the church at the same time. Despite how odd this seemed to him, he shrugged and waved off the strange feeling he had in his gut.

"Let's go, girl," he said to Donna.

He rode past the town square and made his way through the farmsteads owned by the Steward and Froehlich families. They were also missing from their fields—apparently in the church, thought Flint. He finally reached his homestead, guiding Donna into the corral. Flint removed her saddle and then rubbed her snout.

"I'll keep you and your friends here for a while since it's nice out, okay?"

Donna nickered, trotting over to the other horses. Flint watched them eat grass when his stomach growled. He rubbed his slim belly while letting out a sigh, making his way back home; however, he stopped as soon as he reached his porch. He realized that there was something he'd forgotten to pack and take with him on the journey. His widened eyes gazed at the porch's bench and table—no journal. Flint gulped and quietly went inside his house.

No one greeted him. The hall was silent and empty. Flint felt a slight feeling of relief as he hung his hat on the rack, but then he noticed that his trophy had been ripped off the wall. He groaned while he stepped into the kitchen, ready to scream at Amanda; yet she wasn't there. Flint spotted a few shattered mugs on the floor. He had a feeling that this was Amanda's doing rather than the result of someone breaking in and vandalizing his property. His house looked derelict for the first time in his life. Wasn't it he who wanted to abandon his home? It shouldn't be the other way around, he thought.

He was thinking irrationally; he knew his wife and children were probably out in the farm somewhere. And it was better this way because he knew an argument would ignite the moment he'd see Amanda. Flint started cleaning up, removing as much glass as he could with his hands. He then used a broom to sweep away the sharper, smaller pieces into a bag.

Just before he finished, he heard a faint creak. He turned around, noticing Sarah and Tom by the kitchen entrance. The three of them stared at one another awkwardly. Flint looked calm, but his children wore miserable expressions on their faces; they looked as if they couldn't handle another second of life any more. After a few seconds of silence, Sarah and Tom rushed over to their father's arms. Flint embraced his children while they cried.

"What's wrong?" he asked.

"Mo-mom...mom is dead," said Sarah, sobbing hysterically. She looked at her father in despair, tears pouring from her eyes, and went on, "Sh-she hung herself."

Flint felt as though his innards twisted. The anger he had after seeing his trophy ripped off the wall immediately vanished. He backed away, nearly choking. Everything made sense to him. Amanda had found his journal—she read his most private thoughts about Hamarah and his fantasies of leaving to find her.

All the arguments he had with Amanda exploded from his subconscious—they resurfaced into his conscience, making him feel despicable. This was the last straw, he miserably thought to himself: Amanda could no longer live happily after knowing how much he hated her. In fact, she couldn't bear to live at all. He knew family meant everything to her, and since hers was more dysfunctional than any other, she must have felt she'd failed, hanging herself.

He dared to wonder if this was a dream. No, he didn't wonder; he dared to *hope* that this was a nightmare. It was, however, all too real. At least thirty horses stood by the church—most of the townspeople must have been attending her wake, he thought. And while they were doing this, he was out in the wilds like a mindless kid. During his married life, all he'd done was think about himself. He betrayed his wife so many times that it killed her.

Flint staggered against the wall. His children were still holding on to him. Yet he could barely feel them. He almost felt numb. What little feeling he had made him drown further in despair. Suddenly, he pushed his children away. He shook his head, turning to the stairs. Flint wouldn't look at his children; he refused to look at them. All he wanted to do was escape, so he ran upstairs and locked his door as he heard his children cry out to him. He ignored them, hoping he would wake up from this nightmare.

No, he wouldn't be waking up this time; he was already awake. The days of his dreaming were over. The dreamer was wide awake. His fairytale life was as dead as his wife, and he knew that the life he had lived just hours ago would never be the same again. He curled at the bottom of his bed, crying hysterically. One day he was a hero, the next he was a creep on the brink of insanity.

Australia had finally died. Now the whole world was literally dead. Everything was dead to Flint. Maybe his wretched body still pulsed with life, but his soul was dead. And to him, if the soul was dead, then the body was dead too. He remained in his room for hours—for days. His children had stopped crying; they had stopped knocking and waiting for their father to come out. They soon became the parents, taking care of the farm while Flint regressed to being a child. The folks in the desolate town of Desonas continued living except him. He was frozen in time despite him turning sixty, and he made sure it stayed that way.

Flint was nearly starving himself to death. He lived on whatever alcohol was in his home and only ate the food that Sarah would leave for him in the kitchen. Not once did anyone speak of the travesty that took place in their house. Several months had passed, or at least it felt that way to Flint. Time was lost to him. His adventures as a cowboy were over. The dreamer had finally awakened; it was a rude awakening. All of his mesmerizing dreams were lost—gone for what seemed to be forever. The only thing he had left was his sanity, and even that was slowly fading away.

Perhaps he'd already be insane if it were not for one more thing he had in his life. Yes, he had just realized that there was something else other than his sanity—his two children. But at this point, he felt he'd betrayed them as much as he had betrayed Amanda. So much time had passed; they were taking care of the house and farm. And what was he doing? He wasn't doing anything. In the end, he was exactly what Doctor Tutherfield had proclaimed—a narcissistic man who only cared about himself.

He nodded at this realization, on the verge of drinking more alcohol on his reeking bed. Just before taking another gulp, however, he stopped and stared at the bottle with an expression of disgust—he was disgusted with himself. He screamed, hurling the bottle at the wall. Then he cried again. His tormented body desperately wanted to escape reality. He'd always been running away from old age, his late wife, his children, the dead world; he'd been running away from everything in existence.

But just this once he wanted to be irrational and face reality while sober. Despite his odd act of bravery, he soon regretted smashing his last bottle of alcohol. He had a horrible headache and suddenly felt the urge to puke. Slowly rising to his feet, he stumbled to the bedroom door, unlocked it, and wobbled into the bathroom. The moment he entered it, he vomited all over the floor.

Sarah quickly ran up the stairs, holding him. It was the first time since—no, Flint could not remember the last time his daughter had held him. He coughed violently and vomited again. Fortunately, he vomited in the toilet this time. He felt deathly ill, and he certainly looked it: his lurched, skimpy body and face were awfully pale, and his forehead was covered in sweat; he was no longer the strong cowboy he used to be. Flint knew he looked frail, and he had a feeling that his daughter thought the same. Yes, he regretted smashing his bottle of booze. It would've been better if he'd stayed in his room, drinking until dead, he conceded.

"Dad," muttered Sarah.

Hearing her sweet voice felt like a sting from a vicious insect, thought Flint. He wanted to cry again. He was so pitiful; so weak; so ghostly. And yet when he heard her voice, he felt a pulse deep within him—it was the pulse of life. But he hated that pulse. A part of him no longer wanted to feel it. He wanted to scream at Sarah for coming upstairs to help him. He wanted her to forget about his wretched existence. Yet he cried over her shoulder instead.

"Sh-she's gone," he sniveled. "It's all my fault."

"No, dad," she said softly. "It's her fault."

"Huh?" he uttered, almost choking. He could hardly believe what he heard his daughter say. He needed to hear it again. "What?"

"Mom gave up," she said. "Mom will always be in my heart. I will always love her. But suicide wasn't the answer. And it will never be the answer. Even though we have a difficult life; even though the world is barely hospitable anymore, life is still worth living."

"You were always the strong one," he said feebly. He managed to stand straight in the bathroom, leaning against a wall. "I'm proud of you, Sarah."

She smiled, embracing her father. "I love you, dad."

"I love you too," he said, holding her tight.

Now he remembered; the last time he'd held her was on that miserable day—the day he'd come home from his last adventure, only to find out that Amanda had hung herself. He wondered to himself, was she *that* miserable? To kill herself over a journal; over an imaginary woman? He knew the answer but refused to admit it.

"Let me help you back to your room," she said.

He gave her a nod. His daughter unexpectedly made him feel stronger. The pulse of life wasn't so bad after all. And for the first time in months, he felt that he deserved to live. Sarah helped him back to his bedroom. Though, when entering, she tried to hide her face; she wore an expression of revulsion, accidently inhaling the putrid air inside. She laid her father down on the bed and tried fixing the sheets. As she did so, Flint stared at her curiously.

"How is Tom?" he asked.

"He's all right," she said, tucking Flint in with the sheets. "He misses you." She paused for a moment and then added, "We both miss you." Sarah could no longer stand the disgusting odor in the room and lifted the window. She waved her hands a few times and tried to smell the fresh air outside. "That's a little better," she whispered to herself.

"What have I missed?"

Sarah walked over to the bed and sat at a corner next to her father. "Everything is almost the same," she said, putting her hair in a ponytail. She held his hand and said, "I have something important to tell you."

Flint waited for her to speak, but she didn't continue. Instead she simply looked at him with an awkward expression.

"Well, out with it already," he grumbled.

She lowered her head and finally said, "I'm pregnant."

At first, when he heard the word "pregnant" he felt numb inside. Normally, hearing such a thing from his daughter would have made him want to kill Jake for taking her before marriage. But this news strangely felt trivial in comparison to Amanda's death. He stared blankly at his daughter who didn't know what to expect from him. Letting the news settle in, he managed to accept it without screaming.

"Why?" he inquired.

"I needed him," she said flatly. "He wanted me, and I needed him. We were already engaged."

"Are you still engaged?" he dared to ask.

"*Yes*," she said as though it were a stupid question. "As a matter of fact, we're getting married on Friday."

"Huh?" he uttered, faintly coughing. "I don't even know what month it is."

"June," she said, chuckling. "Today is Tuesday, June twenty-fourth. Just don't ask what year it is." This time Flint chuckled. "By the way," she went on, "Steve is going to marry me to Jake. Do you think you'll be able to come and walk me down the aisle?"

Flint finally sat up and said, "I wouldn't miss it even if the world was coming to an end." He thought that was rather stupid to say, since the world had in fact ended long ago. "Ah, forget that last part. Of course I'll be there." He hugged his daughter who gleefully hugged him back. "I just hope Tommy is the best man."

"He is," she said, smiling.

Flint shook his head. "Just a moment ago you told me everything was just about the same." He sighed. "I missed a whole lot."

"You'll make it up by coming to my wedding," she said.

Flint continued to hug Sarah. As he held her, he thought to himself, after all this time, life had managed to go on. Not everything was dead after all. He slowly appreciated the pulse of life. And he finally felt rejuvenated enough to face the real world without wanting to escape into the wilds, his dreams, or by means of alcohol. He made his decision this moment—he would be the father he'd failed to be for so many months.

"Get some rest," she said, kissing her father on the forehead. "We can talk more about it tomorrow."

Flint complied and lay back down on his bed. He let his daughter gently tuck him in again and watched her leave. When she closed the door, he took a deep breath and closed his eyes. The dreary past was finally behind him. He wanted to start over tomorrow, he happily thought. That's right, he conceded—no more alcohol, no more adventures as a cowboy, and no more dreams.

He felt comfortable on his soft bed. It was nice and quiet. And with the window open, he received fresh air with an occasional breeze. After all, June was winter in Australia, and he really needed a nice, cool breeze. Even though he'd been hiding from reality in his room, he had spent most of his time drinking himself to death. But now it was time for him to sleep in peace. While he lay on his bed, however, it started to feel rough—a bit too jagged. He turned around, yet it felt the same.

This rough feeling was the strangest thing, he thought. Just a moment ago his pillow was soft and fluffy. Now it felt hard. And the putrid smell in his room was completely gone. When he breathed the air, it felt absolutely clean. He decided to open his eyes, wondering what this was all about. He probably should've kept them closed because when he opened his eyes he gasped and nearly had a heart attack; he was no longer in his room.

Flint lay on cold granite, his head resting on a jagged boulder. He stood up and felt dizzy and nauseous. The wind blew against him, and mist enveloped him. The fog seemed unnatural, sweeping through the cracked badlands within seconds. Wherever Flint was located, he was far from home. But, somehow, his instincts told him that he was still in Australia.

He squinted, attempting to scout ahead. Despite how hard Flint tried to look, he couldn't see anything due to the mist. He turned around, unexpectedly seeing King Yeramba standing in the middle of nowhere on one leg; his left foot rested along the side of his right knee. He had one hand lifted skyward while the other faced downward. Yeramba's body, as usual, was painted all around with various aboriginal markings.

"I'm done with your games, Yeramba," said Flint sharply.

"Games?" said Yeramba, raising an eyebrow. "It is true: your entire life has been a game. But am I the host? No. I'm afraid that it's the other way around, Anangu." Not once did he flinch or tumble while he spoke in his absurd position. "Open your eyes."

"Stop this!" shouted Flint, approaching Yeramba. "My wife is dead because I confided in you and your ridiculous dreams."

"These are not my dreams," said Yeramba. "They are yours."

Flint, enraged, glanced down and realized that he was dressed like a cowboy with a black duster over his vest. This didn't make sense to him, though it worked out in his favor. He quickly reached for his revolver, pointing it at Yeramba.

"This ends now."

"If you shoot me, you shoot yourself," said Yeramba. Flint was startled when he heard Yeramba who continued, "Do you still think I am an aboriginal?"

"Stop," said Flint, his hand shaking. "Stop this madness."

"I am not the dreamer," said Yeramba. "Only you can put an end to the dreaming. But first you must awaken."

"I *awakened* when my wife killed herself!"

"She was never your wife," said Yeramba.

Flint couldn't take it any longer. He trembled and trembled, and then he pulled the trigger of his revolver. The sound of his bullet being released was like booming thunder. Smoke puffed from the barrel of his gun like a lit cigarette, and the delicate bullet projected out of his revolver, jamming straight between Yeramba's eyes. He croaked while blood trickled down the hole in his head, and he fell flat on the granite. The mist enveloped him, and he disappeared.

"You can't kill me," said a whispery voice.

Gasping as if out of breath, Flint turned around and saw Yeramba standing unharmed in the same exact position he was in before.

"Who the fuck are you?" he inquired, pointing his gun at the aboriginal.

"Now we're getting somewhere," said Yeramba. "I am many things. Sometimes I am the love of your life: Hamarah. Sometimes I am your mentor: Yeramba. But most importantly…"

"Spit it out," said Flint.

"Most importantly, I am you."

Flint squinted, ready to shoot Yeramba again.

"I was so sure that you'd finally awakened on Mount Olga," continued Yeramba. "I was so sure that you'd faced your fears and defeated the evil within you. But you never killed Wanambi. It was only an illusion—I know that now. You climbed Mount Olga merely out of curiosity, ignorant of your situation. Not once did you do it for Hamarah or your old comrades. You did it only to please your ego."

"What the hell are you talking about?"

The sound of a bullroarer suddenly pierced Flint's ears. It was so deafening that it shook the land. Flint dropped his gun and clamped his hands over his ears, kneeling down. When he kneeled down to the granite, however, he gazed at Yeramba who now looked identical to him, except he was naked. Flint could hardly believe what he saw. He stared at his naked self and fell to the ground, screaming in pain. His ears bled while the bullroarer continued to bellow its odd, discordant melody.

After a few seconds, the sound stopped. Flint let go of his ears, gazing up. The aboriginal was gone. Breathing deeply, Flint grabbed his revolver and rose to his feet. He scouted the area menacingly, ready to kill Yeramba. The mist was thickening. No matter where he looked, he couldn't see anything. Flint followed his gut and walked north. The silver spurs on his boots chinked loudly with each step he took. He occasionally turned, aiming his gun around, and continued north.

Flint was angry, anxious, distraught, curious, and tired. Still, he pressed on. Fortunately, when he walked farther ahead, he saw the shape of a mountain whose peak was almost as high as Uluru. Though, he couldn't see it very well due to the mist.

"Where the hell am I?"

He eventually broke into a run. His duster blew back when he sprinted. The violent wind brushed against his old, rugged face as he ran. He was soon panting. His thick, gray goatee felt heavy. His legs—weak and shaky. And despite it being winter, Flint felt as though the heat had begun to pour over his dreary body. Not even winter in Australia held the furious sun back. He gazed up while he ran, but the thick mist and clouds covered the black-spotted sun. Flint slowed down, catching his breath. When he stopped, however, he could finally make out the gargantuan mountain. It wasn't Uluru. No, he wished it were. Standing before him was Kalkajaka, the black mountain of death.

How he ended up in Queensland, he had no idea. But this was the dreamtime. Anything was possible within the dreaming, thought Flint. After catching his breath, he had the nerve to walk forward. He wasn't going to let fear hold him back. The only thing that mattered to him at this point was finding Yeramba and putting another bullet in his head. He'd do it again and again if he had to. The dreaming meant nothing to him. He just wanted to wake up and live out the rest of his days in peace.

Flint was ignorant when he'd climbed Mount Olga during his previous experience in the dreamtime, but he knew that the key to his salvation—returning back to reality—was somewhere within Kalkajaka. As he approached the black mountain he heard whispery screams of torment; he heard echoes of tortured souls who'd been imprisoned within the rock of death. Flint stopped and stood still for a moment, listening to the agonizing voices that were fading. He gazed at the mountain harshly, realizing that this was it—if he walked any farther, he would reach the point of no return; he'd reach the deepest sanctum of his subconscious. Nodding at this realization, he pressed on, entering the darkest realm of his being, where sanity was nonexistent.

The scorching heat increased as Flint approached the mountain. Little by little, the mist dwindled. When it dissipated, steam blew out of the ground's cracks. Looking down, he noticed magma beneath him through the wiry-shaped fissures. Just then, an earthquake started. Flint ran while splintered boulders fell from the black mountain.

He continued to hear whispery voices screaming in agony as he drew closer to the base of the mountain. Upon reaching it, he realized the mountain was covered with black lichen. At first he didn't see an entrance to a cave, so he decided to climb. Though the jagged granite was hot, his leather gloves dampened the heat for him. Glancing down, he saw chasms throughout the grayish mountain and made sure not to fall.

Upon climbing midway, he finally saw a slight opening that seemed to lead into a cave. He felt wary about entering the mountain; however, he'd already journeyed this far. It was time for him to find out what lay inside. He pulled out his Peacemaker and cautiously stooped into the hole, which led him into a nearly pitch-black cavern that reeked with a stench of death so awful that it made him think his booze- and vomit-scented bedroom smelled like a rainforest. A single sniff made him cough and stagger to the side.

At that moment, the cavern lit up with sparks of fire as magma flowed beneath him. His eyes widened when he saw the lava. Steam, once again, billowed out from the cracks. He kept hearing faint sounds of ghostly voices screaming as if being tortured. It was unsettling to Flint, but he refused to give into fear and walked ahead. The heat pressed against his waning body so much that he started to feel dizzy. Still, the air was dreadful. It was so rotten that Flint nearly suffocated in a feeble attempt not to breathe the air. Then he dared to look down and found the source of the stench—thousands of dead bodies.

Flint nearly screamed. He accidently stepped on someone's head, and then he stepped on the ruptured body of another person who seemed to have fallen from one of the large chasms above. The corpses were innumerable, and they were impossible to avoid. Flint began to run, stepping on countless bodies. He wore a ghastly face while steam blew against him. Sounds of hisses pierced his ears. Were snakes living within the mountain of death? The thought simply terrified him. Flint ran as fast as he could, accidently falling down a chasm hidden in the dark passage he'd been dashing through.

He slammed against several ridges, continuing to fall farther down the pitch-black hell that the aboriginals had proclaimed to be a warren of evil. Here, in the depths of Kalkajaka, was Flint's final destination. His fall was interrupted by solid ground. His wail resonated louder than the bullroarer outside, echoing throughout Kalkajaka. Without a doubt, if this was reality, he'd be dead now. The only reason why he was still alive in this godforsaken mountain was because he was within the dreamtime.

Flint painfully uncurled himself and slowly stood up. Although it was extremely dark, the ruby-red lava allowed him to see. His gun, however, was nowhere to be seen; he'd unfortunately lost it in the midst of falling. He walked in a hunch. The stench of death was finally gone. But the blistering heat was still empowering the dark, rickety depths of death, clinging onto Flint in an attempt to roast him and feed him to whatever beast still lurked within these blackish walls of torment.

He eventually heard someone crying; it was the lament of a miserable woman. Flint had heard this voice before. The weeping voice gave him an irrational chill. He then defied the heat pressing against him, urgently trying to find the person who was crying. At the end of the tunnel, curled in a corner, lay Amanda who wept hysterically with Flint's gun in her hand.

"No," he muttered, taking a step back. "No, this isn't fair."

Amanda noticed him and said, "This isn't fair?" She wiped away her tears as she sniveled and added, "What you did to me was unfair!" Amanda nearly stuttered and stammered with each word she uttered. "Yes, this is fair. This is justice, you narcissistic scoundrel!" She lifted the gun, putting its muzzle on the temple of her head. "You never loved me."

"Don't do it," he said, surrendering his hands. "Please don't."

"You never loved our children," she went on. "You never even loved that whore in your dreams. No, you have only been in love with yourself."

"Give me a chance," he pleaded.

"I gave you so many chances," she said, sniveling. She pulled the hammer of Flint's gun, cocking it back. "So many chances..."

"Amanda," he whispered fretfully. "Please don't do this. I lov—"

She pulled the trigger before he could finish, blowing half her face apart. The sound of the gun going off was loud, but not as deafening as Flint's anguishing shriek. He ran to his wife and held her bloody corpse in a tearful outrage, screaming at the top of his lungs. The languish he thought he'd laid to rest had returned within seconds. He was the same pitiful mess of a man he'd become when she had committed suicide in the real world several months ago. Flint lay in the corner, feeling helpless.

"Why do you mourn that which was never real?" asked Yeramba, coming out from the shadows.

The moment Flint heard Yeramba speak, he grabbed his revolver from Amanda's lifeless hand, aimed it at the aboriginal silhouette, and fired the remaining rounds into the shadow. None of the bullets, however, harmed Yeramba.

"Give me back my wife!" bellowed Flint, standing up.

"I already told you, she was never your wife," said Yeramba. He stepped into the dim light, showing his features. Flint gasped and took a step back, seeing himself again. Yeramba, who looked exactly like him, smiled and added, "You still don't get it, do you?" He laughed and went on, "They've been playing you for a fool. This entire world has been a stage, and you are their entertainment—their joke."

Flint felt his heart pound heavily as his mirror image spoke. He remembered everything Browder had told him. And he knew, deep down inside his frail soul, that something was wrong with his life. All of his feelings on the matter had vanished when Amanda committed suicide; he had blamed himself and even considered the possibility that he'd gone mad. But if he was insane, it'd be impossible for him to think clearly, trying to put all the pieces together. Yes, something was definitely wrong. He cast his eyes down, noticing that Amanda was no longer there.

At that moment, Flint came to the conclusion that everything here had been an illusion. His eyes widened, and he realized that he hadn't been defeated.

"It's true, isn't it?" he said. "Hamarah…is she real?"

The doppelganger nodded.

"What must I do to remember everything?"

"You have already stepped into the deepest depths of your subconscious self," said the doppelganger. "You've entered what you were once terrified of—what you never truly wanted to face before."

"Those corpses above," began Flint, looking pale, "they were my comrades during the war, weren't they?"

Once again, the doppelganger nodded.

"They died for me," said Flint despairingly. "I acted as a martyr, and they followed me blindly until the end." Closing his eyes, he could hear their screams again—the bullets, the bombs, the sounds of blowing rubble and death. He staggered as a tear ran down his wrinkled cheek. "And my punishment was this life."

"It's not too late," said the doppelganger. "You can still redeem yourself. I have waited here, locked away in your subconscious mind by the drugs in the bush tucker. You listened to Browder; you knew something was wrong. And now it's time to take back what's yours. Now it's time to avenge those who died for you—it's time to help those who still need you."

"Hamarah," whispered Flint. "Hamarah needs me."

"She is but one of millions who need you," said the doppelganger. "But yes, Hamarah needs us."

"Us?" asked Flint, raising an eyebrow.

"I am you, and you are me," said the doppelganger. "I am your lost memory. Join with me, and we will pick up where we left off decades ago." He raised his hand and curled it into a fist as he added, "Together we'll bring forth a war so menacing that the tribunal will wish they had killed us instead of creating this pathetic charade of a town for their amusement."

Flint stared at his mirror image in awe, nodding at it. Slowly, he approached his mental doppelganger. While he approached him he pondered about many things. He once desperately wanted to forget each and every dream he'd experienced, especially those since November. Life had never been so forthcoming. Wishing for something was one thing, but having it come true was another. Taking a deep breath, he closed his eyes and merged into his doppelganger. It felt like he was in water, drifting freely for the first time in his own consciousness.

In fact, when he merged with him, the entire cavern of Kalkajaka leaked with water. The jagged ground became soft and puffy, as did the walls. Then they burst like bubbles, and in came waves of water, engulfing him. The waves were seemingly endless, and before Flint knew it he was drifting in a blue sea. It was the most intoxicating feeling Flint had ever felt. He was as free and calm as the lucent water.

The indignity and sorrow that he'd had since Amanda had killed herself was wiped away. Suddenly, he wanted to remember everything. His conscience of Amanda's death withered into silence. He pondered about his previous, glorious life. He saw Hamarah clearly in his mind—her Tunisian beauty. She was more real to him than his children. Everything became lucid to him at this point. No matter the situation, he knew that he had to find Hamarah. She was somewhere out there in the dead world. Regardless of what others thought about this, the dreamtime was real—a gateway into his past. And at long last, he became the master of his dreams.

CHAPTER SIX

THE GUNSLINGER

Flint woke up the following day feeling rejuvenated. He walked over to the window and looked out: dawn had arrived. After taking a good long look at the ranch he'd once called home, he turned away, opened his wardrobe, and took out his favorite attire: a beige scully shirt with a suede vest, fringed gloves, shotgun-style chaps made of smooth leather—which overlapped his brownish-blue denim jeans—and oiled chestnut-colored boots. After dressing up, Flint attached his holster.

This was the first time in nearly a year that Flint felt so alive. He confidently stared at himself in the mirror. A new glare of life stirred in his old blue eyes. He'd finally begun to see past this illusory life as a family man that the townsfolk had claimed to be real when in fact it was nothing more than a life of imprisonment. And he knew that if he wanted this to end, he would have to leave Desonas forever. A broad grin formed on his chapped lips as he put his brown-brimmed hat on, tipping it at himself.

He was able to walk with pride, his spurs chinking. Not a moment later, he glanced into Sarah's bedroom, hoping she was still asleep. She was, however, wide awake, sitting with Tom by the window.

"Dad?" called out Tom, surprised to see his father.

"Morning," said Flint, reserved. The trio hugged one another as though nothing bad had happened over the past few months. "What're you two doing up so early?"

"We were just talking about her wedding," said Tom. "Isn't it great?"

"I couldn't be happier," said Flint, glimpsing at Donna through the window. He looked at his daughter and loosely added, "Jake is a good man. He deserves you."

Sarah felt that her father was acting a bit odd—there was a rather cold aura about him this morning, as though he had something to hide. Her father always called Tom "son" but didn't this time, and she felt he'd given her fake compliments about the wedding, trying to say anything just to make her smile so he could go on with whatever he had planned.

"Is something wrong?" she asked suspiciously.

Flint stared blankly at Sarah and then walked over to the windowsill, staring at the ranch again. He kept quiet for a while. His silence made his children feel uncomfortable. As a matter of fact, he wasn't comfortable either. Then he thought to himself, it's now or never.

"I need to leave," he said.

"What do you mean, leave?" asked Sarah. "Leave for a few hours, one day, a few weeks, or what?"

Finally facing his children, he said, "I know you read my journal."

"No," said Tom, quickly shaking his head.

"Yes, I did," said Sarah snappishly. "Marshal Salomon has it now. And he told me that if you go on about it, to tell him."

"Did he now?" said Flint. He smirked at Sarah when she nodded and added, "Well, you can tell him anything you want. Regardless of how you feel, I'm leaving to find Hamarah, and there's nothing you or anyone can do about it."

"If you leave, I'll never forgive you," she said.

Hearing her unsympathetic words, Flint swallowed heavily. There was something about Sarah that made him admire her above all women; she had remarkable principles, he conceded. Still, his love for her wouldn't hold him back from his calling.

"Then don't forgive me," he said, beginning to walk away.

Sarah burst into tears. "But what about my wedding?" She suddenly lost all the strength she had and stuttered, "Y-you said th-that you wo-would walk m-me down th-the aisle. You sa-said you wo-wouldn't miss it ev-even if the wo-world was co-coming to a-an end."

Flint stopped in the middle of the hallway and replied, "The world ended millennia ago. I am leaving, and that is final."

"You selfish bastard!" she shouted, weeping. Sarah had finally cursed at her father. She was so loud that Tom flinched. "You're an ungrateful, self-centered, indifferent, and unfaithful bastard!"

"I know," said Flint, glancing at his sniveling daughter. "The two of you are adults now. You've taken good care of the house and farm while I was a mess these past few months. You have both shown me that this is your place in the world. You belong here. But I don't. The wilds call out to me every day. No matter how hard I try to run, it eats me up. Hamarah is waiting for me. I need to find her."

"You're senile!" she yelled out. "She's not even real! You betrayed mom for a perverted fantasy in your twisted head!" She pushed her father out of the way as she pulled her brother by the wrist. "Come on, Tommy. We're going to tell Marshal Salomon."

Flint stood still for a moment. He listened to Sarah stomp her way down the stairs with her brother until they were gone—the door slamming shut made it obvious to him that he was alone. He felt terrible about Sarah and genuinely wanted to be at her wedding, but he absolutely refused to face the townspeople after everything that had happened. And he certainly didn't want to tell them he was leaving to find a woman who only seemed to exist in his dreams.

He spent the next hour packing for the long journey. First he gathered some clothes in his wardrobe and put it in a knapsack. Then he prepared vegemite sandwiches in another bag with two large wineskins full of water. The last thing he needed was protection—bullets, and lots of them. He went to his old, creaky attic and pulled out some ammunition. Unfortunately he didn't have much. If only he could visit Joey and get some supplies from him; but no, he thought to himself, he dared not face him. Despite how he felt, he needed to overcome his shame and ask his comrade for help.

Flint was finally set and left the attic. When he walked through the hallway of the second floor, he heard the front door open. He stopped, wondering if his children had returned. He'd left his knapsacks in the kitchen, so he'd have to show his face to whoever had entered his house in order to get them. Flint went down the stairs and stepped into his kitchen, surprisingly finding the marshal's wife, Marielle, sitting at the table. And even more surprising to him was that she had his journal.

It looked as though she'd been sitting there for years, soaking up the world's misery. The duo awkwardly stared at each other, silence descending over the room. Marielle, however, broke the silence by throwing the journal at Flint's face.

"Thanks," he said, catching it. "I was looking for this."

"How dare you!" exclaimed Marielle, rising from her chair. She rushed over to him while screaming, "You've betrayed your wife and children!"

"Mmhmm," he muttered, secretly grabbing a knife from the kitchen counter. Marielle reached out to slap him. That instant, he grabbed her hand, twisted it, and put her in a chokehold while placing the tip of his knife by her throat. She shrieked in disbelief. "How long have I been here?" he demanded.

"What are you talking abo—" She choked, Flint tightening his grip on her throat. "Si-sixteen years."

"Are the children mine?" he asked.

Marielle hesitated but eventually replied, "No."

"They don't even know, do they?"

Marielle shook her head.

"Where are they?"

She didn't answer him. Flint squeezed her neck further. Choking violently, her face was beginning to turn red.

"*Where are they?*" he demanded.

"Ron...they're with Ronald," she coughed.

"Thanks."

Flint swerved Marielle around, slamming her face into the kitchen table. He bashed her against the table so hard that it split in half. She was unconscious before she could even drop to the floor. Tossing the knife away, he left his house. He stood on the porch and gazed skyward; the black-spotted sun beamed hard on him. Flint noticed that Donna was still in the corral and walked over to her.

"Sorry, girl," he said, patting her. "I guess they forgot or just didn't get a chance to put you back in the barn. It works out though, since you and I are going on a long journey. But first we're going to wake up Joey because I need some help. Then we'll be off."

Upon mounting his mare, he tugged the reins. Donna galloped toward the town square. Traveling at dawn had always been normal to him, yet there was something abnormal about it this time. At first, he thought it was the unsettling feeling about his past that had caused him to think this way. When he reached the town square, however, his theory changed. Not one person was there, and the buildings' doors were open.

Flint felt that there was definitely something wrong about Desonas. He hitched Donna at a post near The Wild Owl and walked through the batwing doors—no one was there either, not even Walter Hamel.

"Where the hell is everyone?" he asked himself. He left Walter's saloon and stepped into the gun shop. "Hey, pal, you left your door open." No one answered. "Joey?" He went upstairs to check the bedroom, yet his best friend wasn't there. After checking each room, he descended the stairs, searching the cellar. Not finding his comrade caused him to sigh with frustration. "I don't like this one bit."

There were still a few more places for Flint to check. Before leaving, he stocked up on ammunition. He slung a bandolier of rifle shells over his vest. And since he had no bullets in his waist belt, he filled it with magnum bullets. Afterwards, he grabbed a Winchester rifle. Lastly, he left a pouch of coins on the counter. He felt, even though they didn't have an official economy, it was the right thing to do.

"Farewell, my friend," he said, exiting Joey's shop.

He walked across the road and stepped into Doctor Tutherfield clinic. She wasn't inside. Even Ronald Salomon's office was empty. Desonas had apparently been abandoned. Flint stood in the town square with a look of distress. Although he didn't know what was happening, he had to leave. The only person whom he could rely on at this point was Yeramba, so he swung up his mare and traveled in the direction of Uluru, where the aboriginal and his tribe resided.

As he rode south, the sky became cloudier. Seeing this didn't ease his nerves, especially since he was already disturbed by the abnormal nightmare he'd just awakened to. The sporadic sounds of wildlife were his only consolation.

He reached the Wakaya's territory after a few hours of traveling and spotted their totems right away. It would have been helpful to hear Yeramba's bullroarer again, but Flint eventually saw the aboriginals resting on the ground. Relieved, he dismounted Donna and hitched her to a nearby tree. Flint was anxious to speak with Yeramba. When he approached the aboriginals, however, he realized they weren't resting; they were dead. All of them had bullet wounds. Flint saw Jatma, who appeared to be the only one breathing, and rushed over to him.

"Anangu," rasped Jatma, "they...they took—"

"It's all right, don't speak," said Flint.

He kneeled down, trying to help Jatma who groaned in agony. Jatma began to convulse, and then he died. It started to rain after he stopped breathing. Flint shut Jatma's eyes and stayed with him for a while, as though waiting for a spirit to appear and guide the aboriginal into the dreamtime. Instead, the only thing that appeared was a spear. It plunged into the mud-spattered soil no more than two inches away from Flint. He swiftly rose to his feet while spinning out his Peacemaker as three aboriginals approached, screaming at him in their native tongue.

"I didn't do it!" exclaimed Flint. He placed his palm over his sodden vest, shaking his head. "No! Not me! I'm not your enemy! I am a friend!"

The remaining aboriginals continued screaming at Flint. The others who belonged to the tribe lay dead. Even the women and children were dead. Flint was drenched as he gazed at the massacre before him. Meanwhile, two of the three aboriginals kept their weapons lifted high, on the verge of attacking. The one who'd already thrown his spear, on the contrary, walked over to Flint with a look of despair.

"Anangu?" called out the aboriginal.

"Yes," said Flint, putting his revolver away.

"Demons come," continued the aboriginal. "They take Yeramba. Anangu must save Yeramba."

"Where did they take him?" asked Flint. "Where did they take Yeramba?"

The aboriginal pointed at Kata Tjuta. Flint mounted his horse by the time the aboriginal lowered his hand.

"I will find him," he said. "I promise."

Flint took off on Donna and headed straight toward Kata Tjuta. The wind picked up, and it rained heavier with occasional flickers of lightning. Hardly any animals were in sight as Flint tugged the reins of his mare, riding faster through the land. The desert oaks swayed due to the harsh wind as he rode past them. Clouds covered the dark sky. There wasn't a single pocket of light. It was as if the planet was crying because of the loss of its aboriginal children, filling the land with its thundering rage.

Drawing closer to Kata Tjuta, he heard Yeramba's bullroarer. Flint gave out a sigh of relief, following the wind melody. The rain, meanwhile, worsened. The last thing Flint needed was another storm. He finally reached Kata Tjuta, trying to ignore the weather, and pursued the bullroarer's sound that caused the wind to resonate. Yet it was difficult for him to find its source amid the thirty-six bornhardts, not to mention the ruthless storm.

When he arrived at the center of Kata Tjuta, he spotted Yeramba standing on one of the smaller rock formations. It was a relief to see him, thought Flint; however, he'd been tied by a lasso, and he wasn't alone. Beside him were the residents of Desonas. Marshal Salomon, who'd been using the bullroarer, stood among the miners and townsfolk.

"I'm so glad you could make it, Cross," said Salomon.

Flint glared at Salomon and then observed his entourage carefully. Deputy Ted Thornton, Jake Salomon, Joey Stalls, Walter Hamel, Doctor Penny Tutherfield, Daren Linko, Kevin Smith, Martin Aleman, Brock and Bas Panzo, and several other miners whom Flint wasn't familiar with stood there, along with the Steward and Froehlich families. Most alarming to him, however, was Tom and Sarah being with them; though, they weren't armed with guns like the others.

"Dad, stop this madness!" rebuked Sarah. "The world is dead; there's nothing out there. You can't just abandon us."

"She's right, dad," said Tom. "Mom killed herself because of your obsessions."

"Amanda wasn't your mother," said Flint.

Sarah looked baffled. Similar to her, Tom wore a contorted expression on his face. Neither of them knew what to say after hearing their father say something so absurd. Even though they loved him, his words made no sense.

"This entire life of ours has been a lie," continued Flint. "They put us here to mock our desire for freedom. It's possible they even murdered your real parents."

"Are you insane?" yelled Sarah, fed up with her father. "Listen to yourself!" She took a deep breath and said, "I used to have so much respect for you. I had as much love and respect as Tom had for you. But now I understand how mom felt. This is simply your excuse to leave and fantasize about that woman in your deranged journal!"

"Tommy," called out Flint. "You believe me, right?"

"Dad, why can't things return to normal?" asked Tom. "You know, like the way it was when you took me hunting last year with Joey."

"Because I can't turn my back on the people who depend on me," said Flint assertively. "My comrades sacrificed everything for me. Once I began to remember the war, I realized that there can be no turning back."

"War?" said Sarah. "This is crazy."

"What happened to you, Flint?" asked Jake. "The last time I saw you, you were a damn hero. There's no need to make up all of these lies."

"So you don't believe me either, huh?" grimaced Flint. He gazed at Salomon with a look of contempt. "It seems everyone has already been brainwashed into this sick game of yours." He paused for a brief moment while glaring at the others. "Even though I risked my life and saved all your lives in that mine, you still think I'm crazy?"

The titan-steel brothers were the only ones who were skeptical about the situation. They didn't even know what was happening; they cast their eyes down, slightly lowering their guns. Flint stopped glaring at the townsfolk, focusing his attention on Salomon.

"I just want to know one thing," said Flint. "Why did you do it, Marshal?"

"Why?" said Salomon, frowning. "I thought you remembered everything."

Flint shook his head.

"Only pieces of the puzzle, huh?" said Solomon. "One reason, Cross: the tribunal. In this day and age, it's either you agree to die or agree to live with the tribunal."

"And you chose the latter?" guessed Flint.

Marshal Salomon nodded smugly.

"You too, Joey?" asked Flint.

"Isn't it obvious?" answered Joey, his accent gone. "Come on, Flint, wasn't it you who once told me that worth's the name of the game?"

"Well played…"

"Now, now, don't you get all depressed on us, Cross," said Salomon. "We never wanted things to come to this. Our job was simple: to look after you and make sure your rebellious traits were suppressed, that's all. If you just let Penny examine you—" He stretched his hand over to Doctor Tutherfield who pulled out a needle—"then everything will return to normal. No one else needs to get hurt. It's a win-win situation."

Flint raised his magnum at Salomon. The townsfolk readied their guns, aiming at Flint. Normally that wouldn't have affected Flint; however, Salomon seized his daughter and put the muzzle of a gun to her head. "I know she isn't your daughter, but you still care about her. So don't do anything stupid."

"Dad," sputtered Jake. "You promised not to hurt her."

"I'm not your father, Jake, so shut up," said Salomon.

Jake backed away in dismay.

In the meantime, Tom attempted to free his sister. Joey, however, grabbed Tom and held him tight. Salomon kept his gaze on Flint despite the commotion.

"Look around you, Cross," said Salomon. "It's one to twenty-five."

Flint glimpsed around at the townsfolk again but maintained his position and target. He noticed that the only distraught and confused ones there were Jake and the Panzo brothers. The other gunmen were ready to shoot him. They wore the most vicious expressions he'd ever seen; it seemed unreal to him.

"I may be impossibly outnumbered," began Flint, "but one thing's certain: before your goons take me down, I'll have the pleasure of blowing you sky high—so high you'll even see Altjira."

Salomon swallowed. He knew Flint wasn't bluffing. "I'm curious, how did you get your memories back?" he asked.

"You mean to tell me that the great, almighty leader of Desonas can't figure it out?" said Flint in a humorous tone. "Simple enough: Browder warned me about the 'greens' before Joey here killed him. I stopped eating them several months ago."

Salomon turned to Doctor Tutherfield. "Is that possible, Penny?"

"He's lying," replied Tutherfield flatly. "The plants that grow bush tucker near his home were sprayed with the strongest drug we have. No one can recover from its narcotic suppression by not eating them anymore, even if several years passed. Something else caused this, and I think he's hiding it."

"Unlike you, I don't lie," said Flint. "I'm not hiding anything."

"I'm losing my patience with you, Cross," said Salomon. He pressed his revolver harder against Sarah's temple. "No one has to get hurt. Put your gun down, or I'll be forced to splatter her brains all over this rock."

Silence descended over Kata Tjuta.

"All right," Flint finally said. "You win."

He lowered his magnum. The heavy wind pounded against him, causing his clothes to sway while the heavy rain drenched him. It was over—that had been the message; yet Salomon saw the hideous glare in Flint's eyes; those sadistic blue eyes that had made him a prisoner for far too long.

Marshal Salomon had never been more terrified in that second during which Flint had lowered his weapon.

A wicked smirk grew on Flint's lips. Nearly as fast as the speed of light, he lifted his magnum back in the air and blasted Salomon.

There really was no way to accurately describe what had happened to Marshal Salomon's face; it simply exploded. Sarah almost became deaf as blood and brains splattered all over her. She fainted and tilted to the side, falling. Jake caught her, pulling her away to safety. As for the others, they fiddled with their weapons—distraught—and targeted Flint who took cover between two of Kata Tjuta's bornhardts. Tom attempted to break free, but Joey pushed him away and shot him twice. Afterwards, he ran away.

Brock and Bas glanced at each other after they saw what had happened to Tom and knew they had to intervene. The titan-steel brothers aimed their shotguns at the Steward and Froehlich couples and shot them.

In the meantime, Flint ran between the bornhardts as he unloaded an entire chamber of revolver bullets into Kevin Smith's chest. He then turned around, spotting Martin Aleman who stood on top of a bornhardt, aiming his rifle at him. Not a second later, Flint leveled his magnum at Martin and blasted him off the rock.

Flint reloaded his revolver when Daren Linko abruptly appeared behind him, attempting to stab him with a knife.

"I'll have my coins back!" he exclaimed.

"In a few seconds you won't need them," retorted Flint.

He grabbed Daren's hand and twisted it, shoving the serrated knife into Daren's mouth while blowing a hole through his stomach with a magnum bullet. His intestines splurged out of him while he fell to the ground. After reloading his guns, he climbed a bornhardt. Upon reaching the top, he spotted Walter below on a smaller bornhardt. Grabbing his lasso, Flint tossed it down until it fell over Walter's neck and then yanked it back up, snapping his neck. Flint released the lasso and jumped down.

When landing, he noticed seven gunmen scattered on different bornhardts. They noticed him and opened fire. Flint instantly shot six of them with one hundred percent precision, cocking his Peacemaker.

Deputy Thornton, the seventh gunman, was still standing. Flint's revolver was out of ammo, and his magnum was holstered. Thornton smirked, ready to shoot. That instant, somebody blasted him off the mountainous bornhardt with a shotgun shell. Anxiously looking down, Flint saw Bas Panzo. He never had a brighter smile, giving Bas a thumbs up. It was a relief for him to know that the titan-steel brothers were on his side.

All the opposing townsfolk had been wiped out, with the exception of Joey who'd fled when the gunfire started. Doctor Tutherfield was also alive and attempted to leave. Spotting her mount a horse, Flint swiftly pulled out his magnum, spun it, and shot her in the back without even trying to aim. The magnum's force caused her to be jolted off her horse, only to fall dead to the ground.

"It's over," said Bas grimly.

Flint heard him and climbed down. Upon reaching the surface of Kata Tjuta, he shook the Panzo brothers' hands.

"I can't thank you enough for helping me," said Flint.

He abruptly heard his daughter shriek. Flint and the titan-steel brothers rushed over to her. She was crying hysterically next to Tom who lay dead in a pool of his own blood.

"My son!" exclaimed Flint, running over to him.

"Joey did this," said Bas, shaking his head.

"*Tommy!*" cried out Flint, holding his would-be son.

Jake kept silent and held Sarah who sobbed over his shoulder. All he could do was stand there, utterly perplexed by what had happened. The man he thought to be his father had betrayed him, and yet there was also despair within him after seeing his supposed father killed. The titan-steel brothers looked just as confused about the situation; they nevertheless freed Yeramba. Flint couldn't do anything except weep as he held his son's lifeless body.

The rainstorm persisted. Thunder burst with lightning. Wind scrabbled. Earth was giving its last breath of life. Though, nothing seemed to matter to Flint outside the fact that his son was dead. He knew that Tom wasn't his biological son, but deep down inside his indifferent heart, he still cared about him. Despite living in this hellhole of a world for sixteen agonizing years, he'd gained a deep love for Tom. Seeing him dead was unreal—it was a living nightmare.

The titan-steel brothers trudged over to their stagecoach, took out their mining shovels, and started to dig. Jake, meanwhile, stayed by Sarah's side. Yeramba, however, approached the Panzo brothers and held out his hands.

"No dig here," he said. "This sacred ground."

"Everywhere is sacred, shaman," retorted Bas. "If you got a problem with life being just as sacred as this place, then you got a problem with me."

"And me," said Brock coarsely.

Yeramba hesitated at first but bowed and withdrew. He sat by the surface of a bornhardt, humming an indigenous chant. One hour passed while Brock and Bas dug a grave. When they finished, Flint carried his son and gently laid him down in the damp soil. Somehow, even though Tom was dead, he looked at peace. Flint placed his hands on him and cried again.

Sarah surprisingly had stopped sobbing, but her eyes were still bloodshot. She stood still with the others until Flint rose out from the grave. Each of them then grabbed a handful of dirt and sprinkled it over Tom. Yeramba was the only one who refrained from doing that. His path was different; however, he neither intervened nor imposed his tradition. Shortly after, Brock and Bas buried Tom as best they could. Subsequently, they carried a large rock and placed it in front of the grave like a tombstone.

"Thank you...both of you," said Flint.

Giving a faint nod, Bas approached him. "Here," he said, handing Flint back the hunting knife he'd borrowed when they were inside the mine several months ago.

"Thanks again, Bas."

Using the knife, he etched an inscription into the rock that lay next to the grave:

Here rests Tom Cross
You will always be remembered, my son.

Silence descended upon them, disrupted only by the heavy rain. It was getting late, and the storm showed no signs of ending. Flint and Sarah hugged each other after that long, silent minute. They had no words for this tragedy.

Sarah didn't know how to handle her loss; she wondered, was there a way to get through this nightmare? She desperately wanted to feel numb. For the first time in her life she wished, like her father in the past, that this was just a horrendous dream. She knew, however, that this was as real as when her mother had committed suicide.

As for Flint, he'd hoped there was something he could say to make Sarah feel better. But the truth was that no words would ever be enough for this. All he could do was hold her.

"Flint," called out Bas. "What happened? Marshal Salomon told us Browder had been killing the aboriginals and that you sided with him. He claimed you were planning to attack Desonas with Browder. I know this may not be a good place to speak, but I think it's time you told us why everyone went ballistic and tried killing you."

"Browder's been dead for months," said Flint. "Joey killed him. Listen, it's a very long story. I don't even know everything yet; though, before I say anymore, I think it would be best if we find some cover until the storm passes."

Brock pointed at the large stagecoach that he and his brother owned. The survivors saw it and quickly took refuge inside.

"Okay," began Flint, "all I can really tell you right now is that there seems to be a higher power involved. I think there's some kind of government that did this to us...something called the tribunal."

"What's that?" asked Bas.

"I think the tribunal is the seat of power that chose to put me here," said Flint. He sighed and added, "Don't think I'm crazy, but before Browder was killed, he called me Commandant and told me not to eat the bush tucker. There was obviously something put in the ones growing around my farm that blocked my memories. For some reason I still had visions. After listening to Browder, my dreams became more vivid."

"What do you mean?" asked Jake.

"Anangu speak of dreamtime," said Yeramba.

"Yes," said Flint in a somewhat pensive tone. He thought of Hamarah for a moment and then explained, "I had blurry visions about a war within the dreamtime. And somehow, I have a feeling that Browder was with me. I believe this war was real, and it's possible that I may have even been the leader. If this is true, then our lives have been a lie this whole time. We were put here as a mockery by the tribunal, and they clearly put a great deal of effort into this charade to frighten others."

"To frighten others?" said Brock. "You mean we were put here to be made an example of in case others defy them?"

"Right," said Flint.

"But that's crazy," said Jake. "What about Sarah and me? We just turned twenty. That's impossible. How could we have been a part of all this?"

"You couldn't have been," said Flint. "But it's possible that your real parents were a part of it." Jake was taken aback by Flint's response. "Jake, I'm sorry you had to find out this way. I myself can hardly believe what's happening. Every second I keep wondering if I'll wake up and be in Desonas again with...with Tommy."

"Dad, what about mom?" asked Sarah.

"I told you, she wasn't your mother. I know it's hard to believe, but you need to trust me. Most importantly, I need you to stay in Desonas."

"*What?*" she said, startled. "After all that's happened?"

"This isn't about you," said Flint sternly. "It's about me. My entire life here was staged by the tribunal to make me suffer for something I did. And even though I still can't remember everything, all of you would be in danger following me. It's best if you continue your life in Desonas."

With the exception of Sarah, the others were so shocked that they didn't quite grasp what Flint had told them. Despite the fact that Sarah was as flustered as the others, she knew her father was ready to leave.

"Will you ever come back?" she asked, trying not to cry.

"When I find out what this all about, yes," he said, looking at her with sadness.

They hugged each other tightly. Sarah cried again. She felt so lonely. First she'd lost her mother, then her brother, and now her father was leaving. The only person she had left to keep her company was Jake. And with so many of the townspeople dead, she felt the town would fall apart.

"Be strong," said Flint, rubbing her back. "Always remember that I love you. You will always be my daughter." He then fixed his eyes on Jake. "The two of you can have a beautiful life in Desonas."

"We'll look after them," said Bas.

"Honestly, you'll all have to be careful," said Flint. "I don't know what the tribunal will do at this point, but I have a feeling they'll ignore Desonas because I'm the one they want. And that's why it's best for me to leave. Still, I want you to watch your backs."

"You can count on us, Flint," said Brock.

Flint gave them a faint smile, trying to look appreciative even though he was deeply depressed about the death of his son.

"By the way, Marielle is unconscious in my house," he said.

"We'll take care of her," said Bas.

"Does tribunal hunt me?" asked Yeramba.

"No," said Flint. "Just stay away from Desonas and tell no one about me."

Yeramba agreed and said, "Now you go new journey with land of spirits—the creator beings guide Anangu."

Yes, thought Flint, it was finally time for him to leave and find the truth that had been taken and kept from him. He stepped outside when the rainstorm lessened. Sarah hugged him again, and Jake, Brock, and Bas each shook his hand. Yeramba simply bowed. Flint bowed in return and then mounted Donna. He knew Sarah didn't want this; he knew he was leaving at the worst possible time, but his heart was set on finding Hamarah. If he could find her, he felt that he'd be one step closer to finding out more about his past, as well as where the tribunal dwelled. Flint glanced at his daughter one last time, bidding farewell to the life he had lived for sixteen years. He then tugged Donna's reins and rode north.

The others didn't want to leave until Flint was out of sight. Jake continued to hold Sarah who cried, no longer watching. Meanwhile, the titan-steel brothers grimly gazed at the northern wilds where Flint soon vanished from their sight.

In the meantime, Flint pondered about everything that had happened over the past few months as he journeyed north, beginning with his visions of Hamarah. Within days, Flint's life had turned upside down. His son had been brutally murdered, and his best friend had betrayed him. Almost all the townspeople from Desonas had betrayed him. Most of all, it seemed that his life had been nothing more than an illusion.

Nonetheless, today was a victory, he conceded. Flint had finally experienced the genuine freedom he had longed for. He had finally uncovered a part of his lost soul. His memories were gradually returning to him, and that was more than what he could ask for. He still didn't know for sure whether Hamarah was real, even though his instincts told him that she was. But this much he knew: the tribunal existed, and there was a terrible war somewhere out there that he needed to either rejoin or reignite. There were still many questions to be answered; however, Flint was confident he would eventually discover them. A new journey was beginning for the gunslinger. Though, this time, it wasn't going to be within the dreamtime.

PART II
EXODUS

CHAPTER SEVEN

OUTLANDS

Thousands of years ago a region in the Northern Territory through which Flint was riding had once been known as the *Never Never*. It had always been a sweltering land, but the aboriginals nevertheless thought of it as a majestic expanse filled with great spirits. Now it was known as the Outlands—a grayish terrain that was nothing more than a desolate wasteland filled with death, massive gorges, and a thick haze of heat caused by the black-spotted sun. The heat became so intense that little particles of smolder slowly rose from parts of the cracked, crusted-looking terrain.

Flint rode farther north through the land on Donna who galloped cautiously. If it weren't for his mare, he would have dehydrated, fainted, and died hundreds of miles back. He patted her and smiled, grateful to have her. He was, however, concerned about her health since he had yet to find a waterhole in this dead region. He was beginning to feel he'd never find water. Did the rest of the world resemble this environment? If so, then leaving Desonas may not have been the most intelligent decision he'd made in his life.

He had adapted to the extreme heat, yet he was sweating profusely despite it being winter in Australia. The scorching Outlands tested his body's tolerance, and it certainly wasn't different for his mare. On several occasions, Donna slowed down, producing a wobbly gait. Flint gave her most of his water. In fact, he only had one wineskin left, and it was nearly empty. He was hoping it would rain soon. Yet there wasn't a single cloud in the sky.

The wavy heat continued to press against him. Several dust devils whirled in the distance. Flint periodically nudged Donna away from them. They were mostly harmless; though, there was an occasional dust devil that looked dangerous.

During the night, Flint spotted a somewhat safe-looking valley. He tugged the reins and guided his mare toward it. Upon arriving, he hitched Donna to a withered tree. He didn't need to create a fire by the bed he laid out, but when he heard the howl of a dingo, he created it anyway in case there were other dangerous wild animals prowling around in these parts. He lit the fire, feeling just a little safer. Though he wasn't afraid of dingoes, he didn't exactly want a starving animal preying on him. He closed his eyes and eventually fell asleep.

On the following morning, Flint awoke and felt it was much warmer than previous days in the bleak Outlands. No more dreams, he thought to himself. Ever since he'd left Desonas, he hadn't experienced another dream. Unlike before, it didn't bother him. In fact, it made him feel confident. He felt that the last dream he had in Kalkajaka was a new beginning; it was a symbol of him accepting himself and becoming free from the myriad illusions that plagued him since he started living here in Australia.

He thought of Sarah and the others as he ate a sandwich, wondering whether telling them to stay in Desonas was the best idea. Either way they'd be in danger. Though, for the time being, out here seemed worse to him. He wondered whether Joey would come back to kill them; then again, if Joey was smart, which Flint had no doubt he was, then it would make sense for him to forget about the others whom Flint showed little affection for and go directly after him. Yes, he thought, perhaps the so-called tribunal would ignore them since he'd behaved as though they'd meant nothing to him.

After he finished eating, he took a sip of water from his wineskin and then gave the rest to Donna. He no longer had any water; this made him feel uneasy. Flint cursed under his breath, knowing he should have brought more with him. He didn't exactly think this journey through. Nevertheless, he packed his things, unhitched his mare, mounted her, and nudged her to steadily gallop north.

He continued to see dust devils form and dissipate in the distance. The heat worsened and worsened with each passing minute. Flint frequently wiped sweat off his forehead. His heart was beginning to pound as though he'd been traveling on foot. It frightened him to think of Donna's condition. His mare kept galloping. He was proud of her; though, he couldn't help but wonder if she'd be able to maintain this astonishing momentum.

Several hours passed. No clouds had formed. The heat was worse than ever. And there were no signs of life anywhere. Flint's stomach growled fiercely; he was beginning to crave meat. Unfortunately he didn't have any. He took out his last sandwich and ate it while riding forward. Eating made him thirsty. This caused his heart to pound more since he'd run out of water. That's when he acknowledged it wasn't simply the heat that contributed to him feeling fatigued, it was anxiety too—thinking he might die in the middle of nowhere.

Flint tried to keep a sharp eye, scouting the region to see if he'd spot or hear an animal in the far distance. He loved to hunt; in fact, it seemed to him as though he hadn't hunted in ages. If he had to, he'd hunt a dingo or any kind of beast just to have some food for later. He took out his Winchester and slung it around his back, ready to use it if he'd by chance spot an animal.

After a few minutes, Donna slowed down. This alarmed Flint, but he didn't complain or do anything when she reduced her gallop to a canter. The fact that she'd been able to travel this swiftly for so long was a miracle, he thought. He wasn't going to bother her if she needed some rest. Eventually, when the sky changed from blue to an orange tinge, Flint forced Donna to stop by another valley.

This time he didn't set up a fire. He simply hitched Donna to a withered tree and leaned against a large rock, holding his Winchester. He watched the area while Donna took a nap beside the tree she was hitched to until night came. When it was nearly pitch-black outside, Flint heard the distant hooting of an owl. It was hard for him to believe that wildlife still lived in this region considering how bleak it looked, but he wasn't complaining. Flint was tired; however, he stood up and forced himself to scout around, hoping to hunt the owl or anything just to have a decent meal before going to bed.

He searched the area he had taken refuge at for the night, yet there didn't seem to be any signs of life other than the distant sounds of the owl. He took a deep breath and continued to reconnoiter the region, trying to find the nocturnal bird. It seemed to be farther away, so he stepped away from the valley with his rifle lifted. After taking a few steps, the hooting faded. Flint stood stock-still, hoping to hear it again. The owl was long gone. Wherever it went, it was nowhere near him. He cursed and returned to the crater, deciding to lay next to where his mare stood.

The heat pressed against him despite it being nighttime. Flint could barely feel any cool breezes. And the ground where he lay burned as though the sun was still out. He sighed and laid his rifle on his chest. Staring at the stars for a little while, Flint wondered where Hamarah could be. Time went by, and before he knew it, he closed his eyes and fell asleep in the pitch-black Outlands.

The following morning, Flint awoke to a cloudy day. He rejoiced when he opened his eyes, gazing at the gray sky. This meant that it may very well rain soon, and he'd have all the water he would need to keep traveling. Quite frankly, he had no idea where he was going. He'd been traveling on instinct, hoping to find some kind of civilization out here. And since he'd been told that life only existed in the Northern Territory, he had decided this was the path to take. He just needed a little water and everything would be all right again. He eagerly packed his blanket, putting it in one of his knapsacks. He then whistled, walking over to his mare.

"Good news, girl," he said to her. "It's going to rain. Then we'll be as good as new. We just need some foo—" He stopped talking, noticing that Donna lay still by the tree. She did not move at all. He whistled again. "Donna?"

Flint reached her and kneeled down, realizing she was unconscious. He shook her a few times, hoping that she was just sleeping despite the fact that horses sleep standing up; however, she wouldn't wake up. No matter how many times he shook her, she wouldn't budge; she didn't even twitch. Flint gulped heavily, staring at her. She had apparently dehydrated. Even though they'd been traveling for days, Flint didn't think something like this would happen so soon. His horse looked dead. Flint lay next to her and stayed with her for hours.

The sky gradually darkened throughout the morning and afternoon. Flint was praying all day for rain. His prayers, however, weren't answered. His stomach soon growled. He pressed his fingers against his belly, taking deep breaths. This journey was pathetic, he thought. He pondered for a while, acknowledging that leaving his home at a time like this wasn't so wise. It was his narcissism that had made him act irrationally. But no, he said to himself, leaving was the right thing to do because of what had happened at Kata Tjuta. He wasn't insane—he'd been right all along. This wasn't the time to feel guilty or weak; he needed to be sure of himself. He removed his hat for a moment, scratching his head.

"I don't know what to do anymore," he dispiritedly said to himself. He glanced at Donna and gently petted her. She suddenly awoke, giving out a squeaky neigh. "Easy, girl," he said to Donna who convulsed and neighed in a painful outcry. He backed away, distraught by what was happening. "I'm sorry," he muttered. "I am so sorry."

He slowly reached for his revolver, not understanding why she was in so much pain. Not even dehydration or starvation could cause this reaction. He wondered if this was the result of food poisoning; could she have eaten something nearby that was rotten? Flint shook his head as he pulled out his Peacemaker. He regrettably cocked the revolver's hammer back, aimed at his mare, and—no, he couldn't do it. He lowered his gun, hearing Donna neigh louder and louder. Her pain was tearing him apart inside. Flint clenched his teeth as he held in his tears, his finger trembling by the trigger. Then, in one swift movement, as though he'd lost all emotion and guilt, he lifted his gun once more and pulled the trigger.

The gun resonated after going off, producing a ringing echo. Donna's neighs stopped. He could no longer hear the reverberation of his revolver or the cries of his horse. He dared not look down. Instead he stood up, grabbed one of his knapsacks, and walked away. Flint felt worse than when Amanda had hung herself but didn't cry or curl into a hole waiting for death. He simply walked and walked until the crater where Donna had died couldn't be seen even if he turned around to glimpse at it. Yet when he was miles away from Donna, he abruptly knelt to the ground and cried.

"My God," he uttered to himself, sniveling. "I'm a mu-murderer." He shuddered as tears ran down his cheeks. "I killed her." A voice within him tried to tell him that he had to shoot her; it was the humane thing to do. Another voice in him, however, called it murder. "I'm s-so sorry. Please forgive me."

Flint curled up after all. For a brief moment, he thought that he'd lost his emotions by not crying earlier. Now he felt relieved, knowing he was still human. Yes, as long as he suffered he'd maintain his humanity. Flint lay in the middle of nowhere, haggard and dreary due to the treacherous journey. Closing his eyes, he sobbed and surrendered to the sizzling granite. Flint fell asleep earlier than usual.

He awoke a few hours later. It was far past midnight. The ground was dry. It still hadn't rained. Flint roared at the sky, feeling as enraged as the scorched terrain beneath him. He rose to his feet, made sure his Winchester rifle was loaded, and traveled north despite how dark it was. To his surprise, he saw the outline of a mountainous valley ahead. He was hoping some kind of wildlife would be prowling around over there. He pressed on, feeling his stomach ache for food what with its growls. His throat was parched, too, but right now he yearned to have a nice piece of fresh, crispy meat.

As he approached the mountainous valley he recalled the festival that he and his family had prepared for the townspeople. The incredible food he'd eaten back then was what initially made him think about that day back in November. Although most of the folks in Desonas had betrayed him—playing him for a fool—he nevertheless missed them.

He wondered to himself, how were Salomon and the others able to live with themselves? How were they able to smile every day knowing that their lives were a complete lie? Were all of them that afraid of the tribunal? Could the tribunal be *that* powerful? Did they truthfully prefer to be wardens rather than be free? Instead of feeling depressed about what he'd recently done to his mare, he felt livid. Flint thought, if he could just find some kind of sign—anything regarding the tribunal—he'd be content and would deem this journey meaningful. So far, he had nothing; this deeply frustrated him.

Flint finally reached the valley and climbed up a ledge that led him into a tiny cave. He sat down on a rock and listened to the silence, trying to gaze at the stars. It was still cloudy, but he was at least able to see a few stars. He didn't hear any wildlife around the area, making him feel even more frustrated. There was so much turmoil within his mind. Flint abruptly got up and hopelessly threw his rifle. He roared in anger, defying the dead world.

The world, however, wasn't as dead as Flint thought it was. When he finished screaming he heard loud metal clomps. It was the strangest sound he'd ever heard before in his life. While the thunderclap-like sounds of foot stomps continued, he slowly peeked out of the cave, gazing at the desolate, midnight expanse. Flint, however, deeply regretted peeking outside because he noticed a giant humanoid creature encased in body armor approaching him. And yes, it *was* a creature since he didn't know what else to call it.

The thing he saw resembled a man that stood twelve feet tall. It wore thick-plated armor made of titanium, and its helmet resembled a chiseled, stone face with a gas mask. As the being approached him, it breathed as if it were on some kind of life-support system. Its eyes flickered with light as it stomped toward Flint who gasped, backing away. The giant was clearer now—it had oil stains on its robust, copper-tinted suit of armor.

Flint was so startled and frightened by what he saw that he wasn't able to talk or move. He simply stared at the colossal humanoid being that glared at him without uttering a single word. It entered the cave and stood still, observing Flint as though it were studying him so it could dissect him.

"Wh-what are you?" asked Flint, surprised he was able to speak.

The armored being suddenly gave out a deafening metallic sound mixed with electronic reverberations that changed frequencies from low to high pitches. Flint pressed his hands against his ears and ran for his life. When he exited the cave, another armored being approached from a ridge above, raising its giant arm. Flint saw it from the corner of his eye and attempted to jump when it struck him on the side of his face, causing him to fall.

Blood spurted out of Flint's lip as he fell. He slammed his head against the granite, barely able to see. His vision became blurry. The deafening metallic sound finally stopped, but he could hear the two armored beings stomping toward him. He thought he'd conquered his dreams. Why was he back in the dreamtime? This couldn't be real. Yet it felt so real. His head throbbed in pain due to the fall, and his mouth burned as he spat out blood. If he'd taken a direct blow to the head it would have undoubtedly killed him.

Just then, he heard another sound from above—a thudding, vibrating sound. He tried to widen his frail eyes as he lay on the jagged ground. At that precise moment, a red light beamed into his eyes, blinding him. He breathed feebly as heavy steam puffed down, engulfing him. He could have sworn that some kind of machine enveloped in steam was hovering over him, and that the armored beings were on it. But he was too weak to open his eyes again. He gave out one final breath of disbelief before fainting.

CHAPTER EIGHT

HELL'S HOLE

Flint awoke after what seemed to him like numerous hours or even a whole day of sleep. He felt groggy and achy, barely able to move. Again, he heard metallic sounds. And he could feel faint thudding vibrations—the floor on which he lay resonated. Steam billowed, engulfing him. Flint groaned in terrible pain as he attempted to move. He opened his eyes, noticing two armored beings in front of him. One of them was steering a metal wheel while the other examined the Winchester rifle Flint had thrown away back in the Outlands.

He slowly got to his feet and realized that his arms were shackled in thick manacles. The armored beings hadn't noticed that he'd awakened yet, which made him realize he had to make a move quickly. Checking his surroundings, he saw jagged walls. He wondered if he was back in Kalkajaka because it certainly looked as though he were inside a cavern hidden deep within a mountain. There was, however, far too much steam around him to see the lair in detail. It didn't look like the same passage he'd stepped into before. But he was definitely inside some kind of cavern. In fact, it looked so unnatural to him that it made him feel even more confident that this preposterous experience was a result of the dreamtime.

Flint became aware of the vibrations again as he stood still, observing the eerie cavern. Steam continuously drifted up from the hovering machine on which he'd been standing. Out of curiosity he gazed below, noticing that the machine was at least a thousand feet high. It wasn't just a hovering vehicle; it was some sort of airship.

He gasped and backed away, accidently tumbling over what appeared to be a corroded hydraulic motor. Flint nearly fell off by the airship's gunwale, grabbing one of the resonating pistons to give him balance. He'd made so much noise that he alerted the armored beings. The one examining his weapon clomped toward him. Flint froze for a moment, wondering what to do. Then he remembered how he had beat Bas in an arm wrestle, and also how he'd caught and held the huge metal slab back at Panzo Mine. If he still had that kind of strength, it would surely help him.

Lifting his arms, he pulled with all his might and grunted loudly. The armored being took a step back, startled. Little by little, Flint loosened the bolts holding the chains of his manacles. He roared and broke free of his shackles, the thick manacles' ruptured chains hanging down his wrists. Without waiting another second, he confidently approached the creature that was incased in the thick, oil-stained armor.

"Who the hell are you?" asked Flint.

The armored being refused to answer. Instead it lifted its arm and attempted to pummel Flint who evaded him, swerving to the left. He stood on the edge, his heart pounding again. The titanium being turned to punch him. Its fist, however, was halted by Flint's hand. He was insane enough to grab the fist, and he somehow managed to hold it back despite how bulky and heavy it was. The armored being released another deafening metallic sound, causing Flint to stagger. He jabbed his other fist into the breastplate of the creature. And for the first time, Flint heard what seemed to be a human groaning in pain as the armor dented inward. The impact of his punch was so powerful that the armored being flew back and fell off the steamship. While the armored titan fell, it screamed like a terrified man who was as confused and shocked as Flint because of what had just happened.

Flint stared at his hands in awe and then gazed at the other titan who was still steering the ship. Steam swallowed Flint as he walked on the platform of the flying vessel. His coarse face showed every ounce of anger in him when he approached the giant that frequently glimpsed at him while maneuvering the steamship. The robust titanium being eventually turned and aimed its arm at Flint who raised an eyebrow, wondering what it could possibly do to him.

The armor along the forearm abruptly opened, and a contraption rose from it, launching a wide net at Flint. The web-like net enveloped him, causing him to panic. He'd been so arrogant after what he'd done to the other being that it'd caused him to let his guard down; he floundered, trying to remove the net. Before he could do so, however, the steamship jolted and began to fly down since the titan was no longer steering it. This caused Flint to flail and stumble, falling off the mechanical vessel. The armored being hesitated as though determining whether it should grab him, but it withdrew and continued flying the ship to avoid crashing.

Flint screamed when he fell, shrouded by the smog of the exhausts, and slammed hard on a mountainous ridge. He cried out in pain, wondering if he'd broken some bones. A haze of heat swept over him while he attempted to move. He rolled to the side and looked below, spotting molten lava. His eyes widened as he gasped, rolling back against the jagged wall. If this wasn't the dreamtime, then surely he was insane and hallucinating— at least that was what he thought. Nevertheless, he wasn't going to test his theory and jump down into the pit of magma to wake himself up. If this was a dream, he'd see it to the end.

After removing the net, he got to his feet—still aching with excruciating pain because of the fall—and limped along the narrow ledge. A few pebbles fell from above. Flint looked up and noticed that the ridge was severely cracked, as if it would crumble apart at any second.

"I don't believe this," he grumbled.

Flint tried to move out of the way. He gasped in pain, knowing that he was pushing his body over the limits. At the age of sixty, he was supposed to be retired, spending the remainder of his life at home with his would-be family. Instead he was a haggard gunslinger inside some godforsaken cavern of death—not to mention on the run from those eerie humanoid giants. He gazed up, searching for the hovering steamship; it was nowhere in sight.

This couldn't be real, he conceded. This had to be the dreamtime. Yet a part of his mind told him that this was in fact real. What made it seem so realistic to him was the horrible pain. He wondered, shouldn't he have awakened by now? This was a terrifying thought. What if this wasn't a dream? Holding his chest, he took deep breaths. He expected to have a heart attack any moment. Thinking of Hamarah, he managed to calm down. Then, glancing around, he realized how quiet it became. It seemed that he'd successfully escaped those giants.

Just then, he stepped on something slimy. He paused and braced himself against the wall. Flint sighed, yanking his foot out of whatever he'd walked on. Relieved to be free, he pressed on. When he did so, however, his glove stuck to the wall. Flint cursed under his breath, trying to get a good look at whatever held his hand. Staring hard, he realized that his glove was stuck in slime; it was the same slime he'd stepped on a moment ago. In fact, it was the same exact gunk that he had found down in Panzo Mine. His heart skipped a beat when he acknowledged this. He jerked his hand fretfully while trying to stay balanced so he wouldn't fall off the narrow ledge. Though struggling a bit, he finally freed himself.

There was no doubt about it, he thought to himself, the slime in this cave was identical to the ooze he'd encountered when he was with Bas Panzo, trying to free the miners back in March. This slime, however, felt much thicker. He stepped away and shook his head. Not a second later, he heard something hissing.

"No," he muttered, taking another step back. "It can't be."

Growls and hisses filled his ears as he withdrew, nearly falling into the lava beneath him. He quickly pulled out his magnum and shot the cracked wall, causing it to collapse. This was the only thing he could do to rid himself of the grotesque beasts lurking in the cave. One of them, however, leapt across the ruptured ledge, plunging onto Flint who tumbled down with a shriek. He sank his magnum's muzzle into the gooey mouth of the beast and shot it. The creature's head exploded; then its body burst into a glob of slime that enveloped Flint.

He swiftly rose to his feet, still hearing a multitude of growls and hisses in the darkness, and fired his magnum until it was empty of bullets. Flint holstered his magnum and then broke into a run. He could barely see as he sprinted through the cavern of lava, steam, and gunk. This was the last straw for him—with the coming of these creatures, he was sure he'd lost whatever sanity was left in him. It was either that or him being trapped within the dreamtime. But he had been here for so long that he doubted that this was a nightmare. Still, it was the only comfort he had left; the idea that this insanity was a dream was his only sanctuary. And so he convinced himself that it was in fact a nightmare.

Feeling distressed, he couldn't think about this any further and kept running for his life while panting. Realizing that he'd passed the lava, he jumped off the ledge. Upon landing, he saw a tunnel ahead and made his way toward it. He could still hear hisses behind him. He'd never felt more terrified in his life.

He wondered to himself, why would he be scared if this wasn't real? He'd been standing on the precipice of insanity all this time as a result of being in a coma. This idea made him smile since it meant that no one had betrayed him. Marshal Salomon and the other townspeople were decent folk after all. And his wife and son were still alive, waiting for him to recover.

These were all such lovely thoughts. But deep down inside—buried deep within his soul, a voice was calling out to him. It was the voice of insanity. No, it was only insanity because he hated what the voice had been whispering to him. The voice whispered: do not fall into another delusion. Then the voice repeatedly whispered: this is reality; this is reality; this is reality; this is reality; this is reality.

Flint stopped running and screamed. He pulled out his revolver and shot at the darkness behind him, where the creatures had been scuttling after him. When his gun's chamber became empty, he hastily reloaded, taking bullets from the bandolier wrapped around his tattered vest. The hisses were much louder. He looked up for just a second and dropped all the bullets in his hand. Eight creatures were hunched, crawling toward him. Three of them clung to the ceiling while the others stuck to the slimy walls.

"You fucking sons of bitches," he said, staring at them with hatred. "What're you waiting for?" he shouted. "You've followed me this far. Get it over with!"

He knelt to the ground, surrendering himself to the nightmarish fiends before him. It was impossible for him to outrun them. He lay still, acknowledging his fate. Yes, this was reality. He accepted this at the very end, realizing that everything he'd experienced since November had in fact happened; it was all one hundred percent real. He closed his eyes and attempted to think of Hamarah; though he couldn't get a clear image of her smooth, beautiful body. He couldn't even hear her voice. All he could hear were the creatures approaching him, ready to feast on his old, wrinkled body.

Within seconds, an elongated stream of flame spewed out toward the slimy creatures. The beasts screeched, withdrawing. Only one of them was foolish enough to leap into the fire, which instantly devoured it. Flint opened his eyes, sweat pouring down his forehead. He dropped to the rough ground—his mouth wide open—and gawked at the ferocious fire. Then he feebly retreated against the jagged wall, scraping his arms through his torn shirt. As he lay on the granite, several pairs of orange-glowing eyes flickered.

Strident metallic reverberations mixed with high-pitched electronic frequencies rang into Flint's ears. He nearly became deaf as a group of armored beings stomped through the darkened tunnel, continuing to blow flame from their forearms at the fiends. Flint noticed that the titanium beings had tubes attached to their armored hands, connecting to their backpacks—they seemed to have some kind of superior form of flame-throwers. At this point, Flint gave up on figuring things out. He gave up on escaping too because he didn't fight back when two of the ten men in armor grabbed him. One held his left arm while the other held his right. They dragged him to the end of the tunnel where their ship hovered, its engines and pistons rumbling, steam and exhausts of an unknown gas filling the air.

The vessel he'd been taken to was slightly bigger than the one he'd escaped from earlier. Finding himself surrounded by these titans made him feel he was definitely better off being with them rather than staying in this chasm that was apparently filled with the other dreadful fiends. One of the armored men shattered his manacles. For a moment, Flint felt relieved. He thought, maybe they weren't so bad after all. Then another shackled him to the steamship that flew over the sweltering lava. Flint gave out a dreary sigh and slumped down, leaning against the vessel's railing. He desperately wanted to awaken from this nightmare. Instead he closed his eyes and fell into one.

After what seemed to be a few seconds, Flint heard an explosion. He could hear gunfire and countless people screaming. Flint opened his eyes and found himself in a trench filled with dead bodies. The sight made him want to vomit. He backed away and looked up. The sky was charred. To Flint, it appeared as if the atmosphere had consumed every ounce of smoke and flame until it turned blood red. A sizzling haze surrounded him. He finally stood on his feet but kept himself hidden in the trench.

"Commandant!" called out Browder. "We have to retreat! It's over!"

"No, it's not over until I'm dead," said Flint. "You get the others to safety. I'm going to find Hamarah." He pointed at a rundown building to the east. "Before the attack, she was helping me devise a strategy against the tribunal there. Without her, I'm nothing. I need to find her."

Browder stared at Flint with an expression of madness. "If you're going over there, then so am I," he said sternly.

Flint saluted him. "All right, let's go!"

He charged out of the burning trench with Browder. Together they shot at the uniformed enemies with their machine guns. Explosions ignited around them as they pressed onward. The thunderous blasts made their ears ring. They were surrounded by a desolate terrain that no longer bore any life.

Flint didn't stop firing his gun despite the fact that his army had been decimated. Then a bright beam came upon him and Browder from the charred sky, rupturing the ground. Browder helplessly staggered toward an abyss that split open due to the unfathomable blast. Just before he fell, however, Flint grabbed him, pulling him back up.

"Thanks," said Browder, looking pale. "It seems I owe you one."

"You owe me nothing."

Flint carried on, a grim expression on his face as he observed his surroundings. Whatever war they were fighting no longer mattered; it was a lost cause. Detonations ignited around them. The terrain kept splitting while a barrage of explosions came from above. Flint had no time to look. His only concern was to run for his life.

"Do you see that?" yelled Browder, pointing ahead at another trench. "We can take cover down there until we make it across."

Flint agreed, following his comrade.

Corpses were piled on the ground as they ran, still firing at their foes. Another explosion occurred, and this time it was in front of them. Flint fell into a crater, dirt blowing over his body. Just before he was about to faint, he squinted skyward to see what had hit him and Browder. He saw something that was impossible. Deep within the crimson sky that fumed with red death was the outline of a massive spacecraft.

Flint awoke by the gunwale of the steamship that was still hovering through the darkened chasm. He panted heavily and gasped for clean air, as if he'd been transported out of the blazing war-torn land that had become the epitome of char, smoke, and death. He rubbed his face and sat up, realizing he had dreamed again. However, he acknowledged it was a very different dream; it wasn't actually from the dreamtime.

"That was a real memory," he muttered weakly, his fingers twitching. He was in shock after regaining a part of his memory. "I had no control over anything. And that spacecraft...it destroyed everything in sight. Does such a thing truly exist?"

He groaned, noticing his surroundings—the depths of a dark hell, giant men encased in titanium armor, and a steam-powered vessel hovering over magma. Suddenly the idea of a lethal starship seemed possible to him.

"That was an actual memory from the war against the tribunal—the war I lost. How could I have forgotten?"

His head throbbed, sweat dripped down his brow, and blood trickled from his nose. He took a deep breath, trying to calm himself as he pondered about everything that had happened to him since last year. Even though it seemed impossible to him, he finally accepted that this wasn't fictitious. His experiences were real. And since Andrew Browder was in his dream—his long lost memory—he realized that Browder had told the truth after all. Furthermore, he now understood why Browder had said, 'Yes, you even saved my life once. I told you that I'd find a way to repay you. It's the only reason why I'm still here.'

Flint lowered his head. "After all these years, you actually came back to repay me for saving your life," he said pensively. "But you were killed for it. I'm so sorry..."

Lifting his head, he realized that the steamship was no longer hovering above lava. He spotted glimmers of starry lights ahead. As if this wasn't strange enough, the cavernous walls gradually changed to a bluish tinge. These walls, however, weren't jagged; they were straight, solid walls of metal. Slack-jawed, Flint stared at what seemed to be a majestic city.

One of the ten captors in armor clomped over to Flint who listened to its loud inhales and exhales. The titanium being was apparently acting as a guard, making sure he didn't do anything rash. Flint wondered whether the colossal being beside him was the same one from the previous steamship he'd fallen from. If so, that would explain why there were ten of them now. He tried to stand and stretch, but the guard aimed his flamethrower at him. Flint raised his hands, sitting back down. For some reason, he started feeling a bit safe despite being chained and surrounded by titans. The situation became increasingly surreal to him, especially when he gazed at the city of stone and metal that was nestled deep in the dim chasm.

"Where are you taking me?" asked Flint. The guard did not respond; he simply stared at Flint with his orange-glowing eyes, breathing deeply through his oxygen mask. "Are you taking me to the tribunal?"

The guard continued to ignore him. Though the tall beings in heavy armor seemed more human to him than beasts, they apparently didn't speak his language, and they were hostile too. When the steamship entered the city, however, Flint's anger gradually dissipated. He stared at the shimmering, cavernous city in awe. He'd never seen anything quite like this in his life. And he certainly never thought such a remarkable thing could exist. It was like a twilight city made for machines, or a utopian kingdom made for underworld gods.

Suddenly, the chasm he'd awakened to was no longer hell. The walls glittered with a dark blue metal, which Flint guessed was titanium. The star-like lights he once saw in the far distance were now clearer to him; they resembled futuristic lava lamps—some embedded within the walls and others within the ceiling and ground. A great deal of steam filled the air as Flint passed by on the hovering ship. In the distance, he could hear the rumblings of what may have been machines. The reverberations weren't deafening or disturbing to Flint; they surprisingly sounded muffled, as though the great city lived on a steam engine. Even the air smelled fresh to him.

He wondered to himself, had he been underground all this time? Gazing up, he attempted to glimpse at the stars; yet there wasn't even a sky. The dim, cavernous ceiling was blanketed by a clockwork design jointed with spools of gears and wires, as well as thick metal cylinders. Yes, he conceded, this was definitely an underground kingdom.

After observing his surroundings, he looked at the guard who'd been staring at him. Flint wondered if he should be friendly. Maybe what had happened was a simple misunderstanding? Perhaps these men in armor, like him, were survivors of Earth's destruction. Out of curiosity, he bowed to the guard. The sentinel, however, did not react to his friendly gesture.

The steamship gradually slowed down as it approached an abyss that divided the city. On the left side of the titanium kingdom stood several docking bridges where other steamships were suspended in midair, hovering. Sinusoidal-shaped tubes decorated the balustrades of the bridges, which were connected to the steamships' hydraulic systems. It seemed to Flint that those vessels were undergoing some form of maintenance. The ship he sat on finally came to a halt, suspended beside a titanium overpass.

As soon as the steamship docked, the guard who'd been watching Flint unshackled him. He then grabbed Flint, pulling him close. Flint grumbled under his breath what with the sudden heave and walked beside the stomping sentinel without fighting back. The other nine encased in armor clomped in front of him, guiding the way. A few more guards stood on the metal bridges, keeping watch as though they were expecting an invasion.

Flint entered a tunnel that glowed with recessed lighting. Bulky wires and tubes hung along the ceiling. Parts of the walls clanked with oversized cogs. The ground lit up with steam billowing through slit vents. Flint felt a vibration and heard the hum of a powerful machine between the life-support breathing and stomping of his captors. He was still finding it difficult to accept this as reality.

At the end of the passage, the armored beings turned left and activated a door that opened with a loud thump. The guard holding Flint shoved him past the door and entered with his fellow cadre. Inside lay a decorative, clockwork platform. When the door closed, one of the men clicked a switch on a panel, and a sound of pistons filled Flint's ears. The platform elevated, resonating like an ancient slab of stone opening in a secret tomb.

Although eerie to Flint, the city had an artful appearance. It looked futuristic, sanitary, and aesthetically pleasing to his eyes. Even the wires, tubes, gears, and cogs were placed in an artistic manner.

The platform eventually came to a halt, and the door opened. The armored men led Flint through another glittery passage. The dim tunnel was slightly wider than the one far below. As a matter of fact, Flint didn't realize he was so much higher until he exited the tunnel, stepping onto another bridge. He gazed down, spotting all the steamships a few hundred feet beneath him. This startled him, but the guard holding him broke him out of his daze by pushing him forward, barely giving him time to adjust. The abyss was utterly black—no sign of any ground. This made Flint get a chill up his spine. He tried to ignore what lay beneath him and continued following the nine thick-armored beings in front of him.

Crossing over to the other half of the city, he entered yet another tunnel. This passageway looked quite different from the other two he'd walked through. It had elegant burgundy-colored carpeting and bright blue lights. Flint had to admit, this hall was a majestic sight to behold. And at last, he reached a door leading him into a throne room where twelve guards stood—six on each side. The armored men who brought Flint here stepped aside, allowing him to walk ahead on his own.

Flint raised an eyebrow, noticing carpeted steps. Upon the summit of those steps lay a plinth on which stood a throne of sparkling-blue stone. Sitting in the throne was someone—or something—that defied the utopian kingdom he'd been taken to. With the exception of a helmet, it wore full-plated armor. Though it appeared to be a humanoid being, it had extremely pale skin, charcoal-colored hair, and ivory irises. Whatever ethnicity it belonged to, Flint thought it was a freak of nature. He stared at the apparent ruler of this kingdom in disbelief, wondering whether it would eat or greet him.

"Welcome to the city of Soalace," said the man on the throne. The tone of his voice was as empowering as the titanium armor he wore, and yet it had a faint croak. "But you won't feel welcome. Unless, of course, you prove yourself worthy of my hospitality."

"You speak English," said Flint, astonished.

"Yes," said the pale man. "I speak many languages. Et? Tu comprehendere verba mea?" He briefly waited for a response. "Nein?" He gave out a faint laugh. "I suppose you only speak English, Neanderthal?"

"That's right," said Flint. "Why have your men captured me?"

"Ah, my men," said the pale man on the throne. "I am glad you recognize who the leader of this city is. You'll soon learn I don't need to answer to you. However, my guard, Gunthrel, has told me of your escapade by the molten chasm, and it has impressed me. I shall answer your question: my army travels to the desolate surface frequently in search of survivors."

"Survivors?"

"Careful not to ask too many questions," replied the pale man. "You are dressed like a primitive American, and yet you were found walking mindlessly in Australia. I am fascinated by this. How you were able to travel over the scorching surface is beyond me. As for us: we travel through the *undertunnels* to reach other regions of the world's dead surface."

"What does that have to do with survivors?" asked Flint.

The pale man laughed and said, "You're a persistent one, aren't you? The others we find are mostly terrified, especially when they see my face.

But you—no, you are very different. You have an appetite to survive. Otherwise, it would've been impossible for you to have traveled on the surface for so long." He sat quietly for a moment and then continued, "Survivors. Yes, we do occasionally find them scattered around the world. It may be hard to believe but they exist. And when we find survivors—oh, how happy and excited do we become. We call you champions of the surface and send you into the abyss, where our arena is. If you survive, we let you leave. If you do not survive, we eat your remains."

Flint waited for the pale man on the throne to laugh, but he didn't. He was actually quite serious. This made Flint feel uneasy, making him wonder if he was better off not being saved by the armored beings when he was attacked by the slimy fiends in the molten chasm.

"What are you?" he dared to ask.

"I am the evolution of mankind since the death of Earth," said the pale man. "When the sun flares ignited, sundering the world thousands of years ago, my ancestors survived and built the undertunnels. Since then, they worked endlessly to establish a new life where the sun could no longer harm them. They sacrificed everything on the surface. But it made them stronger, and it was passed down to their descendents; it was passed down to me. I am—no, *we* are the greatest creation of nature."

"You eat survivors from the surface and dare call yourself a man?" replied Flint with an expression of absolute abhorrence. "What kind of insane logic is that? You're no different than those mindless beasts hiding in the dark. You're not human. No, you are the fall of man."

"Silence!"

"I am done with these games!" exclaimed Flint, rage in his eyes. "Where is the tribunal? If they want me to suffer for the rest of my life, then just lock me away in some prison and be done with these illusions!"

"Take this senile fool into the abyss!"

The guards immediately approached Flint who swiftly turned, lifting his arms as though ready to fight for his freedom. When he did so, however, the armored guards raised their bulky plated forearms, ready to blow fire on him from their built-in flamethrowers. Flint surrendered, allowing them to seize him. They then took him out of the chamber. As they did so, the pale man stood up from his glittery throne and gazed at Flint with a deranged look.

"There is no tribunal here," said the pale man. "There is only one ruler here in Soalace. I am that ruler. I am Pardashan, and you will remember my name until you scream and croak as a spit of meat on my dinner table!"

CHAPTER NINE
THE THRILL TO KILL

Flint was taken back to the platform on the opposite side of the city. The guards surrounded him, not taking their eyes off him for a second. Once the door sealed, the platform descended to an area in Soalace known only to Flint as the abyss. He gazed at the tall beings encased in armor, snarling at them.

Confused and livid, he wondered to himself, how could the tribunal not have any part in this madness? Although living beings were apparently inside these giant armor suits, they were certainly *not* human. Yes, he thought, they were as vicious and fiendish as the slimy monsters dwelling in the dark chasm that was filled with lava. Flint desperately wanted to escape, feeling that he'd have a stroke if he didn't leave.

The platform finally stopped. When the door unsealed, Flint stooped and rolled between two of the armored beings. He quickly rose back to his feet and broke into a run through the dim passage ahead. He heard the same deafening metallic sounds reverberate from the titanium cadre, but he didn't stagger or clamp his ears. Turning at a corner, he ran through another passage. He dashed past two guards and evaded their hands.

Flint heard their stomps. He knew they weren't far from him, so he didn't stop running, hoping to reach the bridges where the steamships hovered. He didn't even know how to operate them; though, he'd be willing to click any button and attempt to pilot one if he could just find his way to them. Reaching a door, he slammed his hand on a panel embedded in the wall. Though it fizzed due to his unnatural strength, the door opened. Upon stepping into the dim chamber, Flint found himself inside a dungeon.

He simply stopped, feeling lifeless. He might as well have been deaf because the metallic noises behind him didn't make him flinch. Instead he embraced the stomping and reverberations, knowing he wouldn't be seeing the sun too soon. There'd be no escaping—not today. Flint didn't bother turning around while the guards drew closer to him. He stood still, giving up. When they reached him, one of them pounded the back of his head. Flint groaned, his vision diminishing, and dropped to the concrete floor. That was the last thing he remembered.

Several hours later, Flint could hear sounds again. What he heard seemed to be someone or something humming. Then it became clearer—bullets and explosions. He slowly opened his eyes, finding himself in the same ruined area where he'd been running with Browder. The only difference was that he couldn't find him. Flint was surrounded by corpses. He shrieked, backing away from the lifeless people who were once his comrades. The sight of them made him vomit. He lurched, coughing violently. Yes, he was the martyr—he'd always been the martyr, and his comrades had followed him to their deaths.

He gazed skyward, spotting the massive starship suspended amid the clouds, still blasting the land apart. Flint looked eastward and noticed that the structure where Hamarah was supposed to be in was still standing. He quickly ran toward it, hoping to find his beloved soul mate. As he drew closer, he saw multiple enemies dressed in black-red military uniforms; they were shooting at rebels with superior firepower.

Flint stared at their guns, frightened at what he saw. The military no longer had machine guns. Instead they had dreadful firearms known as dimensional cannons: weapons capable of drawing power from other dimensions. When the violet, laser-looking beams touched the rebels, they instantly disintegrated. Though they may have felt a pinch before their demise, they didn't have time to scream. This wasn't a war; it was an unstoppable annihilation.

The beams continued to be fired, one missing Flint by a hair. He gasped, continuing to run. He threw himself into a trench and felt safer, sprinting through the narrow dirt-filled path. The building stood just a few yards away. Scaling the trench, he had a feeling of hope. He then charged toward the structure, excited to see his beloved Hamarah again. At that precise moment, a dimensional missile launched from the starship, blowing the building apart. Flint stared at the exploding structure, feeling his heart sink.

"*Hamarah!*" he cried out at the top of his lungs.

Flint awoke in a cell, tears in his eyes, screaming. He knew the dream he had was also a memory. And of all the memories he could regain, it had to be the one when he'd witnessed his lover's death. He cried in his cell, no longer having the urge to breathe. His mind was beginning to crack. There was only so much he could handle. Age caught up to him, and now he waited for death to take him.

"Hey," called out a man opposite Flint. "It ain't so bad in here, lad."

Flint looked up, seeing a middle-aged man locked in a similar cell inside the dungeon. He was oddly smiling, showing he barely had any teeth. He had a long crooked nose, wrinkled skin, and a feeble body with several scars.

"I don't care about this place," said Flint, trying not to cry. "I just dreamt of a memory that I never wanted to remember."

"Ya don't say?" said the scrawny man, gnawing at his lip. "Ain't no memory so bad that we've gotta git rid of it. There's always sumthin' worth rememberin' if ya ask me, lad. Say, the name's Dale."

"Flint Cross," he said. "Or is it Ethan?"

"Heck, ya can be anythin' ya want down here. I sumtimes call maself Peter Pan. Only thing is, I can't fly. Not anymore, anyways. See, I need sum fairy dust ta git me goin'—then I'm tha real deal."

Flint gawked at the rugged man. After everything that had happened to him, just when he thought things couldn't get worse, he was stuck in a dungeon with a deranged man. Flint rubbed his forehead, trying not to scream. He then closed his eyelids, wiping dried glop from the corners of his eyes. Opening them again, he took a deep breath and observed his cell. It was the cleanest prison he'd ever seen in his life, but it might as well have been the filthiest one considering how vicious the beings in this kingdom were.

"Lovely place ain't it?" said Dale.

"Yeah," sulked Flint. "Feels just like home."

"Ya read my mind, lad!" said Dale excitedly. "But if ya ask me, I think it's better than ma home. See, where I come from, everythin' look like shit."

"Really?"

"Oh yeah," replied Dale. "Hmm, I was on da surface fer how long? Thirty?—nah, 'bout forty-five years. Yeap, I remember now. Forty-five years of shit. Earth ain't ever gonna recover. I promise ya that."

"Why?"

"Why?" said Dale, raising an eyebrow. "I'll tell ya why: 'cus the sun blew it ta hell. Ah, I used ta hear all this aboriginal bullshit 'round Queensland. And that's just it, lad—bullshit! A big load of horse shit. Ain't ya ever wonderin' why it's been so goddamn hot up there? It was 'cus of tha freakin' sun 'n its flares. That damned us all, lad."

Flint thought, maybe this man wasn't so crazy after all. Though, if he wasn't insane, he was surely heading that way. Dale kept talking; in fact, he talked for hours. He just wouldn't be quiet. Though, could Flint blame him? Insane or not, he figured Dale must have been the only human here for years—maybe longer. Who knows how many more were out there? He had a terrible feeling that only a handful of people remained living on Earth, if any.

Dale eventually stopped talking and fell asleep. This was a relief for Flint. He took this short-lived time to appreciate the silence. He leaned against the wall, breathing calmly. After a few minutes of silence, a door opened. One of the guard's came in with a tray of food. This time there was no stomping or loud sounds. When the guard showed himself, he looked similar to the ruler of Soalace. Grimacing at Flint, he slid the tray of food into the cell and quickly rose back to his feet.

"I'm going to enjoy eating you," said the warden, sniggering. "Until then, enjoy your last meal."

The warden laughed again while he walked away, shutting the door behind him.

Flint hadn't eaten since his journey through the desolate Outlands. He brought the tray over, staring at the food. It looked like pudding with worms wiggling inside. He almost barfed when he smelled it, but he was starving and desperately needed to eat something. Grabbing the food, he gobbled it down. Strangely, it tasted good. Whether this was because he'd been hungry, he didn't know. More importantly, he felt relieved not to be hungry.

After an hour, a door opened. The stomping of an armored being entering the dungeon woke Dale up. The warden appeared by Flint's cell, along with Gunthrel who was in his shiny armored suit.

"What do you want?" scowled Flint.

"It's time for your trial," said the warden.

Gunthrel opened the jail cell, grabbed Flint, and heaved him toward another door inside the dungeon.

"Fight hard, Ethan," said Dale.

Flint was amused when his inmate called him Ethan. It was the first time someone had called him by his real name. Gunthrel pushed him through a dim tunnel that led to a rear door. Flint didn't retaliate; he was ready to face whatever trial Pardashan created for him. When he approached the door at the end of the passage, he could hear loud screams. Though, they didn't sound like people being tortured. Upon reaching the door, Gunthrel opened it, and the distorted voices turned into cheers.

Gunthrel stepped into the gargantuan chamber that resembled a coliseum. It was rather bright to Flint when he entered the arena. Lava lamps were nestled into the wired ceiling and glittery walls. He gazed at the audience, seeing at least ten thousand people seated. And at the very top, directly in front of him, sat Pardashan who wore a wicked smile. The screams of the crowd was deafening to Flint, but he was gradually adjusting to the noisy kingdom. Fortunately for him, the audience calmed down when Pardashan rose from his golden throne.

"Another relic has entered our magnificent city," said Pardashan. "Whether or not *it* will be my dinner tonight depends on how smart *it* is." The pale-skinned crowd cheered at what their leader said. He continued, "The first round, which may also be the final round, will be this relic battling against six brutal lurkens. Let the games begin!"

"Uh, what exactly do I need to do?" asked Flint.

Gunthrel opened a compartment in his arm and removed Flint's rifle. He handed it to him without a word and then left the chamber. Just then, another door unsealed across the arena and in came four of the slimy fiends that Flint had been running from in the molten chasm.

"Lurkens, huh?" said Flint. "I guess they're not yowies after all."

He quickly aimed at one of the scuttling fiends and shot it dead in the head. The creature flew back and exploded into a glob of slime. Flint targeted each one, shooting all but one in the head. The last one pounced toward Flint who swiftly rolled to the side, slamming the muzzle of his rifle against its face. Afterwards, he shot the beast in the neck. It screeched in agony, dying a slow, painful death.

The audience was silent, startled that Flint singlehandedly killed six ferocious lurkens. Pardashan grimaced and snapped his fingers at the guards who opened the gates again, allowing twelve lurkens to scuttle out. This time Flint dropped his rifle, swiftly removed bullets from his bandolier—which the citizens of Soalace thought were merely absurd designs on his nineteenth-century clothing—and reloaded his Peacemaker. He then spun it and instantly shot down six of the twelve creatures. Flint cocked his revolver so fast that it looked as if he'd only fired it once. He then pulled out his magnum and blew the others away. He didn't even have to aim at their heads; a single bullet blasted their chests open, killing them.

Once again, the crowd grew silent. Flint holstered his guns, picked up his rifle, and smiled. He was starting to feel right at home, thinking he could do this all day. Many of the patrons were astonished. Some of them even applauded him; however, this made Pardashan scowl and grumble. He stood up, silencing the cheers.

"What is your name, relic?" asked Pardashan.

"I am Flint Cross," he said. "And you'll have to do a lot better than this to roast me as a spit of meat."

Pardashan clenched his teeth and replied, "Very well. I suppose you won't mind skipping the next fifty rounds that I had in store for you. Instead we'll go straight to the last." He snapped his fingers, signaling the guards to open the gates again. This time they kept the gates open rather than closing them after a short time. "Die well, Flint Cross!"

Countless fiends scuttled into the coliseum. However, not all of them went straight after Flint. Most of them climbed the walls, yearning to feast on the crowd. The citizens of Soalace flinched and gasped in horror. Flint shot those that approached him and then gazed up, realizing that the patrons were in danger.

The audience was no longer cheering. Now they were screaming in terror. Time stopped for Flint as he gazed at the extremely pale people. When they shrieked in dismay, a voice within Flint's mind told him that this was his chance to escape. Then another voice spoke to him; it was quite different from the one that told him to run. The voice was telling him to help these people. He wondered to himself, was his conscience an enemy or ally?

Flint realized that the people of Soalace were still human beings. They had changed so much after the sun destroyed Earth, but it wasn't their fault. And though he'd only been in this kingdom for a short time, he'd managed to sense something natural about them—fear. It was natural for any normal being to have fear at a time like this. If he didn't help these people, then he'd be no different than the wretched lurkens that were ready to infest the city with their slime. He was a human being down to the bone, and no matter what, he'd never reject his humanity—his empathy.

Flint reloaded his guns and started shooting down the creatures. Some of them reached the thick windowpane protecting the crowd. The beasts spewed acid on the glass, dissolving it. The audience ran for their lives. Pardashan and his bodyguards were the only ones who didn't flee. The guards reached the decayed glass and used their flamethrowers. In the meantime, Flint kept shooting the remaining lurkens scuttling on the ground.

Pardashan was infuriated at what had just happened. He didn't even care that Flint saved many lives. He sealed the gates and pointed at Flint.

"Seize him!"

"*What?*" responded Flint, enraged. "I just helped you prevent an infestation of these monsters and you *still* want me to suffer?"

Despite the fact that he heard Pardashan say *him* instead of *it*, he was nevertheless fed up with this insane behavior. He reached for his bullets to reload his guns but realized he'd run out of them. Flint stood firm as an armored man approached. He then slammed his fist into the bulky being, sending him across the coliseum.

Pardashan's eyes widened when he saw the guard's armor dent, not to mention seeing him fly back several feet. Another guard approached Flint who grabbed his mechanical hands, flinging him as though he didn't even have armor on. The other guards noticed Flint's unnatural strength and warily approached him. Flint was ready to fight them all, even if they tried to burn him with their flamethrowers.

"Enough!" roared Pardashan.

The remaining crowd and guards were just as surprised as Flint who turned around when he heard the ruler of Soalace speak.

"Your kind doesn't normally have such strength. How is it you possess such might?"

"If you're not linked to the tribunal," began Flint, "then perhaps I'll explain what I know; that is, if you're willing to treat me like a human being."

Pardashan squinted at him. "Perhaps I have misjudged you, Flint Cross," he said. "Yes, I believe you are more valuable alive than dead. Gunthrel will guide you back to my throne room, unless you remember the way."

"I'm a gunslinger, not a psychic."

"Of course," said Pardashan, signaling Gunthrel to escort Flint.

CHAPTER TEN

SOAL FOR COAL

Gunthrel came down to where Flint stood in the coliseum and guided him back to Pardashan's throne room on the other side of the steamy city of Soalace. The kingdom of clockwork, metal, and granite seemed less hostile to Flint since he'd helped its citizens who had been attacked by the fiendish lurkens. Flint stepped into the throne chamber and walked over to the carpeted steps. Pardashan stood up, gesturing at Flint to follow him to the balcony that lay behind the throne, overlooking a chasm lit with an assortment of colorful lava lamps.

"Tell me," began Pardashan, "why did you help my people? You could've used the attack to your advantage and escaped."

"I don't let innocent unarmed people die."

"Is that so?" replied Pardashan, rubbing his white, frail chin. He remained quiet for a moment and then said, "Times have changed, Flint Cross. We are no longer the same noble humans that existed ages ago."

"Noble?" said Flint, trying not to laugh. "Few humans were noble before the sun flares ruined our civilization. I've also unfortunately discovered as of late that they're still scarce. And no," he added before Pardashan could interrupt him, "I'm not referring to you. Do you think I like these clothes? Do you think I like these archaic guns? Do you think I was born and raised on the surface?"

"Isn't every human who has your skin pigment?"

"No," said Flint, irritated. "My life once meant something. Long ago, it was a life empty of illusions. But then I was betrayed, put here by the tribunal."

"You have mentioned this *tribunal* more than once," said Pardashan. "What is it?"

"I myself don't even know," said Flint, frowning. "The tribunal seems to be some kind of seat of power—a dictatorship. I only remember bits and pieces of my former life; they blanked out my memory."

"Why would they do that?"

"Because I started a rebellion," said Flint. "Don't ask me why. I still can't remember my motive. It may have been for the sake of freedom."

"Freedom from what?"

"Some form of tyranny," responded Flint. "Like I said, I'm not sure. All I know is that I started a war with the tribunal. I was the leader. People fought and died for me. Even my beloved Hamarah was killed. I eventually lost the war, and since then I was deprived of everything: my liberty, my dignity, my humanity, my sanity—everything. They put me on this backwater planet and turned me into a joke, giving me a fake name, a fake family, a fake home, and fake friends. Meanwhile, the people who were closest to me were nothing more than backstabbing wardens, put here to watch over me and make sure I'd die quietly rather than be a martyr."

"That is quite a tale," said Pardashan. He really wasn't sure if Flint was making this story up, but he felt Flint had no reason to lie since he'd chosen to help the citizens of Soalace instead of escape when he had the chance. "Tell me, what do you intend to do?"

Flint had been staring at the colorful chasm while listening. When asked that question, however, he turned to the side and stared at Pardashan curiously.

"That depends on you," he said.

"And why is that?"

"You're the ruler of this kingdom," said Flint. "I'm your prisoner, and I have no idea how to return to the surface even if I escaped."

"Despite what you may think," began Pardashan, "I am an honorable man. I'm not like that tribunal you spoke of. In fact, I am willing to grant you one wish for helping my people. It is my form of gratitude."

"Are you sure?" asked Flint, startled.

"I am a fair man," said Pardashan. "Name one thing you desire and I will grant it. If it be returning to the surface so you may find this tribunal of yours, so be it. Or if there is something else you have in mind, ask."

Flint brought his eyes down, staring at the chasm again. He took a deep breath, plagued with numerous possibilities. This was an unforeseen turn of events, he thought. Was it true that he'd somehow gotten on Pardashan's good side? Could he really return to the surface? That was the last thing he expected.

"I have two requests."

"Do not test my benevolence," said Pardashan. "You have helped me, and so I am willing to help you. Afterwards, we are even."

Flint grumbled, thinking hard. "There is a group of survivors in the Northern Territory of Australia," he said. "They live in an old dusty town called Desonas. It would mean a great deal to me if you and your people could leave them in peace."

"Excuse me?" scowled Pardashan, his eyebrows creasing. "Are you certain of this? Those people are no longer a part of your life."

"They are the only real friends I have left," said Flint. "Let them live in peace."

"So be it," said Pardashan, agitated. "They won't be taken or killed by my men if they're ever found. But don't think this *sacrifice* of yours will make me fond of you."

"Sacrifice?"

"Don't be coy with me," said Pardashan. "I won't be granting you any other wishes. If you want to play savior rather than get even with that tribunal of yours, be my guest. But that means you're stuck down here like the rest of us. You'll have to start a new life here and forget about your previous lives in limbo and the surface."

"Fine," said Flint. "It's not like I have a choice."

Pardashan squinted harshly at him. "Gunthrel will be your overseer," he said. "Much work is needed to be done in my city. And a man of your caliber will suit us well. Now leave. I'm done with you."

"As you wish," said Flint, leaving the balcony. He returned to the throne chamber and went down the steps, walking over to where Gunthrel stood.

"One last thing," called out Pardashan.

"Yes?" said Flint, turning around.

"In all the history here in the undertunnels, not once has there ever been a man from the desolate surface of Earth who possessed the strength you have," said Pardashan. "How did you obtain such power?"

"I'm afraid the only ones who may've been able to answer that are dead," said Flint. "But perhaps one day, if I am lucky, I will remember my past. And if I do, I'll gladly tell you."

"Humph…Gunthrel, take him to the Core."

The armored being bowed and led Flint back to the other side of the city.

"Pardashan said you're my overseer," said Flint, walking across the luminous bridge. Not getting a response made him glower. "Tell me, what exactly is the Core?"

"I will explain when we arrive."

Flint thought Gunthrel sounded like a machine, especially with the life-support mask he had on. They reached the other side of the city and entered the platform. When the door sealed, Gunthrel clicked a button on the panel, which made the platform descend. With the exception of his heavy breathing, Gunthrel stayed quiet.

A minute passed, and the platform was still descending. Flint wondered to himself, just how far down does this platform go? It made him panic. After a few seconds, however, the lift slowed down and came to a stop. The door automatically opened, and a dense cloud of steam puffed inward. It was so dense that Flint couldn't see ahead. Fortunately for him, it eventually dissipated.

"This way," said Gunthrel, exiting the platform.

Flint followed him into a resonating chasm with steam filling the air. The floor was made of fine grating. And along the pillars and walls in the chamber were thick metal tubes. Numerous pale men were shoveling what seemed to be coal into fireboxes within boilers, all of which stood next to humming steam engines.

Most of the men looked astonished to see a human from the surface. They surprisingly saluted him and Gunthrel who stomped through the catwalks. To see someone from the surface in the Core of Soalace meant that Pardashan had granted him life and trusted him. That was the only reason why the men here seemed to accept the fact that he came down here, or at least that was what Flint assumed when they greeted him.

Gunthrel eventually reached a boiler far on the eastern side of the chasm. A young man vigorously shoveled coal-like material into the fire-box. When he spotted Gunthrel, however, he laid his shovel down on the grating and left his station. Gunthrel gazed at Flint, pointing at the shovel.

"Listen," began Flint, "I don't mind working, but I'm not fond of people who are cryptic. If you're my overseer, then I expect you to respect me as much as I should respect you. And that means explaining my purpose here in English, not sign language." For a moment, Flint wasn't sure whether Gunthrel was going to hit him or nod. "Did I do something wrong to get on your shit list?"

"Start working."

Flint frowned, grabbed the large shovel on the floor, and dug it into the gray material. He then lifted it and hurled the contents into the firebox.

"Easy enough," said Flint, repeating what he did.

"You didn't have to kill my friend," blurted Gunthrel.

Flint stopped working and sighed. "You can't blame me for that," he said. "In fact, it wouldn't have happened if you didn't capture me. All you had to do was communicate like a normal person."

"Surface dwellers are nothing more than a reminder of man's fall," said Gunthrel.

"Excuse me?" snapped Flint. "You know, I'm getting really tired of your arrogance. All you underground dwellers seem to be indifferent." He remembered when Amanda and Sarah had called him obnoxious, narcissistic, and indifferent. Though only for a moment, he saw himself inside the tall clockwork armor—a soulless husk that had lost its humanity. The thought of him no longer being human frightened him. He looked down, trying to preserve his empathy. "Listen, I'm sorry about what happened."

"Work!"

Flint sighed again. "Can you at least explain what the hell I'm doing? Is this for the city, your ships, or what?"

"It's for everything," said Gunthrel. "Work and I will explain." Flint obeyed, continuing to hurl coal-like material into the fuming firebox with his shovel. As he worked, Gunthrel went on, "You come from the surface and know nothing of our ways. The Core is an ingenious engine. It produces oxygen, filters water, recycles steam, and requires little fuel. You probably think this is coal." Upon seeing Flint nod, he added, "You're wrong."

"Then what is it?" asked Flint, digging again.

"When our ancestors created the undertunnels, they produced an extraordinary material that changed humanity forever," said Gunthrel. "It is what energizes the Core, allowing the flow of steam. It's as precious as our souls; and so we named it *soal*. It is the life of our vessels and our greatest defense against the lurkens. Without it, we're nothing."

Flint slowed down, staring at the material he'd been hurling into the firebox. "It seems my job is much more important than it appears," he said.

"Appearances can be deceiving."

"I know that all too well," said Flint, grimacing. "My life on the surface seemed real—it appeared real. Yet it wasn't. I was deceived until the very end."

"Forget about that life," said Gunthrel. "You are here now. Lord Pardashan chose me to be your overseer for one reason: he acknowledged that you have a great strength despite your age. You can probably work twice as long as our men here. And you *will* work a great deal for the sake of Soalace."

"I'll work when I have to, but I won't be treated as a prisoner," said Flint. "I am a man of freedom, and no one is taking that away from me.

Not the tribunal, not Pardashan, and certainly not you. It was my decision to stay here. But mark my words, Gunthrel, one day I will find a way out of this backwater planet, and I will continue the war I started."

"Every man has a dream."

"Indeed," said Flint, hurling more soal into the firebox.

Gunthrel refused to show it, but he did feel a bit impressed with Flint. "You'll work eight hours, like the others," he said. "Then you can leave through the western catwalk." He pointed to the left, showing Flint the passage. "It will lead you to a hall where the bedchambers are located. You may stay in chamber sixty-two."

"A fitting number for my age," said Flint. "Hopefully the room is cozier than the cell I was in earlier."

"It's too good for the likes of a surface dweller."

"I'm *not* a surface dweller," replied Flint snappishly. "If anything, I am an outlander. Or perhaps the more appropriate term would be *offworlder.*"

"If you say so," said Gunthrel skeptically.

"Anyway," began Flint, still working, "where the hell did those lurkens come from? And just how many of them are there?"

"Ah, the lurkens," said Gunthrel. "They are our mortal enemy. In fact, they are our one and only enemy. There are two kinds of lurkens: the slimy monsters that nearly killed you in the molten chasm, and the more human-looking creatures that hide deeper within the dark shadows of abandoned undercities. I find both to be just as fiendish."

"What's the difference between them?"

"One is mindless, and the other is somewhat sentient," said Gunthrel. "The sentient ones don't have slime or create cocoons. They somehow control the wilder, senseless fiends."

"Why are they so violent?" asked Flint. "And where did they come from?"

"We can only assume that they were a failed evolution of humans who attempted to live in the undertunnels," replied Gunthrel. "Perhaps they couldn't handle the change. They probably fed on one another until they became what they ate—monsters."

"Sounds like your people."

Gunthrel laughed for the first time and said, "We don't eat people. Pardashan was simply amusing himself by trying to frighten you. Otherwise, you wouldn't have had an inmate. Dale works too, though not in this sector. And I can assure you, he certainly hasn't earned the respect you've earned."

"I almost forgot about him," said Flint. "He's a bit crazy but funny. By the way, what sector does he work in, if you don't mind my asking?"

"The waterworks," said Gunthrel. "See these pipes?"

"I only see huge tubes."

"They're actually pipes," said Gunthrel. "People like Dale help keep this city alive in the waterworks, which is a system that leads to the surface, gathering water when it rains. The water runs through these pipes. And while soal is put in the boilers, the steam engines work their magic by supplying us with energy."

"I'm very impressed."

"As I said before, soal is the soul of our city," said Gunthrel. "Without the life of water or the essence of soal, the undertunnels would be as dead as the surface."

"I just have one last question."

"What is it?" replied Gunthrel, irked.

"It's about the lurkens again," said Flint. "There seems to be quite a lot of them. Do they ever attack this city?"

"Do they attack?" said Gunthrel derisively. "Why do you think there are so many guards around the city? Why do you think so many of us walk around in armor all the time? Of course they attack, and they attack us frequently. I told you before: they're our nemesis. As a matter of fact, if they launched a full assault, it is quite possible they'd defeat us."

"I take it they haven't tried that yet?"

"They're not *that* intelligent," said Gunthrel. "Actually, the sentient lurkens may have thought about it, but they're probably too nervous. In fact, they might think that they'd be killed; they are terrified of our flame-throwers. It's the one thing that holds them back. If we didn't have fire, I fear we'd be extinct already."

"They're deadly," said Flint, hurling another huddle of soal into the firebox. "Why don't you launch an assault and get rid of them?"

"Do you think it's that easy? The acid of the lurkens burns right through our armor. We have lost many brothers and sisters fighting against them. Launching a full assault would be no different than every single one of them invading Soalace. Now enough of your questions, Flint Cross. I've said more than I ever should have. You know what to do, and despite how simple it may be, you understand how important it is. In about seven hours, you may retire to your room for the remainder of the day. When you hear a ringing in your bedchamber, it means it's time to return to work."

"What about food?" asked Flint.

Gunthrel sighed and said, "Food is supplied in your bedchamber." He turned, stomping away as he added, "Look alive, people. This isn't coal; it is soal you're working with. It is your life and soul."

Flint gazed at Gunthrel for a moment and smiled at him. Even though they had started out as enemies, he somehow felt that he may have gained a new friend—hopefully his first of many friends here in Soalace. He continued to work, feeling more alive than ever, and didn't stop until seven long hours passed.

CHAPTER ELEVEN

ABOVE LOVE

Since seven hours had passed, Flint laid his shovel by the soal and left his station. He walked over to the western catwalk and followed its path until he reached a corridor that had several doors on each side. This section of the Core surprisingly resembled a hotel. Flint had to admit, Soalace had an elegant appearance even in the engine sector. He searched for room number sixty-two. Upon finding it, he tried opening the door.

Flint's eyes widened when he recognized the same hole in the door that he'd seen back in Panzo Mine. It was a confirmation that the undertunnels reached as far as there. No wonder the miners had come across the lurkens, he conceded. They'd dug so deep that they had accidently penetrated an undercity. It all made sense to him. Yes, he thought, that would explain why the architecture was so sophisticated. Then he was plagued with a terrible realization—that area in the undertunnels had been abandoned, infested with the lurkens. Perhaps the derelict undercity was once greater than Soalace, Flint wondered to himself. If so, this meant that Gunthrel wasn't honest; the lurkens were spreading and slowly defeating them.

"What am I doing?"

He realized he'd been standing in the corridor thinking like a madman after working so many hours. He put his hand into the hole, and a translucent light waved through his wrinkled body, scanning him. When finished, the door unlocked. Flint stepped into his bedchamber in awe. Inside was silent. He didn't hear a single sound of the steam engines, nor did he feel any vibrations. The walls were one hundred percent sound proof and sparkled with beauty like the upper levels of the city.

"Unbelievable," he said to himself.

He noticed a panel on the wall beside an indigo table, and below the panel was a recessed shelf with an empty tray and cup. Flint walked over to it, seeing that there were two buttons on the panel: food and water. This was a dream come true. He clicked the food button, and the same pudding-like food he'd eaten before in the cell drooped onto the tray. He quickly ate it and then poured some water into the cup, drinking it in a single gulp.

"I can do this all night."

Feeling ecstatic, he clicked the buttons again. Unfortunately for him, only a little extra food and water came out. It apparently had a limit. He hoped that it would automatically refill within a few hours. In the meantime, he ate and drank the remaining sustenance. Shortly after, Flint lay on his bed. It was a canopy bed with an exceptionally soft mattress on a glittery, stony bedstead. He took off his tattered clothes, covered himself with a warm blanket, and fell asleep in less than a minute.

Over the next few weeks, Flint worked hard. He had a simple job but felt proud about it since it was so important. Living in such a strange place soon became normal to him, and the pale humans he lived with were now more real to him than those he'd lived with in the town of Desonas—at least those who'd betrayed him. Living in the city of Soalace actually seemed to be a life worth living to him. He felt safe from the extreme heat, the occasional violent storms, and he never had to worry about having food on the table. As long as he worked hard in the Core of Soalace, he was always able to return to his bedchamber and have sustenance.

Sometimes he thought about Sarah and Jake in his room. Though he had no idea how they were doing, he felt it was best that they stayed on the surface. If they had followed him all the way to the Outlands, then they could have been killed either by the harsh weather or by the lurkens.

"I hope you're happy, Sarah," he said on his bed.

His life in Soalace didn't start out well, but it eventually became a comfortable home for him. He doubted things would have turned out just as well if the others had been with him. Yes, thought Flint, he had definitely made the right decision by telling Sarah and the others to stay in Desonas.

The only thing that he occasionally missed was hunting. Though, when he thought about his hunting days, it reminded him of Joey. An urge to kill filled his veins whenever Joey came into his mind. He'd feel so angry and miserable that it actually made him hate the idea of ever hunting again. And so, little by little, even his most precious sport—the game that once made him feel one hundred percent free—faded into his subconscious.

Flint gained a new life here in the city of Soalace, a city occupied by those whom he now called *steamwalkers* since they were the masters of steam technology. He soon gave up on his past lives and looked forward to each day. Though he'd occasionally have dreams that reminded him of his past, they would never reveal anything new about his previous lives. In due time, he no longer cared. And so his mystical dreams faded away. Instead he started to have more natural ones about his life in Soalace.

Eventually, two years passed. Flint had turned sixty-two, the same exact number of his bedchamber. He was getting older. And even though many of the pale humans in Soalace were very young, he felt that this was a place worthy of a gentleman his age. Somehow, he felt better about his age being here. Living and working in the Core gave him a great deal of pleasure, not just because he was helping fellow under-dwellers live comfortably by working with soal, but because he felt the Core was an old place. He felt that it was like his second heart, giving him a sort of "second wind" to life.

Another thing that made Flint happy was his friendship with Gunthrel. Over time, they'd become decent friends. Gunthrel wasn't just his overseer any more. In fact, Gunthrel came to respect him so much that when he asked if Dale could have his own bedchamber instead of a cell, he agreed to it. Flint was, by far, the hardest working man in the Core. This amazed his coworkers since he was in his sixties. No other man at that age could work so efficiently; it was as if he were a machine. The steamwalkers sometimes referred to Flint as *Heart of the Core*, and it amused him.

A few months passed. Flint no longer thought about Desonas. He even stopped thinking about what had happened to Hamarah. Life in Soalace was so important to him that he'd finally decided to let go of everything, as though his past had been an illusion. Soalace was his reality now. Then, one day after working in the Core, he dreamed. Yet this one was vastly different than anything he'd experienced before.

Like most dreams, he found himself in a place without knowing why or how he'd gotten there. He wore a burgundy robe that had laced designs on the cuffs and collar. Although it was a robe, it seemed to be some kind of militaristic uniform. Flint stood in the lobby of a skyscraper. Just then, a chime emanated behind him. He turned, entering an elevator that had opened. It was encased in glass with lights along the plating.

Flint clicked the ninety-eighth button, which was the highest floor in the building. The elevator closed and took him up. A circular white city of dome-shaped buildings stood before him—it was majestic and utopian looking to him. He also saw a vessel flying into the greenish atmosphere. This made him realize that the planet wasn't Earth.

Upon reaching the ninety-eighth floor, he stepped out of the elevator, walking through a carpeted corridor. He approached a pair of doors that swayed into the walls. Entering the atrium-like chamber ahead, he saw three men seated on a balcony. A fourth chair was among them but remained empty. And beside the balcony hung an embossed emblem depicting a hand rising up, its palm seizing the stars.

"There he is," said Laskov, an elderly man dressed in white.

"Welcome back, Ethan," called out Kuralan, the second man who was slightly younger than Laskov.

"I apologize for my tardiness," said Ethan.

"It is quite all right," said Tarak, the third elderly man. "Considering that you're the Commandant—and the new Commander-in-Chief of our proud nation—we expect you to be quite busy."

The balcony descended while he approached. He saluted the tribunal and stood still, awaiting orders.

"Don't be bashful," said Tarak. "Have a seat."

Ethan was shocked and said, "But—"

"No buts," interrupted Kuralan. "Your success to colonize Vorilian IV has truly made us proud. This is the next step in the history of humanity's exploration into the stars. And none of it would have been possible without you."

"You grace me too much," said Ethan, bowing and then taking a seat.

"Now that you have proven your ability to seize the future," began Laskov in a croaking tone, "is it time to begin humanity's final evolution."

"I beg your pardon?" said Ethan, confused.

"Take a deep breath," said Tarak. "This news won't be easy to swallow, especially since this has been debated many times."

Ethan listened, bracing himself for what they were about to tell him. He wondered to himself, what did they want him to do? All his life he'd faithfully obeyed the tribunal—the true leaders and voice of humanity. He felt anxious and nervous, not knowing what to expect from them.

"Since the dawn of human consciousness we have tried to understand the laws of nature and its secrets," said Tarak. "We survived the harsh chaos of Mother Earth at the beginning of our existence. And we proudly conquered Earth."

"But we didn't stop there," said Kuralan.

"We reached out to the stars," said Laskov faintly. "We knew that we were destined for greatness."

"Greatness indeed," said Tarak. "Even though the sun defied us and destroyed our most precious home, we prevailed. We have proven ourselves to be the masters of life. Even death is having difficulty catching up with us, thanks to nanotechnology. We as the tribunal proved this by living for over three hundred years, guiding humanity through the stars. There is, however, one thing that still remains—our greatest nemesis to which we've never been able to defeat. But this will finally change with you, Commandant."

"Humanity believes in you," said Laskov.

"Which is why we've made you Commander-in-Chief and asked you to come here," said Kuralan. "The time has come for the military to make its most glorious move."

Ethan, though flattered, was growing too anxious. As much as he respected the immortal tribunal, he couldn't help feel that they were essentially rambling. He already knew all this—it was history 101. He wanted to know his orders: the reason why he was here.

"Sir?" said Ethan in a calm yet slightly restless tone.

"Evolution," said Laskov. "As you know, thanks to dimensional technology, our brightest physicists have discovered another dimension—unparallel to ours. Do you know what this means for us, Ethan? There are different humans there; they are superior and filled with insurmountable potential. Yes, it is time to fuse our dimension with theirs. Despite the risks, doing so will create what we refer to as *dimensional synthesis*, allowing us to physically and mentally unify with the humans from the other side and transcend into one ultimate race...call it godhood."

"Synthesis is essential to our survival," said Kuralan. "And we want you to convince humanity that such an evolution is necessary."

Ethan felt as though his heart sank. It was true—humanity had just invented the most powerful and sophisticated technology in the world of physics. But did the tribunal truly want him to take advantage of every person who loved him for the young leader he'd become and betray them by ripping their freedom and lives away? Yes, humanity needed to evolve because the vast majority of humans were still the same blood-thirsty animals they were millennia ago. Yet shouldn't such a change be natural? Why, after all this time, would the tribunal want him to manipulate the laws of nature and play God with every living being in the universe?

"You are the voice of humanity, and I am your body," said Ethan. "But please forgive me for wanting to ask this one question: Why?"

"Think about it, Ethan," said Kuralan. "We have seen everything within the universe. It is the 54th century, and not once have we ever come into contact with any scientific evidence that a superior being or race exists in this dimension."

"Our imperfection is the one thing that has always held us back," said Laskov sadly. "We would have stood united and reached the stars ages before the sun destroyed Mother Earth if we were perfect. It is time for the final evolution."

"You are the only one who can do this, Ethan," said Kuralan.

"Me?" said Ethan, taken aback.

They were wrong, he thought; he needed to take more than one deep breath for this. What with the rumors he heard from scientists in the past, this union could cause the entire cosmos to collapse. If he was to truly carry out this order, he felt that it would not only eliminate freedom but possibly destroy all life in the process.

"Do not underestimate yourself, Commandant," said Tarak. "The people do not hear our voices. They see you and only you—a young man filled with life. We may be your voice, but humanity does not think of it this way. Like authors, we are an invisible hand, writing the law down. And you are our publicist: our Commander-in-Chief."

"You have brought humanity to a new age of existence, Ethan," said Kuralan blissfully. "To create an analogy using our ancestors' beliefs, Vorilian IV is the paradise that we've been searching for since cast out of Eden."

"And now that we have returned, so to speak," said Laskov, "we can close that old book and start writing a new one."

"One in which we are gods," said Tarak. "Forget about genetic equilibrium; we shall transcend in ways beyond anyone's comprehension."

"The people will always listen to you, Commandant," said Kuralan.

"It may seem impossible," began Laskov, "but in about twenty years— our physicists estimate—the dimensional gateway will be operational. Then together as a nucleus we shall transcend and evolve as we were always meant to."

Ethan gave them a faint nod, but it was a lie. He had always agreed with the tribunal. Yet, after hearing his orders, he became disgusted with them. They were old, pompous dictators who defied death; they had lived for so long that they could no longer recognize how precious life in its innate state was. And they were certainly no longer capable of experiencing empathy—the human condition that allowed people to understand one another. In their arrogance, they would destroy the tower of mankind, forgetting that its foundation was the very nature surrounding them.

"*Never!*" cried out Flint Cross, rising from the chair that the tribunal had allowed him to sit in. He gazed at the relics of mankind with fury. "I will *never* betray humanity!"

The tribunal disintegrated, and every object in the room started to wither away. Slowly, the military emblem crinkled and fell, flapping down with holes due to age; then it dissolved on the rusty floor. Afterwards, the lights flickered and blacked out. Flint stood alone in the derelict chamber. With the exception of hearing his heart pound madly, it was silent in the room. Not a second later, he heard someone clapping behind him. He turned around, looking at Ethan—a slightly younger version of himself.

"Now you understand why you're on this backwater planet," said Ethan.

"*No!*" bellowed Flint, his voice resonating.

He awoke on his comfortable bed in Soalace, screaming hysterically. Flint wept, filled with despair. Now he understood everything; he defied the tribunal for the sake of humanity. It didn't matter to him if his orders were from a god. He simply couldn't find it within himself to take away others freedom and play with their lives. And so he did the impossible: he ignited a revolution to overthrow the tribunal. The war that he'd ignited against the military—against the tribunal—was the final, ultimate war in the history of mankind.

And despite the outcome, the war wasn't over just yet. Oh no, thought Flint with the rage of a demon, they will all pay dearly for this treachery. Flint got off his bed, almost falling on the floor. He limped forward, briefly staggering, and strode out of his room. Flint ran into the Core, screaming and crying in an ululating tone.

"Pardashan!" he cried out, falling on the catwalk. "Pardashan!"

No one had ever seen Flint act this way. He'd been living in Soalace for a little over two years, and not once did the steamwalkers think he would ever break down like this. He'd always been known as *Heart of the Core*, the most dedicated man. Now he lay on the floor, screaming as though he'd lost his mind. Even his best friend, Gunthrel, approached in a wary manner, startled by his behavior.

Flint continuously cried out for Pardashan. But his lamenting voice was more than just an outcry; it was a voice filled with regret, hatred, release, and fear. If this were any other man who was pitifully weeping on the floor, Gunthrel would have instantly locked him up. However, the man before him was Flint Cross—*Heart of the Core*. And he was also his best friend. He felt he had no choice but to take him to Pardashan.

Within the next hour, Flint had managed to calm down from his sudden outburst. He sat outside the throne room with bloodshot eyes. After waiting a few minutes, Gunthrel approached and signaled him to enter. Feeling relieved, he entered Pardashan's chamber.

"Thank you for seeing—"

"I'm not doing this as a favor," interrupted Pardashan, sitting on his throne. "I only agreed because Gunthrel said you were screaming like a madman."

"I'm sorr—"

"Do not interrupt me, Heart of the Core," said Pardashan sternly. "Yes, I know all about your merry life down in the abyss. It's quite romantic and utopian. But I do not care what you do with your life. You chose to stay here for these two...three years, however long it's been. I really don't remember, nor do I give a damn."

"But—"

"If you interrupt me again," began Pardashan, his veins bulging, "I will throw you out of my city."

This time Flint remained silent.

"You once helped me during that accident down in the arena, and I in turn helped you. From that point on, we were even. I do not play favoritism. No one sees me anytime they want, not even Gunthrel. I am the ruler of Soalace. Everyone bows down to me and only me. Maybe you think you're some hero down in the Core, but you're only one of thousands keeping the city alive. So what if you finally lost your mind? So what if you

DARK SANITY

croak and die? We never needed you before, and we don't need you now. Is that understood, *Heart* of the Core?"

"No," replied Flint, clenching his teeth and walking closer to the steps of the throne. "No, it's not understood."

"Eh?" uttered Pardashan, surprised by his reaction.

"I am a man of freedom," said Flint. "In my world, there are no dictators or tribunals. I'm done with the abyss. From this day forward, I will no longer answer to anyone. And if I suffer or die because of this, so be it. I die a free man."

Pardashan laughed. "Were you down there for three years rehearsing to say this to me? Just where do you think you live, heaven?" He laughed again and then abruptly stopped, glaring at Flint as though he were ready to kill him. "Earth is dead. The sun is dead. There is nothing outside of these walls but death. Soalace is the only home left for humanity. And even this sacred sanctum is dwindling because of the lurkens that are gradually growing in numbers. It is only a matter of time before they invade my city and destroy the remnants of humanity."

"Is that what you want?" asked Flint. "I can help you."

"Help?" responded Pardashan, trying not to laugh.

"I remember the man I used to be," said Flint. "I remember my past and purpose. That's right, I remember everything. And I know of a beautiful world far away from this dead planet that would ensure your survival."

"You must be senile," said Pardashan. "Yes, you've finally lost it."

"You know very well that I'm not insane. The planet is called Vorilian IV, and I helped colonize it before the tribunal betrayed me."

Pardashan raised an eyebrow, a dubious yet curious expression on his face.

"They wanted to take away the soul of man and bury it," added Flint, his hands faintly trembling.

"And let me guess, you chose to fight for it?"

"You know the kind of man I am," said Flint. "You may hate it, but this is how I've been from the beginning. I have always defended freedom. The tribunal decided to take that away, and I chose to fight for it. My war isn't finished yet, Pardashan. I tried to start over, but my memories won't

let me." He curled his hands and continued, "Help me leave this chasm—
help me build a starship based on your steam and soal technology. If you
do this, I promise I'll guide all of you to paradise."

For the first time, Pardashan gulped heavily and stared at Flint with
hope. "Perhaps some of your words have truth," he said. "However, thousands of years have passed since we withdrew into the undertunnels. It
may be too late for us."

"It's never too late," said Flint. "We can help each other."

Pardashan grimly shook his head. "To build a steamship worthy of
taking us to the stars, we'd need a tremendous amount of soal and, most
importantly, titanium."

"It seems like you have more than enough soal to me."

"The problem lies with titanium," said Pardashan. "The foundation
of Soalace is from the superior metal. Since the lurkens have grown so
far in numbers throughout the undertunnels, we can no longer mine it to
expand."

"Then we fight for it."

"Are you insane?" shouted Pardashan.

"Many seem to think I am, but I'm not. I still have a few years left in
me, and if a sixty-two-year-old man is willing to fight for it, then I'm sure
your people will be up for the challenge too."

Pardashan stared at Flint with a crazed look. "In all my years, I have
never met a man so hell-bent on helping others. Why are you doing this?"

"The simple answer: I need you, and you need me," said Flint. "The
complicated answer: I don't like leaving something unfinished, especially
when the universe is at stake. The tribunal killed my beloved Hamarah,
took away my soul, and left me to rot on this dead planet. This is not acceptable. But more than anything, an old aboriginal friend of mine once
told me that there is one thing more important than love—one thing
that's above love."

"And what's that?"

"Duty," said Flint.

Pardashan exhaled, rose from his throne, and stepped down to where
Flint stood. What he'd been told was hard to believe. Yet something within

his gut told him that Flint was telling the truth. After all, what sane surface dweller would ever believe that a city exists deep within Earth? Surely the opposite could be said: what sane under-dweller would ever believe that a city could exist in outer space?

"A land where no lurkens can harm us ever again?"

"A land where no lurkens can harm us ever again," repeated Flint, nodding. "I will lead you and your people out of this hellhole and guide you all to paradise."

For the first time since they had met, they shook hands. This was the end of Pardashan's tyranny. Taking a leap of faith, he lifted Flint from the Core and gave him the rank he had in his previous life—Commandant. From this point on, they decided to work together to build a steam-powered starship that would guide them to Vorilian IV. Before doing so, however, they would first need an insurmountable supply of titanium, and that meant dealing with the lurkens.

CHAPTER TWELVE
THE WAY TO ALLAY

During the following weeks, Gunthrel taught Flint how to use the mechanical armor that he and his fellow guards had been using for decades. Flint eventually discovered that they never needed the life-support system—it was simply used for purifying air so they could breath as though they weren't wearing armor. In time, Flint fully understood the machinery in Soalace and was able to help build power suits and flamethrowers for the steamwalkers.

The flamethrower was, without a doubt, the most powerful weapon available when using a power suit. However, it would be equally dangerous for him and the guards of Soalace to use it should they come into contact with hordes of lurkens. Flint knew that they needed long-range weapons too. So he convinced Gunthrel to start manufacturing soal-based bullets, titanium rifles, pump-action shotguns, and double-action magnums. They weren't just getting ready for a fight—they were getting ready for a war.

As soon as two magnums were constructed in the engineering sector, Flint grabbed them and spun them with delight.

"Those are a bit too small for my power suit's hands," said Gunthrel.

"Don't worry, I made these for myself," replied Flint. "The shotguns and rifles will be perfect for you and the others."

With the exception of one shotgun and rifle, which were custom designed for Flint, every weapon made in the engineering sector was triple their size. The steamwalkers inside their power suits were thrilled to have these new weapons. Now they had ranged firepower and didn't have to worry about using flamethrowers unless a few lurkens would evade their shots. And with Flint teaching them how to use these guns, they became marksmen.

In time, Flint assisted Gunthrel and the others in constructing firearms instead of simply instructing them on how to craft them. It helped him keep his mind calm. And while he worked beside Gunthrel, he told him about his life back in Desonas, as well as his experience within the dreamtime. Gunthrel could hardly believe Flint's tales, especially about how he'd been betrayed, but he knew that Flint was telling the truth. Flint earned a great deal of respect while he helped the steamwalkers manufacture weapons and bullets.

After another week, Gunthrel made a special power suit for Flint. It was essentially the same design as the other armors, except it was tinted black.

"Do you like it?" he asked.

"I think it's incredible," said Flint. "But, to be honest, I wouldn't be much of a gunslinger if I wasn't on foot. Rest assured, there will come a time when I'll use it. But for now I'm going to play cowboy like my days in Desonas."

"Sounds fun," said Gunthrel.

Flint had been wearing overalls most of the time since working in the Core; however, now that he was a part of Soalace's military, he felt it was time to wear something that suited him. He took the tattered clothes he'd worn when he first arrived at Soalace and decided to ask Darla, one of the many tailors in the city, if she could help him patch up his clothes.

Fortunately for him, many people in Soalace admired him because of all the things they'd heard about him ranging from being *Heart of the Core* to the military mastermind against the lurkens. Darla was one of them.

He used a platform that brought him near Pardashan's throne room and found her shop nestled into the granite. Flint removed his old cowboy clothes from a knapsack while he entered her store.

"Why hello there, Flint," said Darla, an extremely pale lady with blonde hair.

"I'm sorry to bother you, Darla," he began, "but could you fix my clothes? They're a bit old and damaged."

"I could try," she said, taking a look at the clothing on her counter. "Here in Soalace we don't have too much leather. But I'll scrap up what I can find and will try to fix it, unless you don't mind me crafting a new one with other materials?"

"Do whatever you'd like," he said, unconcerned. "I'd just be happy to wear something like this again."

"All right, I'll do my best."

"Thanks a lot, Darla," he said. "I owe you one."

She waved a hand and replied, "With you getting ready to kill all those lurkens? No, you don't owe me anything."

Flint smiled, bowed, and exited her shop, returning to the dark abyss to continue crafting weapons. And within a few days, Darla visited him in the engineering sector, proudly presenting the refurbished cowboy garments to him.

"This is unbelievable," he said, astonished.

"I'm so happy you like it," she said. "Just make sure you kill plenty of those lurkens with it on."

"Believe me, I will."

He went straight to his bedchamber and put the clothing on. Afterwards, he attached his holster and bandolier, filling them with soal bullets. Lastly, he holstered his titanium magnums. He didn't have his hat, but this was good enough. Flint looked slightly older, and he could feel it in his bones. Though, just as he'd told Pardashan, he still had a few more years left in him.

Flint was ready to decimate the lurkens. He knew that this was the path he had to take in order to get his life back—the life that had been stolen from him by the tribunal. Flint thought to himself, setting things right and bringing justice to those who had abused the law, as well as the sanctity of life, was his final objective. But to do so, he had to first help the steamwalkers get back their territory where myriad rich veins of titanium lay. This was the only way to allay his soul, he eventually concluded—the way to getting his old life back; only then would he be able to return to the realm of space.

And so the time had finally come to embark on his journey into the molten chasm. He traveled to the dock where dozens of steamships were suspended, vibrating. Pardashan stood on the summit of the city, watching groups of armored men board their hovering vessels. Among the cadre of hunters was Flint who had Gunthrel and four others beside him. Once they were aboard, they turned and gazed up at their leader.

"Brothers," began Pardashan, "we've lived in Soalace since birth, as our ancestors before us. This great city has given us solace. And it has enriched our souls with soal. But the lurkens threaten our magnificent city. They swarm throughout the entire underworld and plague our once thriving undertunnels that stretch to every continent in the world. Just a few weeks ago we didn't have the courage to leave and take back what is rightfully ours. But one man changed our path. One man—a surface dweller, an under dweller, and an offworlder—changed our destiny. His name is Flint Cross. And today he fights beside us. Today we fight for the same freedom that he fights for! Today we begin the eradication of the lurkens!"

There were many cheers and praises.

When the army grew silent, Pardashan called out, "Flint, do you have any suggestions before we embark?"

"I am honored you seek my advice," said Flint. "I suggest we stay close to one another and in the light. When or if we enter dark tunnels where there is no light, use the flares in your armored suits. Shoot every lurken with your ranged weapons unless they manage to get within melee range, which I *think* would be a good time to use your flamethrowers."

Some of the men laughed, sensing humor from him.

"That is all," added Flint.

"Then it is time," said Pardashan.

He stepped into his mechanical power suit, which attached to his skin and sealed once he sat inside, and then stomped onto a steamship. The militia cheered as he activated his steamship, being the first to leave Soalace's dock. Shortly after, the army followed him. Earth's chasm lit up as though the sun was rising inside while the steamships glided through the undertunnels. It was the first time in centuries since the army of Soalace had gathered together like this.

Flint had never been a part of their underground expeditions; he was astounded and truly inspired by the sight of so many ships united. Even though this hadn't originally been his war, it reminded him of the insurrection he ignited in space decades ago, and it made him yearn to leave even more.

"One step at a time," he whispered to himself, taking a deep breath.

It wasn't long until he and the army passed Soalace's boundaries. The colorful lava lamps were no longer around. Now they had to rely on the light coming from their steamships, guns, and armor. They still had decent vision, but it was disturbing for most of them to enter places in the undertunnels that had no light since it was a reminder that the lurkens had taken over these areas and drained the energy inside. Flint spotted slime dripping along the granite, causing him to grimace.

Suddenly, an ear-piercing chant of hisses and growls filled the cavernous undertunnels. It was as though thousands of lurkens had been waiting for them, hiding within the shadows. They pounced toward the steamships from the jagged ceiling and walls. Several armored men winced; though most of them aimed their rifles and fired.

"They're everywhere!" bellowed Gunthrel, shooting at the creatures.

"All the better," said Flint, blowing them away with his magnums.

Flint reloaded and continuously blasted every lurken he saw with one hundred percent accuracy, as though he were an automaton. He was even more accurate than the armored men, and they had sensors and extra lighting built into their mechanical suits to help. Flint holstered one of his magnums, steering the steamship while shooting lurkens with his other gun.

A few lurkens boarded the hovering vessels. The armored men, however, burned them to ashes with their flamethrowers. Innumerable flickers went off as fire and bullets dispersed. The steam produced by the vessels created a dense haze. Fortunately for Flint and his comrades, by the time it clouded their vision, the remaining lurkens withdrew. Once the hisses and growls faded, the militia cheered.

"This is only the beginning," said Pardashan. "Be proud, but do not let this small victory blind you with arrogance. Stay alert."

"What next?" asked Gunthrel.

"The molten chasm is upon us," said Pardashan. "I think it's time for us to split into two groups."

"Are you sure?" asked Flint.

"Trust me, Flint," said Pardashan. "I know these undertunnels better than anyone. When we reach the molten chasm the path will become much more narrower, making it difficult to fly all of these steamships through."

"Which groups will stay, my Lord?" asked one of the steamwalkers.

"Those who are above shall follow me," said Pardashan. "The rest of you who are lower will land on the ridges and enter the undertunnels on foot."

"A ground and air assault?" said Flint. "I like it."

"Flint," called out Pardashan. "You shall be the one to lead the ground force. As always, be careful."

Flint nodded.

"Let's move out!" commanded Pardashan.

The vessels hovering near the ceiling continued to fly ahead. In the meantime, Flint and his army descended toward the lower ridges. Once they landed and docked their steamships by the jutting cliffs, they disembarked and stomped onto the cracked ground. Most of them started using their flamethrowers, burning away the dense cocoons and oozy slime that clung along the walls.

Moments like this made Flint wish he were using the power suit Gunthrel had made for him. He nevertheless loved being free, relying on his own body. This time he had his shotgun out. It wasn't long before he and his men heard hisses again. The steamwalkers fired into the darkness using their heavy rifles. Fortunately for Flint, the armored men were so tall that he didn't have to worry about them accidently shooting him. He also fired, manually pumping his shotgun while each shell dispersed into the slimy lurkens.

Despite how many lurkens were being blown away, dozens upon dozens of them kept coming out from the shadows. At times Gunthrel and his fellow steamwalkers had to use their flamethrowers when the fiends got closer than they wanted them to be. Flint eventually ran out of shotgun shells and lifted his rifle whose sling was around his chest. With his rifle he was able to shoot down many more lurkens.

Flint and his militia pressed on, sporadically firing at the few beasts that mindlessly approached. They eventually passed the molten chasm and entered a dark tunnel on the right, reaching an ancient subway. In fact, after walking through the tunnel for a mile, Flint saw a rundown steam train.

"I didn't know you use trains," said Flint.

"*Used*," said Gunthrel. "When the lurkens spread, they ruined most of the tracks with their slime. Then they took over the subway system our ancestors had built."

"We've got company!" shouted one of the steamwalkers, firing his rifle.

Hundreds of lurkens sprang out from the shattered windows and unsealed doors of the decrepit train. The militia launched flares and fire at the fiends. Flint climbed to the top of the train and shot them from high ground; the flares made it much easier for him to see. He jumped from car to car, firing his magnums. One of the fiends approached him from behind, ready to bite his neck. Gunthrel, however, spotted the creature and shot it down.

"Watch your back!"

"I'll try," he said to Gunthrel, startled. "Thanks."

Flint turned back to the front, reloaded, and continued to jump from car to car. He and his army pressed on, letting their flares guide them.

"Damn, this train is long," said Flint to himself. He eventually noticed massive amounts of slime on the next car and cursed under his breath.

Flint jumped down, rolled to the side, and shot at the train. "These bastards make everything their home."

"They have no conscience," said Gunthrel.

Flint and Gunthrel blasted the remaining lurkens side by side while the rest of the army spread apart, launching more flares. They eventually reached a part of the darkened tunnel that had collapsed. They had no choice but to climb atop the train. Flint decided to go inside. It was spacious, and he was excited to explore it; however, he quickly became disinterested due to the cocoons inside, so he exited and joined his comrades above.

"If only we could use one of these trains to travel faster," said Flint.

"It would be safe and efficient if all the lurkens were gone," said Gunthrel. "Sadly, that is not the case. But perhaps one day."

Flint nodded, liking that idea.

Once they passed the area of the tunnel that had collapsed, they jumped back down. The steamwalkers then launched another set of flares and cautiously searched the tunnel. More hisses and growls filled their ears. They spotted some of the lurkens hiding in the corners and fired at them. A huge sinkhole lay in the center area where they were fighting. Flint gasped at the sight of it. Just when he thought he'd reached the deepest region in Earth, there was still yet another chasm.

Flint reloaded his magnums and continued to blast every lurken in sight. He was starting to feel drained but pressed on. The slimy fiends were relentless. They wouldn't stop coming, and they showed little fear. Luckily for Flint and his army, the lurkens weren't too smart.

"Will they ever retreat?" asked one of the steamwalkers.

"They don't know the meaning of retreat," said Gunthrel.

"Too bad," said Flint, blasting them with ease. "I'll do this all day if I must. I won't stop until they're gone, or until I'm dead."

Gunthrel laughed and replied, "That won't happen."

"Why is that?" asked Flint, still firing.

"Because you're the Heart of the Core."

Flint smirked. "You always know how to motivate someone," he said.

"It's a gift," said Gunthrel, blowing a creature's face off with his bulky shotgun. "Watch out for the sinkhole!"

"I spotted it already," said Flint.

The others, who didn't know yet, observed and noticed the sinkhole. They launched more flares, this time toward the sides so they wouldn't fall into the central chasm. For the most part, they were easily defeating the lurkens with their ranged weapons. Only a few armored men were wounded due to the acid that a few fiends had managed to spew on them before getting burned to ashes.

After passing the abysmal sinkhole, they left the subway in the undertunnels and walked over to a precipice. As soon as Flint and the others approached the cliff, they spotted the second army of men who were on their steamships. Pardashan flew his vessel down to where Flint and Gunthrel stood.

"Excellent work," said Pardashan.

"Thank you, my Lord," said Gunthrel.

"Where to next?" asked Flint.

"Follow the ridges," said Pardashan. "You may need to climb a little, but there should be another tunnel ahead."

Flint and the other steamwalkers complied, following the narrow trail along the ridges of the dark chasm. And, as Pardashan had assumed, they had to climb since parts of the trail were severely damaged. When they started to climb, however, they heard more hisses. Another horde of lurkens pounced out from various holes nestled into the jagged walls of granite and scuttled toward the steamwalkers.

"Obliterate them!" commanded Pardashan.

The army on the steamships aimed their rifles and fired at the lurkens. Some of the men climbing held on to tiny ledges while shooting with their other hand. Flint was among them, using his magnum. He blasted six lurkens with one gun, holstered it, and continued to climb. Shortly after, he used his other hand to hold on to the granite, pulled out his second magnum, and shot down another six fiends.

"I'm on a roll," he said, grinning.

"How many did you get in total?" inquired Gunthrel. "A hundred, two hundred, or maybe three?"

"Shit, I don't know," said Flint, climbing beside him.

"Ah," uttered Gunthrel with amusement. "Well, you'd know if you used the power suit I made for you."

Flint chuckled, reaching a place to stand. "How many did you get?" he asked.

"Six hundred and fifty-one."

Just as Flint whistled, another horde of lurkens pounced out of the tunnel ahead. Gunthrel used his flamethrower, setting them on fire. The creatures screeched and fell.

"Six hundred and fifty-nine."

"Yeah, yeah," said Flint, rolling his eyes. "Keep bragging."

Gunthrel laughed and continued to shoot the remaining creatures with Flint. By the time the others reached the top, the lurkens in the area were dead. This time Pardashan and his forces docked their steamships by the cliff where Flint's militia stood and joined them as one army.

"We shall rest here for the remainder of the day," said Pardashan. "Provisions are on our vessels. Take them only when needed. Gunthrel, assign your best men to form three squadrons to patrol the perimeter in shifts while the others rest."

Gunthrel obeyed, beginning to gather a watch group.

In the meantime, Pardashan went on, "We have finally begun to taste victory! Get some rest, eat when hungry, and remain steadfast!"

The militia listened to Pardashan. The three squadrons Gunthrel had formed took turns patrolling the areas. They took lamps from the ships and placed them around the perimeter and occasionally launched flares farther away to make sure no lurkens were prowling about. But no creatures attacked them. This was a miracle to Flint and the steamwalkers. They were expecting multiple surprise attacks, and yet they had several hours to recuperate.

On the following day, they shut off their lamps and moved out. Pardashan led the army into the tunnel ahead. Upon entering the next section of the undertunnels, they noticed that it was completely covered in slime. They couldn't even see the walls. Only parts of the ground hinted a base of granite since it was jagged.

Flint stared at the sight and gulped heavily. The slime was so thick that it made him feel as if he were stepping into the nasal passage of a gargantuan beast. But he knew that wasn't the case, it simply appeared that way.

"Do not be frightened," said Pardashan. "This is telling us that we're getting closer to the second city."

"How much titanium is in there?" asked Flint.

"Enough to build a thousand vessels," said Pardashan. "But beware, Flint, the old city is where the sentient lurkens dwell. And I assure you, they will not give up their territory without a fight. Nonetheless we shall prevail. Men, ignite the undertunnels!"

Over the next few days, the army blew fire on the thick slime until they could see their precious granite. Afterwards, they pressed forward and repeated Pardashan's strategy. As they drew deeper and closer to the ancient kingdom, lurkens emerged again to defend their lair. The steamwalkers, unyielding, obliterated the horde.

Flint and his comrades experienced several battles each day. Fortunately for them, hardly any men were lost. They rested when needed and then continued their expedition. Flint thought the city was only a few days away based on what Pardashan had said before. On the contrary, it ended up being more than a week's worth of traveling through the undertunnels. He wondered to himself, perhaps it was only a few days away if they'd been using the train he had found before? Nevertheless, he held himself together and fought with as much passion and determination as the steamwalkers.

And at long last, after two weeks' time had passed, they reached a cavernous tunnel that showed them the entrance to a primordial city. The steamwalkers launched another set of flares, approaching with caution.

"This is it," said Pardashan, "the elder kingdom of Allay." He gazed up at the colossal gates with an emotional expression and added in a frail whisper, "You shall finally be at peace, Clarienus." His face soon returned to its usual stern look. "Bring out the crates. We need all of the remaining ammunition, flares, and lamps at our disposal."

The steamwalkers who had crates attached to their armored backs swiftly spread out and laid the crates down. Others burned the slime that surrounded the city's entrance. As they did so, however, an ear-piercing chorus of hisses and growls rang behind the oozy, stony walls. The militia reloaded with haste and saw the largest horde of lurkens arise from the gates. Flint felt distraught for the first time since the war had begun. Not wavering, he took out his rifle and targeted the fiends.

"This is the alpha and omega of our war!" shouted Pardashan. "We stand together in the chasm of death, and we shall give it life once more!"

The steamwalkers cheered and fired at the swarming lurkens who scuttled toward them with blind rage. Myriad flashes of light flickered as guns went off. Screeches and screams filled the cavernous lair. Flint and Gunthrel, as usual, fought side by side. This time Pardashan joined them. Only a few of them died. The horde of lurkens fell, but then another swarm emerged.

"Is there no end to them?" asked one of the steamwalkers.

"They will keep coming!" replied Pardashan. "Nevertheless, we will keep pushing until they either become extinct or withdraw into the deeper regions of the undertunnels!"

One of the fiends suddenly crept up from Pardashan's flank and spewed acid on him. He blasted the lurken with a shotgun shell and gasped in great pain as parts of his gauntlet and skin melted.

"My Lord!" cried out Gunthrel.

He, Flint, and several others rushed to aid their leader.

"I'm still alive," said Pardashan, rasping through his tinted helmet. "Press on and show these beasts no mercy!"

Gunthrel roared and charged forward, ramming himself into one of the stony gates. The strength of his attack caused a part of the gate to crack. Others followed his spontaneous tactic, charging toward the gates. They repeatedly slammed their armored fists into the walls until the entrance collapsed.

The army launched their remaining flares and infiltrated the infested city. Most of them fired from long range while others blew flame on the slimy walls and ceiling, disgusted by the sight of slime. The raging inferno soon spread, causing cocoons and several hidden lurkens to catch fire. In due time, the entire city was lit up like a furnace.

Flint ran along one of the many bridges and stopped at its crest, firing at several lurkens that were climbing from the sides. While shooting, he recalled his experience in Panzo Mine. He gawked at the architecture and had a terrible feeling that Brock and Bas had probably begun to accidently dig into this region. There were no other areas in the undertunnels that had the same architecture as this within Panzo Mine. And he remembered seeing veins of titanium. Flint felt queasy and shook his head, trying to stay focused. He reloaded his magnums and continued to fire.

The hisses and growls soon faded. Pardashan and his men cheered while they walked across the bridges.

"I doubt any of the platforms still work," said Pardashan. "The city may have water, but it has fallen asleep without soal. It is time to climb down to the Core and awaken our long lost kingdom."

With the exception of Flint, the steamwalkers jammed their fists into the granite and climbed down. Gunthrel, however, approached him and playfully cleared his throat.

"Care to join me?"

"I would be delighted," said Flint.

He climbed onto the armored back of Gunthrel who then descended to the abyss. Only a few lurkens attempted to attack them. Flint swiftly blew them away using one of his magnums while hanging on Gunthrel's pauldron. They soon saw the ground and leaped off the old wall, landing on slimy grating. Oddly, this area wasn't as infested with slime as the other areas. The militia nevertheless remained vigilant, entering the inactive Core.

Flint gazed at the chamber in awe. Without a doubt, it was twice the size of the Core in Soalace, and it was the biggest lair he'd ever entered in the undertunnels. The silence inside the chamber gave him a creepy chill.

"I have a bad feeling about this," he said.

"Relax," said Gunthrel. "It seems safe here."

The lights embedded in the jagged walls abruptly dimmed on, and steam filled the once lifeless chamber. Many of the militia stepped back, hearing a deafening screech. At that exact moment, a pale green-skinned humanoid woman emerged from a plinth. She raised her hands while hissing and thousands of slimy lurkens peeked out of holes in the granite. The armored men lost their morale, realizing how vastly outnumbered they were.

Pointing his magnum at the sentient lurken, Flint shouted, "Draw them away or I'll put a bullet of soal in your skull!"

"Put your weapon down!" exclaimed Pardashan, removing his armor.

"What?" replied Flint, startled.

"She's my sister," said Pardashan.

Flint felt his heart sink. His eyes widened in disbelief, utterly baffled. He slowly lowered his weapon, taking a deep breath.

"I know you can hear me, Clarienus," called out Pardashan. He dropped his weapon and cautiously walked over to the pale green woman. "It's me, your elder brother. We didn't come to harm you."

Clarienus stooped to a hunch while she sniffed Pardashan, faintly growling. The hordes of lurkens stayed slightly hidden but still hissed at the remaining army.

"Can someone please explain what the hell is going on?"

"Flint," began Pardashan, "I want you to keep your mouth shut until I resolve this." He stared at his sister and continued, "You still remember me, don't you? We are not here to harm you, Clarienus."

Gazing upon him with teary eyes, she growled ferociously.

Pardashan went on, "I know you feel I've abandoned you, but I am back." He showed his frail palms, surrendering. "Please—"

She abruptly swung one of her claw-shaped hands against Pardashan's face, gashing his left cheek deeply. Flint instantaneously lifted his magnum. Gunthrel, however, lowered Flint's hand, shaking his head at him.

"We are not here to harm you," said Pardashan, kneeling. "Please believe in me as you always have and command the lurkens to leave this place."

Clarienus stared at her pitiful brother, crying and roaring in anguish. Shortly after, she hissed and waved her arms as though she were performing a ritual. Little by little, the lurkens jittered back into the holes. Their sadistic growls faded, and then they were gone.

"Now!" yelled Pardashan.

Gunthrel targeted Clarienus and shot a tranquilizer dart into her neck. She screeched in pain, staggered, and fell to the slimy floor, unconscious. Pardashan gently lifted his sister and rejoined his army. Not a moment later, the steamwalkers burned whatever slime remained on the steam engines and grating.

Flint, meanwhile, gazed at the armored men with a crazed look. "Can someone please explain what the hell this is all about?"

"Do you think soal always existed?" said Pardashan. "Soal was once no different than the metamorphic rocks deep within Earth." He gently laid his sister down and put his damaged suit of armor back on. "When our ancestors abandoned the surface and created the undertunnels, they knew that they'd need a new source of power to live. And in most cases with science, to get what you want, you must play with fire."

Flint began, "Are you insinuating that the first time you created soal, it was—"

"Poisonous," finished Pardashan. "It mutated our ancestors. Though most of us remained sentient, others lost their humanity and rapidly turned into lurkens. Not all of them, however, are monsters."

"Like your sister?"

Pardashan nodded, lifting Clarienus and placing her over his shoulder. "One day, in our ignorance, toxic soal was produced in this city," he said. "We had to evacuate. Being the ruler of this city, my sister felt that it was her, as you put it, *duty*, to stay until her people evacuated. She was foolish—altruistic like you. I believed she'd leave; however, she...she never did."

"So, you're going to take her back to Soalace?" assumed Flint, staring at Clarienus with a crazy look on his face. "And why didn't you tell me any of this before?"

"This isn't your war, Flint Cross," said Pardashan. "While you may have chosen to stay and help us, you entered a realm that you're mostly ignorant of. And I'm positive that we'll be just as ignorant when we reach yours."

"My realm," muttered Flint, almost forgetting about the sole reason he'd been helping the steamwalkers. "Yes, I suppose you're right."

"But don't think for a second that I'll be as selfless as you," said Pardashan. "The war you started is yours alone. My people will be led to paradise, as you promised. You'll get what you want—returning to space. From then on, you are on your own."

"So, you're really going to do it?"

"What's this?" replied Pardashan, shaking his head. "You've been here for three years and still haven't realized that I honor my covenants?"

Flint barely understood what was going on, especially after learning that the mutants he'd been killing were once human. Upon realizing Pardashan was a man of his word, however, he let everything go. Instead he gave a faint nod, grinning. Pardashan was as much an honorable man as he. Flint became full of life. This was, without a doubt, the path to regain his freedom. He'd helped fight a war that was never his just to taste freedom again, and now he was ready to face his own war.

CHAPTER THIRTEEN
HELL'S FAREWELL

One week later, Flint and the remaining army returned to Soalace. They celebrated their greatest victory and started burning away the slim and ooze that still lingered in the undertunnels leading to Allay. Once they finished, they mined the titanium in the abandoned city and brought it over to Soalace using their steamships.

Flint, in the meantime, created a blueprint of a steam-powered starship. Since he'd been able to remember more of his past life, other things came naturally to him—such as designs of dimensional weaponry. And since he'd learned of soal, it was easier for him to help Pardashan and his people build a hybrid state-of-the-art military vessel that combined their soal and steam engine machinery with dimensional technology.

Explaining such concepts to the scientists and engineers of Soalace came so naturally to him that it actually made him feel uneasy. He was a military mastermind in his past life, not an engineer or scientist. How did he understand such intricate technology? Using it was one thing, but knowing how to create it? This greatly disturbed him, but he placed these questions on hold for now and continued teaching the steamwalkers how to build such a technologically advanced craft.

Whenever they made significant progress, Flint would travel to Pardashan's throne room to inform him. The only thing that worried him each time he went there was Clarienus who lay beside the throne like a pet. Flint had no idea why Pardashan allowed her to live, much less roam around free. He wondered to himself, what if she wasn't as sentient as Pardashan claimed? What if she'd cry out to the lurkens again and bring them here? Despite his distress, he dared not share his concerns with Pardashan.

When it came to life in Soalace, Flint kept his opinions and thoughts to himself. He was happy enough to know that Pardashan was willing to let him return to his previous life. Since the great ruler of Soalace had finally accepted him and no longer acted like a dictator, he didn't want to test his patience or munificence. And he especially didn't want to get involved in Pardashan's personal affairs, even if he thought keeping Clarienus here was insane. He simply told him about the ship's progress.

Several months passed. The engineers and scientists of Soalace worked endlessly to build the soal-fueled starship. They were constructing it where the arena once stood. Given that it had been ruined during the lurken incident three years ago, Pardashan allowed them to demolish the arena and use it as an engineering chamber to construct the vessel. The only difference was that they expanded the chamber, making it bigger than the Core, which was perfect for building a starship.

And finally, after another year of endless labor, the vessel was complete. Flint went to Pardashan's chamber to inform him of the incredible news. As usual, Clarienus lay beside the throne. Flint approached and bowed at Pardashan.

"You're starting to look your age, Flint," said Pardashan. "Even with that fancy attire of yours, I can see it in your face."

"The ship is complete," said Flint, ignoring the comment about his wrinkles.

"Is it?" he replied skeptically.

"Pardashan, this is the greatest achievement in the history of your people. I stare at it every day in awe, and the time has finally come for us to leave."

"It's been about two years since you started constructing it," said Pardashan, drumming his fingers on the arms of his throne. "Even though I have let you wonder around to make that toy of yours, I've changed my mind about leaving."

"*What?*"

"You're old, Flint, but you're not deaf," scowled Pardashan. "You heard me. If you want to leave, that is your choice. I'm still keeping my end of the bargain by letting you go. However, if I want to stay here, it is my decision."

"But why?" asked Flint. "I don't understand."

"You don't understand because this was never your home," said Pardashan. "You want to leave because your soul cries out every day for freedom—the chance to return to your home and continue your life. Can't you see? I am already free; I am already home."

"We put so much effort into the size of the ship," said Flint fraily. "Even the windows have been strengthened to withstand the heat and glare of the sun."

"I don't care," grumbled Pardashan.

"Oh, I see..."

He strangely felt broken. Just a few seconds ago, he was excited to leave the underground chasm he'd been living in for the past four years. Yet when it was time for him to finally leave, he felt as though someone betrayed him again. But he knew the real reason why he suddenly felt so miserable, and it was because departing would mean leaving behind the only true friends he had. Life was funny, he thought. One moment the steamwalkers were trying to kill him and the next, they were good friends.

"Leave when you want," said Pardashan.

"You don't even want to see the ship?"

"My goodness," sighed Pardashan. "You're more sentimental than a woman. How do you expect to defeat such a powerful enemy who rules space? With your sappy semantics?"

"I just wanted you to see the ship."

Pardashan laughed. "Fine," he said. "Come now, Clarienus. Let us see this steamship that the old offworlder has created."

Clarienus anxiously hopped up and trotted in a hunched manner behind Pardashan who leisurely stepped down his throne, following Flint. The trio traveled to the other side of the city and entered a platform, descending into the depths of the abyss. When the door opened, Flint exited and guided his company through what was once the dungeon; now a laboratory lay before them. The trio eventually reached a door leading to the engineering chamber, at which point Flint clicked a console to open it.

Pardashan was tapping his feet, waiting for the door to open so he could see the starship and be done with Flint's sappy behavior. The door finally unsealed, and Pardashan entered with his sister. When he saw what stood before him, however, he no longer felt the need to tap his feet or rush back to his throne. Flint saw his expression and smiled, knowing the sight of the starship impressed him.

Standing before them was a gargantuan spacecraft with the same design as Soalace. It had a glittery hull made of titanium. The windows were thick and tinted black. The weapons along the side of its wings were massive cannons, and at each of its corners stood cylinder-shaped pillars from which steam billowed. The vessel also had interstellar propulsion engines by its aft.

"This isn't a steamship," said Pardashan. "It's a damn city."

Flint was the one who laughed this time. "And we have a Core that's just as beautiful as the one here," he said.

"Did you name it?" asked Pardashan, approaching the ship and touching its frame.

"With your permission, I'd like to name her Soalace II."

"Just call her Soalace," said Pardashan. "After all, she was built in my city and is an extension of its soul."

"Soalace it is," said Flint.

Pardashan began, "Well then—"

An alarm suddenly went off. It was a deafening sound Flint had never heard before. At first he thought it was coming from his starship, but then he realized that the recessed lights on the ceiling here were flashing.

"What the hell is that sound?" asked Flint, covering his ears.

"Impossible," said Pardashan. "That siren was only used once a decade ago. It was made to be used whenever a massive invasion of lurkens would swarm into our city."

"I knew it," said Flint, glaring at Clarienus.

She screeched, dropped to the metal floor, and cried hysterically while she held her brother's leg.

"Don't act out of ignorance, Flint," said Pardashan. "You didn't think my sister was the only sentient mutant in the world, did you? There are millions more of them, and most of them like what they've become."

"Millions?" said Flint, his mouth agape. "And you want to stay?"

"How was I supposed to know that they'd invade my city?" said Pardashan. "My sister controlled the ones in this region. It's possible that when she called off the lurkens they fled to another sentient mutant who seized control of them."

"It doesn't matter anymore," said Flint. "We need to leave—now!"

"We're not going anywhere without a fight," said Pardashan. "If you want to wait, you wait. But I don't run from anyone, especially mindless mutants."

Just then, Gunthrel entered the chamber. "My Lord!" he called out, running to them.

"I know what's happening," replied Pardashan snappily. "Clarienus, be a good sister and stay here." He left the engineering chamber and went on, "We need to join the others and destroy those wretched fiends once and for all."

The trio made their way to the kingdom's armory, stocking up on weapons and bullets. Flint, as usual, holstered his magnums. Shortly after Pardashan was in his suit of armor, they traveled to the docks. When the door opened, they heard numerous guns going off, as well as monstrous hisses and growls. Flint reached the bridge with the others, firing at the fiendish creatures.

The amount of lurkens scuttling into the city was almost unbelievable to Flint. He stood on the bridge, dismayed. He'd never seen so many lurkens together. Whoever was controlling them clearly wanted to take over the undertunnels of Australia. But this wasn't his war, and he wasn't ready to die just yet.

"Pardashan!" called out Flint. "You know what's needed to be done. Don't let your pride be the death of your brethren."

"I don't run from anything!" bellowed Pardashan.

Flint cursed under his breath while he fought alongside his armored friends. He knew that Pardashan wasn't going to listen to reason. Pardashan was too stubborn and proud to leave at a time like this. And so it was left to him to do what was wise. He left the docks and made his way back down to where the hybrid starship was located. Upon reaching the chamber, he approached his fretful team of scientists and engineers.

"Activate the ship," he said sternly. "I need all of you to man your posts, and I also want you to alert the citizens of Soalace to evacuate here."

The scientists and engineers complied, activating the spacecraft. Flint, meanwhile, exited the chamber and ran to the elevator platform, using it to return to the docks so he could continue helping his comrades. He reloaded his magnums, firing the moment the door opened. There were so many lurkens that some of them were prowling along the bridges and passageways.

Advancing to the docks, Flint heard a noisy siren indicating an evacuation. That instant, one of the many scientists spoke through the city's amplified loudspeakers:

"If you can hear me," began the scientist, "it is imperative you evacuate to the Soalace spacecraft immediately. I repeat: it is imperative that you evacuate to the Soalace spacecraft immediately!"

Flint rejoined Gunthrel and Pardashan, using his rifle to shoot down as many lurkens as he could before needing to reload. He noticed a great number of armored men on the floor with half their bodies melted due to the lurkens' acid. Flint grimaced, feeling enraged by this sudden and absurd incursion, killing every creature in his sight. In the meantime, the scientist repeated her message, and the siren continuously rang.

"If we survive this," began Pardashan, "I'm going to kill you, Flint."

"Say what you want, and do what you have to do," said Flint. "But no matter where I go, the vow I made years ago remains the same: to help people."

"I've always admired you, Flint," said Gunthrel, blasting lurkens with his rifle.

"There's nothing to admire about a man who's insane," said Pardashan. "Mark my words, Flint Cross, your sentimentality will be your downfall."

"If that's true, so be it," replied Flint. He reloaded his rifle and continued to fire. "It's the one thing that makes me remember that I'm human. As long as I can feel—as long as I can hear the cries of others, I'm still human."

"Humph," uttered Pardashan, blowing lurkens away with his shotgun. "I suppose that is important if you want to defy that tribunal of yours. But you won't be able to succeed alone."

Flint tilted his head. "Are you insinuating—"

"Insinuating, insinuating, insinuating," repeated Pardashan. "This promised land of yours better be worth it."

"Trust me, it is," said Flint.

"Then what are we waiting for?" said Gunthrel.

Pardashan entered a code into his power suit, alerting his armored comrades fighting beside him to evacuate.

"Let's go!" he said.

Gunthrel and several other steamwalkers held the line while the majority escaped. Flint ran beside Pardashan, shooting lurkens climbing up the walls. At that exact moment, two fiends leaped onto Pardashan from the ceiling. He grabbed one, blasting its face apart with his shotgun. The other jumped away, spewing acid on his breastplate. Flint shot the mutant off the bridge and then held Pardashan whose armor and chest melted.

"Pardashan!" exclaimed Flint.

"My sister," rasped Pardashan. "Don't harm her." Flint looked as pale as Pardashan who stammered in a croaking tone, "I lied to Gunthrel. You know that, right? The truth is that I have always envied..."

Pardashan stopped speaking, and the twinkle in his eyes waned while his chest continued to melt. Flint shook his head and cried out in rage.

Gunthrel and a few others realized what had happened. They became frantic, roaring at the sight of their leader's demise. It was so chaotic, however, that not many of them saw what had become of Pardashan. Even those who mourned his death had to leave or else they'd be killed too.

Gunthrel stared at Pardashan's corpse in disbelief; yet he had no choice but to accept his master's fate and escape. In the meantime, Flint and the steamwalkers continued to clear a path to the platform. Upon reaching it, they sealed the door and descended deep into the abyss. The fiendish hisses and growls faded. Silence fell for a moment, punctured by a lament from the men in armor.

Flint had teary eyes, trying to hold himself together as the platform descended. He simply listened to the armored men who wept. Hearing them cry shook him up. He'd never heard them cry before. Since his time here in Soalace, he wondered whether they were capable of empathy. When he heard the steamwalkers' lament, it made him realize that even though they'd mutated and evolved living underground for thousands of years, they were still human.

The platform finally reached the bottom, and its door unsealed. Flint, Gunthrel, and the others quickly made their way through the laboratory. Although they felt safe being so far down, they knew that the lurkens could probably find their way here. Making haste, they reached the chamber of the starship. Seeing the gargantuan vessel burst with life and steam made them feel relieved. A door on the front of the ship swayed open, and a ramp lowered as they approached. The moment Flint and his companions boarded the vessel, the spacecraft sealed.

Just then, the thick pipes around the outer chamber sizzled and melted. Countless lurkens crawled out of them, scuttling toward the steam-powered craft. Fortunately for the steamwalkers, the ramp of their ship had already lifted.

Flint, however, didn't want to risk their acid damaging the hull. He dashed through the spacecraft filled with rotating cogs, pulsing lights, steamy pipes, spooled wires, glittery conduits, and grating that vibrated due to the engines' hum. Most of the people he passed were terrified. Flint wanted to comfort them yet had no time to do so. Keeping his pace, he promptly reached the control room. Though several scientists and engineers were stationed here, they didn't know how to fully operate the starship. The only one who was a master of its design was Flint.

"Are you ready to leave this hellhole?" he asked.

Even though calling their home a hellhole was an insult to them, they nonetheless nodded anxiously, ready to go anywhere as long as the lurkens wouldn't be there. Flint took a seat by the central chair, placing his fingers above a kiosk embedded in the slanted dashboard. A translucent interface in the form of a web appeared before him. Lifting his hands, the web spread, displaying numerous possible actions available to him. He stared at the interface of his vessel for a moment and then pressed multiple semi-transparent buttons.

Within seconds the vessel's force field activated; it pulsed outward, knocking the lurkens on its hull down to the ground. At that precise moment, Flint ignited the propulsions, decimating the lurkens via the surge of fire that blasted out. The scientists and engineers clapped while Flint cautiously ascended the ship. His cannons automatically aimed at the remaining lurkens climbing the walls of the outer chamber, disintegrating them with dimensional beams, which were able to be fired after absorbing tremendous energy from the city of Soalace.

Flint hoped to find a new independent power source if he'd be able to leave Earth, but for the time being he tried to remain focused on the present situation. The city of Soalace flickered as dimensional beams continued to blast the lurkens. While flying the starship up, he manually aimed the cannons at the ceiling, absorbed the remaining energy from the city, and released a surge of beams into the granite. The cavernous ceiling didn't crumble, it simply disintegrated what with the power of the dimensional beams.

"Activate the polarized shield," commanded Flint.

One of the engineers listened, clicking a translucent button beside her. Doing so extended the titanium hull, sealing its windows. Once sealed, the hull merged with the windows, allowing the passengers to see as if it were night outside the ship—this allowed minimal light or radiation filtering through the windows, especially since all of them, including Flint, were fatally sensitive to sunlight after living underground for so long.

Taking a deep breath, Flint increased the speed of the starship and slowly ascended it out of the undertunnels. For the first time in four years, Flint could see the surface again. He smiled as he piloted the vessel, feeling relieved. The others rose from their gray enamel seats, staring at the desolate land in awe. The sun beamed hard on them. With the polarized technology activated, however, it didn't harm them. The steamwalkers stared at the black-spotted sun with expressions of incredulity and hope.

"I can't believe it," said Gunthrel, entering the control room.

"Believe it," replied Flint.

"If only Pardashan could see this," said Gunthrel despondently.

"Gunthrel," called out Flint, trying not to sound depressed. "Pardashan's last wish was to make sure his sister was protected. I need you to ensure her safety. Take her to Pardashan's room and keep her there."

"All right," replied Gunthrel. "But what happens now?"

"I have some unfinished business in Desonas before we leave this godforsaken world," he said, his brow creasing. "Feel free to join me after you see Clarienus to her quarters."

"Sounds good," said Gunthrel, walking away.

Flint, meanwhile, clicked a panel displaying an atlas of the world. An area in Queensland pulsed on the map, showing him his current location.

"I haven't forgotten about you just yet, Sarah."

He flew the ship over the desolate landscape of Australia, toward the town of Desonas. It was some distance away, but the starship was capable of incredible speed. Within ten minutes he had flown from Queensland to the Northern Territory in Central Australia. As soon as Uluru was in sight, he slowed the vessel down. His heart pounded. He was feeling anxious to see Sarah and the others again. Though, he wasn't sure how they'd react seeing a starship.

Flint continued to slow down the vessel as he approached his destination. And at long last, he could see Alice Springs—what had become Desonas. Flint rotated the propulsions and descended the black- and indigo-tinted spacecraft several yards away from the dilapidated town. It was just as dusty and desolate as he'd remembered. He exhaled deeply, lowering the ship's ramp. Just then, Gunthrel stepped into the control room.

"Clarienus is safe."

"I'm glad," said Flint. "I believe she was innocent. The others will adjust to her, but time needs to pass."

Gunthrel concurred and asked, "Is this the place?"

"Yes, it is," said Flint. "It's been four years since I've seen this town." He stood up from his pilot chair and looked at the others while he went on, "I won't be gone too long. Keep an eye out for anything strange."

"Strange?" said one of the scientists.

"I don't know how much has changed since I've been gone," said Flint. "Strange could be a horse, a half-naked aboriginal, or another starship that may try to attack." Having said that, he left with Gunthrel, leaving the crew shaky. "I'm going to need my power suit."

"You enjoyed that, didn't you?" muttered Gunthrel. He then cleared his throat, stopped in the middle of the corridor, and said, "Wait. What did you just say?"

Flint smirked and repeated, "I'm going to need my power suit."

"Well, it's about damn time," said Gunthrel. "You're lucky I transported here before the incursion."

"Great," said Flint. "Where is it?"

"Follow me."

They went to the ship's armory, which wasn't too far from the control room. Once they entered the chamber, Flint spotted the power suit right away and stepped inside it. Upon him activating it, its plating smoothly attached to his wrinkled skin, and he was able to walk around with ease, clomping like a titan.

"Looking good," said Gunthrel.

"Thanks," said Flint, his voice sounding heavy through the mask. "Let's go."

They walked over to the ramp, stepped down until outside, and jumped off the hovering starship that was slightly shrouded with steam. Flint stared hard at the town square for a while and then approached it with Gunthrel.

"So many memories," said Flint huskily.

He thought about the townspeople and remembered the life he had in Desonas as though he'd just left yesterday. It had, however, been four long years. He remembered his hunting days with Tom and Joey; he remembered Marshal Salomon persuading him to search for Browder; he remembered his days in the wilds with the aboriginals; he remembered Amanda who had hung herself because she had felt he loved an imaginary woman more than her; and he remembered that most of the townsfolk had betrayed him, playing him for a fool.

"It's overwhelming, but I'm glad to see Desonas again."

"Doesn't look like much," said Gunthrel.

Flint unexpectedly laughed. He needed that, especially after thinking about all of his dark memories.

"Gunthrel, you're the best."

He finally reached the square. Desonas looked derelict, as though it'd been abandoned for years. Nearly all of the buildings were dilapidated. The only structure still intact was the church. Flint abruptly felt distressed, gazing at the church that looked a bit too well preserved. He slowly approached the town's house of worship, raising his soal-based rifle. Standing before the doors, he opened them and stomped into the dim church that had candles lit. Gunthrel followed, staring at the stained-glass windows that depicted angels coming out of the sun.

"Ah, did the tribunal finally say I can go home?" inquired Steve Harrison, looking at the advanced-looking power suit. "I've done everything they asked of me."

"Even you," said Flint, enraged.

"I beg your pardon?" said Steve, not recognizing the voice. "Even you? Oh, of course," he said, chuckling. "You mean even I am allowed to go home, right?"

"Even you were in on this game."

Steve Harrison tilted his head, confused. Just then, Flint's power suit kneeled down and unsealed. When the preacher saw Flint's demented face emerge from the power suit, he gasped and backed away to the altar.

"Fli-Flint!" rasped Steve. "You're alive!"

"My name isn't Flint," he said.

"Th-they forced me," said Steve. "I didn't have a choice, Ethan." He sneakily clicked a button on the altar, opening a secret compartment that had a dimensional gun inside. "I swear to God."

"You swear to whom?"

"God!" said Steve, sweating and warily gripping his advanced gun. "You believe in God, right?"

"If I choose to be a theist or an atheist, that's my business," said Flint. "And the same goes for anything else, especially life. No one...*no one* under *any* circumstance has any business taking that precious gift away from people or manipulating their genes and splicing them without their consent. I don't care if it's the tribunal."

"How quaint and honorable of you," said Steve, cautiously pulling his dimensional gun closer.

Flint squinted viciously and asked, "Where is Sarah?"

"Oh, I'm afraid you missed her and the others a few months ago," said Steve. He pulled the gun more, trying to be as quiet and discreet as possible. "You see, Joey told the tribunal what had happened; they weren't very happy. The military had to come and take your daughter away." He chuckled derisively and added, "But wait, she isn't your daughter. So I'm sure you don't care if she, her husband, and the Panzo brutes are slaves for the rest of their lives, right?"

"Wrong."

At the same moment that Steve lifted his gun, Flint spun out his magnums. Within a split second, Flint aimed them at the preacher and unloaded their chambers, blowing his body apart and sending his corpse through a stained-glass window. Flint's face burned when the sunlight beamed into the church. He turned away and took cover, entering his power suit.

"I know this is your business," began Gunthrel, "but shouldn't you have disarmed him and questioned him more?"

"He wasn't going to tell me a damn thing," said Flint.

"Are you sure?"

"I'm old, but I'm not blind yet," said Flint. "I saw that idiot reaching for a weapon. Trust me, his intention was to either shoot me or die. No one is going to betray the tribunal after what they did to me. Steve had to be stopped, just like Salomon and his goons."

"I see," said Gunthrel. "Well, what's next?"

"Vorilian IV," replied Flint.

"All right, lead the way."

The duo returned to their vessel. By now the steamwalkers had learned of their leader's horrible fate. Gunthrel was the only one closest to a leader since he'd always been Pardashan's right-hand man, so the people in the ship were relieved to see him back on board.

After settling down, Flint returned to the control room with Gunthrel and started to fly the vessel skyward. The passengers fixed their eyes on the windows, staring at the blue sky that soon turned black as they entered space. Flint heard a few people sigh in awe of the breathtaking view. While the starship flew past the moon, they saw a shiny blue interstellar mist ahead. And though beautiful, there were a lot of asteroids floating miles apart, all of which had a redness to them. Knowing the sun's history of deadly flares and not locating Mercury or Venus on the star map, Flint rationalized why he spotted asteroids instead of planets.

"My goodness," he whispered to himself.

He had to admit, it was almost unbelievable. Yes, he conceded, *almost* was the right word because he *did* believe. He no longer doubted himself. Flint knew the difference between dreams and reality. And this was, without a doubt, reality. The tribunal had tried to turn him into a senile fool who didn't know what to believe. However, he'd finally found himself again. After all the nightmares he'd experienced in Desonas and Soalace, he got his life back—his identity and his freedom. And now it was time for him to make the tribunal regret their authoritarian scheme of forcing humanity to undergo synthesis.

PART III

REVOLUTION

CHAPTER FOURTEEN
BOUNTY HUNTERS

The realm of deep space flickered in silence, showing its seemingly limitless stars. It was a dark realm, just as dark and sinister as those who inhabited it in the 54th century—the tribunal made sure of that. Since the end of the war two decades ago, they used their ruthless military to wipe out autonomy, preparing the human race for dimensional evolution.

Anyone who may have desired anything other than synthesis had either been imprisoned or killed. No man or woman was brave enough to shout in public that they wanted the tribunal to be overthrown unless they were ready to be gunned down by the military or bounty hunters who covertly worked for the tribunal. After two decades, however, one man was insane enough to challenge the military. He loved to shout out loud how psychotic and fanatical the tribunal had become. That man's name was Flint Cross, and he immediately became the most wanted man in the universe.

The tribunal became outraged by the whispers of an outlaw named Flint Cross—the same fictional man they had created for the sake of showing humanity what happens to people who reject science and the next evolution of consciousness. Not only was the military searching for the avatar named Flint Cross, but bounty hunters were after him too.

One year had passed since Flint led his underworld companions to space. They'd been hoping to find refuge on a planet called Vorilian IV. As it turned out, Vorilian IV was a quadrant of space. After reaching it within half a year, Flint helped his companions settle in a world on the outskirts of the Vorilian sector, which they called New Earth. When they settled down, Flint set off on a smaller spacecraft. Since then, he'd been causing chaos in Vorilian IV.

On a dusty barren planet known as Maveron, bolts of orange lightning emerged in a spot of its fallow-colored sky. This bizarre phenomenon only occurred whenever a spacecraft was descending into the planet. Hardly any ships came to this desolate planet that looked as dead as Earth, so when the deprived people who lived there stared at the flashing sky they felt it wasn't good since only the dictatorial military possessed vessels capable of interstellar flight.

At first it looked as though a glittery black- and indigo-tinged mountain with bornhardts for wings was descending. Mist formed and wrapped around the mountain—no, it wasn't mist, it was smog. Patches of light burst within the whistling steam produced by engine burners of what was now clearly a spacecraft to the people who stood on a canyon full of parked vehicles.

The starship slowly reached the grimy canyon, hovering slightly above a cliff where the vehicles were parked. It gave out a vibrating hum from its engines. Then the ramp of the vessel opened. Steam billowed, engulfing the ramp. Shortly after, a silhouette of a man appeared within the dense steam. The onlookers by the parking area—ready to enter the lit-up, dingy- and rusty-looking saloon that stood across from them—stared at the man who exited the vessel, stepping onto the granite of the canyon.

His black clothes made him look like a futuristic cowboy; he wore a duster over his vest, fringed gloves, shotgun-style chaps that overlapped his jeans, and knee-length boots with silver spurs. He also wore a high crowned, wide-brimmed hat shrouding his beard and facial features. None of the people here had ever seen this man before, but the moment they saw him they knew he was Flint Cross.

The gunslinger's spurs chinked with each step he took. His duster fluttered back while wind and dust swept about him. When steam dissipated around him, he faintly lifted his head, showing his strong, wrinkled face. As he walked toward the saloon his vessel automatically sealed and landed below the cliff on a protruding ridge.

Flint pushed open the batwing doors of the rusty saloon and entered it, finding himself in a nightclub with multicolored laser lights and people dancing wildly and sensually to deafening cyberpunk music. Though the patrons were either drunk or drugged as they elatedly danced, they broke out of their trance when Flint walked by. He didn't even have to budge anyone to reach the counter; they simply stepped aside, staring at him as if they'd seen a man who'd been shot dead, only to rise back up from his grave.

"Holy freakin' shit," said a scrawny man with a mohawk, standing by the second floor's balcony. "That's fucking Flint Cross!"

His voice was muffled by the music, but a beautiful Tunisian woman nearby heard him, gazing down at the legendary Flint Cross who'd come back from the dead after twenty years. Most of the patrons in the saloon calmed down; they continued kissing, dancing, drinking, and taking drugs. Flint, meanwhile, sat on a stool by the bar counter. The bartender, smoking a thick cigar, observed the gunslinger and approached him.

"What'll it be?" asked the bartender.

"Just some water," said Flint.

The bartender raised his eyebrows, took hold of a grimy pitcher, and poured him a glass of brown water.

Flint stared at it, grimacing. "I asked for water."

"On this planet, this is water made in heaven," said the bartender.

"More like shit," scowled Flint, grabbing his cup and taking a sip. Despite how filthy it looked, it actually tasted clean. "Hmm, not as bad as I thought it'd be."

The bartender snorted and walked away, preparing a drink for somebody else.

"Wha' tha fuck iz tha'?" blurted a man sitting beside Flint. "Ya come 'er ta git fuckin' drunk 'n laid, nah drink sum pussy shit water."

Flint heard every single word that the scrawny, tattooed man beside him said. However, he didn't turn or tilt his head. He acted as though he were deaf and continued to drink his water in peace.

"Ehey, I'ma talkin' ta ya, old man," said the scrawny patron. "Oh, 'n wha' tha fuck iz thiz, *Halloweeeen*?" He stared hard at Flint who paid no mind to him whatsoever. "I don't lik' when beaople ignor' me." The drunkard clenched his teeth, watching Flint finish the rest of his water. He then pulled out a sleek knife. "Eh, 're ya fuckin' deaf?"

Flint spun out a magnum, shoving its muzzle down the drunkard's mouth. The scrawny tattooed man floundered and dropped his knife.

"I suggest you leave me alone," said Flint.

The drunkard shuddered, falling off his stool. He got back on his feet and ran out of the saloon. Flint holstered his magnum and slammed his glass on the counter. The bartender refilled his cup.

"Thanks," said Flint.

He was about to gulp down his water in peace when the Tunisian woman from the second floor advanced, seized him, and made out with him passionately. He didn't know why a stranger would do such a thing; then he felt her shove something in his mouth with her tongue.

"Je suis désolé, monsieur, j'ai pensé que vous étiez quelqu'un d'autre," she said, gazing at him sensually, only to walk away.

Flint raised an eyebrow, watching her approach the dance floor. She started kissing a blonde woman, grabbing her breasts. Flint shook his head, turned back to the bar counter, and felt something in his mouth. He glanced around, making sure no one was looking, and let what was in his mouth fall on the counter. It was a folded piece of paper with crinkles. Flint waited a few seconds and then unfolded it, noticing a sentence written in English:

If you want to know about Hamarah, take care of those six bounty hunters on the second floor and find me downstairs.

The moment Flint saw the name *Hamarah*, he felt his stomach twist, and his heart began to beat with a pounding that matched the electronic music. Reading the rest of the note made him squint. He dared not glimpse at the second floor. Flint stayed still for a while. He eventually put the note away and drank his water as if nothing fazed him. Afterwards, he gave the bartender ten credits and stood up from his stool. He then casually shuffled out of the saloon.

When he stepped outside, he continued to walk in an oblivious manner. Several passersby stared at him with absurd expressions. One of the half-naked women giggled, pointing at his hat. Flint walked over to the cliff and pulled out a charcoal chip, clicking it. Upon doing so, he heard the batwing doors slam open. He stared at the dusty panorama of Maveron, a seemingly endless valley littered with naturally carved canyons, sandstone spires, towering mesas, and skyscraping bornhardts. And as he gazed at it with an arrogant look on his face, he heard a bunch of footsteps crunch against the sooty, dirt-covered ground.

The six men behind him wore rusty red-brown armor. None of them wore helmets. They appeared to be fairly young—in their thirties—and looked extremely rugged and crude. One of the six men spat on the ground. The others either grimaced or sniggered at the sight of Flint and his ridiculous clothes.

"Joey sends his regards," said the man who spat.

That instant, Flint jumped off the cliff while clicking his charcoal chip again. The bounty hunters stared at him with dumbfounded expressions, watching him jump to his death. Just then, they heard the bustling sound of a reverberating engine. Running to the cliff, they saw Flint rise on a hovering soal-fueled motorcycle that billowed searing steam into their faces. They screamed in pain and withdrew.

Only one of them managed to lift his hands, firing dimensional beams from his armored forearms. The violet-colored beams, however, missed Flint.

"Get him!" exclaimed the unharmed man.

The group of bounty hunters strode over to where their vehicles were parked. As soon as they approached their automobiles, the roofs opened, allowing them to jump into the driver seats. Once the vehicles started, they shifted into aircraft-shaped vessels and took off, tailing Flint into the elongated valley.

In the meantime, Flint flew his hovering motorcycle through a steep-sided canyon filled with rock arches and dust devils. The brim of his hat flapped as he sped forward with a grin on his face, waiting for the bounty hunters to approach. And approach they did. Cannons the size of Flint's hovering motorcycle jutted from the wings of their vessels. The bounty hunters launched multiple dimensional beams at him. These lethal rays were twice the size of those fired from their armor.

Flint veered left and right, swiftly dodging the deadly beams. He checked his rearview mirror, pulled out one of his magnums with his right hand, and fired over his shoulder without looking. Four of the six soal bullets he fired pierced an engine of a vessel, causing it to explode. The bounty hunters looked pale at the sight of their comrade's demise and decided to take Flint more seriously.

The bounty hunters continued to fire but from a distance. Flint continued to evade their beams. He quickly holstered his empty magnum and took out his other, firing over his shoulder again. This time none of the bullets hit his foes. One of the bounty hunters laughed and zoomed forward, riding alongside Flint. He lowered his window and aimed his dimensional pistol at Flint who pulled out a shotgun from within his duster, blowing the man's face off.

The headless bounty hunter slumped against the door, his vehicle crashing and exploding on a mesa's summit. Flint, meanwhile, flew his steam-powered motorcycle between two narrow escarpments. The bounty hunters recklessly followed him. After firing a few beams, one of them accidently bashed a wing against a protruding ridge, causing him to spin out of control and blow up against the rocky cliff.

Flint swerved through the curving ravine while the three remaining bounty hunters tried to shoot him. As soon as Flint passed the ravine, he reached an area in the valley decorated with clusters of arched rocks. He easily flew through the loops. Two of the three bounty hunters rose from the region and stayed in the sky while the other stayed below, tailing Flint.

A few seconds later, however, he entered a loop slightly smaller than the previous ones, and the wings of his ship tore off against the sides of the arched rock. The archway collapsed, and the bounty hunter's vessel plummeted. He screamed and covered his face with his arms, exploding when the vehicle hit the ground.

The last two bounty hunters remained in the sky, waiting for Flint to leave the cluster of arched rocks. When he flew through the last one, he steered his motorcycle skyward in a loop, aimed his shotgun at one of them while upside down, and blasted the engine. The ship instantly blew up. Flint reloaded his lever-action shotgun with one hand and shot at the remaining bounty hunter, flying his steam-powered bike straight toward him.

It looked as though they were performing hawk-dove, shooting at each other while on a collision course. One of the beams eventually zapped through Flint's motorcycle, splitting it in half. Flint quickly stood up before it disintegrated and jumped onto his enemy's vessel.

"What the fuck?" said the bounty hunter, aiming his pistol at the roof and firing.

The beam missed Flint by a hair, at which point he slammed his fist through the roof. He grabbed the bounty hunter and snapped his neck. Not a second later, the ship started to aimlessly descend. Flint tore off the top with his unnatural strength, flung the lifeless bounty hunter into the valley, and took control of the craft.

Flint smoothly turned the vessel around and flew back to the saloon. After a few minutes, he reached the cliff and landed in the parking lot. Several people outside stared at the half-ruined ship in dismay, many gasping when they saw Flint emerge from it. He fearlessly walked past the patrons who looked like they were either thugs or drug addicts. Only a few stood by the door, not moving out of the way.

"If you don't want to get brain-fucked by the tribunal, step aside," grumbled Flint.

Although many of the thugs and prostitutes maintained a deadly glare, they decided not to interfere, walking away. Flint reentered the saloon. The cyberpunk music wasn't loud to him anymore. Once again, people stared at him as if they saw a wraith. And a wraith he was, dressed in black, jostling through the crowd with wrath in his eyes. Not one person got in his way while he approached the stairs in the back.

Flint went down the steps, finding himself in a brothel. A man with a dark complexion was having sex with an Asian woman in the hall. They didn't seem to care if someone watched. The naked woman, lifted against a wall, screamed wildly while her client penetrated her. Flint, slack-jawed, raised his eyebrows at the sight and walked by them without a word. Others were having sex in bedrooms that had no doors.

Eventually, as he walked through a graffiti-covered corridor, the Tunisian woman who'd given him the note peeked out of a bedroom and pulled him in. She only wore stockings, panties, and a nearly see-through bra with her nipples poking out. The woman rubbed his chest, smiling while giving out a faint moan. Flint, however, grabbed her hands and pushed them away.

"Thanks for the tip," he said. "But I'm not here for sex."

"Of course you're not," said the Tunisian woman with a French accent. "I wasn't sure if you were going to live…I'm glad to see you again."

"Forgive me if I don't remember you."

"It's me, Anissa," she said.

Flint stared at her blankly.

"So, it's true," she added, "they took your memory away?"

Flint nodded with a regretful sigh. "Yes," he said. "Though, over the past few years I've been able to remember certain things. Hamarah's death being one of them."

"She's not dead," replied Anissa.

"*What?*" he said, gazing at her in disbelief. "That's impossible. I remember everything from that day as though it happened yesterday. She was waiting for me at the command center, hoping to discuss a new strategy when the military surprise attacked us. Andrew Browder and I were running through the trenches, making our way to her. Then a battleship came. It descended and destroyed the building."

"Maybe you thought she was there," said Anissa. "But my sister is very much alive and hiding with the resistance."

"My goodness," said Flint. "You're her sister?" Before she could nod, he added, "Wait a minute, did you just say—"

"Resistance," she said. "It isn't much, but yes, there is a resistance."

"Can you take me to them?"

"Take you to the resistance?" she said crudely, putting her hands on her hips. "Look at me, Ethan. I'm just a prostitute. I don't have a starship."

"But I do," he said, grinning.

CHAPTER FIFTEEN
SCIENCE IN DEFIANCE

Flint exited the dingy saloon with Anissa and approached the cliff, pulling out his charcoal chip from his vest. He clicked it several times, inputting a code, and the precipice resonated with the rumbling of an engine activating. A cloud of smog billowed from the crag, and a mountainous steamship ascended. Anissa stared at the vessel in disbelief.

The craft's ramp lowered, and Flint climbed aboard. He noticed Anissa looked wary, so he extended his palm. She took his hand, boarding the vessel. Inside looked a bit old, though it still glittered and pulsed with life. Anissa observed the interior of the steamship in awe as she followed Flint through a corridor. The clacking clockwork, rumbling of the soal-fueled engine, and humming of the automatic Core filled their ears. It was a natural sound to Flint, contrary to Anissa who felt it was bizarre; however, the reverberations of the vessel became trivial when she approached the pilot chamber. That instant, Clarienus jumped out while hissing.

Anissa shrieked, falling onto the floor.

"No," said Flint sternly. "She's a friend, Clarienus." He helped Anissa up, who clung to the wall, frightened. "Be a good girl."

"Is that an alien?"

"Aliens don't exist in this dimension, remember?" said Flint, amused. "It's quite a long story, but she's a mutant human from Earth."

Anissa began, "That's no hum—"

"You're late," said Gunthrel, entering the corridor. He clomped through the walkway in his power suit and glared at Anissa. "Who's this?"

"She's a friend," said Flint. "Anissa, this is Gunthrel."

"H-hi," said Anissa, startled by his size.

"Any friend of Flint is a friend of mine," said Gunthrel, bowing. "Clarienus, be nice to her. It seems she'll be with us for…?"

"For a while," replied Flint, guiding Anissa to the brass-tinted pilot chamber. "There's a resistance after all, and she's going to show us where they are." Upon entering the pilot room, he added, "All right, Dale, take us out."

Dale smiled in his tattered overalls, still missing most of his teeth, and flew the steamship out of Maveron.

"Where to, Ethan?" he asked.

"Rutica," answered Anissa.

"Well, well, ya got yerself a fine lady," said Dale, glancing at her. "Tha name's Peter Pan, but ya can call me Dale if ya'd like."

"Nice to meet you, *Dale*," she said. "I am Anissa."

Anissa wondered if she was better off staying in the brothel. She was in a strange vessel with advanced technology that she'd never seen or heard of before, a mutant and giant were on board, and the pilot seemed to be insane. Flint was the only person she trusted, and yet even he tested her trust because he was oddly dressed in nineteenth-century clothing. She nevertheless decided to have a little faith in him.

"Hamarah is alive," said Flint with elation, looking at Gunthrel. "She's been in hiding since the war ended."

"It's astounding she's managed to hide from the tribunal this long," replied Gunthrel. He patted Flint on the shoulder. "I'm happy for you, Flint." He clumped over to a control panel and took a seat. "We're running low on soal. I'll contact the mothership for replenishment."

"Sounds good," said Flint. "Dale, do you see Rutica on the map?"

"Yup," he said. "It's sumwhere in Vorilian—oh, I just got a fix. Yer not gonna like it, Ethan. It's at tha heart of tha military."

"If we come across any vessels, we'll greet them with love," said Flint, taking a seat. He heard Dale guffaw, which reminded him of Joey's laugh. Then he wondered to himself, where is that scoundrel? One of the bounty hunters had mentioned his name. This meant that Joey must be in charge of the hunt. But that was just fine because Flint loved hunting too and was ready to kill Joey for his betrayal. "I'll man the weapons should anything happen," he added, taking control of the armaments' interface. "Set the course, Dale."

Anissa, meanwhile, warily sat next to Flint. She tried to ignore Clarienus who mindlessly hopped around the pilot chamber, howling.

"I agree, Clarienus," said Flint, "this is going to be another adventure."

The steamship flew through the fallow sky, leaving Maveron's atmosphere. Not only was the vessel flying fast, but it had a haze of smog enveloping it in space. The spacecraft resembled a comet while traversing through the cosmos. In due time, the crew reached a star cluster where Rutica was located.

After three long hours, Anissa started feeling safer. She occasionally watched Flint handle the vessel's controls but mostly gazed at space through the tinted window that had polarized technology, allowing her to stare directly at nearby stars without being harmed by their luminous, blinding light. She eventually turned her attention back to Flint. This time she fixed her eyes on him with an expression of curiosity.

"So," she began, "how come you came to the saloon on Maveron?"

"Don't you know?"

"If I did, I wouldn't be asking," sulked Anissa. She snorted when Flint laughed at her response and went on, "I thought you were looking for me. But you lost your memory. So, I really don't know why you traveled there."

"I've been visiting a lot of places within the past few months," he said. "I always make sure they're somewhere around the outskirts of Vorilian IV to avoid a direct confrontation with the military. As for your saloon, I went there hoping to find out from the locals which planet the tribunal are located on."

She gave out a cold laugh. "That kind of information is probably classified. I sure as hell don't know. And by the way, don't you think hanging around a saloon while dressed like that is risky?"

"Well," he began, "I didn't think a bunch of bounty hunters would be there. But these days the tribunal wants me dead, so I'm likely to find trouble anywhere I go."

"Why are you so hell-bent on this revolution?" she asked.

"Does it matter?"

"Yes!" she exclaimed. "It does matter! It matters when the military is ready to kill you over a stupid theory!"

"It's no theory," he said. "Before the war, as Commander-in-Chief, I was an overseer in the science division. I've seen dimensional technology firsthand. The ability to fuse with those from another dimension is very real, and it is a serious threat to our individuality. Whatever you've heard about concerning a superior race is bullshit. More so, synthesis may cause our universe to collapse. I won't let the tribunal do this to humanity."

"Humanity?" she scowled. "You talk as if you're no longer human."

Acknowledging his abnormal strength and thinking of all the people he'd killed and must kill to prevent dimensional synthesis, he responded, "Maybe I'm not."

"Huh?"

"Forget it," he said, sighing. "You live your life, and I live mine. I don't judge you for the person you are. So, why should I be judged?"

"Right on, lad," said Dale.

"Whatever," she said, sulking. "I don't care anymore. I just want to stay alive. And if I need to suck a man's cock to live longer, so be it. It's better than dying for a lost cause."

"Lost cause?" said Flint. "Things are *very* different now."

"Oh?" she said curtly. "Very different? The only difference is you're practically alone in this weird revolution of yours. More than half of your original resistance are slaves. And the few who're still alive are hiding."

"They're doing the smart thing," said Flint. "They're probably just waiting for the right moment to strike. And, by the way, I am far from being alone."

"Indeed," said Gunthrel.

"Sorry," said Anissa. "Okay, you're not alone. You have Peter Pan to fly you around, Tin Man from Oz over here to hold your hand when the military attacks, and some kind of human-mutant pet that doesn't even know what's happening."

Clarienus howled in a lamenting tone.

"You should apologize to her," said Flint. "You hurt her feelings."

He chuckled when she sighed with frustration. She rose from her seat and went over to a corner window.

"Listen," went on Flint, "I never asked you to join my cause. In fact, you're the one who got involved and decided to come aboard my vessel. I'll bring you back to Maveron as soon as you show me where the resistance is hiding."

Anissa didn't respond. She just crossed her arms and remained standing for a while by the corner. She felt what Flint had said was fair enough but made no sign of appreciation. The only thing she could do at this point was be patient and wait until the steamship would arrive at Rutica. She occasionally paced; though, looking at the others made her feel nauseous, so she eventually stayed still and simply continued to stare at space, trying to ignore the fact that she was in an insane asylum.

By the next hour, she finally spotted an orange-green planet in the far distance. "That's it," she said, feeling relieved.

"Now that's a beautiful sight," said Flint. "Dale, take her in nice and easy. We don't want to alert anyone."

"Too late," said Gunthrel.

Flint, disturbed by what his comrade had just said, stared at the sensors. "I don't see anything. What're you talking about?"

"Not space," replied Gunthrel. "I've spotted something leaving Halvon—it's the planet neighboring Rutica. It's flying *real* fast and I calculated its trajectory, which is heading directly toward us."

"Shit!" cursed Flint. "I should've been more careful."

"That's why you have me on board," said Gunthrel. "It's just one, at least for now. It'll be in range within a minute."

"This can't be happening," groaned Anissa.

Dale shrugged at her response. "Wha'd ya expect? This is tha heart of military space." He glanced over to Flint and asked, "What ya want me ta do, Ethan?"

"Change your course," said Flint.

"Right," said Dale, decelerating and turning the steamship.

"Are you fucking insane?" snapped Anissa. "The only way to stay alive is to outrun the military and hide! Why are you slowing down?"

"I don't want them being suspicious of us traveling to Rutica," said Flint. "If they see us escaping to the planet they might think something important is there. I won't let the resistance down again."

"They probably already know!" she yelled.

"They're in range," said Gunthrel.

"I can see," said Flint, staring at the cruiser.

When the vessel reached the steamship, it halted. A red light activated from the military spacecraft, scanning the mountainous smog-covered ship in front of it. Then one of the ensigns in the cruiser approached the commanding officer on the main deck.

"Captain," called out the ensign worriedly. "Our sensors are showing nothing. They seem to have some kind of shield prohibiting us from seeing their technology."

The captain rose, staring at the unknown vessel with a distraught expression. "I've never seen anything like this before," he said, gulping. "It's like a floating city enveloped in a nebula." He stood silent for a moment and then commanded, "Return to your post, Ensign."

"Aye, sir," replied the ensign, going back to his seat below the command deck.

"Have the resistance been this busy?" pondered the captain. He opened a voice channel on his console. "This is Captain Armstrong of the military starship Hewlett speaking. Who are you, and what is your destination?"

A visual screen activated, showing Clarienus growling and hissing ferociously. Many of the crew gasped and winced when they saw her.

"What in God's name is that?" said the ensign, horrified.

Captain Armstrong flinched when he heard the unforgivable three-lettered word that had been banned decades ago and pulled out a dimensional pistol, zapping the ensign into dust.

"No one speaks that name," said the captain. He turned off the visual screen and glared at the vessel. "There're no such things as demons or aliens. It must be a trick. Lieutenant Coleman, use the ST-8 and bring the ship in," he added, looking behind him. "We're going to board it and find out what this is about."

Lieutenant Coleman complied, launching a green spherical beam that hit the steamship. The ray ignited and exploded into a shield-like field, spreading all over the mountainous vessel until its power died out.

"Goodness gracious," said Dale, slack-jawed. "It looks like they've stunned us. We're sittin' ducks even if ya told me ta git outta here."

"Everything's been deactivated," said Gunthrel with aggravation. "Even the weapons."

Flint attempted to click his interface but nothing worked. Then the vessel trembled and motioned toward the military ship.

"They're using a tractor beam?" said Gunthrel. "Why aren't they attacking?"

"Ah," said Flint. "They don't know I'm here. They just see a new toy. And, like children, they want to play with it." He smirked and continued, "Activate the emergency generator. We're low on soal anyway. We might as well go out in a big bang."

Gunthrel agreed and turned on the emergency generator, reactivating the Core. Just then, the steamship trembled violently—it connected to the military vessel. Dale tried to fly away, but there was nothing he could do since the tractor beam was still in effect.

"They're boarding the ship!" exclaimed Gunthrel.

"I don't believe this," said Anissa. "I was better off getting fucked by men with AIDS than coming here."

"It's time to show them some love," said Flint, ignoring Anissa.

Gunthrel concurred, opening a compartment in his armor and removing a dimensional cannon. He then dashed with Flint to a corner in a cog-covered corridor where the cruiser clamped on to their vessel via its hatch. Upon taking position, Gunthrel inputted a code in his suit: *Gamma*. Within seconds, the military blasted open a wall inside the clanking corridor and entered. They wore burgundy uniforms and carried plasma guns.

Before they could even examine the interior of the foreign vessel, Flint peeked out of his corner and shot down nine men using his magnums.

"Take cover!" shouted one of the soldiers, "it's Flint Cross!"

Gunthrel also peered out from his corner, blasting them with his dimensional cannon. The violet beams caused them to disintegrate.

"They've got dimensional technology!" shouted another soldier.

"Don't switch to their weaponry yet," said Lieutenant Coleman. "The captain wants us to capture the ship and that specimen for study!"

"Gamma, we need you now!" exclaimed Gunthrel, continuing to fire and take cover.

In less than a minute, a door unsealed on the opposite side of the corridor. A squadron of steamwalkers emerged, blasting the military soldiers with dimensional cannons. The men who were still alive retreated to the hatchway.

"There are fucking aliens on board!" cried out a soldier.

"*What?*" said Lieutenant Coleman furiously.

He was ready to assassinate his own man for being superstitious when Gamma squadron came through the hole he'd created to infiltrate the foreign vessel. The twelve-foot tall armored beings stomped into the military cruiser's hatchway, shooting the soldiers. They then gave out a loud metallic sound that was deafening to the remaining men. Flint had already gotten used to it in the underground city of Soalace, so the high-pitched reverberations were music to his ears as he charged with his magnums, blowing holes into the chests of dismayed soldiers.

"Fall back!" commanded Coleman. He exited the light-pulsing hatchway and ran back to his vessel, activating a voice channel. "Captain! Flint Cross is on board this ship, and he has an army of...I don't know what they are, but they have dimen—"

"I've already called for backup," interjected Captain Armstrong. "Hold out as long as you can without dimensional weapons. I don't want that ship to accidently be destroyed. It may have vital technology that we can use against the rebels."

Coleman complied, taking cover and firing cautiously.

Flint also took cover, reloaded his magnums, and then sprang out as he shot and shouted, "Surrender at once and stray away from the oppression of the tribunal or face the wrath of Flint Cross!"

"You're a madman, Ethan!" yelled out Coleman, hiding. "It's too bad I have to put you down the old-fashioned way! If I were the captain, you'd be space dust right now!"

"Then what're you waiting for?" roared Flint, blowing away another group of men.

Coleman grimaced while he peered out of his corner, firing his plasma gun at one of the steamwalkers. The beams, however, simply dissipated upon impact.

"These *things* are completely impenetrable!" said Coleman, frustrated.

"We need to use dimensional weapons!" said one of the soldiers.

"Negative, soldier," said Coleman. "Ignore the armored men—target Flint Cross! I want that man dead!"

Just then, Clarienus scuttled through the hatchway, ripping soldiers apart with her sharp claws. Upon reaching the military ship, she climbed onto the ceiling and pounced on Coleman, biting his neck. A few soldiers who saw Clarienus ran for their lives. When the remaining unit realized that Lieutenant Coleman was dead, they activated their advanced dimensional weapons and opened fire. Although they were too slow to catch Clarienus, they were able to blast several steamwalkers, disintegrating them.

"Idiots!" yelled a soldier using a plasma gun amid his brigade. "Why are you disobeying the captain?" His regiment ignored him, frantically shooting. "Do *not* miss! If you damage our ship, or that foreign vessel, the captain will have us court-martialed!"

Reloading his magnums, Flint stepped away from his corner. He sprinted forward with a heinous glare, firing at the remaining military men. Countless beams passed him. Some of the steamwalkers beside him disintegrated. The deafening metallic sound rang again. Flint pressed on, aiming and pulling the triggers of his magnums. Smoke blew from the muzzles of his guns, soal bullets piercing his targets. They were either blown in half by the power of the magnums or poisoned by the soal, which killed them in seconds as they bled on the grating.

"Bad news," said Dale, speaking to Flint on a private communications channel. "A fleet of twen'ney-four ships appeared on tha sensors."

Flint grew pale. "Time to get the hell out of here," he said.

"Why?" inquired Gunthrel.

"They have reinforcements," answered Flint. "If they can't take our ship by force, then I'm sure they'll destroy it."

Flint, Gunthrel, and the remaining steamwalkers of Gamma squadron started to withdraw back to their vessel. Clarienus was the only one who lingered, killing the rest of the soldiers who dared not run. Once she finally killed them, she scuttled away and returned to the steamship. As soon as she entered, Gunthrel attempted to reseal the blasted wall. Flint, meanwhile, returned to the cockpit.

"It ain't looking good, Ethan," said Dale.

"I don't understand how we're still alive," said Anissa.

"After what we just did to them, so am I," said Flint. "We're gonna need to do something extraordinary to get out of this."

"Like what?" asked Dale.

"I don't know," said Flint, staring at the twenty-four starships that were approaching on his sensors. "They're going to shoot us down any second."

"We're nearly out of soal," said Gunthrel, entering the chamber.

Flint's eyes widened. "That's it!" he said excitedly. He clicked the vessel's control panel, expanding the interface. "Gunthrel, do you remember what I did in the city of Soalace before we escaped?"

Gunthrel shook his head.

"All right, no time to explain," he said, continuing to click buttons. "Dale, fly us into the heart of that fleet."

"Say what?"

"Trust me," said Flint.

"Are you insane?" cried out Anissa.

"People keep asking me that," sulked Flint. "This is the only chance we've got at getting out of this alive."

Dale listened and attempted to fly the steamship away. Fortunately, the tractor beam was no longer active. He turned the vessel and flew it straight toward the military fleet. As he did so, the captain of the Hewlett screamed.

"Why isn't the tractor beam active?" he asked.

"I thought we didn't need it anymore when Coleman infiltrated the ship," replied one of the ensigns. When he saw the furious look on his captain's face, he immediately reactivated the tractor beam. "The ship's too fast—we're out of range!"

The captain pressed his fingers against his forehead, trying to stay calm. "They won't be able to escape," he said. "Our reinforcements have arrived."

In the meantime, Dale continued flying toward the military fleet, sweat dripping down his face. Anissa wept while Clarienus let out a monstrous dirge. Gunthrel shook his head, not sure if he should remain passive. Flint was the only one who grinned; it was a maniacal grin. He leaned forward at the windowpane, glaring at the twenty-four starships lined up in a blockade.

"Just a little closer," muttered Flint, his grin expanding. "Almost there."

He blocked out Anissa's wailing and Clarienus' sing-song dirge from his mind. Several military cruisers opened fire, releasing dimensional beams. Dale attempted to evade them, but some rays blasted the force field, deactivating it. The steamship shook violently.

"Flint!" shouted Gunthrel, losing faith in him.

"You're all dead!" roared Flint, cackling as though he'd lost his mind.

In the blink of an eye, Flint expanded his web of controls and inputted a code, making the ship's Core absorb all the dimensional energy from the fleet of starships just as he'd absorbed the kingdom of Soalace's energy before. The energy was redirected into the dependent Core, causing every cruiser, with the exception of the distant Hewlett, to shutdown. Not one second later, the dimensional energy pulsed outward, disintegrating the entire fleet.

"Impossible," said the captain of the Hewlett, staring at the glittery particles of the fleet in disbelief. "He has dimensional technology built into that vessel. Retreat!"

Flint noticed the Hewlett beginning to turn and fly away. "Oh, no you don't," he said. "I have yet to absolve you of your sins." He aimed the dimensional cannons of his steamship at the retreating vessel and used the remaining energy in the Core to launch one final beam. The thick violet-colored ray shot out, blasting through the Hewlett, leaving only soldiers' ashes.

"Fairy dust," said Dale.

"Space dust," said Flint, correcting him.

The crew cheered and applauded Flint who couldn't help but keep his grin. Anissa shed tears of joy while Clarienus howled with great delight, barely understanding what had happened. Dale guffawed and clapped, amazed. Gunthrel and his fellow steamwalkers raised their guns in victory. The celebration, however, was short lived. Just a few seconds after they had begun to cheer with relief, an alarm went off.

"Oh my goodness, what's happening now?" asked Anissa, fed up.

"Soal," said Gunthrel.

"Right," said Flint, sighing. "We're on the verge of running out of soal. It's used to fuel our steamship. Damn it, I knew we should've replaced the Core with another power source. It worked well in the undertunnels, but it just isn't the same in space."

"We have less than five minutes," said Gunthrel.

The alarm continued to ring, causing the lights in the cockpit to flash red. Dale flew fast toward Rutica. Little by little, the smog enveloping the vessel thinned out. Hardly any exhaust fumes emitted from the titanium cylinders atop the steamship, at which point the vessel rumbled fiercely. The orange-green planet gradually appeared bigger to the crew.

"Oh my God," scowled Anissa.

"You're still a believer?" asked Flint, grinning at Anissa who rolled her eyes.

"Um...now'd be a dandy time ta give me tha coordinates," said Dale.

Not wasting any time, Anissa gave them to him.

"Alrighty," he said, gleaming. "We'll be there in a jiffy."

"I sure hope so," said Gunthrel. "We have two minutes left."

The crew remained seated, bracing themselves as the steamship entered Rutica's amber-tinged sky. Hardly any clouds were visible to the crew. At first that didn't matter to them, but when the steamship's smog dissipated, Dale lost control. The crew screamed, gazing at the tiny-looking land while they fell thousands upon thousands of feet in the air. They had wished to see clouds because at least they wouldn't have realized that they were descending toward land. The terrain expanded quickly as they fell.

"Do something!" yelled Anissa, crying hysterically.

Flint desperately tried to think of a way out of this. Yet he had no ideas. The pressure of the descent made him as mindless as Clarienus. He was terrified, like the others. He'd hoped to pull off another fancy tactic; though, there was nothing left to do since the vessel's soal had run out. And the dimensional power that was once within the hybrid Core had been drained during the attack. Flint didn't scream or close his eyes despite his fear. Deep down inside, he refused to accept death. Even if he'd die right now, it was a big bang, as he'd hoped. However, he rejected the thought of this being the end of his revolt. He ignored his rational mind and preferred to be irrational, staring at the approaching landscape. That instant, he spotted a greenish circle that turned out to be an ocean of some kind.

"Water!" exclaimed Flint.

He cheered and jumped for joy. Then he staggered and flew against the wall as the vessel dove into the lake that had resembled an ocean from afar. The seats broke off from the floor, and the crew fell against the grating. The vessel sank deep into the lake. Only the roof and a few of its cylinders protruded from the green-blue water. Although the water cushioned the crash, the steamship nevertheless sank fast, its base smashing hard against the lake's surface.

Flint gave out a feeble groan. He was barely conscious; he couldn't even move. Opening his eyes, he noticed his crew on the floor. Though they appeared to be unconscious, he wasn't sure if they were. Then he glanced at the cracked window, noticing they had in fact sunk into the lake. Water gradually filtered through some of the smaller cylinders that were submerged. Flint knew what was happening, yet he couldn't move. He felt weaker, and his head throbbed. After a few seconds, he closed his eyes and passed out.

CHAPTER SIXTEEN

THE SOULLESS MESSIAH

After an hour of being unconscious, Flint awoke and found himself inside the flooded steamship over Gunthrel's shoulder. His comrade lifted him to the surface of a platform one level below the vessel's roof and then put him down. Violently coughing out water, Flint groaned and gasped for oxygen.

"Are you all right?" asked Gunthrel.

"I think so," said Flint weakly. He turned around and searched the platform. No one was there. "Where are the others? Are they alive?"

"Anissa's fine."

"And the others?" asked Flint.

His helmet downturned, Gunthrel answered, "Dale's unconscious, and Clarienus refuses to leave."

"Shit," cursed Flint. "Wait a minute, Clarienus can breathe underwater?"

Gunthrel nodded at him.

"She's probably better off here," said Flint. "We don't want her to scare anyone." He rose to his feet, wobbling. Gunthrel grabbed him, holding him steady. "Thanks. I must've hit my head pretty hard." He rubbed his forehead and added, "Let's get out."

The duo climbed a ladder through a hatch and stepped onto the titanium roof that faintly sparkled. Anissa was holding Dale, but when she saw Flint she gently laid Dale's head down and rushed over to Flint, hugging him.

"I'm so glad you're alive," she said.

"So am I," replied Flint. He looked ahead and noticed fourteen survivors of Gamma squadron scouting the area. "Glad we're not alone."

"I told them to go ahead," said Gunthrel.

"Good idea," said Flint. "Who knows if the rest of the military was alerted by our little incursion, not to mention crash landing here."

"We'd better hurry," said Anissa.

Gunthrel grasped Dale and carried him astride over his bulky pauldrons. Flint and Anissa leaped into the green water, swimming to the shore. The waves sporadically fell over them while they swam. They eventually reached the sandy shore, breathing heavily.

"That water is icky," said Anissa.

"At least we can breathe," said Flint, observing the region.

The area where they stood was a beach. Farther away, however, lay a wilderness teeming with life. Flint and his friends rejoined Gamma squadron and walked toward the jungle. When they entered it, most of the steamwalkers bashed branches apart since they were getting in their way.

"Is this where your resistance is located?" asked Gunthrel.

Flint shrugged and glanced at Anissa who seemed to be lost in thought. She was walking mindlessly through the wilderness like Clarienus.

"Anissa," called out Flint, snapping her out of her daydreaming. "Is it here?"

"Sorry," she said. "I don't remember where exactly they are. But yes, they're somewhere around here."

"Should we spread out?" asked Gunthrel.

They abruptly heard numerous dimensional weapons activate. That instant, an army of camouflaged men rose from the dense bushes. They were all aiming their weapons at Gamma squadron. When they noticed

Flint among the giants in armor, however, they appeared slightly less anxious to shoot. Nevertheless, their sudden approach caused Flint and his comrades to raise their weapons.

"Hold your fire!" said one of the camouflaged men. He stepped out of the bushes, warily approaching his targets. "Flint Cross?"

"That's me," he said, cocking his magnums. "Now don't come any closer."

"We're on the same side," replied the camouflaged man. "Stand down, men!" He lowered his weapon and added, "The name's Jeremy Woodson."

"This man is in dire need of medical attention," said Flint, pointing at Dale.

"We can help," replied Jeremy. "But before we leave, I'd like to know one thing—should I call you Flint or perhaps Ethan?"

Flint shrugged. "Call me whatever you'd like."

"Ethan it is," said Jeremy. "And I'm sure those who remember you during the war will be calling you the same." He waved his hand while turning around. "Come, I'll take you to our base of operations. I'm sure you went through a lot to find us."

"Through hell and back," said Flint.

Jeremy and his camouflaged troops guided Flint deeper into the forest. Though they had to travel several miles, Flint took the opportunity to explain everything he'd been through since his days in Desonas. Jeremy shook his head several times—the word *flabbergasted* would be an understatement to describe his reactions to Flint's tales, but it nevertheless did justice.

"I don't know how you're still alive, but thank goodness you're here," said Jeremy. He continued to guide Flint and his entourage through the woods. Upon walking one more mile, he stopped and added, "We're here."

"Huh?" uttered Flint, glancing around and only seeing the dense forest.

His comrades were just as confused and frustrated. They then heard a loud mechanical snap as though every branch in the forest had splintered; the land on which they stood abruptly descended like an elevator. With the exception of Anissa, Flint and his company were amazed. The ground beneath them appeared to be a camouflaged platform that looked as real as the rest of the forest's terrain.

"Very interesting," said Gunthrel.

Flint agreed, gazing up and seeing another artificial platform of soil and grass slide over the hole above to keep the base hidden.

"I hope you don't mind being underground again," said Jeremy.

"Are you kidding?" responded Flint. "Though it may not be the paradise we wish for, it reminds me of a fine home I once had."

Gunthrel and his fellow steamwalkers concurred. Although the architecture was vastly different than Soalace, it nevertheless made them feel at home. When the elevator reached the bottom, it clanked, and a brass door unsealed. Jeremy, along with his militia, led Flint and his comrades into the secret base.

"I need a doctor to look after this man," said Jeremy, pointing at Dale.

Several people in the tunnel approached Gunthrel who gently laid Dale on the floor. The group of men in greenish-brown clothes picked Dale up and took him to one of the underground infirmaries.

After walking through another dim tunnel for a minute, they entered a large chamber that resembled an old underground shelter for homeless people.

Flint saw countless men, women, and children on the floor with tattered clothes and old makeshift beds. Seeing them this way tore him apart. He wondered to himself, was this the kind of life people had to live just to be free? No one in the universe deserved this fate, especially the innocent. He stared at the refugees with teary eyes, trying not to cry. Flint forced himself to be strong since these people needed him now more than ever.

When they saw him, it was like seeing an angel arrive. No normal man was dressed like a cowboy in the 54th century—only one man, and that man was Flint Cross. They instantly got to their feet, flocking to him. And those who didn't spot him right away soon did when they noticed others running toward him.

"Flint Cross!" they cried out with relief.

Numerous people tried to touch his hands while he passed by with troops. Seeing him was a symbol of hope, respect, and freedom. Men, women, and children of diverse ethnicities from Earth surrounded him. Flint smiled and waved at as many of them as he could. Upon witnessing this, it became evident to him that the people before him represented the last family of love in the universe. Standing still for a moment, staring at the remaining rebels and refugees, he wasn't sure if he should be happy or pity them.

"This way," said Jeremy, speaking louder than usual to make sure Flint could hear him over the elated crowd. "Though it's been two decades, I'm sure there's someone who would like to see you."

"Hamarah?" said Flint ecstatically.

"I don't know who that is," replied Jeremy, "but perhaps our leader may know; he's been around a bit longer than us younglings. Follow me. I'll take you to him."

Though disappointed, Flint complied, trying to smile at the multitude. He entered another tunnel where more people flocked to him. There was so much commotion that other rebel troops came to see what was going on. They then saw Flint and shouted for joy, raising their weapons while praising him.

"Seems like you're Pardashan in these parts," said Gunthrel.

"Never," said Flint. "Pardashan, may his soul rest in peace, was a man who stood against the odds and lived for you and your people."

"Much like someone I'm walking next to," said Gunthrel.

Flint shook his head, slightly blushing. He and his comrades continued walking through the maze-like tunnels, following Jeremy. Eventually, they reached the end of a passageway that led to a chamber filled with rebel tacticians. Some of them were using computers while others studied cosmic grids displayed along the walls.

Upon seeing Flint, however, they stopped what they were doing and ran over to him, shouting and cheering in disbelief. One of the men who looked as wrinkled and old as Flint approached him in the midst of the crowd. Flint didn't recognize him, but there seemed to be something familiar about the aged man who smiled, shedding tears of joy. He hugged Flint in disbelief.

"Welcome back, Ethan," said the elderly man.

"You must forgive me," began Flint, "but after the war ended...after being imprisoned, the tribunal—"

"Took away your memory," finished the elderly man. "Yes, I know what the tribunal did to you. It's a miracle to see you alive." He shook Flint's hand and said, "I am Gregory Browder, the leader of this resistance."

"Browder?" said Flint.

"You remember the name?" asked Gregory.

"My God," said Flint, staring sharply at him. "You're his brother, aren't you? You're Andrew's brother."

Gregory nodded and, with a hopeful expression, asked, "Is he with you?"

Flint looked down while shaking his head in misery. "Joey killed him before I could do anything," he said.

"No," muttered Gregory, his lips quivering. "No, it can't be."

"I'm so sorry," said Flint dismally.

Gregory took a seat, tears rolling down his wrinkled cheeks. He then stammered, "When I first heard rumors of a man rising by the name of Flint Cross—a name the tribunal had given you—I hoped with all my heart that he was with you; that the two of you had managed to escape the military's grasp. Ethan, tell me, who is this *Joey* who killed my brother?"

"In this universe, I have no idea," said Flint. "But he seems to be the one responsible for hiring bounty hunters who've been hunting me down for the past year."

"What?" said Gregory, standing back up. "Could it be the Commandant?"

"Commandant?" said Flint, perplexed.

Gregory Browder approached a small computer in the back of the room, typed into it, and displayed an image of a middle-aged man in a military uniform. As soon as Flint saw the image, he fiercely squinted at it. Although the man no longer had a mustache, he was, without a doubt, Joey.

"Is that him?" asked Gregory.

"Oh, yes," said Flint, gritting his teeth. "That's him all right." He clenched his hands into fists as he continued, "I've been waiting a long time to put a bullet in his head. Where do we find him?"

"His real name is Cain Sullivan," said Gregory. "He's the current Commander-in-Chief of the military. And, unfortunately, like the tribunal, we can't approach him."

"Then how do we lure him out?" asked Flint.

Gregory stared at the crowd of people and sighed. "I don't know," he said. "None of us know how. We'd probably have to do something drastic to get his attention."

"Like what?" asked Flint, approaching Gregory with a face of curiosity.

Gregory looked as though he were deeply lost in thought. "Like destroying Titan," he finally said.

"That's impossible," said Jeremy. "We'd be wiped out in seconds."

"He's right," said one of the tacticians in the room. "The military is probably waiting for us to make that mistake."

"Wait," said Flint. "What exactly is Titan?"

"It's the prison that holds the rest of the resistance," said Gregory. "Everyone is there, including Andrew's son, Michael."

"Michael Browder?" said Flint. "If the rest of the resistance is there, then that means my daughter may be there."

"You have a daughter?" asked Gregory, startled.

"Well," began Flint, conflicted by the truth, "she's...yes, she's my daughter. I need to rescue her. And if doing so frees Michael and the others, as well as helps lure Jo—Sullivan out, then Titan needs to fall."

"We barely have an army!" protested Jeremy.

"And we only have one military ship!" objected another tactician.

The rebels grew noisy, complaining and debating whether they should initiate an attack or stay in hiding. Flint, however, walked over to a plinth in the chamber and raised his hands, a flare of hope in his eyes. When the people saw this, they became silent and stared at him with questionable expressions, which told him that he only had one chance to prove why they should risk their lives.

"Look at where we are," said Flint. "Is this the life you want to live? Is this the life you want for your children, and the children of their children? Do you want this to be an endless cycle? Do you want to hide forever?

Synthesis is upon us. Sooner or later, we need to stand up and fight for our humanity."

Just then, he flinched and wondered, was he even human? No, he didn't believe so. In fact, in this underground base he was the only person who had unnatural abilities, such as his abnormal strength and near-flawless accuracy. Realizing that he had no humanity made him feel empty. He had no soul—like the tribunal. He suddenly felt like one of the many machines in the chamber, incapable of having human values. This frightened him. It made him miserable, and it ate away at his sanity. Yet he refused to steal hope from these people. It didn't matter if they weren't perfect because it was "natural" not to be. And to him, the nature of imperfection was an integral part of being human, even if he himself was somewhat of an outcast.

"I know many of you may be terrified to lose what little remains of our freedom," Flint went on. "Despite what happened in the past, the war never ended. In spite of what the tribunal did to me two decades ago, I came back. And I came back to finish what I started. Follow me to Titan, and we shall continue where we left off. Follow me, and we shall show the tribunal how great we are despite our flaws!"

About half of the crowd cheered. Those who didn't simply gave a slight nod when they heard the others, and then many of them decided to join in the cheering. Most of the rebels were now praising Flint.

"All right, people, settle down," said Gregory. "If we're going to do this, we'll need to devise a strategy."

"I'm fresh out of ideas," said Jeremy.

"I don't mean to pry," began Gunthrel, looking at Flint, "but what army is going to be attacking that Titan place?"

"Your army," said Flint, winking at him.

Gunthrel sighed. "It's a smart idea, but is it fair to my brethren? You guided them to a new home, and—"

"And you agreed to join me," interjected Flint. "I'm sure Omicron squadron would like to show the military some love. We still have the mothership, remember?"

"But is it the right thing to do?"

Flint tilted his head and calmly said, "I promised to guide your people to a world without lurkens; however, you must realize that the military rules this universe with an iron fist, and as long as the tribunal is in power, your people will always have to worry about synthesis, just like my people. Is that what you really want?"

"No," said Gunthrel, frowning. "But I still think it's wrong to abuse my brethren."

"I'm not abusing them, Gunthrel," said Flint defensively. "If we don't do something to stop the military, we'll all eventually suffer the consequences. Hiding won't save your people. Not now...not ever."

Gunthrel gave a faint nod. He was still upset with Flint for planning such an attack with his own people without even consulting him about it until now, but he nevertheless agreed that this had to be done. Trying to look at the bigger picture, he managed to put his resentment aside and listened to the voice of reason.

"You're right," he said gruffly. "Thanks to you finding a planet that doesn't have much light, for the very first time my people can explore a world without worrying about using armor to survive. I'll...I'll contact Soalace."

"Thank you," said Flint, relieved. "What you're doing is helping your people, as well as mine." He gave him a warm smile and then turned to Gregory. "I wanted to ask you something earlier, but so much has happened since I came." He paused for a moment, afraid to ask. "What happened to Hamarah?"

"I'm very happy you remember her," said Gregory. "Unfortunately, she hasn't been with us since the war had—"

"Where is she?" asked Anissa tersely.

"I don't know," replied Gregory in an irked tone. "Besides, why would you care? You've never been interested in this war."

"Excuse me?" snapped Anissa.

"Please," began Flint, intervening, "no fighting. We just wanted to know Hamarah's whereabouts. Perhaps she's still hiding."

"I'd like to believe so," said Gregory.

"But I don't understand," said Anissa. "I received a message from her a week ago telling me she was here."

"What?" said Gregory. "That's impossible. She hasn't been here in decades."

"Forgive the intrusion," said Gunthrel, "but is it possible the military contacted Anissa under the guise of Hamarah to confirm any suspicions about this place?"

"Wouldn't they have attacked by now?" said Jeremy.

"This is troubling," said Gregory. "I thought you came because you remembered where this place was located."

"No," said Flint. "Anissa had the coordinates."

"Something's not right," said Gregory. "If the military does in fact have something to do with this, then we need to—"

The installation trembled with sounds of explosions, and an alarm went off. Although the rebel troops were panicky, they attempted to get their weapons. Many of the refugees, however, screamed and ran aimlessly. Flint and his companions were the only ones who were somewhat composed.

Gunthrel and his squad promptly activated their dimensional cannons. Flint, meanwhile, pulled out his magnums and approached the tunnels where Jeremy, Gregory, and the other rebel troops took position. The underground base continued to tremble due to more explosions. Not a minute later, the ceiling cracked and collapsed. Silence fell. Most of the rebels lay dead. Flint was the only person who still moved through the rubble, but one of the thousands of military soldiers approached him and blasted him with an ST-8 stunning rifle. Flint immediately cringed and fell unconscious.

CHAPTER SEVENTEEN
HALVON'S INFERNO

Several hours passed, and Flint woke up. However, he couldn't open his eyes. He tried to move but couldn't. Was he blind? He felt numb, as if he were paralyzed. Was he crippled? Moments later, he attempted to scream for help. Yet his mouth remained closed. In fact, he couldn't even hear anything. Was he deaf? All he could do was think, and the only thoughts going through his mind were terrifying.

At last, he heard a metal door open. He was able to hear several footsteps enter the room, or at least he assumed he was in a room. The people who came inside approached him and spoke another language. He didn't know which one it was, though it sounded like German.

Flint started to feel relaxed since he realized he wasn't deaf after all. He thought, perhaps he would be able to move around and see in a little while. In the meantime, he tried to be patient. Then he heard machinery being activated. The sounds resembled either medical instruments or a ship's engine. Though, since nothing vibrated, he felt that he wasn't on board a ship. But he still couldn't open his eyes, so he wasn't sure. Another tool turned on, resembling a drill. The people surrounding him continued to speak in a foreign language.

Within the next few seconds, Flint was finally able to feel something. He experienced a ticklish feeling on his forearms and fists. He twitched, wanting to laugh. Yet his mouth would not open. Perhaps doctors were giving him drugs to relax? Flint wondered why he wasn't able to breathe. But he was in fact breathing or else he'd be dead. Then he felt something in his throat. Was it a tube connecting him to a life-support machine? Why did he need it? He finally opened his eyes and saw his youthful body torn apart by what must have been caused by explosions during the war twenty years ago. Parts of his arms were missing, and the doctors were inserting synthetics into him. Flint shrieked and fainted on the operation table.

After what seemed like a week, Flint awoke inside a reeking chamber cuffed in manacles that were connected to chains linked to the ceiling. Standing before him was a paunchy warden in a military uniform.

"Where am I?" groaned Flint.

"You're where you should have been twenty years ago," said the military man. "Yes, all this time I should've been torturing you like the rest of your pathetic followers."

"Titan?"

The man flinched and asked, "How do you know that name?" Flint didn't respond, which infuriated the warden. He readied his whip and said, "It doesn't matter. Either way, you're a dead man."

"I beg to differ," said Flint, breaking free of his manacles.

Before the warden could react, Flint pulled on the chains, severing them from the ceiling. He then swung the loose chains at the man's face, knocking him out. Flint strode across the room and quietly opened the door. Before escaping, he peeked to see if anyone stood there. Fortunately it was empty.

Flint assumed that his guess was correct—he was in Titan, the prison where his followers from the war had been imprisoned. The military had done him a big favor, he thought to himself. He searched the penitentiary, trying to be as stealthy as possible. Flint went up a spiral staircase of stony steps and eventually found a doorway leading outside.

As soon as Flint stepped outside, he noticed the prison consisted of four massive towers that had spire-shaped roofs. The towers were connected by bridges, and below lay a mining pit. Gazing at the pit, he noticed hundreds of prisoners were being forced to dig and find minerals. He grimaced and scouted the rest of the prison, spotting a spacecraft docked on an octagonal platform by the eastern tower.

He sneakily made his way across. Upon reaching the eastern tower, he saw a guard by the starship. Flint took a deep breath and climbed down to the side of the bridge. He dared not look down as he hung along its ledge. Luckily for him, since he had a strength that, for the first time, didn't confuse or frighten him, he easily climbed sideways to where the sentinel stood. He then whistled, alerting the guard. When the soldier peered down to find out what the wind-like noise was, Flint grabbed him with one hand and choked him to death.

Climbing up, Flint dragged the dead sentinel into the vacant ship. He then searched the vessel, finding his hat and guns. After putting them on, he spotted bombs in a corner. When he saw them, he had a feeling that those were what had been used to destroy the rebels' base. His face became contorted, thinking about all the innocent people who'd died. Were his steamwalker comrades also dead? That thought terrified him. He grabbed four bombs and left the ship. Trying not to be seen, he went around the outer prison, instinctively setting up the bombs. It was evident to him that he'd used them during the war two decades ago. Although he had no solid memory, being able to activate them was proof enough for him.

After setting the last bomb, he put the detonation chip in his pocket and made his way to the southern tower from where he had originally escaped. He was hoping to find other prisoners. When he entered the tower, however, an alarm went off. Flint froze for a moment and then ran up the stairs, trying to hide. Several guards found him, at which point he pulled out his magnums and shot them. Guards continued to enter the southern tower, firing at him. Flint was running out of bullets to defend himself. He eventually felt that he had no choice but to hide again. Although he had no idea where to go, he went down a seemingly endless spiral staircase until he reached a floor containing a tunnel. Upon seeing the passage, he entered it.

Even though the path was dim, Flint saw a map chiseled on the left wall. Based on what he could see, the area he stood in seemed to be a passageway to other towers. And an arrow on the stony map indicated that across from him was the northern tower. He swiftly made his way through the tunnel, hoping to find Gunthrel or his daughter. When he reached the other side, a loudspeaker in the dungeon activated.

"Flint Cross," said a voice through the loudspeaker, "you impressed me when you found a way off Earth. But now I am agitated and tired of the tribunal's game. I have all of your pesky rebels outside, lined up and ready to die. If you do not turn yourself in within the next minute, I will start to blast them one by one."

Flint gritted his teeth and ignored the threat, thinking the man was bluffing. He walked around, noticing empty cells. The tower was silent. There were no guards here, causing him to feel uneasy. He tried thinking of a plan but nothing came to mind. When a minute passed, he heard beams and horrid shrieks via the loudspeaker. Flint felt nauseous, realizing he'd made one of the biggest mistakes in his life—assuming he knew the warden's level of tolerance—and tried to find the tower's exit.

He continued to hear dimensional beams, as well as the outcries of his comrades. Frantic, he sprinted ahead. Finally, after searching nearly every corridor, he found a door and approached it. Upon opening the metal door that led outside, he noticed myriad prisoners lined up along the side of the long, wide bridge of the northern tower. And in front of him were at least a hundred guards wielding dimensional weapons. One of them was dressed in an elegant military uniform rather than the rags that the others wore. He smirked, leisurely walking over to Flint.

"Ah, the legendary Flint Cross has surrendered," he said. "My name is Bartholomew, and I have been in charge of Titan for the last twenty years."

"I'm happy for you," said Flint.

Bartholomew struck Flint across the face with his hand. "Don't be too happy," he said. "Today is your execution, and I've gathered your loved ones here to witness your death." He laughed with a wicked smile. "Yes, that's right. Today is the day it all ends."

"I wish it were."

Once again, Bartholomew struck his face. "With a mouth like yours, I'm surprised the tribunal kept you alive. Eh, I suppose they made the right choice. It was better to have let you withered away on Earth than to have made you a martyr. But now it no longer matters. People are tired of hearing about you. This execution will only make you a martyr to these pitiful prisoners, and they're going to rot here." Bartholomew cackled, pointing his gun at Flint. "Any last words?"

"Well, since you've asked, I was hoping to say a prayer."

"A prayer?" replied Bartholomew, laughing hysterically. "My goodness, you really are as insane as the Commandant had said. In just a few days *we* shall be the ones being prayed to." He sighed and added, "This truly is an end. Today will be the last day man reaches out to a god."

Flint gave a faint nod, pulled his hand out of his pocket, and joined his palms, clicking a tiny chip. "In the name of the Father—" The eastern tower suddenly detonated. "In the name of the Son—" The western tower exploded. By now the guards were panicking. "And in the name of the Holy Spirit—" The southern tower blew up. Witnessing mass hysteria, Flint produced a demented grin. "Doesn't anyone want to pray with me?"

Upon asking, the northern tower exploded. Just as the explosion sent him into the air, he pulled out his magnums and blasted Bartholomew with all twelve rounds. Bartholomew didn't even have a chance to scream; his body simply blew into pieces, and whatever remained of him fell into the super pit. Flint landed in a roll onto the bridge's cement, holstered his empty guns, and picked up Bartholomew's dimensional cannon, blasting the frantic guards with one hundred percent precision.

Many of the prisoners were cheering and praising Flint in disbelief. They then took up arms, fighting alongside Flint. Several of them were being disintegrated by the dimensional beams of the remaining guards, but the survivors counterattacked with their beams. Then a starship emerged from below. Flint jumped on the front of the vessel, bashing its hood so hard that it dented, causing the engine to malfunction.

The starship started to explode. Flint, meanwhile, performed a back flip onto the bridge and recharged his dimensional cannon, blasting a few starships descending from the gray- and crimson-tinged sky of Halvon. A deadly blaze surrounded him as he sprinted across the bridge, firing at other vessels rising from the pit.

"Let he who is god-worthy strike me down!" he roared with a mad look in his eyes.

A fleet of starships were now descending from the scorched sky. This, however, didn't stop the madness of Flint Cross. He simply picked up a second dimensional gun and fired both weapons at the approaching ships that attempted to shoot back at him. Each vessel disintegrated from a single zap. Although the battleships were nearly millions of feet away, Flint didn't even have to aim once. Before any of the pilots could get a lock on him, violet beams pulsed through them, disintegrating them along with their spacecrafts.

Despite the fact that there were no more vessels, Flint continued to fire skyward, roaring like a complete maniac. The sky was filled with flames and particles of what used to be dozens of starships. Flint did not stop firing until he heard a soft voice that saved him from losing his sanity.

"Father, stop!" shouted Sarah, approaching him. "They're dead. They can't harm us anymore."

"Sarah?" muttered Flint, no longer shooting.

He turned around, dropped his weapons, and hugged her while crying. Jake, Brock and Bas Panzo, and Yeramba approached him.

"Anangu regain spirit."

"Yeramba," said Flint, startled. "I am sorry they brought you into this." He calmed down, embracing the others. "I'm so glad you're safe. I don't know what I would've done if something had happened to any of you."

"How did you do all this?" asked Jake.

"I don't know," replied Flint. "It's like a demon took over me."

"No demon," said Yeramba. "Angry spirit."

Flint laughed. "Yes, an angry spirit." He then looked ahead and noticed Gunthrel limping over without his power suit. "Gunthrel!" Flint ran to his comrade and helped him stand. Never had he seen Gunthrel look so weak; he'd been so used to seeing him as a colossal titan in bulky clockwork armor that he'd forgotten his best friend was still human. It looked as though he'd been tortured over the past week. "Are you all right?"

"I'll live," said Gunthrel frailly.

"How did we get here?" asked Flint.

"It was so sudden," responded Gunthrel. "Unfortunately, I was right. We were simply the bait to prove the military's suspicions. The bombings—the explosions—everybody died that day except me and my men. Our armor protected us. But we couldn't fight. There were thousands of soldiers. We had to surrender. Then they made us remove our armor, shackled us on a ship, and brought us to this wretched place. I didn't even think you survived."

"Gunthrel," said Flint apprehensively, "please tell me that you contacted Soalace before this insanity happened."

For a brief moment, Gunthrel had a stern face. Then he looked at Flint and smirked. His devious grin was the answer Flint was hoping to get. Shortly after, Brock and Bas helped carry Gunthrel to a safe area that wasn't burning while Flint hugged his daughter again.

"I'm so relieved to see you again," said Sarah.

"I thought I'd never find you," said Flint emotionally. "I nearly searched everywhere in the Vorilian quadrant for you."

"Joey and Steve betrayed us," said Jake. "Can you believe it?"

"Steve is singing a new hymn outside his church," said Flint.

"But what about Joey?" asked Sarah.

"He's still out there," said Flint, gazing at the charred sky. "Though, after what I just did here, I'm sure he's going to come out from the shadows. In the meantime, we'd better get out of this hellhole and wait for Gunthrel's reinforcements."

CHAPTER EIGHTEEN
HUNTING THE HUNTER

Flint and the others managed to reach the central bridge of Titan, the only area that wasn't about to fall apart. Upon reaching safety, Flint explained to Sarah and his friends from Desonas what had happened when he traveled to the Outlands of Australia, as well as his experience in Soalace, and his revolution against the tribunal. They could hardly believe his tales, but it was evident that they were true.

After six hours passed, the mothership approached the planet. Soalace had a haze of smog enveloping it in the void of space. The interstellar steamship looked as if it were a mountainous metropolis blanketed by a glittery blackish-blue nebula drifting through the cosmos. The vessel majestically descended into Halvon's atmosphere. It was perfect timing because more military vessels were approaching. By now, the steamwalkers aboard Soalace had become masters of dimensional technology and blasted the military vessels. Once they were destroyed, Soalace docked. A ramp lowered shortly after, allowing Flint and his comrades to enter. The survivors then gathered in one of the many chambers inside Soalace to recuperate.

"Flint," called out one of the rebels, "is it true that you can't remember anything?"

He gave a sad nod and replied, "I can barely even recall the war. Only bits and pieces have returned. Other than that, I just can't seem to remember much. Please forgive me for not remembering any of you."

"I understand, as I'm sure the others do," said the rebel, patting Flint on the back. "It's just so wonderful to see you again."

"We thought you were dead," said another rebel.

"I can assure you that I wasn't far from death," said Flint. "Now, I know this may seem impulsive, but I feel that it's time we launch a final assault. If anyone knows where the tribunal is located, I need to know."

"It's not that simple," said a young man with a brown beard.

Flint curiously glared at him. "You're one of the few who look too young to have been in the war with me before. If you don't mind my asking, what is your name?"

"Michael," he said. "Michael Browder."

"Browder!" cried out Flint, overwhelmed with joy. He approached Michael and shook his hand. "I am proud to say that I remember your father; he saved my life once."

"My father?" said Michael anxiously. "Do you know where he is?"

Flint hesitated to answer but eventually replied, "I'm sorry." The expression on his face told Michael all he needed to know, causing him to slouch and cry. Flint held him and continued, "I've suffered terrible losses as well, Michael. But right now we need to be stronger than ever. If there is anything you know, it will help us defeat the tribunal."

"As I said, it's not so simple," said Michael, wiping away a tear. "The tribunal lives on a special planet at the heart of Vorilian IV." He sighed and went on, "The planet's called Parronus, and it has a unique force field that only Judgment is able to fly through."

"What is Judgment?" asked Flint.

"It's the Commandant's starship," said Michael. "It's the only vessel capable of entering the planet's shield with full clearance."

"Then we need to get aboard Judgment," said Flint.

"That's nearly impossible," said Michael. "Even if we got the Commandant's attention, it would be impossible to hijack his vessel. One dimensional beam alone can kill us."

"Then we'll need an advantage," said Flint, looking through a window and gazing at one of the military starships docked on a ruptured platform. "Gunthrel, have the engineers put that ship in the docking bay." The moment Gunthrel nodded at him, Flint added, "All of you have been through more than enough. When the time comes, we'll strike. Until then, I want you all to rest."

Before he could leave, Sarah called out, "Dad, where are you going?"

"To the flight deck," replied Flint. "We need to get out of here as soon as that military ship is aboard."

"Can we come?" she asked.

"Sure," said Flint, smiling. He guided Jake and his daughter to the cockpit, letting them sit beside him. While he showed them the controls, Gunthrel entered the room in a new power suit, joining him. "Nice armor," he said. "Is the ship docked in our bay yet?"

"Thanks, and yes," said Gunthrel.

"Then it's time for us to leave," said Flint, operating Soalace's interface. "I'm setting a course to Rutica."

"What?" said Gunthrel. "Why?"

"After what the military did, it's the last place they would think we'd go to," said Flint. Even though Gunthrel wore a helmet, Flint had a feeling that he had a crazed look. "I know it sounds absurd, but trust me. Besides, we have a friend to pick up."

"Clarienus can wait," said Gunthrel.

"She's not the only reason why we're returning," said Flint. "We need to hide for a little while, especially for my plan to work."

"And what plan is that?" asked Gunthrel, slightly irked.

"You've never been a hunter, have you?" said Flint. "There is a lot more to the hunt than simply searching for your prey. One must first have bait to play the game."

That was all Flint had to say. No one understood his motive, especially Gunthrel, but they trusted him since he'd managed to free them from prison. Flint wore a wicked grin on his face while he ascended Soalace into space, ready to begin hunting the hunter.

In the meantime, on the green planet of Parronus, Joey entered the tribunal's atrium-like chamber in a burgundy uniform. The tribunal sat above on a large balcony. Laskov and Kuralan were hooked up to life-support machines. Tarak was the only one of the three who still didn't need a machine to keep him alive, but he looked as though he were on the verge of needing one. Joey approached and kneeled before the tribunal.

"I received your transmission and came as fast as I could," said Joey. "How may I be of service?"

"You know very well why we contacted you," said Laskov, breathing heavily.

"Rise up, Commandant," said Tarak in a croaking tone.

Joey got to his feet and asked, "Is this in regard to that rebel scum?"

"So, you're not as dimwitted as we thought you were," responded Kuralan, also breathing heavily through his life-support machine. "Your bounty hunters and subordinates of our glorious military have failed to hunt down Ethan."

"One of my captains captured him," said Joey. "But he somehow escaped."

"Obviously," said Laskov, displaying an image of the ruined penitentiary of Titan. "The symbol of Flint Cross has become even more powerful than we've ever imagined."

"You're the idiots who made him this way," mumbled Joey.

"What did you say?" snapped Kuralan.

"I said it's surprising he has managed to live for so long," replied Joey. "To be honest, at his age, I'm surprised he hasn't died of a heart attack. Rest assured, I'll personally deal with this problem."

"You had better," said Tarak. "Or else this will be the last time you leave Parronus with the name Cain Sullivan."

Joey bowed, trying to hide his gulp, and left the chamber to hunt down Flint.

Meanwhile, on the amber-tinged planet known as Rutica, Soalace had just landed on top of the sunken starship. Its substructure's cylinder-shaped pipes attached to those of the smaller steamship's roof, becoming one vessel. Clarienus was jubilant to see Flint and Gunthrel again. And though Flint had told his daughter and fellow rebels about her, they were still distraught by her appearance. They nevertheless managed to accept her since she looked so happy, innocently hopping around Gunthrel.

Shortly after the reunion, the mothership ascended and flew over to where the rebel base was located. Flint still remembered the coordinates. And just as he feared, the entire region had been destroyed. Not only was the base in ruins, but the entire jungle that had once surrounded it was burnt to ashes.

Upon landing the vessel, Flint exited it and stepped onto the smoldered terrain. No longer able to smell fresh air, he crumbled to the ground, crying. So many innocent people were brutally murdered simply because they had embraced their imperfect nature—their humanity.

He thought, perhaps Anissa was right; she would have been better off continuing to sell her body in Maveron. Then he thought of Dale and shook his head.

"Rest well in Neverland," he said, desperately trying to embrace the few good memories he had. Despite his greatest efforts to think positive, he remained on the rubble. Thousands of innocent people were dead because of him. Even the rebel troops had been killed; they had died without even being able to defend themselves. This wasn't a war; it was a mindless slaughter. Gazing at the ruins, he feebly muttered, "I can't believe they're all gone."

"They will live in our hearts," said Michael Browder, approaching. He placed a hand on Flint's shoulder. "Remember what you told me? We need to be stronger now more than ever in order to win this war."

Flint agreed, standing up with a frail countenance. "You're right, Browder," he said. He finally turned, looking at him with a stern face. "I'm glad you're here. You're as strong as your father." His comment made Michael smile. "Let's go," continued Flint. "We have a lot of work to do."

Over the next few days, Flint and his army dismantled the military starship they'd taken and incorporated its ST-8 stunning technology into Soalace.

Gunthrel occasionally checked the ship's sensors to see if any military ships were nearby. Fortunately nothing showed up. Flint's plan, at least for now, seemed to be working out; though, Gunthrel and the others still weren't quite sure what Flint had in mind other than wanting to gain control of Judgment, the only ship known to freely enter Parronus. Although the ST-8 stunning weapon may do the trick, thought Gunthrel, it'd be impossible to get close since Judgment had superior range and firepower. A single dimensional beam from Judgment could cause their force field to malfunction and disintegrate their interstellar steamship. The rebels continued to worry. Nevertheless, they decided to keep trusting their leader.

After a week had passed, Michael Browder checked the sensors with Gunthrel and saw something pulse on his screen.

"Ethan!" he shouted.

Flint strode over to Michael and asked, "What is it?" He anxiously checked the scanner and saw a dreadnaught vessel entering the star cluster where Rutica was located. "What do you think that is?"

"I checked the ship's code," said Michael with poise. "You may not believe it, but it's Judgment."

"Oh, I believe it," said Flint. He sat in the pilot seat, opening a communication's channel that was linked to the entire steamship. "This is Flint Cross speaking. We have spotted Judgment entering our star cluster. Even though it's still a great distance away, we must leave before the Commander-in-Chief has a chance to get the initiative. Be ready for anything."

The soldiers in the steam-powered starship ran to the armory. Within minutes they were loading weapons and suiting up in thick armor. There were so many armors available that the steamwalkers allowed the rebels to use their power suits. Among them were Brock and Bas. This time they were literally titan-steel brothers.

"Ready to blow off some steam, brother?" asked Brock.

"And then some," said Bas, loading his pump-action shotgun.

Shortly after the crew was ready, Flint departed from the amber planet and observed his scanner. According to what it showed him, not too far seemed to be a large nebula. He increased the steamship's speed, flying toward it. As it turned out, there were actually a few nebulas. Most of them were purplish and blue. Although the scanner scrambled with all the energy surrounding Soalace, this made Flint smirk with a maniacal expression.

"Are you ready for the hunt, Joey?" he said, gazing out into the dark, hazy space.

Meanwhile, an ensign aboard Judgment observed his scanners and saw something pulse away from Rutica, flying toward a group of nebulae. He confirmed that it didn't have a military code, anxiously turning around.

"Commandant," he called out. "I have spotted an unidentified spacecraft flying toward the Hypo Nebulae."

"Engage that ship immediately," commanded Joey. He rose from his chair and walked over to the front of his starship, gazing out into the silent space. "Let's make a bet, Flint. I'm willing to bet all the coins on Earth that you'll be dead within the next hour, just in time for me to sit down and have lunch."

After a half hour passed, Judgment entered a nebula. The scanners scrambled. Yet the pilot continued to fly forward. Joey drummed his fingers on the arms of his chair, squinting at the colorful, hazy nebulae.

"So, you've taken my bet seriously," said Joey, scowling. "Very good, I was afraid you'd be deaf and senile at the age of sixty-five. I'll enjoy ridding you from space once and for all." A few soldiers glanced at him with concerned expressions on their faces while he spoke to himself, but they quickly looked back at their screens when Joey tilted his head. "Ensign, take us into that purple nebula."

The ensign complied, flying the ship over to the large purple cloud that was amid indigo and violet nebulae. The scanners were still jammed, and no communication channels functioned. Even the pane at the front was faintly showing signs of haziness as the vessel flew through the interstellar cloud that looked like a gateway to a dimension of paradise. Shortly after entering, however, Joey spotted a ship ahead.

"I've found you!" he exclaimed. "Fire at will!"

The dimensional cannons along the wings of Judgment charged and released thick beams at the drifting steamship, disintegrating it. Joey laughed, looking at the particles and dust of what remained of the mountainous vessel.

"What a disappointment," he said, sighing. "I was hoping to at least be a little engaged with our bet. Oh well, too bad all the coins on Earth are worthless."

A spherical beam suddenly shot out from a blue nebula from the side, blasting the vast starship. Electrical energy flowed through Judgment, and within seconds the entire spacecraft was stunned.

"What is the meaning of this?" said Joey fretfully.

"In almost every hunt, one must use bait to entice his prey," said Flint. He stood by the front windowpane of his dimensional mothership, which no longer had the other ship attached. Grinning wildly, he went on, "You were my prey, and you fell for my bait like a mindless fish. Now it's time to die like a man, Joey." He faced his crew and shouted, "Prepare for battle!"

Joey roared with so much anger for falling right into Flint's trap that he slammed his fists against the thick windowpane, nearly cracking it.

In the meantime, Soalace advanced and attached itself to Judgment; this was something Flint had learned after his experience with the Hewlett. Flint and his rebels charged over to the hatchway. Gunthrel and Omicron squadron were already there, waiting for their leader.

"This is it, men," said Flint. "This is the moment we've been waiting for. Aim well and avoid destroying the ship at all costs."

He gave the signal, and Gunthrel blasted Judgment's hatch open. The rebels stepped onto the iron grating of Judgment and immediately fired at the military soldiers inside. Flint, as usual, pulled out his magnums and fired his soal bullets at them. Within seconds, it was an all-out war aboard Judgment.

Countless beams pulsed back and forth in the chamber. Dozens of military soldiers and rebels disintegrated. The steamwalkers of Omicron squadron pressed on, flanking most of their enemies. The remaining military forces started to flee and take cover. Flint and his army charged forth, relentlessly firing at the soldiers. Reinforcements soon came from the upper decks of the vessel and joined the onslaught. Flint only took cover when he needed to reload. Otherwise, he was at the frontlines blowing soldiers away with his magnums.

Flint's militia eventually split into two groups. Omicron squadron handled enemies who attempted to flank them while Flint and his rebels pressed onward. Every time Flint took cover, reloading his magnums, he'd witness someone in his army disintegrate. It shook him up to see people who'd followed him for decades die so rapidly. He grimaced, continuing to blast every enemy in his sight.

After an hour of warfare and charging through Judgment, Flint finally found steps that led to the pilot chamber. With the exception of Gunthrel, Omicron squadron stayed on the lower levels, battling against the remaining military soldiers. Though the majority of Flint's army had been decimated, Sarah, Jake, Michael, and the Panzo brothers were still with him. This at least made him feel a bit relieved.

They took cover by the entrance of the pilot chamber. Flint peeked out and then charged into the room, ready to kill the remaining cadre of infantrymen.

"Where are you, you back-stabbing son of a bitch," he said, not seeing anyone.

A violet beam suddenly projected toward him from behind, missing him by an inch. Flint took cover, as did his comrades. Joey, meanwhile, stood on an upper deck. He continuously fired weak beams from his dimensional gun, hoping to kill Flint while trying not to destroy his vessel. One of his beams shot through Gunthrel, disintegrating him.

"*Gunthrel!*" cried out Flint.

"Hunting a bear is easy prey," said Joey, scowling. "But hunting a human is another story." He shot once more and then withdrew to a corridor behind him. "Hunt me down if you dare, old man."

Flint held the remnants of Gunthrel's ashes, crushing them into his palm with tears in his eyes. When his comrades approached him, he held out his other hand, halting them.

"This asshole is mine."

No one dared question him after seeing the demented look on his face. They left the pilot chamber and joined Omicron squadron to finish off the remaining military soldiers. Flint, in the meantime, went up the staircase and stepped onto the upper deck. He approached the tunnel Joey had gone through, cautiously peeking out. Ahead of him stood another staircase. He made sure his magnums were fully loaded and then charged forward. When he reached the stairs, Joey tried to zap him. Flint hastily took cover.

"How does it feel committing mass genocide?" shouted Joey, continuing to shoot. "Your insanity has killed millions of healthy, sane people who wanted to transcend!"

"Murdering innocent civilians who embrace their humanity and want to stay the way they are is hardly sane, Joey!" yelled Flint, firing back from a corner.

"My name isn't even Joey!" he bellowed, launching a beam that split the stairs.

"In that case, I'll start calling you maggot!" retorted Flint, aiming sharply and blasting Joey's left hand off.

Joey screamed in agony, blood pouring out of his wrist. He dropped his dimensional gun in shock and ran into his personal quarters while holding his bloody wrist with his right hand. He saw another gun by the delicate stained-glass window that stood near his bed and reached for it. That instant, Flint shot it away. Joey flinched and stepped back, frailly leaning against the glass as he groaned and bled profusely.

"Okay," said Joey, feebly chuckling. "You win, Flint." He breathed heavily, beginning to hunch. "Looks like you never needed to retire after all—you still got a few years left in ya. How about we team up like the old days and fight the tribunal together. How about it, partner?"

"Worth's the name of the game," replied Flint, cocking his magnums. "And right now, you're worth nothing."

Joey stared at Flint's demented face and screamed at the top of his lungs while charging to choke him with his remaining hand. Without feeling any emotion, Flint pulled the triggers of his magnums and put six bullets into Joey who flew back, crashing into the glass. His furious scream turned into a screeching croak when he fell down several flights, slamming against the first floor's cold, metal grating.

Flint approached the shattered glass and gazed down, staring at Joey's crippled body. He menacingly stared at the corpse of a man whom he once thought was his best friend—a man who ended up killing his true best friend, as well as his son. He felt empty staring at the corpse, and it was because he no longer cared about the sweet satisfaction of revenge; he simply wanted to see Joey dead. After a long hard look, he turned away, never looking back.

CHAPTER NINETEEN
CYBERNETIC MAYHEM

The rebels were victorious at infiltrating and seizing control of Judgment, the most powerful and significant ship in the military. This victory, however, came at a great cost. Dozens of men who followed Flint had lost their lives, including Gunthrel. Flint was the only person who mourned his death more than Clarienus and the steamwalkers. Sarah tried to comfort Flint, except there was nothing she could say or do to put a smile on his face.

After a day of mourning, Flint decided to gather the survivors of his rebellion. Though he didn't smile, he felt relieved to see Michael Browder among them. Jake stood beside Sarah, and the Panzo brothers joined the meeting as well.

"Yesterday was a tremendous victory," said Flint. "And though we have lost heroes who will always be remembered, we must not waver. The tribunal remains in power. They have been in power for more than three hundred years. If we destroy them, the military will surely fluster and fall apart. Only then shall we finally taste true freedom."

The rebels cheered, praising their leader's words.

"From here on, we may very well gaze upon the face of death," continued Flint. "All of you have already risked everything. You've proven your loyalty and your courage, which is why I won't be disappointed if anybody here stands down at this point. Unlike the tribunal, I give you the freedom to choose: come with me to face death itself or stay here and start a brand-new life until synthesis."

"Are you insane?" responded Michael.

Flint chuckled for the first time since he took control of Judgment. "Several people have asked me that," he said. "To be honest, I don't know the answer."

"We're with you until the end," said Michael. "Isn't that right, men?"

The rebels cheered with absolute conviction. Even Omicron squadron, which had no real part in this war, concurred and raised their bulky arms with loud cheers, ready to do battle once more. Flint nodded at his crew, feeling confident that the tribunal's days were numbered.

After the meeting, the rebels gathered weapons and armor from Soalace and transferred them over to Judgment. In the meantime, Flint made sure Clarienus stayed in her bedchamber for her own good. Then he searched the ship to find Sarah and Jake. He found them in a room near the armory.

"Listen," he called out, entering their chamber. "I truly meant what I said before: about you having freedom. But I beg you as your father—" he glanced at Jake, "and father-in-law, to please stay here."

"Dad, when we lived in Desonas things were so different," replied Sarah. "This life in space—it was inconceivable. I even blamed you for mom's…mom's death. But you were right all along. No, you were more than right. Everything you're doing now is affecting our lives and the lives of future generations." Sarah tried her best not to cry, but she couldn't help it when she tried to tell her father something important. "My baby. Don't you see? They took my baby away from me and killed her. So you see, this is bigger than you."

"My God," said Flint, holding his daughter who continued to cry. "Sarah, I had no idea. I am so, so terribly sorry that you were forced into this."

"You didn't force us into this mess, Flint," said Jake. "The tribunal threatens us all. Even if we left to start a new life, we wouldn't be safe unless the tribunal falls. I've no doubt that they killed our parents. We had no part in the war. We weren't even teenagers. And still the tribunal took us away from reality, treating us as if we were cattle for their amusement. I need to be a part of this."

Flint accepted his words with a strong countenance and then abruptly broke down crying. His daughter held him while he cried. Jake felt awkward; the only thing he could do was place a hand on his father-in-law's back.

"I miss Tommy," said Flint, shuddering. "I got you back. But not my son."

"You're wrong," she said. "He's with all of us, like my child. And as long as we fight for freedom, Tommy will be with us."

Flint gave a faint nod, holding his daughter. "I told you before, you were always the strong one," he said. Managing to stand straight and control himself, he glanced at Jake. "I'm blessed to have the two of you in my life."

"We're in this together, Flint," said Jake, hugging him.

His daughter and son-in-law had suffered greatly, conceded Flint, just as he'd suffered. But there was more to life than pain. Life also had joy. Except, to finally experience such joy with his family for the rest of his life, he'd have to eliminate the tribunal. Only then could he have his family back, as well as his freedom. Flint smiled at Sarah and Jake, shedding a tear of hope. And then together, as a family, they boarded Judgment, ready for the final battle.

Judgment departed from the Hypo Nebulae sector, and the civilians of Soalace waved goodbye to Omicron squadron, hoping their brethren would be victorious and that they'd see their loyal guards again on New Earth.

Flint piloted Judgment, flying toward the heart of Vorilian IV—planet Parronus. He knew there was something special about that particular world. He then wondered to himself, what if the reason why he couldn't find Hamarah was because she'd been imprisoned and tortured all this time on that wretched planet? The thought infuriated him. Either way, Parronus was his final destination.

By the next hour, he could see Parronus with his own eyes. The green planet sparkled with life. He remembered that he'd been there before when he was the Commandant—a puppet for the tribunal. The dream he had a few years ago in the kingdom of Soalace was a confirmation of him once visiting Parronus. And as Michael Browder had said, his sensors picked up a force field enveloping the planet. When he drew closer to the world, however, the shield automatically deactivated. The sacrifices of his people—as well as Gunthrel—were not in vain after all, he told himself.

Spotting the white colony that he'd once seen in his dream, he grimaced and steered the starship toward it. The majestic city looked as though its citizens had never seen a day of war. Without mercy, he blasted every building in his sight with plasma beams. Flint didn't want it to simply disintegrate and vanish—no, that would be too kind, he thought. He wanted to see the heavenly city burn.

"Yes," he said aloud with a deranged face, "I will blast all of you to kingdom come!"

The city didn't even have defense weapons to shoot down Judgment. Apparently, no one had ever thought that such a monstrous thing would occur. The populace ran for their lives while Flint destroyed houses, parks, fountains, roads, statues—everything. There was only one building he left alone: an ivory skyscraper where the so-called immortal tribunal dwelled; it was also the only logical place where Hamarah could be imprisoned.

After several minutes of blasting the colony, military soldiers finally rushed out of the tribunal's domain with dimensional weapons. Flint saw this and clicked an alarm, signaling people to be prepared to use an escape pod should something happen to Judgment. The soldiers fired at the ship, but its force field held up.

By now every rebel was wearing a power suit. Most of them used the escape pods simply to help Flint from a ground position. They seemed to be just as crazy as him, or at least that was how he felt. Now the vessel's shield showed signs of failing. Flint clicked a panel on Judgment's interface, activating another alarm that alerted the crew that the ship's destruction was eminent. He targeted the ivory skyscraper, selected auto-pilot, and ran to the armory. His twelve-foot tall power suit was still there.

"This is for you, Gunthrel," he said, entering it.

He clomped his way over to the escape pods and stepped into one. Flint clicked a button to escape, yet the capsule he stood in did not budge—it seemed to be jammed. He continuously pressed the button, but it still didn't work. At that point, he made his way to the ramp of the ship and noticed a battleship approaching.

Activating his magnetic boots, he exited the ship and clomped up the hull while removing a dimensional cannon from a compartment in his power suit, charging it. He then aimed it at the vessel, blasting it into particles. Upon reaching Judgment's roof, he spotted more starships. They attempted to shoot Flint who strode over to the ship's aft, counterattacking.

"Go to hell," he said, charging his cannon to maximum power.

An array of beams lit up the sky. Battleships gleamed in a violet radiance before being disintegrated. Dodging numerous beams, Flint reached the aft of his spacecraft, disengaged his magnetic boots, and leapt off, hurling himself into the air. While in midair, Flint blasted three battlecruisers and then activated his thrusters as he approached one of the few military vessels remaining in the sky. Since the thrusters slowed his fall, he landed safely onto the cruiser closest to him, recharged his cannon, and fired at the remaining fleet.

"They didn't even know what hit them," mocked Flint, thumping forth atop the military ship, his dimensional gun illuminating the atmosphere with a barrage of beams.

When the flotilla turned into glittery particles, he disengaged from the vessel he'd been standing on and hurled back toward Judgment. Performing a flip as he soared through the sky like a bullet of mass destruction, he zapped the last ship and reinitiated his thrusters, trying to slow himself down. Instead of landing on the side of Judgment's hull as he'd hoped, he crashed through a polarized windowpane. Just then, the vessel collided into the base of the skyscraper and exploded.

If anyone had remained on the ship, they were surely dead or burning to crisps. Only one person broke free of the rubble, and it was Flint Cross inside the power suit Gunthrel had made for him. The armor, however, had been severely damaged, and it was on fire. It had served its purpose, thought Flint, forcefully opening it. When attempting to exit it, he felt something keep him at bay. A large piece of shrapnel was stuck in his abdomen. He bent it and gasped in horrible pain, removing it. At that moment, the flame spread to his body, setting him ablaze.

Flint screamed as he got out of the clockwork power suit whose cogs clanked no more, its breathing apparatus no longer filtering oxygen. He threw off his duster and swiftly rolled down to the floor, trying to put out the fire. By the time the flame had doused, soldiers were upon him. Before shooting, however, they gasped in terror, not seeing a man but a creature whose flesh was burnt, revealing corroded synthetics. Flint grinned manically, pulled out his magnums, and fired at the distraught soldiers.

Blasting them, Flint shouted, "Where are all of you going? This is your chance to show me your godhood!"

Taking cover, he reloaded and then charged back out while continuing to blow away the remaining military soldiers amid the violent flames and rubble. As always, he never needed to aim when shooting. The soldiers started to flee, thinking he was some kind of demon being able to fight in his condition. Flint reloaded again and shot the last troops in sight.

Just when he thought there were no more enemies around, two hovering tanks descended toward him. The large turrets of the tanks turned, aimed at Flint, and released dimensional beams at him. Flint instinctively leapt sideways into the air and preformed an aerial cartwheel, gunning down the crew of each tank. Only the drivers were left when he landed.

"Why can't you die?" roared one of the soldiers, trying to ram Flint.

"Try harder, asshole," said Flint, swerving away while reloading his guns and firing at the driver who retreated down the hatch of the tank.

Holstering his magnums, he climbed one of the hovering vehicles, bent its long-barreled gun, and then leapt off it. He'd leapt so high that he landed onto the other, smashing and denting the hull with his fist. Its engine got crushed, splintering into shrapnel. The tank glided down and crashed onto the ruptured street.

"Is that all you've got? This militia is pitiful!" shouted Flint, jumping off the damaged vehicle with a look of lunacy.

At that moment, Flint gripped the hull with all of his strength and tossed the crippled tank into the other. A massive explosion erupted when the tanks collided. Flint stared at the explosion, finally accepting the fact that he was no longer completely human. The pain eventually caught up to him as he stood still. The crash, the stomach wound, the fire that briefly engulfed him—it had all taken a toll on him; he wasn't sure how much more life he had left in him, but he vowed to at least take out the tribunal before his death. Just then, he faintly heard dimensional beams behind him—his comrades who had used escape pods before the crash were still fighting bravely, even in the face of death.

Feeling satisfied, he limped forward and entered what remained of the white skyscraper's lobby. As it turned out, a few soldiers were waiting for him and started shooting at him. Hissing in pain, Flint forced himself to slide over to a pillar. He peeked out and blasted a couple of them. He then rolled over to another pillar and blew away a few more enemies on the second floor by the balcony. Spitting out blood, he got to his feet, reloaded his weapons, and charged out into the open—guns blazing—shooting every last one of them while he shouted:

"There is only death upon synthesis!"

Barely breathing, blood oozing down his charred flesh and partially melted synthetics, he approached an elevator and clicked a button on the console beside it. Upon the elevator arriving, he stepped inside it and entered the code *Evolution* on a panel. He leaned against the wall as the lift's door sealed. While the elevator ascended to the tribunal's floor, Flint gazed at the burning city and smiled at it. He did not smile long, though, since it pained him.

The door opened, and Flint exited the elevator. He limped through the light-pulsing hall, toward the tribunal's assembly room. When he entered the atrium-like chamber, eight soldiers rose from the sides of the second floor's balustrade, aiming their weapons at Flint who abruptly stopped. He glanced at them and then noticed the tribunal seated ahead.

"Well done," said Tarak, clapping in his chair.

"You have successfully wounded the evolution of man," said Laskov, speaking through a speech-generating device.

"Wounded?" said Flint. "I was hoping you'd say the word *destroyed*."

"Destroyed?" said Tarak in a croaking tone.

"My goodness," said Kuralan, breathing through his life-support machine. "You truly are mad, Ethan."

"We've spent centuries leading humanity through the stars," said Tarak. "Since the dawn of our evolution, we have been able to rise and conquer everything—even death. We cannot be destroyed. We are immortal."

"You are our only mistake," said Laskov. "You are the last degenerate cell in the body of man that has failed to evolve."

"Because I chose to embrace human nature?"

Flint unexpectedly felt a rage within him that was so monstrous and powerful that it gave him the strength to lift his magnums, defying his crippled body. He then shot down every soldier, roaring at the top of his lungs.

The tribunal panicked as they saw their guards get blown away. Before they attempted to leave, Flint removed a burnt knife from his tattered black vest and hurled it at Tarak's throat. He choked on his blood and croaked his last breath, slithering down his chair. The other two tried to leave on their mechanical chairs, but they were slowed by their weighty life-support machines. Flint holstered his guns and approached Laskov and Kuralan, forcefully removing the tubes in their mouths. He then tossed down their machines while he bellowed:

"We cannot become gods!"

Those were the last words the tribunal heard before they suffocated. Flint fell to the floor, barely able to take the pain. He was on the verge of fainting when he abruptly heard a rumbling sound emanating behind the burgundy curtains that hung at the back of the chamber. With the last of his strength, he managed to get back on his feet and limped past the curtains. Before him lay an ivory-coated room with crystal machinery. Electrical currents were jolting wildly out of its blue crystals into a hovering gateway.

Groaning and gasping for air, he limped farther into the room, toward the gateway that was suspended in midair. Inside the gateway hung a prism resembling the colors of a rainbow. He approached it and shot at the crystals, causing them to crack and shatter. That instant, the dimensional machine trembled and started to shutdown; however, before doing so, Flint was pulled into its threshold as if it had a mind of its own.

CHAPTER TWENTY
SYNTHESIS

Flint majestically hovered through a dimensional tunnel. It was semi-transparent, allowing him to see the dark realm of space and its distant stars. As he floated through the prism that pulsed with energy, his body gradually healed. He could see numerous planets as he floated deeper through space. The stars sparkled before him, radiating an eternal light. He soon passed a white dwarf, staring at it without getting blinded.

He thought that this was the most beautiful sight and phenomena he'd ever experienced in his life. To him, it was as though dream and reality became one. This felt so real to him, and yet it was a dreamy feeling. He then reached a cluster of colorful gas clouds, similar to the Hypo Nebulae sector; the only major difference was that this interstellar region of space had an orange- and red-colored gulf of cosmic dust.

The nebulae vanished shortly after, as did all the planets and stars. Flint was distraught by their sudden disappearance. For a while, he stared into nothingness. Before him was an empty realm where no life existed. Utterly frightened, he wondered what had happened to the universe. At that precise moment, new worlds, moons, and stars appeared. This was a tremendous relief to him.

Each planet he saw had a different color. The serene spacescape before him was an even more magnificent panorama than he'd experienced upon entering the semitransparent rainbow-colored tunnel. Once again, the planets, moons, and stars vanished. Flint stayed calm, trying to be patient. After several seconds, the celestial bodies returned. And, as usual, they were different than the previous ones. With this experience, he felt as though he were traveling through other dimensions.

This time he witnessed the birth of a star, its stellar core shining. Upon passing the newly forming star, his somewhat middle-aged body started to slow down. He spotted a green planet not too far from the newborn star. When he looked at the world, he began to fall toward it. The velocity of his body flying made him feel as if he were falling due to a presence of gravity. He refused to scream despite the fact that he was afraid. At that moment, he saw another gateway hovering near the green planet. His journey through space and time was coming to an end, he realized. And then, in the blink of an eye, he entered the spherical gateway and dropped into an ocean.

Flint was flustered, swimming up as fast as he could. It wasn't long until he reached the surface, gasping and breathing fresh air. The waves pushed him forward instead of sucking him in, and he hurled onto a sandy shore. Flint remained flat on the ground for a while, catching his breath. He gazed at the sky, noticing it was green. Somehow, he had a feeling he'd been here more than once. Yes, he thought to himself, this was definitely Parronus. The white colony, however, wasn't standing before him, not even its rubble. Instead there was a beach house a mile away.

The moment Flint noticed it, he felt his heart skip a beat, and his eyes widened. He then broke into a run toward the beach house with countless thoughts. He wondered to himself, could Hamarah be there? Was this in fact Parronus? It definitely seemed like it. But then, in the far eastern expanse—opposite the ocean—he spotted Uluru and Kata Tjuta. Upon seeing them, Flint stopped running and stared at them in disbelief. He looked at the sky again; yet it was still green, not the blue sky of Earth.

He didn't understand what was happening, nor did he know for sure where he was. But he nevertheless continued running toward the beach home. As he drew closer to the house, it became evident to him that it was the same one from his dreams. He'd dreamt of being on the balcony years ago during his time in Desonas.

At last, he reached the house. He tried to catch his breath, anxiously going up the stairs. It was so quiet. The only sounds he heard were the waves crashing down along the shoreline. Still, he did not see Hamarah anywhere. He then opened the house's front door and stepped inside. It was silent inside. Flint observed the interior and saw photographs of him and Hamarah in frames that hung along the walls.

When he looked at the photos, however, he felt as though a sharp piece of twisted metal was stuck deep in his throat. He couldn't breathe, realizing that Hamarah was a younger form of Amanda Cross. He backed away, bumping into the wall behind him. A frame fell, and its glass cracked. He wore a look of horror and ran upstairs. Once he reached the second floor, he heard a strange humming sound emanating from the bedroom.

His heart pounded again, and his head throbbed in terrible pain. He wasn't sure what he'd find in the room. In fact, he didn't know if he wanted to find out; but he was willing to take a risk if there was even a slight chance to see Hamarah again. He warily entered the bedroom. No one was there. The house had been empty for ages. He'd hoped Hamarah would be there, humming a lovely tune while waiting for him. He was wrong. The source of the eerie sound was from a dimensional rift by the ocean-view balcony.

A voice within his mind was beginning to whisper something to him. He tried to block it out and ignore it. Yet a part of it stuck with Flint, telling him a deep miserable truth that all the photos had shown him downstairs. He closed his eyes, trying to listen to another voice. Yes, he thought, this second voice was exactly what he'd wanted to hear. It was telling him that Hamarah was here with him. And when he opened his eyes, an ageless Hamarah sat before him—she was by the windowsill in a see-through gown, smiling at him with sensual eyes.

"Hamarah!" he cried out.

"Ethan!" she also cried out.

Together they ran into each other's arms, kissing passionately. Flint could hardly believe that this moment had finally come. After what had happened to him on Parronus, he'd lost faith, no longer believing he would find Hamarah. But since he'd been sucked into the dimensional rift, he was somehow able to be with her.

Flint felt so relieved to finally see Hamarah outside of his dreams. When he saw her body through the gown, he felt the urge to grab her, put her on the bed, and make love to her. She was the only one who attempted to speak while Flint took off her gown, kissing her soft voluptuous breasts.

"You did it," she said, moaning and taking his clothes off. "After three long centuries, the tribunal is dead."

"Yes," he whispered, caressing her delicate skin.

"The military is deeply wounded," she began in a murmur, "but it hasn't fallen just yet, Ethan. Someone will have to keep fighting."

"Browder will continue the war," he said, kissing her all around her body. "He will fight on and protect those who have been suppressed. And because of him, Sarah and Jake will be able to start a new beautiful life together. They'll have a family, just like you and me. Wouldn't that be wonderful?"

"Yes," she purred, moaning loudly.

"I love you, Hamarah."

"Oh, and I love you," she said blissfully.

Feeling so much pleasure, Flint closed his eyes. Though, when he did so, he could no longer hear or feel her. A burning sensation he'd been feeling around his groin traveled to his upper body. He gasped on the bed, feeling his chest tighten and burn as if a knife were cutting through him. Flint couldn't breathe. He started to convulse. His eyes blinked rapidly, froth coming out of his mouth. Then he fell flat on the floor. After a few seconds, the convulsions stopped. He coughed violently and breathed in a heavy, rasping tone. Little by little, he regained his composure.

Opening his eyes, he found himself in the dysfunctional synthesis chamber, just beyond where the tribunal lay dead. The building shook, on the verge of collapsing. Blood dripped down Flint's burnt face, his vision blurry. Barely able to breathe, he gagged, wondering what had just happened. Could it be that he'd hallucinated? Or was his experience the result of a synthesis glitch before breaking down?

At that moment, two voices arose within him. He shook his head, trying to shake them away. He wasn't sure which one he should listen to, if any. The second voice eventually faded away. Only the first voice remained—the voice of reason. In this final moment, he'd finally accepted the frightening realization he'd had at the beach house. Just as he'd lost his memory as Ethan and became Flint Cross, Hamarah had lost hers and became Amanda Cross.

He cried miserably. All this time, he was searching for a woman who'd been in front of him his whole life in Desonas. He'd been so certain that the woman in his dreams was different from Amanda Cross that he subconsciously separated the two. Though his memory had been severely tampered with, he nevertheless blamed himself for her death.

The pulse of life he'd managed to regain a few years ago quickly withered away again. Suddenly, destroying the tribunal no longer satisfied him. Winning the war against the military became worthless to him. Freedom was trivial because he'd lost the only precious thing left in this world.

Amid his torment, he wondered why he'd experienced such a wild hallucination—being with Hamarah at the beach house. A voice within his mind told him that he knew the answer: he'd fantasized of a greater outcome to this war. He yearned for so much more, yet his body lay ruined. There was nothing more he could do except find tranquility in the final moments of his life.

Flint Cross may have once been a gunslinger and revolutionist. Now, he desired to be a husband again. Hamarah was waiting for him, he conceded, and now he was ready to join her. He was content with this outcome, no longer questioning his sanity, and so he closed his eyes and finally surrendered, knowing his mission had been fulfilled.

EPILOGUE

EUPHORIC HORIZONS

With the tribunal defeated, the war came to an abrupt end. Since dimensional synthesis had been prevented, life continued in the universe. The rebels celebrated their victory across the Vorilian quadrant. And though they lost their leader, they embraced what he stood for—freedom. In due time, Michael Browder and his rebels brought humanity to a new era of prosperity. Though the steamwalkers were welcomed to join, they valued their independence and remained isolated as they had always been.

Yeramba was eventually brought back to Earth by the steamwalkers via their mothership. Brock and Bas Panzo loved their homeworld, but since civilization no longer existed there, they decided to live on Parronus with the rebels and helped rebuild the capital. Within less than a year it was rebuilt. And though they were never able to find Flint after the collapse of the tribunal's skyscraper, a memorial dedicated to him lay at the center of the capital city. Billions of people from other planets soon moved there, living in harmony.

In the meantime, Sarah mourned the loss of her father and attempted to start a new life with Jake on Soalace. Since a full supply of soal lasted for several months, the interstellar ship became known as a vessel of exploration into the unknown. Sarah and Jake decided to become explorers on this city-sized spacecraft, seeing what the universe had to offer.

Together they visited myriad worlds, collecting materials for their ship. They were even able to help the steamwalkers recreate soal from planets' resources, allowing them to continue their journey without needing to refuel on New Earth. Yet after five years of exploring countless galaxies, they felt it was time to return home.

Soalace reached Vorilian IV within seven months. When their home-world was in sight, two boys with black hair and sky-blue eyes ran to the observation window in the pilot chamber, looking at it with excitement.

"Tommy...Ethan," called out Jake, approaching his children. "How many times do I have to tell you? No running in the pilot chamber."

Just then, Clarienus leapt down from the ceiling, playfully licking the kids.

"Ah, so you three are playing without us?" said Jake, raising an eyebrow.

Sarah chuckled while walking beside her husband and reached down, lifting up her four-year-old twins.

"Mommy, look!" said Ethan, pointing at the indigo planet ahead.

"Is that New Earth?" asked Tom.

"Yes," she answered, smiling. "We're finally home."

The Cross family was once dysfunctional. Humans weren't perfect. Nothing could ever truly be perfect. Although dimensional synthesis may have evolved the human species, it would have caused the destruction of the cosmos. And thanks to Flint, upon the precipice of insanity, he'd managed to put an end to synthesis, giving his family and everyone in the universe a chance to find peace.

ABOUT THE AUTHOR

Paul L. Centeno was born and raised in New York City. During his early teenage life he wrote twelve short stories, several of which he used as a foundation to create his first fantasy novel, *The Vagrant Chronicle*. As a young adult, he studied at Herbert H. Lehman College where he earned a BFA in Creative Writing and Philosophy. After becoming a graduate, he worked with Gabriel Packard, associate director of the Creative Writing MFA Program at Hunter College, to master his craft. *Dark Sanity* is his third novel. He presently lives in New York City with his wife. Visit his website at www.PaulCenteno.com.